RAPTURE'S EDGE

J.T. GEISSINGER

RAPTURE'S EDGE

A NIGHT PROWLER NOVEL

Published by Montlake Romance

PO Box 400818
Las Vegas, NV 89140

ISBN-13: 9781611099133
ISBN-10: 1611099137
Library of Congress Control Number: 2013931730

CONTENTS

To Jay, for
sixteen years of happily-ever-after.

Take me as I am.
I offer scars, imperfections—
touch me and embrace my flaws
I am your beloved
You look at my failings and see stories
legends, maps of me before you.

I will tell the tales, my lover, only
whisper where I will find you
and I will come out of hiding.
Or we can play cat and mouse…
pursuing, escaping
one another until we collide.
I'll follow your trail and
you follow mine.

From *My Lover Is Mine*
by Aly Hawkins & Bryan Ashmore

PROLOGUE

Of all the places in all the world to spend a clandestine night alone, the Louvre museum in Paris is quite possibly the finest.

Of course, to do so is illegal.

Visiting hours are nine in the morning to six in the evening every day except Tuesday, with slightly extended hours on Wednesdays and Fridays. But for visitors with certain special abilities, visiting hours mean exactly zero.

Because when you can vanish into mist and nothingness by the mere focus of your will, a great many rules and regulations applicable to others cease to impress you.

It was one of these "special" people—beings, rather, or more accurately *creatures*—who happened to be contemplating a sculpture by Michelangelo titled *Dying Slave* at twenty minutes to three on one starlit, crystalline December morning, hours before daybreak and even longer before the tourists would begin to line up outside again. At almost eight feet tall, the dramatic, bone-hued marble sculpture of a naked man bound at wrist and chest was described by the plaque beneath as "the moment when life capitulates before the relentless force of dead matter."

Brilliant, mused Eliana Cardinalis as she stood before the statue, admiring the uncanny representation of that fleeting moment just before death. *I know just how he feels.*

As naked as the dying marble figure she was so arrested by, she wasn't cold or uncomfortable or in any way self-conscious. She was, simply, content. Alone—blessedly alone and free of the watchful eyes and whispers that normally followed her—her natural curiosity and good humor returned. She'd rambled through the cool, echoing corridors of the museum for longer than strictly necessary for the task at hand, but a pastoral Monet had called to her, then a fierce Caravaggio, then a glassed display of Egyptian funerary implements laid over woven palm leaves in a fascinating, ghoulish row.

The canopic jars—ceramic receptacles for storing the inner organs of a mummy—had made her snort in disdain. Dead was dead, but her kin, the ancient Egyptians, wholeheartedly believed in life *after* death, a leap of faith Eliana found seriously lacking.

Stupidly lacking.

She knew from firsthand experience that leaps of faith were nothing more than acts of willful self-delusion. Nowadays, she operated on two simple principles: *I'll believe it when I see it* and *It's better to ask forgiveness than permission.* Both had served her far better than the blind faith of her childhood.

Faith was a luxury she could no longer afford.

But she hadn't always been a cynic. Born and raised far below ground in a dark, sprawling labyrinth of incense-scented catacombs no human eye had ever seen, her education in the lore of ancient gods and secret spells, of rituals steeped in magic, had been thorough and effective. She prayed to all the old gods and left offerings of handmade lace and ripe fruit for the new, she lit candles in honor of dead ancestors, she watched with all her kin on the once-monthly *Purgare* nights as the silk-wrapped ashes of the unfortunates who didn't survive the Transition bobbed slowly down the Tiber on balsawood planks until they vanished from sight around a sinuous bend in the dark river. She accepted all she was taught by her elders with the open-armed trust of childhood, because even at twenty-three when most would have considered her a woman, Eliana had been still in many ways a child.

Then three years ago everything changed.

Now, from necessity, she was all grown up.

But she wasn't thinking about any of that as she stood in silent contemplation of the Michelangelo. She was thinking she'd better get moving because the night guard would make his scheduled appearance around the far corner of the sculpture hall in exactly three minutes and seventeen seconds, and she had a painting to steal before he did.

With a sigh of regret, she turned from the statue and made her way silently down the shadowed marble hall, enjoying the feel of the cool air on her naked skin. She rounded another corner and stopped abruptly as she caught sight of Canova's famous statue. Erotic and beautiful, the marble work titled *Psyche Revived by Cupid's Kiss* depicted two mythological lovers ensnared forever in a passionate near-kiss.

Seeing that—Cupid's languorous embrace, Psyche's sensual, pliant surrender—sparked an unwanted memory that pierced her heart, sharp as knives.

Demetrius.

Her stomach twisted into a knot. Heat made her face feel molten. Then abruptly, without sound or warning, the flesh and bone woman that was Eliana dissolved into mist.

She didn't even need to consciously think it anymore—*Vapor*—Shifting was as natural to her as breathing, as natural as the first time it had happened to her at thirteen years old when her *cunaria* had tried to force her to eat boiled eggs and she'd balked. One minute she was sitting at the polished stone table with her lips smashed together in disgust, the next—*poof!*

Vanished.

Only the strongest of her kind could Shift to Vapor, and so she was grateful, but to this day she loathed eggs.

Vapor was only one of her many Gifts, but one that offered a precious benefit the others didn't: escape. Now, relieved of the terrible burden of feelings, she floated in a ruffling pale gray plume for a moment, regaining equilibrium. Disconnected from a body, she was still herself—her mind remained, as did the strength of her will—but there was no heartbeat, no respiration, no emotion or digestion, just the lovely and calming sensation of freedom from gravity. Of herself, weightless as air.

An applied thought—*up*—and she drifted toward the ceiling, far enough above the lovers below that they became slightly less offensive. She turned away and surged off through the vast darkness of the museum, a shimmering cloud of Vapor headed toward room 77 and the Romantic paintings, where one of her other powerful Gifts would come into play.

A Degas was the prize tonight. Not too famous, not too large, it would still command a good price on the black market and wouldn't be too easy to trace by the authorities, or too hard to remove from the wall.

Contrary to popular belief, museum security systems are typically some of the worst. Unlike the movies, which would lead one to believe a field of invisible lasers and infrared cameras are de rigeur, the reality is closer to the sorry duo of underpaid, badly trained security personnel and mechanical gates. Most jewelry stores are far more secure, as are all banks; Eliana knew this from experience.

And for a woman who could not only dissolve into a wisp of air but who was able—even better—to become invisible in the cover of shadow while still retaining a physical body that could lift and carry a painting, the temptation of stealing into buildings that were closed, locked, and legally verboten became too great.

But that wasn't the primary reason. Money was the primary reason. Crass, yes, but she needed money to continue her father's research, and her people needed to eat, so she'd resorted to using her Gifts as a way to avoid starvation.

It wasn't as if they were going to start feeding on humans, after all, no matter how much her brother, Caesar, tried to convince her it was their birthright, and that the sorry creatures were quite tasty. *Think of them as cows,* he'd argued again not two days prior. *You like beef, don't you?*

Yes, she liked beef, but she liked humans, too. For the most part. Either way, she wasn't going to eat them. It just seemed like one of those things you don't do.

She'd thought of getting a job to bring in money, but quickly realized how ridiculous that notion was. Not only did none of the *Ikati* have any work experience or what could be deemed "skills" by an employer, they were too different from humans. They stood out.

An ancient Zulu word from their even more ancient homeland in the darkest heart of Africa, *Ikati* meant "cat warrior," and it was a near perfect description of Eliana and her kind. Sleek and lithe and powerful, able to move without sound on two feet or four, able to strike a killing blow before their prey ever sensed danger, the *Ikati* were part of the human world but not *of* it, and even in clever disguise it was evident for all to see.

The eyes gave it away. Flashing and feral, alight with a predatory gleam even when they smiled, Eliana and her kin of the Roman catacombs had eyes of deepest midnight, a black so deep it was fathomless. The most stalwart of human men had been known to falter in his step when one of her kind looked a moment too long in his direction.

So the eyes were a problem, but so was nearly everything else. The way they spoke, the way they walked, the way the very air seemed to hold its breath around them. Even at night when they usually went out their differences were apparent, so Eliana and her little band of rebels kept apart from the rest of the everyday world as best they could.

One day soon, however, the world would become well acquainted with them. Then everything would change.

Until then she'd have to keep stealing.

And there—just around another quiet corner, hanging benignly on the wall in a square gilt frame unprotected by glass—was the Degas.

The first thing to rematerialize was her lips, and they were smiling.

She took shape as a woman again, her feet alighting soundlessly on the stone floor with the casual grace of years of practice. Her senses surged back: the dull tang of cloistered air in her nose, the stone cool and smooth beneath her feet, a faint car horn from the traffic on the Rue de Rivoli that never dissipated, even at this hour. Her stomach growled with a hunger pang, and she realized she hadn't eaten in hours.

She'd just reached up and grasped the painting—ethereal light and shadow around the voluptuous figure of a retreating woman—when she heard a trio of faint noises and froze.

Snap.

Click.

The *creak* of leather shoes.

For a split second her heart stopped beating. It started up again and took off at a thundering gallop.

She wasn't alone. Someone was *here.*

Eliana didn't even have time to turn before the darkness was sundered by a dozen wide yellow beams of light, aimed at her back. The soaring wall in front of her was bathed in brilliance, and the row of gilt frames caught the light and reflected it back in blinding glints of gold. She whirled around with one hand raised to shield her eyes, and just before she heard the loud report, in the infinitesimal second between the sting of gunpowder in the back of her throat, the flash of dazzling white and the pain that ripped through her bare calf, sending a flare of agony through her entire body, she heard a male voice shout something in French.

She crumpled to the floor. Blinded by the lights, unable to run or stand or even breathe, Eliana watched in horror as a dozen armed gendarmes ran crouched from hiding places on either side of the long corridor.

Police. Humans.

She touched her calf, felt the wound there, a ragged, wet slice through skin and muscle. She raised her hand, and for a suspended, horrible moment she stared down at it, slick with blood, her mind wiped utterly blank.

The male voice came again, still shouting at her in frenzied French, and she realized what he'd said before. A cliché she'd heard a dozen times in the American movies she loved, the old Westerns where it was easy to tell who the bad guys were because they always wore the black hats.

He'd shouted, "Stop or we'll shoot!"

As she watched the booted knot of armed gendarmes creep closer—guns drawn, eyes rabid—to where she crouched naked and bleeding on the floor beneath the Degas, Eliana had the brief, ironic thought that he'd gotten that perfectly backward.

ONE
Ice Serpent

Seven days earlier

For the fourth time in as many weeks, the police paid a visit to Gregor MacGregor.

They had their reasons, of course. He wasn't what could be called a good man—he wasn't the worst, either—but he was an excellent *business*man, and the type of business he specialized in never failed to attract the scrutiny of the authorities. Women, weapons, drugs, or thugs, Gregor could satisfy nearly every nefarious desire of his well-heeled clientele, and it had made him outrageously wealthy.

He managed his various business enterprises from the plush confines of a black leather recliner situated behind a massive, gleaming desk in an office on the top floor of a high-rise he owned in central Paris that housed a nightclub and a bordello, among other things. The police knew about the nightclub but not the bordello; only the very rich could afford to step beyond the opulent gold leaf doors that led to the garden of delights hidden deep in the bowels of the building, and they weren't inclined to talk.

Because Gregor had been subjected to these impromptu visits by the police on dozens of occasions, he was more irritated than worried. They never found anything incriminating; he was much too careful for that.

What bothered him about this particular visit, however, was the man who sat in a shadowed corner of the office on his custom Louis Vuitton silk divan, smoking a cigarette, watching him with hawklike intensity from blue eyes as clear and cold as an arctic sky. Wearing a black suit, black oxfords, and no watch or rings or adornment of any kind except a pair of small round spectacles, he'd never accompanied the police on any of their other surprise visits, and something about this man didn't sit right.

Gregor had grown up in the dodgy end of Edinburgh to impoverished parents who had eight children in quick succession until his father disappeared—fled, more like—and he'd been forced to survive as best he could. By the time he was ten years old, he'd committed nearly every crime imaginable and was well acquainted with all manner of thieves and cutthroats.

So he knew a soulless bastard when he saw one.

Gregor turned his attention back to the man seated across the desk from him. Tall, impeccably dressed, and utterly French, he was the chief of police's right-hand man, and a royal pain in Gregor's ass. "This is bordering on harassment, Édoard. I'm a law-abiding, tax-paying citizen of this country. I tolerate it because I've got nothing to hide, but if you keep up these witch hunts, I'll call my lawyer."

The blandly handsome Édoard smiled, revealing a row of perfectly straight, white teeth, a little too big for his mouth, like Chiclets. "Tax-paying, I'll give you. We've already looked into that. *Law-abiding*, however..." The Chiclet smile grew mocking. "You and I both know that's a stretch."

They stared at each other. Behind him on the divan, the blue-eyed man lifted his chin and, like the fire-breathing red dragon on the MacGregor family coat of arms, exhaled a long, gray plume of smoke.

Flanking either side of Édoard's chair were two standing gendarmes, glancing around his luxurious office in obvious envy. Gregor wondered why Édoard never brought the same men twice. Maybe he hoped new recruits would see something the old ones hadn't?

"What do you want?" His Scottish accent still added faint music to his speech, even after two decades in France, but its charm was lost on Édoard, whose smile never wavered.

"We're looking for a thief. An art thief, to be specific." His gaze flickered to the oil painting hanging on the wall behind Gregor's head. It was large and abstract; Picasso in his blue period. Original. "I understand you're well connected in the art community."

A laughable understatement. Art was a small and insular community, and he was both a dealer and a collector. Some of the deals were even legitimate. But to Édoard he only said, "This *La Chatte* I keep reading about in the press?"

"The very same."

Gregor shook his head. "Don't know him. Can't help you there."

"You do realize, MacGregor," said Édoard, his voice slightly lower than before, "I can make life much more difficult for you than I have. I can have men in here every night. I can have your every move watched. I can crawl right up your ass and plant a flag there if I like, and there's not a thing you can do about it. So please, take a moment to think it over." He paused, and that slick smile stayed affixed to his face as if it were carved on. "Perhaps you've overheard something in your travels. Perhaps there's someone you don't particularly like who might have some interesting news for us. Perhaps there might even be something you'd like to"—his brows lifted, hopeful—"confess. Even the smallest tidbit of information will do wonders for my general sense of leniency. You do enjoy all your expensive toys, don't you?"

His gaze slid to the Picasso. "You wouldn't want your art collection and your penthouse and your nightclub and your Ferrari to suddenly be seized by the government due to a paperwork error, would you? An unfortunate mix-up that would certainly take months, possibly years to untangle?"

Like a snake, anger unfurled in a slick, cold coil in Gregor's stomach. A reptilian slither that wound its way up through his gut and into his chest until his lungs were constricted, it was as familiar as his own face in a mirror. With it came the equally familiar, nearly overwhelming urge to beat something to a bloody, unrecognizable pulp.

Luckily for Édoard, the urge wasn't *completely* overwhelming.

With the steely control of a man who'd once stabbed a rival to death with his platinum Mont Blanc pen and hours later used the same pen to sign his name with a flourish on a check with six zeroes at the mayor's annual charity ball, Gregor mused, "Did you know that hydrofluoric acid is one of the only things that can completely decompose human bone? It can also dissolve glass, it's so corrosive. Even if as little as a few inches of your skin come into contact with it, you'll die within hours. Reacts with the calcium in your body, causes systemic toxicity and tissue death. It's untraceable, too."

Édoard's bland smile died a quick, ugly death. He sputtered, "Are you…are you *threatening* me?"

"What?" Gregor blinked, feigning innocence. "Sorry, I was just thinking about this thing I watched on TV last night. Amazing what you can learn from those crime shows."

From behind Édoard came a low, amused chuckle. Gregor glanced at the man in the black suit and found him smiling, a flat slash across his face that did nothing to warm the frozen intensity in his gaze. With those sly, vulpine eyes and the clouds of smoke billowing around him, the man was reminding Gregor more and more of an ice serpent conjured from some glacial version of hell.

Édoard sprang from the chair. "Have it your way," he snapped. "I'll be back in the morning with a warrant. Plan on spending all day here. We're going to need access to all your files."

Muttering oaths, he jerked his head toward the door and turned. The two gendarmes followed on his heels. "Agent Doe!" he barked over his shoulder, then he stepped through the door and vanished.

The man in black rose from the couch with quiet, confident economy. He took one last drag from the cigarette and then dropped it to the handwoven Turkish rug beneath his feet. With the toe of his gleaming black oxford, he unapologetically ground it into the thick pile. He clasped his hands behind his back and regarded Gregor with those chilling blue eyes. When he spoke, his voice was a perfect complement to that look—cold and lifeless, with a pronounced German accent that could make even the most lighthearted child's song sound like a funeral dirge.

"French cigarettes are as feeble as everything else in this country."

Gregor leaned back into his chair and gazed at the inscrutable Agent Doe. "Including the police."

"Ha. How right you are," quipped Doe without an ounce of affront. He walked to the door, unhurried, his hands still clasped behind his back.

"You're not one of Édoard's, then," said Gregor. "But he called you 'agent.' You're with the government?"

Doe reached the doorway and paused. "I am with the government in the exact same way that you are a legitimate businessman."

This statement bothered Gregor. The way he pronounced *with the* as *wit zuh* bothered him. *Everything* about the man bothered Gregor. Like a physical itch on his skin, he felt the intense, irritating need to know exactly who this man was and what he was up to. "Doe is an unusual name for a German," he persisted. "What's your first name?"

The agent gave him another of those dead smiles. He stepped over the doorway threshold and said, "John." He disappeared through the door and swung it shut behind him. It closed with a thud that faintly shuddered the row of floor-to-ceiling windows.

John Doe?

From behind him a voice said, "Watch out for that one. He'll skin you alive and make a lampshade out of your hide if he gets the chance."

Gregor smiled but didn't turn. He wanted to savor the moment.

He remembered the very first time he'd heard that silken purr of a voice. It was three years ago. He'd been at Bulgari with his son Sean and his son's pneumatic bimbo-of-the-week

Nicollette, shopping for a Christmas gift for his now blind, elderly mother he'd installed in a big house he'd bought for her in Monaco, when his idiot offspring had thought it a capital idea to try and steal a ten-thousand-euro watch as a Christmas gift for *himself.*

Try being the operative word. It was a clumsy attempt, at best, and a gargantuan security guard had him by the collar before he'd made it ten steps.

Like his father, Sean had been in trouble with the law since he was a child but had none of his father's intelligence or ability to learn from mistakes and devise new, better ways of operating outside the confines of the legal system. He was a petty thief, a dumb one at that, and had it not been for the intervention of an angel he'd still be rotting in jail to this day.

Gregor didn't know exactly how she'd managed it; he didn't know because she wouldn't tell him, and though he'd mulled it for years he'd never solved the riddle. The only thing of which he was certain was seeing with his own disbelieving eyes when his son palmed the watch and slid it in his coat pocket as Nicollette distracted the salesgirl from the selection on the white velvet tray. Then he turned and began to walk toward the door. Then the security guard nabbed him, wrestled him to the floor, and searched him while Sean lay silently still, tears rolling down his red cheeks.

But there was no watch.

It wasn't in his pocket or anywhere on his person, and in the end the guard was forced to let him go. The evidence had disappeared into thin air.

They were all back in the limo, just about to pull away from the curb outside the store, when he heard a light tap on the tinted window. Gregor pushed the armrest button, and it slid silently down, revealing in degrees the most astonishing face he'd ever seen, peering in.

Wide-set eyes of blackest night, canted up at the corners like a cat's. Thick, shoulder-length hair chopped rough and dyed indigo blue by someone who obviously hated her. Skin the color and creamy consistency of café au lait. A delicate nose and a wide, intelligent forehead and lips almost outrageously full that brought to mind certain body parts he'd like to have them wrapped around.

Gregor didn't think she could accurately be called beautiful—she was too exotic, too many planes and angles in features that were proportionate but atypical—but he knew without doubt he'd never seen anything remotely comparable. He felt like he was a Neanderthal gazing at a Salvador Dali painting; he had no frame of reference and didn't quite understand it, but he recognized the genius nonetheless.

For the first time in his life, he *almost* believed in the existence of God.

His surrealist masterpiece said, "I think this belongs to you." She lifted her hand, and from one tapered finger dangled the gold and diamond watch Sean had taken. It glinted with mocking cheer in the afternoon sun.

When he glanced back at her, she had a faintly amused tilt to her mouth. Gregor felt the sudden, violent urge to kiss those pornographic lips. Instead he said, "No. You're mistaken."

Her brows rose. "Am I?"

She laughed a low, throaty laugh that sent a shiver all the way down his spine. He ordered the driver to keep the car running, opened the door, stepped out into the crisp autumn air, and struggled to inhale a single breath of it as his gaze traveled over her body. Head to toe she was encased in black—stiletto boots, kidskin gloves, and enough skin-tight, curve-hugging leather to satisfy the kinkiest of BDSM enthusiasts, complete with a high-collared jacket zipped right up to her chin.

All that leather armor couldn't mask the pain in her eyes, though. He stood on the sidewalk next to her and marveled at how someone with the balls to be so defiantly uncommon could be so sad. Her lips smiled, but her midnight eyes held a terrible sorrow he was deeply moved to want to erase.

"Perhaps I'll keep it, then," the sloe-eyed stunner said, and slid the watch over her hand and clasped it in place on her wrist. She admired it for a moment, turning it in the light, and then looked back at him, pinning him in the deep melancholia of her eyes. "You wouldn't happen to know anyone who could help me sell something like this for a little profit, would you?"

The amusement again. Because he wanted desperately to assure it would stay, he replied, "As a matter of fact, I would."

Then he sent the driver with a tearstained Sean and a pouting Nicollette on their way.

Three years ago. Gregor knew the woman standing behind him now had known exactly who he was that day, had most likely followed him, waiting for the chance to propose to him what she did eventually propose, here in this very office after she'd pretended to let him convince her to come. Though they'd done business together regularly since then, she was as much a mystery to him now as she was that very first day, a bewitching ghost who drifted in and out of his life, ever silently, ever unexpectedly, leaving behind a faint scent of clover and winter roses that haunted him for hours afterward.

She haunted him.

Gregor, a man of calculating pragmatism who didn't believe in spirits or the supernatural or anything that could not be purchased with cold, hard cash, still wasn't entirely convinced this otherworldly creature was real.

"Just another one of Édoard's lackeys, princess," he said to her now, slowly swiveling around in his chair.

In soft shadow against the far wall, she stood watching him, regal and enigmatic as the Sphinx. He called her princess because although she stole for a living and dressed like a dominatrix and downed whiskey like it was going out of style, she was obviously highborn, a feline Audrey Hepburn, elegant and lithe. There was something elementally feral about her, too. Something that spoke of nighttime prowls and moonlit hunts.

Something almost...predatory.

He'd never known anyone who could be silent the way she could, who could look at you—*into* you—as if contemplating how you'd taste.

It was disturbing. Also—profoundly exciting.

She wore sleek, androgynous black, as always: a supple, thigh-length belted leather coat that molded to the lean lines of her body, black gloves, and short black boots with enough buckles and straps to handily double as bondage wear. Beneath the coat her long, gleaming golden legs were bare. She'd told him once that pantyhose made her feel claustrophobic—she had to feel the air on her skin—and he'd instantly summoned the vivid image of her sun-dappled nude body stretched out on green grass under a tree in the woods, arching her back and holding her arms out to him, wiggling her fingers in invitation like a lusty dryad.

He couldn't help these thoughts. He had a girlfriend, Céline, he was more or less devoted to, but in the presence of this woman who called herself Eliana—he wasn't entirely convinced that was her real name—all his willpower crumbled.

It should have worried him.

Being a man, it intrigued him instead.

"I don't think so." She stepped forward from the shadows, and for the first time Gregor noticed she carried a long cardboard cylinder under one arm. "He's dangerous, I'm sure of it."

Gregor rose, crossed to her, and took both her hands in his own. Beneath her gloves, they were chilled. He didn't bother asking her how she'd gained access to his highly secured building. Just another of her mysteries, never to be decoded.

"Don't worry about him," he murmured, gazing down at her. "It's good to see you again, princess. How are you?"

She grimaced and dropped her gaze to their joined hands. "You know I hate it when you call me that, Gregor. I'm about as much a princess as you are." After a moment, she gently removed her hands from his. "And how I am is worried about *you.* They're getting too close. One of these days—"

"One of these days nothing," he interrupted firmly, brushing her concerns aside. "They don't know anything, and they never will. Have I ever failed you before?"

She looked up at him, and something hot flared in her eyes, which was immediately veiled when she lowered her lashes, deftly avoiding his scrutiny.

He was tempted to put a finger beneath her chin and force her to meet his eyes, but he knew that would be a mistake. Aloof and proud—though never haughty—she didn't do emotions well. As a matter of fact, he'd never met anyone more restrained. Only rare glimpses of sadness and quickly snuffed anger ever escaped her chilly reserve, and it made him wonder what she was hiding. In his experience, only people with something to hide or something they were trying to forget kept themselves locked down like she did.

In Eliana's case, he suspected it might be both.

"No. Of course not, Gregor. I only meant that maybe we should stop for a while. I don't want to put you in any danger—"

His guffaw cut her off. "Danger is my middle name! Get it right! I'll not be havin' any more of that nonsense. Now, girl, show me what you've got there under your pretty little arm."

Her lips curved to a faint, wry smile. Her lashes lifted, and she regarded him with those eyes, dark as a swan's. Then without another word, she moved to his desk, removed a plastic cap from the cardboard cylinder, and withdrew a canvas from within. She laid the cylinder aside and carefully unrolled the canvas until it lay flat.

He came up behind her and stood looking down over her shoulder. Had the cylinder contained the Holy Ghost itself, he would not have been more stunned. "*The Card Players*," he whispered.

"I know you're partial to Picasso, but this Cézanne spoke to me," she murmured. One finger of her gloved hand reverently traced the frayed edge of the old canvas. "Intense, isn't it?"

"This was sold to a private collector in Qatar last year," he said, still stunned. "How did you get it?"

Her head turned a fraction, and he saw the glint of mischief in her eyes as she gazed up at him. He smiled, feeling his insides soften under the warmth of her look.

"The Cat has her ways, eh, princess?"

"She does indeed, Mr. MacGregor." Moving away to take a seat on the other side of the desk, Eliana settled herself in the chair, folded her hands in her lap, and said, "Can you sell it?"

"Can I sell it?" He raised his brows in mock indignation. "Is the pope Polish?"

She blinked, bemused. "No. But I'll take that as a yes."

Gregor sat in his comfortable chair and beamed at her. "You bet your biscuits I can sell it, princess! Same terms?"

She smiled. "Ten percent. Agreed." Her smile faltered, and for a moment that old sorrow welled to the surface again. "However…I'd like to take the ten in trade this time."

Gregor was intrigued. "Trade for what?"

She tucked her hand into the pocket of her coat and from it pulled a piece of paper, carefully folded. She leaned across the desk and handed it to him without a word.

Curious, he unfolded the note. When he read its contents, he was even more shocked than moments before. "Eliana. What the *hell* are you going to do with this many guns?"

Utterly composed, that terrible sadness still lurking behind her little smile, she quietly said, "What people always do with guns, Gregor."

They gazed at each other. Outside in the cold, winter Paris night, it began softly to rain.

"And the rest of it?" He peered at the list. "Rocket-propelled grenades? Smoke bombs?" He looked up at her again, incredulous. "*Land mines*?"

She exhaled a long, slow breath and looked away. She removed her gloves, finger by finger, and ran a hand through her thick, twilight-hued hair. He noticed for perhaps the millionth time that she never wore makeup, but he'd never seen anyone who needed it less. Like a firefly, the woman actually *glowed.*

"Wars can't be fought with sticks and stones."

Gregor jerked forward in his chair, really alarmed now. "Wars? Who you going to war with, princess?"

She remained silent, gazing at him now with rebuke. There were questions they didn't ask each other, information that was never exchanged, and they both knew he'd just violated that inviolable rule. But dammit, this was different! If she was in trouble—the kind of trouble that required this much heavy artillery—he wanted to help. He *needed* to.

"Let me help you. Whatever this is about, I can help."

Her answer was swift, cool, and unequivocal. "No."

Outside, the rain picked up. It began to beat against the windows in staccato bursts, smearing the city beyond into plots of wavering black and yellow.

"I don't like it," Gregor declared and tossed the note onto his desk.

Eliana didn't even blink. "You're a businessman. This is business. You might not like it, but you'll do it." Her head tilted to the side in a birdlike motion he'd seen a million times before when she was puzzling something out, and he knew that something now was *him.* When she spoke again her voice had softened to the consistency of warmed butter, and he knew she had his number: flattery and female helplessness were a potent combination for him, even if both were patently insincere. "Won't you, old friend? For me?"

"Stop trying to dazzle me, Eliana, this is serious!" Truly aggravated now, he leapt from the chair and began to pace behind it.

"Why are you lecturing me, Gregor?" she said, harder now. "If I were a man, would you even hesitate?"

He swung around and stared at her. His gaze swept the lovely landscape of her body, her bare crossed legs, the perfect oval of her face. "You're *not* a man. Obviously."

By the way her face flushed and she stiffened, Gregor knew he'd offended her. *At last, we're getting somewhere,* he thought. Maybe that wall would come down after all.

"So my lack of a penis is the only problem here?" The bitterness in her voice was unmistakable, and surprising. Eliana stood and drew on her gloves, all the while shaking her head and making little noises of disgust. "My entire life I've had to deal with that crap from my family. I *will not* tolerate it from my business associates."

She looked at him and drew herself up to her full height, which, for a woman, was substantial. At six foot three, he didn't tower over her nearly as much as he did everyone else.

"Thank you for all your help in the past, Gregor. I wish you the best. Good-bye."

She briskly began to roll up the oil painting still laid flat on his desk.

He leaned over and grabbed her hands. She lifted her gaze to his, all cold fury and steel, and he met her steely look with one of his own.

"Nay, girl, I'll not have you walkin' out on me in such a snit."

Whenever he was really emotional, his speech always reverted to the cadence of his childhood, rolling *r*'s and dropped *g*'s and the slow, musical lilt of a native Scotsman. Because he lived in France where everyone looked down on him because of his country accent, even the housemaids, he'd improved with years of practice but couldn't be bothered to concentrate on the properness of his speech at times like these.

"If it's guns you're needin' it's guns you'll have, but I'm tellin' you I don't like it, and if you get into trouble I need you to promise me you'll let me know so I can help."

She recoiled against his grip with a sinewy strength that surprised him for one that looked so delicate, but he pulled back and refused to let her go until she relented. "Promise me, princess," he insisted, his voice very low in his throat.

Finally, after long moments of staring at him in livid, unblinking silence, she quietly said, "I like you, Gregor. I always have. But if you don't take your hands off me in the next five seconds, you're going to see a very ugly side of me. A side I can't guarantee you'll survive seeing."

Then she murmured something in Latin, which he understood, because the Catholic mass his mother dragged him to every Sunday when he was a child had always been in Latin.

"*Nec mala te amicum. Placered non faciunt me.*"

Translated: "I don't want to hurt you, old friend. Please don't make me."

She lowered her head a fraction of an inch, and he imagined her eyes silvered against the light, like a cat's. A tingle of fear—something Gregor had not felt in many, many years—raised the hair on the back of his neck. Before he could form a reply, there came a loud knock on his closed office door. He and Eliana broke apart as the door swung open to reveal his girlfriend, Céline, clasping her teacup Yorkie to her ample chest.

As it always did when it caught sight of Eliana, the dog began first to growl, then to tremble violently in Céline's arms. She shushed it and sashayed toward them, weaving across the rug in a slinky red Dior dress she looked sewn into and a pair of Louboutin sandals he knew had cost him an arm and a leg. The monthly bill for her black American Express card was more than the GDP of some small countries.

"Daddy, I want to go out!" she implored him in pouty French. She gave Eliana a quick, sour once-over, which Eliana wholeheartedly returned, and then turned her attention back to him and tossed her long, platinum blonde extensions over one shoulder with a practiced flick of her wrist. "How much longer are you going to be?"

"We're actually done here," said Eliana flatly, her face drained of emotion. She turned and moved to the door, abandoning the painting on his desk.

"Eliana," Gregor entreated.

He wanted so badly to say, "Don't go," or "Please stay," or some version thereof, but under the shrewd, watchful eye of Céline, he didn't dare. He might have been the gangster in the room, but between these two goddamn women he was as helpless as a newborn kitten. Each of them had one of his testicles gripped firmly in a delicate, ruthless hand.

At the door Eliana paused. She looked back at him over her shoulder, and something in her face softened. She glanced down at the painting she'd left on his desk, and he realized she'd done it on purpose, as an offering. If she'd taken it with her, he'd never have seen her again.

"Gregor," she said.

of an elevated boxing ring. One of the bare-chested men in the ring was now spread-eagle on the mat, unconscious. The other—a beast of a male with chest and arms covered in tattoos that rippled with every movement of impossibly huge muscles—stood over his opponent, panting, looking down at the still body with crazed eyes, bared teeth, and all the geniality of a shark in a feeding frenzy.

"You can't deny his dreams are getting worse," Lix persisted as they watched D wave another opponent into the ring. He'd already been through three, and the training session had only started twenty minutes ago. Two *Legiones* dragged the unconscious male out of the ring, leaving a long smear of crimson on the white tarp. Another young male took his place, a tall, sinewy soldier nearing his twenty-fifth birthday who the *Bellatorum* were considering inviting to join their ranks if he survived the Transition. Which most likely he wouldn't; less than one percent of them ever did.

The Transition hung like a hangman's noose over the head of every half-Blooded *Ikati*. When fused with its human counterpart, *Ikati* blood was warped from the initial purity that allowed their unique characteristics to flourish. Twenty-five years to the minute from birth, and the half-Blood lived…or didn't. Just like a clock ticking down to zero hour.

Constantine remained silent. He knew what Lix had said about D's dreams was true because he'd heard the screams with his own ears. An almost nightly occurrence, D's dreams—more correctly nightmares, though he never said what they were about—weren't the dreams of ordinary people.

D was Gifted with Foresight, a talent he'd had since birth that had of late been torturing him with visions of which he refused to speak. It had everyone on edge, and not just because his screams echoed eerily through the winding corridors of the catacombs, fading to silence around dark corners while the children in bed pulled the sheets over their heads.

The things D dreamed came true. And if his terrified screams were any indication, something awful was headed their way.

"Does he ever talk to you about her?" Lix murmured, watching as D's new sparring partner began to circle him in the ring. D stood still, hands with taped knuckles lowered to his sides, tracking his opponent's every move with only his eyes. They shone with a murderous light.

"He barely speaks to me at all anymore," replied Constantine. Then, lower, "Not that he was much of a talker before, but now he's perfected the silent treatment into an art form."

Lix nodded his agreement. Then, as D threw a vicious punch that slammed his opponent into the ropes where he clung, wavering for a moment, before he fell face-first onto the tarp and lay still while the crowd went wild, he said, "He's going to kill one of them, Constantine. He's supposed to be training them, but it's like he wants to *kill* them. We have to do something about this. We've got to get Celian involved."

Constantine watched as D, who'd apparently had enough of beating trainees senseless for the moment, jumped the ropes and leapt down from the ring. The crowd, still cheering, gave him a wide berth as he stalked away into the gloom of the far corridor and then broke into a run. After only a few long strides, he was swallowed by blackness.

The gathered *Legiones* began to disperse and make their way out of the sparring chamber and into one of the dozen winding tunnels that fed it. The catacombs where the Roman colony made their home included miles and miles of those tunnels, deep beneath the city, dark and chilly and scented faintly of mold and more strongly of the incense that burned everywhere in gold censers to mask it.

"Maybe it's not anyone *else* he wants to kill, Lix."

Even in the semi-gloom that was the constant of the catacombs, he saw Lix blanch. He turned to Constantine, his long hair falling, as always, into his eyes. "He would never… do that," he said, scandalized. "It's forbidden."

"You know as well as I do that D doesn't give a damn about rules. Ours, the gods', anyone's. I hope you're right, though, brother." He sighed, feeling a lead weight settle into the center of his chest. "I really hope you're right. But we're going to have to do something about him soon—before we find out the hard way."

The therapeutic waters that fed the underground baths of the thermae were bubbling hot and faintly salty, as always, but for D they provided little relief. His muscles would be helped, but that wasn't where the real ache lay. He settled his heavy bulk lower into the water, dragged his hands across his face, and closed his eyes.

Eliana.

Her image sprang to life beneath his lids. She was on the forefront of his mind every moment. Sleeping, waking, fighting, eating…he carried her with him always, and the need for her was like a sickness that had spread to every organ, eating him alive.

There would be no relief from it until he found her… or died.

He'd been in love with Eliana so passionately and for so long that the pain of her disappearance three years ago had transfigured itself into a morbid kind of obsession, burning and black and weirdly alive, like an agonizing cancer in his gut that was slowly devouring him from the inside out.

It was relentless, this obsession. He thought of nothing else. He dreamt of nothing else. He ate and breathed and lived for one thing only, and that was the day he'd find her and apologize for the mess he'd made and explain that contrary to what she thought, it wasn't him who'd done the terrible thing that had driven her away in the first place.

Unfortunately, D had no idea where Eliana had gone. Rome was a huge city, ancient and sprawling, with a million places to hide. Or disappear altogether. But he knew the city and the particular musk and heady sweetness of her scent equally well and had high hopes he'd be able to find her before too much time had passed. Before things got even more complicated.

Before things got dangerous.

He failed, though. Every day and every night for years he'd searched, all for naught. He scoured the city, the surrounding countryside, as far north as the Alps and as far south as the tiny island of Malta, but not a trace of her could be found. He knew there was the possibility she'd left the country, though he couldn't really get himself to believe it. Like all predatory animals, the *Ikati* had a home range. He thought she'd stick close to hers.

Wrong. She was gone. And he had no idea where she went.

That and the dreams he'd been having about her were killing him.

"*Bonum vespere, Bellator,*" said a soft voice. D's head jerked up.

On the smooth rock floor on the opposite side of the thermae pool stood a young woman, robed in red. Dark haired and dark eyed like all of their kind, she also was very young. And very lovely. In layer over pale, wavering layer, light from the moving waters danced over her face, her body, the walls of the room. He searched his memory for her name…Iris. Former member of the *Electi.* Celian had disbanded the harem when the old king had died, but the *Bellatorum* were still sought after by the unmated females for sexual partners and breeding studs; the warriors were the most Gifted, and their genes were in high demand.

Among other things.

D nodded a curt greeting.

Encouraged, she smiled at him shyly and walked around the ledge of the pool, gazing down into the bubbling pale green water, sending him an occasional glance as she moved toward him. He saw the curves of her body beneath the flowing robe as she walked and imagined she might be nude beneath it.

Eliana.

His body responded. Naked in the hot water, he grew hard.

Iris stopped beside him. Silent, he looked up at her. She said, "May I join you?" Without waiting for a response, she opened her robe and slid it over her bare shoulders. It billowed into a pool of red silk around her ankles and settled against the wet stone.

Nude, she was more than pretty. She was ripe and perfect as a summer peach.

She crouched and swung her long legs over the side of the pool, and D watched with dark, gnawing need as she arched back and shook her hair from her face. She sat on the edge, leaning on her hands, her feet in the water, flat stomach and full breasts and a little smile as she looked down at him with an eyebrow raised like a cat with all the cream.

D stood abruptly. Water streamed from his naked body, and Iris lost her smile as her gaze traveled over his chest, down his abdomen, even lower…

Her eyes widened. Her mouth formed a startled O.

D grabbed Iris around her slender waist and dragged her into the hot water, holding her pinned against him. She was surprised but didn't struggle; D knew he'd earned such a deserved reputation for brutality from his battles in and out of the ring that Iris would not be expecting gentleness from him. And maybe that's what she hoped.

As he pulled her head back with a hand in her hair and lowered his mouth to hers, D idly wondered who'd sent her. Lix? Constantine?

When her tongue touched his, he decided it didn't matter. He needed this. It had been so long, so long since he'd even touched a woman, and she felt so good. So plush…

Eliana.

He pulled back from Iris's soft mouth with a muttered oath. She looked up at him, confused. "*Bellator*?" she murmured hesitantly.

He didn't bother with an answer. His body was still hard, aching for release, and now wasn't the time to drown in memories of a lost love or think about his dreams that vividly depicted her in trouble, in pain…but never *where.* Holding Iris tight against his body, D sat on the submerged rock ledge of the pool and pulled her down with him. He kissed her again, harder than before, desperate to block out everything but this moment.

Hot water swirled around their bodies. Her legs came around his waist. Her breasts pressed against his chest, and D let out a low groan as he felt her press against that throbbing ache between his legs. He needed this…he needed this so badly…

Eliana.

This time his curse was nearly shouted. Iris pulled back, that sweet softness in her face hardening into something else altogether.

"*Bellator,*" she said in a businesslike tone. "How do I displease you? Tell me and I will change it."

He wanted to laugh. He didn't think asking her to change into another woman would go over so well. He brushed a strand of damp hair from her flushed cheek and said, "You don't displease me, little one. You're beautiful." He tried out a smile. It felt strange on his face, alien, like it didn't belong there. "You know that."

The softness came back to her face, and she smiled. Her arms wound around his neck, and she began, slowly, to rock her pelvis against his. He felt her heat even in the hot water, and a growl rose in the back of his throat.

"Let me please you, *Bellator,*" she whispered, leaning close to stroke her tongue along his bottom lip. "Take what you need from me." Taut nipples brushed his chest, and D lifted his hands to cup her full breasts, pinching those enticing nubs between his fingers. She gasped and tightened her legs around his waist and then kissed him, deep and demanding. His erection grew even bigger, aching for her, for release, for a moment of forgetting, for—

ELIANA!

D shoved Iris away with so much force it sent a wave of water splashing against the rock rim of the thermae behind her. She stood and cursed, sputtering in indignation, wet hair dripping into her face.

He leapt from the pool, grabbed a towel and his clothes, and with a murmured word of apology and shame like cold fingers wrapped around his heart, got the hell away from the alluring Iris and the demons she roused in what was left of his black, ragged soul.

THREE
Little Prizefighter

Two days later and almost a thousand miles away, in a secret underground city much like the one in which she'd been born and raised, Eliana spun on the ball of one booted foot, snapped out the opposite leg, and landed a perfect, vicious kick to the jaw of her opponent.

It sent him staggering back across the dusty limestone floor into a sea of bodies crowded together in an irregular circle against the shadowed, graffitied rock walls of New Harmony.

The crowd roared its approval and flung him back toward her.

"Had enough yet, slick?" she murmured as he went down on one knee. Sweating and panting, he looked up at her through a thicket of tangled blond hair and grinned.

"Not even close, Butterfly. I'm just getting warmed up."

He stood and paused just long enough for her—and all the other women in the crowd—to admire his toned physique: tight muscles in tight jeans and a tight black T-shirt, all of it theatrically showcased by candlelight from hundreds of votives tucked into niches in the rounded walls that spilled a warm, flickering glow over the cavernous room. Golden blond as an angel, he had a dimpled smile to match, warm chocolate eyes, and a laugh that could melt an iceberg.

What was it she'd heard the catagirls—the groupies of the underground fight scene—call Alexi? Oh yes. *Ripped.* Also *fine* and *ohmyGodsohotithurts.*

He didn't hold back as he leapt forward with a roar, arms outstretched, teeth bared, intent. She admired him fleetingly again—such animal grace and ferocity, almost like one of her kind—and then snapped into focus as instinct took over and a ripple of power shuddered down her spine.

Sensual and delicious, it sent goose bumps crawling along her skin.

She crouched into it, coiling, drawing down close to the ground, her eyes and ears and nose wide open and focused on him as he neared, seeking, calculating every nuance of his expression, every twitch of muscle and nerve that broadcasted his intent as clearly as a loudspeaker.

He was almost on her, reaching out, almost had a hand fisted in her hair—

—but she dodged his grip in one lightning-fast move and twisted away, smiling.

He skidded to a stop and swung around, growling his frustration, gravel grinding and spitting chunks beneath his heels. He whipped around and then lunged at her again, this time diving low to try and kick her legs out from under her with a sweep of his powerful legs. She leapt clear, executed a somersault in the cool air high above his head, and landed in a perfect three-point crouch, one hand and knee balancing her weight, one leg stretched out, her other arm held aloft behind her as counterweight, disturbing not even a single mote of dust as she settled silently on the ground.

Collectively, the gathered crowd gasped.

"Showoff," Alexi muttered, glowering, but Eliana could tell by his tone and the gleam in his eyes that he wasn't really annoyed.

He lived for this.

A successful man in the real world aboveground, Alexi was also one of the smartest people Eliana had ever met. He held postgraduate degrees in electrochemistry, applied mathematics, and computer science. By the age of twenty-one, he'd bought and sold his first company. By twenty-eight, he held patents in robotics, augmented reality and holographic technologies, and cryopreservation. And now, at thirty-two, he was CEO of an international conglomerate that was pursuing, among other things, the key to cold fusion.

Like most people of genius intellect, he was drawn to the odd and the eccentric, the unexplained and the unexplainable. So naturally he was drawn to the catacombs, and to Eliana, a riddle he was determined to solve.

Fight Club was his favorite movie, and fighting in the catacombs fed the highly competitive, thrill-seeking side of his personality. Eliana suspected he fancied himself the better-educated, European version of Brad Pitt.

He was. His combination of looks, smarts, and brawn was devastating.

"Five hundred says she pins you in sixty seconds," Melliane called out from somewhere in the crowd behind her. A chorus of voices chimed in, arguing and yelling over one another, clamoring for a piece of the action. Eliana smiled; tonight the take would be good.

"A thousand if she does it in ten!" an anonymous man with a whiskey-soaked voice shouted above the noise, and that's what finally decided it for her.

She rose to her feet in a single, fluid unbending of limbs and felt the animal rise to an almost unbearable peak within her, sinking tooth and claw into her muscles, her nerves, straining against her skin, hissing out with her own exhalation, writhing to be set free. Her eyes fixed on Alexi's, and for a moment she was sure he saw it, too, the beast that lived ever long just beneath her skin. His brown eyes widened for a moment and then narrowed, preparing.

Finish it! the beast hissed. Without hesitation, Eliana obeyed.

One long stride, two, three…a sudden rush of cool wind as she moved, the blur of bodies in her peripheral vision, the bulk of Alexi ahead of her, the muffled roar of voices from all sides, the smell of hot wax, damp rock, and humans. In a heartbeat she was on him, heat and muscle and the heady scent of clean skin and cologne and sweat, his hard arms tightening around her back as she slammed against him and knocked them both to the ground.

His breath huffed out on impact, but he didn't loosen his grip. She gave him bonus points for that.

"Sorry, slick," she whispered against his ear, "but play-time's over."

Then she flipped onto her back, dragged him along with her, threw her legs around his neck, and squeezed.

The roar of the crowd was deafening.

He tried with all his considerable might to pry open her thighs, but his face got redder and redder by the second, and then veins began to bulge in his forehead and neck. Beneath him she mouthed it again—*sorry*—and gave him a little apologetic shrug.

Finally he tapped out, and she released him. He fell back against the dusty limestone, coughing and laughing at the same time, brown eyes watering, both hands at his throat.

"Hellcat!" he rasped.

If he only knew. Eliana glanced to her right and saw Mel—a dark-haired sylph sandwiched between two hooting, fist-pumping men—her arms crossed over her chest, nodding in satisfaction. She winked at her, and Mel's face split into a grin. She danced over in a few swift strides and offered her hand. Eliana took it, stood, and brushed the fine limestone dust off the back of her favorite black leather pants and out of her hair.

"Took you long enough," Mel murmured with a quick glance at Alexi. Two of his friends were helping him from the floor, but he pushed them away, cursing loudly, preferring to get to his feet under his own power.

"Just long enough to let him save face," Eliana murmured back as Alexi shot her a penetrating sideways glance and then turned away to slap one of his friends on the back.

"Somebody buy me a drink—I just got my ass kicked by a girl!" he shouted.

"Again!" someone shouted back, and he hollered a good-natured curse at the man. Eliana was the only one who ever beat Alexi in the weekly matches, but she beat everyone else, too, even the monstrous MMA cage fighter who'd once come to test her skills, so it almost didn't count.

She was a freak of nature, that's all. It's always easier to dismiss the freaks.

A knot of moon-eyed, squealing catagirls in heavy makeup, miniskirts, and midriff-baring tops shuffled in his direction. He glanced in her direction to make sure she was still looking and then put his arm around the nearest one and nuzzled his face into her neck.

Eliana sighed. If she had been in love with him, his ploy might have worked. As it was, she only felt the same vague pang of guilt that she was so broken she couldn't feel anything at all, even for someone she'd been so intimate with.

No—she'd never been truly intimate with Alexi. It pained her to admit she'd used him as a foil for her own black, bottomless loneliness. For a few chaotic months before she came to her senses and turned him loose, they were inseparable, her ebony to his ivory, her dark to his light.

Then, when the gifts started coming, flowers and candies and that beautiful filigree ring he called a "friendship" ring, she ended it. She sent him back to the catagirls who followed him wherever he went like a school of hungry remora.

She wasn't good for him, and he deserved to be happy. Alexi, for all his swagger and chest-thumping, was a good guy. She hoped they could get to a place where they were truly friends, but she was beginning to doubt the possibility. It had been over a year since they'd been together, and his eyes still restlessly followed her.

He still wanted to solve her riddle.

"He's got the right idea, anyway." She turned her attention back to Mel, who was watching her carefully, something she'd caught her doing on more than one occasion. Eliana knew Mel worried about her, but the cornerstone, unspoken rule of their friendship was *don't ask, don't tell.* Relationships were one of a dozen topics Eliana did not discuss, with anyone. Ever.

"About?"

"Drink. Let's go get one."

Mel nodded. "Give me ten and I'll meet you at the Tabernacle." She grinned, and it made her face look even more impish than usual. "I've got to collect the money." She turned and danced away in that particular way she had, almost skipping over the ground, her long, plaited black hair slapping lightly against her back.

Right, Eliana thought, turning away. *Keep your eye on the prize, Butterfly. Eye on the prize.*

Beneath the glitz and glamour and city lights of Paris, there exists a cool, quiet world of freedom and possibilities. Les Carrières de Paris is a deep, intricate web of nearly four hundred miles of abandoned limestone quarries, pits and old wells, subway and sewer networks, canals and reservoirs and aqueducts that leak into the surrounding rock and make the walls weep silent tears. It is a beautiful, mysterious, and some would say frightening subterranean paradise; it's been said the gate to hell can be found there, just beyond the catacombs named the Empire of Death for the six million nameless souls buried in its dark embrace, moldering bones jumbled in vast, dusty piles at the bottoms of wells and stacked in macabre precision along dark walls, common as discarded seashells.

These catacombs form the arteries and intestines of Paris. Ancient and eerie, they're decorated with wall carvings and acres of neon graffiti, bone sculptures and dripping stalactites, all of it illumed by thousands of candles tucked into niches whose flames never waver because the air is so still. It is an underground kingdom few know of, and fewer still ever see.

The few who do risk arrest—entering the catacombs has been illegal for many decades—keep the secret of their entry spot closely guarded. Through the mouths of abandoned railways, down manholes that fall away into darkness, in the basements of old buildings and churches and banks, the "cataphiles" come seeking relief from daily life in the spiritual night of the underworld. Freedom and anarchy reign, all the cataphiles have nicknames to conceal their true identity, and they share a single, simple philosophy:

"To be happy, stay hidden."

Eliana and her group of two dozen were exiles, and they were well acquainted with hiding, so life in the catacombs suited them perfectly. For now.

As she made her way through the crowd, people fell back to allow her passage, and whispers followed in her wake. "You ever see anyone move like that?" murmured a tattooed, lanky young man to his muscled friend who stood beside him. They stared at her like she might suddenly sprout horns.

"Told you, man," the muscled one said with pride. "The Butterfly's a legend in the underground. Never been beat."

Eliana raised a hand to the back of her neck, imagining she could feel her own tattoo there, the vivid indigo and black butterfly that spread its wings between her shoulder blades and earned her the nickname. *Phengaris arion* transformed its original shape, was painted the colors of night, and teetered on the razor's edge of extinction; they had a lot in common.

Leaving the heat and crowd of the amphitheater behind, Eliana made her way down a winding corridor, ducking under an outcropping of sewer pipes and carefully avoiding the crumbling stone support columns wedged between the floor and the low ceiling above. There had been many cave-ins over the years—the old quarries had been overmined and were as fragile as a dry skeleton—so she stayed well clear. Down a narrow passageway where the light sank to murky green and a few more twists and turns around corners she knew by heart, and suddenly the walls fell away and the room opened into soaring, silent space.

The Tabernacle was the closest the underground had to a church. It was a sanctuary, though a nondenominational one, where thousands of unnamed people had left mementoes of loved ones they'd lost over the years. Photos and trinkets, poems and wedding rings, yellowed letters with curled edges and tear-shaped stains...a million dusty memories lined the walls and littered the floor, and everyone who entered this place spoke in a reverential hush.

Everyone, that is, except Caesar, who never failed to make a dramatic entrance wherever he went.

He stumbled into the room on the arms of two girls from an egg-shaped access tunnel several yards away. As soon as he spotted her, he shouted, "There she is!"

The girls were covered in dust, their shoes caked with muck, their bare arms and legs streaked with mud from the limestone powder and moisture that invaded every crack and crevice, but between them Caesar was spotless, his clothes unwrinkled, his hair in its usual perfect shape. "How's my little prizefighter?"

It echoed off the walls, dying slowly into silence. He was slurring a little, weaving a little, and the girls were supporting most of his weight.

Wonderful.

"Brother," she greeted him stiffly.

"Sister." He smiled, a slow, mocking curve of his sculpted lips, and then bent his head to the ear of the girl on his right and whispered something. She giggled and stole a quick glance in Eliana's direction, and then the trio stumbled off into the shadows of the far wall where several couches were hidden behind stacks of old wooden crates some long-ago cataphile had erected.

"Don't let him get to you," Mel said softly, coming up behind her.

"It's fine," Eliana lied, breathing hard through her nose. "I'm fine." She brushed away the hand Mel had placed on her shoulder—she could handle humiliation, but *never* pity—and turned to face her.

Mel held up an old-fashioned silver flask and wiggled it. "Victory drink?"

Eliana took it without hesitation, unscrewed the cap, and swallowed a long draught of liquid. A rotgut hooch made from fermenting pears and potatoes, it burned like acid going down. Coughing, she handed it back to Mel. "Ugh! Did you cook that up in your shoe? I like to think I'm the kind of girl who can drink anything, but this stuff is volcanic. Why can't my victory drinks ever be champagne?"

"Champagne tastes on a beer budget." Mel shrugged. She tipped the flask to her lips and swallowed. Her face screwed up just as Eliana's had, and she hacked a lung-clearing cough. "Besides, Ms. Pouty Pants, with the way we drink, in a few months someone would have to get a bulldozer in here to dig us out from under the mountain of empty bottles."

Eliana paused, considering that. She had a point. Neither of them drank to the point of stupidity like her brother, Caesar, did; they drank just enough to take the edge off and get beautifully blurred. Sometimes it even worked. "Volcanic moonshine it is, then."

Mel handed the flask back to her, and she drained it, grimacing, as Mel watched.

"Alexi asked me where you'd gone."

"Pfft. He was so draped in women, I'm surprised he even noticed I'd left."

Mel's mouth twisted to a rueful smile. "He always notices what you do, E."

"Yeah, well, ancient history notwithstanding, I hope he doesn't catch something from those catagirls he was with. They didn't exactly look…virginal."

Mel laughed, a decidedly witchy cackle that was at odds with her appearance. She was shorter and daintier than her lean, long-limbed friend, with beautiful waist-length black hair she wore in a French braid. Matched with her doe-like prance and a snarky, irrepressible sense of humor, Mel's travel-size frame lent her the general air of a mischievous woodland creature, a sexy trickster elf who might lead you out of the forest to safety or right over the edge of a cliff.

In other words, a wolf in sheep's clothing.

Though she was six years younger than her friend, and Mel was perfectly capable of defending herself, Eliana felt violently protective of her. She considered Melliane the sister she'd never had.

"Look who's talking trash!" Mel cried in delight. Dark eyes dancing with mirth, she pointed a finger at her. "Pot, meet kettle!"

"Shut up," Eliana answered good-naturedly, and then she froze as the sharp, unmistakable sound of flesh smacking flesh broke the stillness. It was followed quickly by a low moan, a growled admonition, and then eerie silence. Mel glanced over at the high stack of crates Caesar and his two companions had disappeared around, but Eliana didn't have to look. She'd heard it all before, and it made her sick to her stomach.

"Let's get out of here." Mel's pretty face had darkened. "I don't want to stay for the freak show."

Me neither, thought Eliana as they quickly turned and headed for another access tunnel that would lead them out of the catacombs and into the basement of the abandoned abbey where they slept. *I already know how it ends.*

FOUR
The Logical Conclusion

"Caesar's late again."

Eliana absently poked the tines of her fork into the gelatinous yolk of the fried egg on her plate. It quivered and split apart, oozing over the porcelain in a spreading stain of yellow. She shuddered, disgusted. Chicken stillbirths. Who liked these hideous things?

Silas did, apparently, because he cut into his own with surgical precision and ate half of it in one bite. Mildly he said, "He's sleeping in."

This didn't fool her; Eliana knew Caesar too well. Sleeping in meant sleeping it off. He'd spent another night carousing with the catagirls—new ones, ones who didn't know his particular tastes—or at the infamous Moulin Rouge, where the girls were paid handsomely to cater to those kinds of tastes and the men who possessed them. It had been five days since she'd witnessed the ugliness at the Tabernacle, and he'd only made one of their morning breakfast meetings.

It was their long habit to take breakfast in the back garden of the DuMarne, the old, sprawling abbey they'd moved to when they'd decided to take refuge in Paris after fleeing Rome three years before. A beautiful ruin, cavernous and neglected but in no danger of being sold because of its historical value, it was the perfect temporary hideaway for their little colony. The access to the catacombs was an added bonus they all took advantage of; they were creatures of the underworld, after all, even more so than all the other human cataphiles who went there to cavort and hide from real life in the cool, succoring dark.

"Maybe if he didn't spend so much time sleeping I wouldn't have to spend so much time working," she said. As it usually did when the subject was Caesar, her stomach tightened to a fist.

"You don't like the fighting?"

She glanced up at Silas to find him staring at her in sharp-eyed assessment. His shoulder-length black hair, gathered in a neat queue with a slim leather tie, framed a square-jawed, imposing face that others described as handsome but she saw only as hard. And preternaturally intelligent; Silas never missed a thing.

He was a dozen years older than she, and she'd known him all her life. A servant before they'd fled the catacombs three years ago, he was now second-in-command to her brother, the Alpha, and had been invaluable to them both in the years since. He was utterly capable and loyal, and if she had the occasional strange vibe from him, she tried to dismiss it as nerves.

To be sure, her nerves were not what they used to be.

"The fighting is…well, it's a distraction." She shrugged. "And it's just for show, no one ever gets hurt." Egos were really the only thing that ever took any damage. In the weekly matches at New Harmony, she fought for money, not for blood.

Silas wiped the corner of his mouth with a napkin, still watching her intently. "So it's the stealing you object to. You don't like being a thief."

She grimaced. "Of course I don't *like* it, Silas. It's dishonorable. Even a child knows stealing is wrong."

He smiled at that, a faint curve of his lips that might have been either amusement or disdain. "You're only stealing oil painted on canvas, Eliana. It's hardly a stain on your morality. And in any case, the ends justify the means. Your father knew that. Sometimes we have to sacrifice our own… lofty ideals…for the greater good."

He would consider honor a lofty ideal. To him, there was only one benchmark by which everything was measured: Is it *useful?* If the answer was yes, regardless of the situation or ethical questions or opinions of others, it was adopted. She'd never known anyone more clinically pragmatic.

"The greater good of my brother's fondness for beating prostitutes?"

Silas's smile only deepened at the acid in her tone, the look of disgust on her face.

"Your brother's little peccadilloes notwithstanding, he's willing to do whatever it takes to see your father's dream of freedom for all our kind come to pass. We all share the same philosophy; unfortunately, *you* are the only one with the

Gifts to get us what we need." His eyes softened, yet somehow grew more intense. "Believe me, I'd take the burden on myself if I could."

Uncomfortable under his penetrating stare, she glanced away. "We have almost enough money now to finance the construction of the stronghold. Once that's completed—"

"Then you'll stop," Silas said, reading her mind. The man really didn't miss a thing.

How irritating.

"Then I'll stop," Eliana agreed, nodding. And do what, she wondered. Garden?

Again with that uncanny intuition, he said, "Perhaps then you could consider..." He trailed off, lowering his gaze to the plate of food on the table in front of him. He toyed with the half-uneaten egg. "Starting a family." His voice was oddly neutral. "Taking a mate."

"A *mate*? You make it sound so romantic."

A muscle flexed in his square jaw. "You're too smart to think marriage is about hearts and flowers, Eliana. Perhaps for humans it is, but romance is a luxury creatures like us can't afford. We have to be more clearheaded, look at choices through the lenses of logic, not emotion. Our continued survival depends on creating the next generation, especially now—"

"Seriously?" The fist in Eliana's stomach started to burn. "It's not enough that I steal and fight to support us—now my *uterus* has to support us, too?"

He stared at her, his eyes coal black and flinty. "Your *uterus* aside," he said, deadly soft, "there is a war coming. Survival of the fittest is the only thing that matters now, *principessa*—"

"Don't call me that, Silas," she hissed, jerking forward in her chair. He knew she hated to be called that, knew how much it reminded her of the past. "The day my father died I stopped being a princess—"

"A war that will cost many lives," he forged on, calm and dogged, pointedly ignoring her anger, "and leave us even weaker than we are now unless there are children to replace those lost. And since females only go into Fever once a year and many times do not get pregnant, every Fever that passes is a lost opportunity. You've had three since we left the catacombs of Rome—"

"Silas!" He'd been *counting.* The thought made her shudder.

"—and soon you'll have another. The clock is ticking, Eliana. And no one else in this colony is better suited for you than I am. Our marriage is the logical conclusion."

Eliana stared at him for long seconds, both repulsed and curiously deflated by the sudden realization that Silas was talking about marriage to *him.* Which made absolutely no sense at all; most of the time she was convinced he didn't even like her.

She said, "That has got to be the least enticing proposal of marriage ever uttered in the history of life on this planet."

A faint crease in his cheek indicated he was holding back laughter. Or was it a sneer?

"That's not the only reason you should consider it, though."

Her brows climbed. "There's *more* to this fuzzy, heartwarming declaration of yours? I'm on the edge of my seat."

He tilted his head and looked at her from beneath a thicket of black lashes, that slight crease in his cheek growing deeper as his lips curved into the faintest of smiles.

Something about it set her nerves on edge in a way she couldn't quite put her finger on.

"I guarantee things won't always be as they are now," he said softly. "Your brother is...unbalanced. Don't look at me like that. You know it's true."

She enunciated each word carefully. "What is your point, Silas?"

He stretched out his arm, leisurely, unhurried, inspected the manicured crescents of his fingernails, and straightened the cuff of his crisp black shirtsleeve. Then, almost casually, he said, "When his goals for the production of the antiserum and the construction of the stronghold have been fulfilled and you're not quite so necessary to him anymore... marriage to me..." He hesitated, and Eliana sat there staring at him in growing dismay, feeling her heart thrum in her chest. "You know the influence I have over him," he murmured, his voice almost seductive. In contrast to his silky voice, his smile grew positively chilling.

He lowered his arm and lifted his gaze straight to hers. "I could offer you protection."

So. There it was.

With as much dignity as she could muster, Eliana lifted her chin and gazed in stiff silence at the rose garden, a profusion of white blossoms nodding in the cool morning breeze. Their scent sweetened the air but did nothing to remove the sudden, sour taste in her mouth.

Though he was eldest and a boy and therefore automatically held in higher esteem by the custom of their people, Caesar had been born Giftless, and so their father—brilliant, brooding Dominus who prized honor above all—had favored Eliana. He never said it, but it was crystal clear through years of sour looks and cold shoulders that their father considered Caesar a failure, a stain upon the honor of his powerful Bloodline.

Dedecus. A disgrace.

Eliana had done her best to shield Caesar from the relentless disappointment that emanated from Dominus. Caesar, though unGifted, was smart enough to recognize the disdain that oozed from their father like pus from a sore, and he resented Eliana all the more for trying to protect him from it.

No matter how she tried to bridge the gap between them, Caesar was as unpredictable as a crossbred dog, and she was never quite sure from one moment to the next if her olive branches would be met with smiles or snarls.

She knew he was flawed—worse than that, possibly—but he was the only family she had left. Her mother had died giving birth to her, her father had died only three years ago, and she had no other siblings and no immediate family since they'd fled Rome. Without him, she'd be alone.

Utterly alone.

It was her deepest fear, and one of which she was even more deeply ashamed. It made her feel like a coward, and right after liars, she despised cowards more than anything else on earth.

"I'm his Blood," she said, soft and vehement, more to herself than to Silas. "Beneath it all, he loves me. I don't need protection from him."

Silas's brows shot up as if she'd just said something very stupid. "Jealousy has darkened his heart," he answered, almost managing to sound truly regretful. "Who can say what a jealous king will do, even to those he loves?"

Heat flashed over her, scalding hot. She gripped the edge of the table so hard her knuckles turned white. "Who the *hell* do you think you are, trying to threaten me into marriage, trying to turn me against my own—"

"Morning, kiddies," a languid voice drawled from behind her. Eliana turned slowly in her chair to glare at its owner.

"Caesar. How kind of you to join us."

If he noted the sarcasm in her voice, he didn't acknowledge it. Clad all in white, with the winter morning sun behind him flared into a nimbus around his head, he appeared like a seraph, otherworldly and darkly dangerous. He'd inherited their father's breadth of shoulders and powerful, elegant frame, their mother's sculpted lips and eloquent eyes. Golden-skinned and long-limbed, he was gorgeous, and as one could easily tell by the insolent way he moved and spoke and even *breathed*, he knew it.

"Having a little argument?" he asked lightly as he seated himself at the table. He gracefully unfolded his napkin and placed it on his lap, picked up his fork, and leaned over Eliana's plate to spear a piece of ripe melon. He popped it in his mouth and sat back in his chair, watching the two of them with bright, laughing eyes.

"We were just talking about the stronghold," Eliana said, still stiff and seething, glaring now at Silas. "We'll need to choose a final location so we can get started on the architectural plans."

"Well," said Caesar around the melon in his mouth, "we've all agreed on the Congo basin in Africa, which is apropos considering that's where the *Ikati* originated." He sighed. "Though I admit, I'll miss France. The people here are so…friendly."

The women, he meant. The paid ones. "But the final *location*," Eliana insisted, but Caesar cut her off.

"I think it's more important we discuss the name."

Caught off guard, Eliana blinked at him in surprise. "The *name*?"

He took his time selecting another piece of melon from her plate. "Hmmm," he said, sifting through her food with his fork. "An important country needs an important name."

Silas and Eliana exchanged a look. "Country, my lord? Our planned stronghold might be a little small to call itself a country—"

"If the Vatican can be called a country, so can Zion," pronounced Caesar, eating two pieces of melon in quick succession. Eliana had the urge to smack the fork out of his hand and tell him to get his own damn plate, but she contained it by curling her hands into fists in her lap. "It will definitely be the more important of the two, in the long run."

"Zion," Eliana repeated. "How dramatic. And maybe a tad too biblical, don't you think? We'll have the apocalyptic wackos descending on us in droves. All those Mayan calendar doomsdayers will think we're the next best thing."

"Actually, it's perfect," purred Silas, with a sideways glance in her direction. So he'd chosen sides and was punishing her. Her fists curled tighter in her lap. "Zion refers to the world to come," he continued, "the promised land, the spiritual and physical homeland of an oppressed people, wandering and longing for safety."

Eliana glared at him. Though her father had ensured she'd had the best education—arts and language tutors and mathematics and science instructors and even a Japanese *gendai budō* master paid handsomely for his visits and his silence—Silas and Caesar inevitably spoke to her as if she were mentally challenged. It was the unfortunate and infuriating collateral damage of living in a patriarchal society that had remained unchanged for thousands of years: women were second-class citizens. Or possibly third, behind the livestock.

With a clenched jaw, Eliana said, "I know what the word means, Silas."

"Then we're in agreement." Caesar's teeth shone brilliant white as he flashed a smile. "Good!"

No discussion, no agreement, just Caesar doing exactly what he wanted. As usual. Trying very hard to breathe calmly around the sudden pounding in her chest, she said, "And the location?"

Caesar's answer was a waved hand. "I've hired the architectural firm to start the plans for the main compound and outlying buildings. We're making inquiries into the availability of a tract of land large enough for what I envision. Room to grow is important; once the disgruntled members of the other colonies find out what we're about, we'll need it." He chuckled. "I imagine there are a lot of them who are quite sick of hiding like rats in the basement."

"And how exactly are the other colonies going to find out about us?" Eliana asked. "We've never talked specifically about how we're going to get the word out to those who want to live openly with humans, as we want to, how we're going to provide them safe transport from their own colonies, protect them from their Alphas who'll definitely want to kill them for deserting—"

Another waved hand from Caesar. "Let the men worry about the details, Ana. You just keep on bringing home the bacon. Which reminds me," he said, snapping his fingers together. "There's a new Degas at the Louvre you should take a look at. It would be perfect for your little human pet."

Gregor, he meant. That's what he called him: *human pet.* It was better than what he called most other humans. To him, they would ever only be three things: pets, playthings, and breeders. It was where their ideologies diverged sharply. Eliana believed they should live alongside humans because the two species were equal, as were all the creatures of the earth, but Caesar thought they should live alongside humans so the *Ikati* could be worshipped as they were long ago in ancient Egypt.

They were once considered gods, and he had not forgotten it.

"The Louvre? That's pushing it, don't you think? It's a little...high profile."

Caesar's answering smile was nearly a sneer. "It should be easy enough for *you*, Ana. Vapor, invisibility...everything comes so easily for you. It'll be a cinch."

He leaned back in his chair and smiled at her, slow and mocking, and that look made her face flush with blood. *Enough. I can't take any more of our dysfunction today.* She rose from the table and shoved back her chair. "I'll look into it."

Unfortunately, her voice didn't come out quite as smoothly as she wanted, and she knew he was pleased she was upset when his smile grew larger.

"Tonight," he said lightly. The look in his eyes was anything but light, and Eliana understood this wasn't negotiable. "Get it done tonight. There's another payment due to the lab."

Their eyes held for a moment, until finally she nodded. He nodded back, satisfied, and turned his attention to Silas.

"We've got enough of the serum now to inject all the half-Bloods from the old colony. There's no reason they wouldn't jump at the chance to survive past the Transition and join us. Now we just have to get the word out to them. We'll have to think of something…special."

Dismissed. She'd just been dismissed. Without another word, humiliated and burning with hand-shaking, throat-squeezing, chest-crushing anger, Eliana turned and walked away.

Silas's black, black eyes followed her until she swept out of sight beyond an ivy-draped corner, heading back inside the abbey.

His Gift was subtle, but—on those whom it worked—devastatingly effective.

Less powerful than the outright mind control of the Gift of Suggestion, the ability Silas had learned over long years to wield with the deadly precision a ninja wields a katana was more a whisper than a shout, a gentle nudge than a shove, the coy glance of a maiden that garnered the same result as the bolder, more lusty stare of a whore.

In other words, it was elegant.

He had no name for it and no use for one; it wasn't as if he'd speak about it aloud, in any case. He wasn't prone to that horrific new age compulsion so many humans were afflicted with: sharing. He was, however, prone to plotting. Prone to planning. Prone to a dark, satisfied chuckle when some outcome he'd orchestrated came to glorious, inevitable fruition.

Silas chuckled a great deal.

The one black spot in his otherwise great satisfaction with his Gift was its limitation. There were certain minds, certain hearts, too strong or closed or stubborn to be swayed. In Eliana's case, he suspected it was all three, but she'd never been affected by the subtle pressure he sent her way, little nudges of intent sent out in invisible waves, gentle as a lover's touch. No matter how he tried to influence her emotions, she would not be swayed.

Her brother, on the other hand, was an entirely different matter.

Caesar, his eyes lingering on the place where Eliana had disappeared beyond the wall, said, "Still playing hard to get, is she?"

Impossible to get, more like. Silas was no fool; he knew she didn't love him—would never love him. He knew also that she still pined for that knuckle-dragging warrior they'd left behind in Rome. But no matter. Love was for children and fools, and he was neither. Love didn't play a part in his plan. Caesar, however, did.

He said in a quiet, dejected voice, "Is it that obvious she doesn't want me?"

Caesar laughed, delighted. "Don't worry, Silas. It doesn't matter what she thinks she wants. She'll be yours eventually."

Silas could almost hear the indulgent head-pat in Caesar's tone. He said innocently, "If only I could be as certain as you are, my lord. She's damned stubborn once her mind is made up."

Caesar's laughter died. He gazed at Silas for a long moment, silent and still as a coiled snake, sunlight glinting blue off his black hair. "She's only a female, Silas. She doesn't get to choose her fate."

Silas raised his brows and blinked, the picture of breathless anticipation, and Caesar said, "Let her think she's in control for now; it doesn't matter. In fact, it suits our purposes. We need her content for the time being. But once we get to Zion, she'll be yours. You continue to oversee the production of the serum and successfully carry off the little coming-out party we have planned, and I promise you, she'll be yours." He smiled, hard as stone. "No matter what she wants."

A smile crept over Silas's face. Great Horus, manipulating him was almost *too* easy; the boy's will was a weak, slithery thing, easily pushed aside. Truly, the two of them were no match for him and everything he had planned. Knight to rook, pawn to queen, it was all just a game, and one at which he excelled.

He was already six moves ahead of them both.

Knowing exactly what Caesar needed to hear, Silas said in a humble voice, "Your father would be very proud of you, my lord. You're just as ruthless as he was."

In the morning sun, Caesar's black eyes glittered with malice. "He was too easy on her. I trust you won't make the same mistake. My sister requires…a firm hand." They gazed at one another, and Silas heard loudly what had been left unspoken. His smile grew wider and more rabid.

"I couldn't agree more, my lord. I couldn't agree more."

He looked forward to proving to them all exactly how firm his hand would be.

FIVE

Death Wishes and Penis Envy

The best thing about whiskey is the speed at which it works.

"Easy, killer," said Mel dryly, prying the silver flask from the death grip Eliana had on it. "Don't make yourself sick."

Too late, Eliana thought. But she wasn't sick from the alcohol. Leaning against the bare rock wall of the fighting amphitheater they'd ironically nicknamed New Harmony, Eliana let Mel take the flask and then wiped her mouth with the back of her hand. Her gaze wandering around the shadowed space, she wondered aloud, "What's a worse way to die, do you think? Eaten by a shark or burned at the stake?"

Mel paused with her hand in midair, staring at her with one eyebrow cocked. "Ah. We're in that kind of mood, are we? Let me guess…jerkass number one, or jerkass number two?"

Eliana exhaled hard, and whiskey fumes seared her nose. "Both."

"Double-team." Mel nodded sagely. "That'll do it every time." She looked down at the flask in her hand and then thrust it back. "You definitely need this more than I do."

"I'm pretty sure I finished it," Eliana said mournfully.

She'd fled to the catacombs after her breakfast with Caesar and Silas, and she'd been prowling around for hours, hoping to find someone to spar with, thinking a good fight would lift her mood. No such luck. The candlelit corridors were all but deserted with the exception of the two of them. Mel had found her just a few minutes ago, kicking down a row of empty bottles someone had lined up along a crevice in the rock. Carved gargoyles leered down from the ceiling, staring with empty eyes, and all along one wall someone had painted a beautiful, cresting tsunami, swallowing cliffs and villages in Japan.

Monsters and mayhem. It perfectly suited her mood.

Eliana put her hands over her face, rubbed her throbbing temples, and sighed. "In my next life, I'd like to have a penis. Whoever wrote that song about it being a man's world was spot on."

"Death wishes and penis envy. You *are* having a bad day." Mel's sarcastic voice gentled as she studied her face. "What happened?"

"What always happens. Caesar happened."

Mel let it hang there for a minute and then very quietly said, "Eliana, you know you're the reason we all left Rome, right?"

She lifted her head and looked at Mel.

"Not your brother, not Silas, not this shining great plan to live in the open with humans that you're all so gung ho about. None of us cared about any of that. We left because you were leaving. *You.*" Her voice dropped even lower, to nearly a whisper, conspiratorial. "You're the Alpha of this colony, Eliana, whether you realize it or not. Silas was just one of your family's *Servorum* back home, even though he acts like he owns the keys to the castle now. And it's well known that your brother is unGifted and...problematic. You could formally challenge him—"

Eliana clapped a hand over Mel's mouth and held it there, horrified. "Don't you dare say it!" Though she'd hissed it as low as she could, her voice seemed amplified in the cavernous, echoing space. She had to take several long, deep breaths before continuing. "He'll have your head on a stick in ten seconds flat if he thinks you're conspiring to...to..."

Her voice muffled beneath Eliana's hand, Mel said, "You're stronger than he is. You'd win."

"Shhh!"

Mel shrugged. Above Eliana's hand, her black eyes were solemn, but filled with challenge. "Besides, you're the real breadwinner around here. He'd starve to death without you."

"Mel," she warned, but before she could say more there came the sounds of voices and footsteps from one of the corridors that spilled into New Harmony. Someone was coming.

Eliana stood and ran a hand through the choppy blue tangle of her hair. "Please, not another word!" Mel rose beside her, folded her arms across her chest, and made a vague gesture with her shoulders that seemed to say *for now.*

"Butterfly!"

Alexi, coming through the low archway of the access corridor, pulled up to an abrupt halt. Beside him looking around in awe at the graffitied walls and rows of stalactites that hung from the high, arched ceiling like monstrous rows of teeth was a girl in a short leopard-print miniskirt with teased blonde hair and a deep tan that appeared to be sprayed on. She had the kind of voluminous breasts typically seen on models in men's magazines and long nails painted an alarming neon pink. Their hands were clasped together, but as soon as Alexi caught sight of Eliana, he dropped the girl's hand as if it burned.

Oh gods. Not today. Not now.

"What fun!" snickered Mel beside her. "Ken and Hooker Barbie!"

Eliana elbowed her in the side. "We were just leaving, slick," she called out, edging toward the corridor behind them. She reached out and grabbed Mel's arm, but she wouldn't be budged. Clearly, she wanted to stay for the fireworks.

The girl muttered to Alexi, "Who's slick? And who's *she*?"

Another tug on her arm and Mel relented with a sour look. "I've got five hundred on my girl for Friday night, slick, you in?"

Alexi looked at Eliana. "I'm always in," he said solemnly, and the double meaning couldn't have been clearer.

"Good luck with that," said Mel under her breath, and then she smiled brightly and waved good-bye as Eliana dragged her off into the corridor.

When Alexi and his flavor of the week were out of ear-shot, Eliana said, "You're terrible. Stop baiting him, will you?"

"Why? It's fun to poke the bear and watch him dance."

"Be nice."

"Is *he* being nice by dragging every single low-rent skank in Paris down here to rub in your face? I think not. Therefore, he deserves everything he gets." Mel made this pronouncement with a queenly wave of her hand. "God, it's like he clones them or something."

"He's just…trying to get a rise out of me. Because he cares. It's sweet, in its own sick, twisted way."

"Sweet? Are you serious?" she scoffed. "It's a cheap, immature trick. He deserves to have his boy bits cut off for that kind of behavior."

"*Mel,*" Eliana warned, but her friend only laughed, a merry snort that echoed off the rock walls around them.

"Don't worry, I'll leave his boy bits unharmed for the time being. But he's on my *list,* E, along with a few other people who will remain unnamed."

She sent Eliana a dark, loaded glance, and she suddenly remembered the task she'd been assigned. "Speaking of those unnamed people, they've decided I should hit the Louvre tonight."

Mel stopped dead in her tracks, and Eliana turned, surprised, to look at her. The corridor they were in was dark and winding, filled with the sound of trickling water and long, crawling shadows, but Eliana could easily make out the dismay on Mel's face.

"The *Louvre*! Why there? That seems so risky!"

Eliana sighed in agreement. "I'm glad I'm not the only one who thinks so. As if I had a choice," she muttered as an afterthought. "Anyway, security personnel can't see me in the dark. Cameras can't capture an image of me. Plus, I can Shift to Vapor if I need to. Really, what's the worst that could possibly happen?"

It was a rhetorical question, of course, and one Mel didn't have an answer to, but as they turned and began the long walk back to the upper levels of the catacombs and the hidden entrance that would lead them into the basement of their abandoned abbey, Eliana couldn't shake the dark, nagging feeling that, somehow, she was about to find out.

SIX
The Cat

Heart pounding, D shot up in bed and blinked into the cool stillness of the dark room, trying to regain his equilibrium. Trying, without success, to swallow around the cold, devouring terror that clawed at his throat. An echo of a scream died into silence off the curved rock walls as he sat there sweating and panting with the sheets rucked up around his waist, and D realized it must have come from him.

The dream was the worst he'd had yet.

Fighting panic, he dropped his head into his hands and concentrated on getting himself under control. Images still battered him relentlessly—gunfire, blood, men with weapons descending on the naked, terrified figure of Eliana crouched against a wall like a cornered animal. There was nothing he could do, but every nerve ending in his body screamed for him to do *something.*

Because like the others before it, this dream was a harbinger of things to come.

He swung his legs over the side of the cot and pushed off. Naked, he went to the footlocker at the end of the bed and pulled on the pair of black cargo pants and shirt he'd tossed there hours earlier. He laced up his boots and crossed to the dresser on the other side of the room that held the various weapons he always carried, laid out in a careful row on top. He strapped them on in the same order he did every time: Glock nine-millimeter on his right hip, kukhri—tip dipped in poison—on his left, push daggers in each of his boots, folding knives tucked into pockets in his pants. He was a walking arsenal and, as one of the king's elite guards, had been most of his adult life.

Not that there was a king to guard any longer, but that hadn't reduced the threats to their colony. If anything, the king's death increased the threats tenfold.

He ran a hand over his head, his dark hair shorn so close to his skull it couldn't accurately even be called a haircut, and grabbed the keys to his Ducati from the small wooden bowl where they were always kept. He needed a ride. He needed a drink, as well. Ignoring the fact that they were all basically under martial law and forbidden to leave the catacombs without express permission from Celian—once the king's main enforcer, now the leader of the *Bellatorum* and de facto ruler of the colony—D had been making clandestine reconnaissance trips ever since Eliana had disappeared.

He groaned aloud. Even *thinking* her name hurt.

With a curse, he spun on his heel and made his way from the Spartan sleeping chambers the *Bellatorum* used into the chilled gloom of the main corridor of the catacombs.

Fifteen minutes later he emerged in the shadows of the subterranean basilica of Domitilla that the *Bellatorum* used as their own special entrance and exit to the catacombs and came face-to-face with a pair of nasty-looking guards lounging against the ancient Doric columns. Young, muscular, and glowering, they sprang to attention and trained the sights of their automatic rifles on the center of his chest. D noted with no small satisfaction he was at least a head taller than both of them.

Then again, at over six foot five, he was at least a head taller than almost everyone.

"Gentlemen," he said calmly, looking first at one, then the other.

One of them cleared his throat, a froggy sound that echoed softly off the crumbling stone walls. "Can't let you pass, D."

D's brows rose. "That so?"

"Celian's orders," the other one offered apologetically. Restless, he shifted his weight back and forth between his feet. D smelled his anxiety, both acrid and musky, a hint of spice on the air, and made the instant assessment that these two were all sizzle and no steak.

In other words, easy pickings.

"You were at the training session the other night," said D, eyeing the more obviously nervous one. He nodded, a curt affirmative, and adjusted his grip on his rifle. Little beads of sweat had broken out on his upper lip. "Enjoy it?"

The guard glanced at his companion, and D continued. "Heard that soldier I knocked out is doing better."

"Which one?" said the other guard, smiling grimly. He was the bigger of the two, also nervous but determined not to show it, standing there with his legs spread wide and his square chin jutting out like a dare.

Okay, thought D. *You first, then.*

Before either one could react, D Shifted to Vapor, shed his clothes in a pile on the ground, reappeared behind the cocky guard, and tapped him on the shoulder. The guard spun around, right into the unleashed power of D's fist. He dropped like a stone, and his rifle went clattering over the cracked marble.

The other guard took one look at D's massive, naked, tattooed form and promptly dropped the rifle. He held up both hands. "Just make it quick," he said. "And do me a solid—tell Celian I put up a good fight, will you?"

D almost smiled. He liked this kid. So instead of punching him in the face—which would leave him with a bruise blooming blue and purple over one side and probably a few crushed bones like his friend lying at their feet—he used an old standby…the sleeper hold. Steady, applied pressure to his carotid artery, and after a few twitches, the kid was out like a light.

Just as D finished getting dressed again, he heard a noise behind him. He spun around and saw Constantine leaning against a marble column on the other side of the basilica, slowly clapping in mock applause. His expression was one of amused disbelief. He pushed away from the column and walked toward D.

"Great show. I think Celian really needs to rethink his containment strategy." When D didn't answer, he said with exaggerated sarcasm, "Going somewhere?"

D shrugged and crossed his arms over his chest. "Stir-crazy. Needed to get out."

"Figured as much."

"You spying on me again, grandma?"

Constantine chuckled. "Something like that. Mind if I join you?"

D paused, examined the expression on Constantine's face, and then said, "Not really a question, is it?"

Now Constantine's chuckle was wry, as was the smile that split his face. "You're pretty sharp for a blunt instrument, you know that?"

"Got all the looks in the family, too." At that, they both chuckled. "Ladies first," said D, gesturing toward the hidden door that led to the outside world and freedom. "And if I hear one word about a curfew, I'll smack that movie-star smile right off your face."

"Good to know you haven't lost your sense of humor, D. The thought of you landing a punch on me is seriously hilarious."

Constantine gave D a friendly shove, and D shoved him back, grinning. Then they both walked out into the starlit Roman night.

Three hours and two bottles of Glenlivet later, D's mood had sunk a notch below black.

"You want to talk about it?" asked Constantine, watching D stare blankly at the empty glass in his hand.

"When have I ever wanted to talk about it?" D muttered. The camaraderie from hours earlier had evaporated along with the scotch, and D was surlier than ever. He knew from experience that drinking only dulled the pain but didn't numb it, and that ache beneath his breastbone would need something stronger to kill it than an eighteen-year-old single malt. A machete might do the trick.

"So we're just going to sit here all night and stare at the walls?"

D glanced up at Constantine, and a hot flash of anger lit through him when he saw the pity on his face. "I seem to remember it was you who insisted on coming," he snapped.

"If I'd known your little pity party was going to be this much fun, I wouldn't have."

D bristled and sat up, glaring at Constantine. "I'm not feeling sorry for myself!"

"Right, you're just drinking this much because you're *happy*."

"Screw you, Constantine."

"Get real, D. You need to get a grip on yourself, brother. This can't go on forever..."

Constantine kept talking, but D didn't hear the rest because his attention was diverted by the flat-screen television hung above the pool table across the room. It was tuned to a news station, and the picture on the screen froze his blood to ice.

Eliana. Good God, it was *her*.

Hands cuffed behind her back, dressed only in a man's wrinkled white button-down shirt, she was being hauled out of a police car by a pair of uniformed gendarmes sporting enough weaponry to outfit a small army. Though her head was turned, he saw her clearly in profile, and the image instantly seared itself into his mind. The proud lift of her chin, the elegant line of her neck, the elongated limbs that lent her the look of a ballerina, pixie-like and delicate. She was exactly as he remembered, except for hair dyed the color of lapis lazuli and an ominous bloodstained bandage wrapped around one bare calf.

The television was muted, but the caption on the screen screamed, “French police apprehend notorious thief!”

Everything around him vanished.

Gone was the dim, smoky room with its rickety tables and tacky décor, gone was the humid fug of cigarettes and stale beer, gone was the flickering neon Peretti sign in the window and the empty scotch bottle on the table next to his left hand. There was only her. Every nerve, every cell and atom of his body came into brilliant, throbbing focus and began to roar: *Eliana! Eliana! Eliana!*

Frozen, he stared at the television and watched as the two gendarmes swiftly maneuvered her—limping—past a crush of shouting reporters and up a wide flight of marble steps toward the double glass doors of the entry to an enormous brick building. Just before she disappeared through the doors, she glanced over her shoulder and looked directly into the camera.

Wide-set doe eyes, liquid soft and black as midnight, stared at him. *Through* him. D’s heart stopped dead in his chest. He shot out of his chair and at the top of his lungs shouted the only word that came to mind.

“Shit!”

Despite this outburst, none of the other bar patrons chanced a glance in his direction. He came to this dive bar fairly regularly, and they’d more than once seen the huge, glowering, tattooed male beat someone to a pulp for no discernible reason and had learned to keep their eyes averted or risk a beating of their own.

“Nice,” said Constantine dryly as he drummed the fingers of one big hand on the scarred, sticky tabletop between them. His back was to the television. "Is that just a general observation, or are you experiencing some kind of emergency with your bowels?"

"It's her! On television! It's *her!*" D sputtered past numb lips.

Constantine closed his eyes for a second longer than a blink and sighed. "You've had about a liter of scotch, D. You're seeing things. Why don't you take a seat and we'll—"

"*Turn it up!*" D shouted at the skinny bartender, silencing Constantine and launching the bartender into motion. He leapt over the counter and flung himself at the television as if his life depended on it. His shaking fingers found the volume knob, and as Constantine, frowning, turned in his chair to look, a female reporter's modulated voice filled the dim, smoky room.

"...eluded authorities for the past several years in what has become the most infamous string of art thefts in France's history. Some of the country's wealthiest citizens and political figures have been victimized, including the prime minister himself, Francois Fillon, whose personal collection of original Picassos valued at more than five million euros was stolen from his home last year while he and his wife were sleeping."

The picture changed to a scene of a grinning, middle-aged man standing shirtless and tanned with a glass of champagne on the glistening deck of his massive yacht.

"At this point it isn't known if she was working alone," the reporter continued as the picture switched back to the crowd milling around the front of the brick building, "but for now the thief known simply as *La Chatte* is in custody, and we imagine Paris's beleaguered police chief is heaving a very loud sigh of relief that this protracted chase is over and the elite's personal fortunes are, once again, safe. Reporting live from the Paris prefecture of police, this is Lisa Campbell with CNN International News. Back to you, Bob."

D stood staring at the television long after Bob-the-balding-reporter had segued into another story. His breathing was erratic, his heartbeat was wild, and his hands twitched by his side, but all that was secondary to the storm of howling white that raged in his skull.

La Chatte. The Cat. Infamous, elusive thief.

Eliana, love of his life, source of his joy and his pain and three years' worth of the kind of soul-searing agony he wouldn't wish on his worst enemy, was *La Chatte.* Now in police custody in France.

D's big hands curled into fists at his side.

In spite of his bulk and the array of weaponry hidden beneath his long black coat, Constantine rose gracefully and soundlessly from his chair. "D," he said sternly, reading what was plain on his face, "don't even think about it."

D's gaze narrowed. Though most of their kind were beautiful to the point of being meaningless, Constantine—he of the glossy black hair and glorious cheekbones and long, feminine eyelashes—outshone them all. At the moment, D had a mind to wreck that perfect face with a devastating punch to the middle of it.

"Don't *you* even think of trying to talk me out if it," he snarled. He took a step back, and his chair skittered back across the faded checkerboard linoleum with a nerve-scraping screech.

"Celian won't allow it," answered Constantine. The subtle adjustments in his stance and the calculation in his eyes signaled he'd made the instant shift from brother to sparring partner. It wouldn't be the first time they'd gone toe to toe, and it likely wouldn't be the last. "And she's wanted by the Council of Alphas—"

"Fuck the Council!" D bellowed. Two humans sitting at a booth in the back stood up and made their way quickly toward the back door.

Constantine set his jaw and leveled him a steely, intense look that would have drained the blood from anyone else's face. D, however, didn't bat an eye. Very quietly Constantine said, "Think about this for a minute. If we've seen her on television, they've seen her, too, and they're on their way. None of us are authorized to act on this, especially not you. And you know what happens if you go rogue, brother. They'll take you out before the *Bellatorum* can even blink. You saw how serious they were. You do *not* want to get in the way of The Hunt."

The Hunt. A group of eight of the deadliest hunters picked from the four other *Ikati* colonies, tasked with one thing: find the missing *principessa,* her brother, and the small group of loyalists who'd vanished with her three years ago, and bring them in to face the Council.

For interrogation. For elimination.

D's heart twisted at the thought. "You think I'm going to let them *touch* her," he snarled, every inch of him bristling, "you're crazy! I'm going. *Now.* With or without your blessing. So you better step back if you want to keep your head attached to your body."

They stared at each other silently, two muscled, menacing males in black, both alike and yet so different. Same height, same breadth of shoulders, same air of danger, and those black, black eyes. Born and bred in darkness, they were warriors and had a warrior's fearlessness and sense of pride, and also the willingness to die for what they believed in.

Constantine believed in duty. What D believed in was far more dangerous: love.

"Great Horus save us," Constantine finally muttered, "from idiots in love."

Though he doubted even the god of war and protection whose symbol all the *Bellatorum* had tattooed on their left shoulders could change D's mind once it was made up. He ran a hand through his hair and stared at D another moment longer until he shook his head and sighed. "And you *are* an idiot, you know."

"No argument here," D answered, still bristling with anger.

Constantine's mouth twisted. He regarded his brother, thinking of the pain he'd been in the past few years, though of course D had never voiced it aloud. Ironically named after an ancient Greek orator, D often went days without speaking at all. As if the shaved head, multiple tattoos, eyebrow piercings, and air of murderous rage weren't enough, his silence lent him an even more frightening aspect. A glance from him sent most people running.

Constantine saw past that, though. They'd known each other since birth, and though not brothers by Blood they were brothers in spirit, and as D lost hope, Constantine saw him slowly, surely dying, day by miserable day. He'd thought D would get over her in time, forget her, but Eliana and the memory of what could have been haunted him like a ghost.

And now that ghost had been captured by the Paris police.

"But two idiots are better than one," Constantine decided, loyalty winning out over logic. "I'll go with you."

D's body relaxed a little, and the tension went out of his shoulders. Just because they'd sparred in the past didn't mean either one looked forward to another go-round. "No. I have to do this alone." He paused. "You know why."

Three years' worth of history passed between them with a single, pointed look.

"Don't be an asshole!" Constantine snapped.

D met his gaze head-on but didn't respond.

"Are we really going to do this again? Here?" Constantine gestured to indicate their surroundings, the dive bar he despised but came to because he didn't want his best friend and brother to drown his sorrows alone. "Fine, then, let's do it! If I didn't shoot that son of a bitch, you'd be dead. We'd all still be living like slaves. Your girl would be married to some idiot from the *Optimates* that you'd want to kill every time you got near him—"

"I know," D interrupted. "You saved my life. You saved *all* of us. I know."

"But you'll never forgive me for it," Constantine said flatly.

D paused for the barest of seconds. "I hated that bastard as much as you did. More."

That was just an evasion, and they both knew it. A few more seconds of silence crackled between them while everyone else in the bar paid close attention to their drinks and pretended not to listen. Finally, Constantine muttered a low oath. He said, "I'll cover for you as long as I can. Ten, twelve hours tops, then Celian will figure it out and send the *Legiones* after you. But The Hunt won't wait that long, brother. They're probably already on their way. So be careful. And be quick."

There was a time when the two would have exchanged a quick, hard, back-pounding hug when one or the other was going off into battle. But now they only exchanged stiff nods. Too much anger, too much blame, too much unsaid left festering between them. Now, finally, the real battle would begin.

D turned and made his way toward the door.

After only a few paces, he broke into a run.

SEVEN
A Grim, Bloodless Line

If she wasn't injured, Eliana might have Shifted to panther and torn the police officer's head right off his body.

Unfortunately, she *was* injured. The bullet had gouged an agonizing divot in her leg, and tearing off his head would have to wait. Though she'd heal quickly from a relatively clean wound like this—within a day, most likely, as fast healing was common to all her kind, but even more pronounced in her immediate family—even a much smaller injury was enough to trap her in human aspect, so Shifting was impossible. The more pressing problems were getting her leg stitched up, getting the humiliating handcuffs removed, and getting something better to wear than the button-down shirt that stank of stale sweat and fried food. When standing, it fell to mid-thigh and did a decent job of covering her nude body. When sitting, however…to put it delicately, her lady parts were about to make an appearance.

And the officer had definitely noticed. Though why he'd be so interested now was a mystery, as he'd already seen her entirely naked at the museum.

Damn it all to hell. She *knew* the Louvre was a bad idea.

The officer seated at the table across from her said something to her in French. She pretended not to understand him, so he switched to English. "How is the shirt for you, pigeon?"

Pigeon? Cockroach of the skies? Deeply insulted, she asked, "How was the box of donuts you managed to smear all over it, pig?"

His cheeks flushed red. She was gratified to see it. In the corner of the room, another officer leaning against the wall snorted.

There were six of them in all. Uniformed, armed, obviously feeling very pleased with themselves that they'd finally caught the infamous *La Chatte.* The interrogation room was small and cold, devoid of anything except a metal table, two metal chairs, and a small camera mounted high on the wall above the door. A large window covered one wall, and though it was blacked out she assumed it was two-way glass. Her own reflection mocked her there, a testament to her first failure.

No matter. It was only a question of time. Just a short while until she healed and she could Shift to Vapor and slip out the door, the window, through a ceiling vent. She had only to survive long enough—

"Our little kitty has claws, eh, gentlemen?"

It was the officer in the corner who spoke, his voice soft and amused. He spoke in French, and though she'd pretended not to understand it before, somehow she knew that he knew she actually did. She slanted him a sideways, assessing glance. He was good-looking, this one, tall and finely made with thick brown hair and penetrating green eyes that didn't seem to miss a thing. He watched her with those avid eyes now, ignoring her bare legs and concentrating instead on her face.

She'd have to be careful with him. Human men didn't have the keen senses her kind did, but every once in a while one of them surprised her. At the very least he was trigger-happy; he was the one who'd shot her.

And then, in a flash, she recognized him. The man from Gregor's office that night a week ago, the one who'd threatened the subpoena—

"Let's try again," said the first officer seated across from her, the one whose shirt she was wearing. She turned her attention to him. He was shorter and chubbier than the rest of them, with hairy forearms and what could only be described as dead shark eyes. Black and flat, they bored into her like knives. "And for the sake of expediency, I'll dispense with all the bullshit." He paused, evidently for dramatic effect. "We know everything," he said.

Eliana narrowed her eyes, waiting.

"Everything," he repeated more forcefully, leaning forward over the table. Beneath the rolled-up cuffs of his shirt, the backs of his pudgy, pasty hands were damp with sweat. "We know exactly who you are...and exactly what you've been up to."

"I see," she said, feigning a calm she definitely didn't feel. Her heart was beating so hard in her chest she thought they all must be able to hear it. "I must be in very deep trouble."

His shark eyes narrowed. He didn't like being mocked.

"As a matter of fact you are." His tone dropped. "But if you cooperate, you may earn yourself some leniency come sentencing time."

Eliana resisted the urge to respond with a withering comment about fat, donut-eating primates not being able to intimidate her. *Goddess Bastet,* she silently prayed, smiling at the officer, *please send a plague for this one. Preferably involving flesh-eating bacteria.*

Holding his gaze, she murmured, "Oh, I'd *love* to cooperate. Cooperation is one of my favorite things, especially when it's with someone like you. Someone so smart. And so obviously..." She glanced at his doughy arms, and her smile turned faintly mocking. "Strong."

He blinked rapidly, and the flush in his cheeks deepened to scarlet. Like a preening peacock, his chest puffed out, and she had to restrain herself again, this time from rolling her eyes.

She'd never understand a man's ego. It was their universal Achilles' heel.

"But I'd like to ask a question before we get started." She felt the lasered attention of the handsome officer in the corner as easily as she saw the chubby one in front of her lick his lips.

"Er...ah...yes," he stammered, then cleared his throat. "What is it?"

She cocked her head left. "You don't actually have any evidence against me, do you?"

It hung there in the following silence, reverberating like a struck drum. To their credit, the men standing around the room didn't react, not a muscle was moved, but she tasted their sudden discomfort like a metallic tinge in the air and had all the confirmation she needed.

"No surveillance video, no fingerprints, no eyewitnesses. Nothing," she said softly.

"We caught you red-handed in the Louvre, pigeon." The chubby officer's face had turned a mottled shade of burgundy. He was blinking fast again, and it made him look like a fat baby bird. "Trying to steal a famous piece of art. We have all the evidence we need to put you away for a very long time. *Échec et mat.*"

Checkmate? Clearly this one didn't actually play chess. She did, however, and played it well. Her father had taught her when she was twelve years old, had told her every great general and military strategist in history had used the tools learned in chess to win a war: always keep your goal in mind; have a plan but stay flexible; think at least three moves ahead; protect your assets; and last but most importantly, don't trust your emotions, because they lie.

She'd learned that final lesson the hard way. The very *hardest* way of all.

Her gaze went to the handsome, green-eyed man in the corner. He wasn't smiling. In fact, his face had darkened, and his mouth had thinned to a grim, bloodless line.

"How do you know I was trying to steal a painting?" she challenged. "Maybe I just got locked inside the museum before it closed—"

"Naked?" Green Eyes interrupted, hard.

"—because I fainted in the ladies' room and didn't wake up until the lights were out and everyone was gone, and in my state of panic at being alone in the dark I wandered around the museum trying to find a way out—"

"Naked," he repeated, even harder.

She lifted a shoulder. "Some people cry when they get scared. I get—"

"Naked," he finished, and now he sounded like he really wanted to break something.

She smiled at him, a cheerless curve of her lips. "Exactly. It's a tic. As I was saying, maybe I was trying to find a way out of the big, dark, scary museum—it's over seventy thousands square meters, you know, which is a lot, especially in the dark—and I wound up in front of the Degas and was distracted for a minute from my extreme fear and disorientation and just stood there admiring it."

"With your hands on the frame," interrupted Chubby in a high, disbelieving voice. "Trying to lift it from the wall!"

Eliana looked at him. "I never touched that painting."

He made a sound like he was choking on something and jerked his hand to indicate everyone else. "We saw you! You had your hands right on it—"

"It was very shadowy in there. Maybe your eyes tricked you. Have you dusted it for prints?"

No one said anything. One of the standing officers shifted his weight from one foot to the other.

"No? Well, don't bother. Because unfortunately you're not going to find any."

They wouldn't because they *couldn't.* Intangibility in shadow allowed her to sneak around undetected, leaving no fingerprints…she was as invisible as air.

In the shadows, that is. When pinned in the highly focused beams of flashlights—like the one Chubby and company had wielded—she could be seen plain as day.

She'd heard of this only once before. Her great-grandmother on her mother's side was also a Shadow Walker and had also been an accomplished thief. That was where their similarities ended, however; to hear the story told, her great-grandmother stuck to jewels and absolutely loved thieving.

It was said she wore so much of her pilfered booty she jangled when she walked.

Green Eyes addressed her directly. "You like to play games, don't you."

It was a statement, not a question. Beneath the soft tone of his voice, she felt the challenge and also sensed a dark, growing undercurrent of excitement.

Holding his gaze, she leaned back in the chair and crossed her legs. The shirt rode up even higher on her bare thighs, and that searing gaze flickered down to her legs. When his gaze traveled back to her face, it was bright and burning hot.

It did something to her, that look. An old memory flickered in her mind, beautiful dark eyes that looked at her with that same, fevered hunger. She quashed it as quickly as it surfaced.

The memory of those eyes and who they belonged to was even more dangerous than capture by humans.

"I like to do all kinds of things," she answered, staring unsmiling at him. "What did you have in mind?"

He stiffened. His nostrils flared. Judging by the sour tang that suddenly permeated the air, she'd really pissed him off. In one swift motion, he shoved away from the wall. "Everyone out," he snapped. He crossed his arms over his chest and stood staring at her, his face now hard as a slab of granite.

"Édoard," Chubby protested, turning to him with knitted brows, but Green Eyes cut him a glare so vicious he snapped his mouth shut and rose stiffly from the chair.

"*Vous l'avez entendu*," Chubby snapped to the other four standing officers, and one by one they filed out the door. Chubby slammed it shut behind him, leaving her alone with the unpredictable, agitated Édoard.

They stared at each other for what felt like an hour. The only sound was the whisper of air through a ceiling vent. A muscle in her bicep began to cramp and twitch, and she longed to stretch her arms overhead and massage it. But of course, the handcuffs prevented it.

Then into the tense silence he abruptly said, "What are you?"

Not who, but *what.* Startled, she blinked. "Excuse me?"

"You heard me," he said, unmoving. He looked at her—really *looked* at her—as if trying to slip inside her body using only his eyes. It was unnerving. She knew it wasn't the chill in the room that made her skin prickle.

"What I am is hungry, hurt, and not in the mood for word games," she said flatly, trying to keep the sharp pang of worry she suddenly felt out of her voice. *What are you?*

He just stared at her.

Her gaze skipped away from his and fell on the small camera above the door. There were no shadows in this harshly lit room; they'd have her on video now for sure.

Seeing the direction of her stare, Édoard turned, walked over to the door, reached up, and flipped a switch on the side of the lens. A tiny red light beneath the camera faded to black.

Her brows shot up.

He turned back to her with that intense green gaze and leaned over the back of the chair his chubby companion had just vacated, his knuckles white as they gripped the curved metal. Beneath the glare of the fluorescent lights, his brown hair shone a beautiful shade of burnished bronze.

"You're different," he accused, startling her again. "*Everything* about you is different," he went on, his terse voice softened by the lilting French accent. His gaze scoured her. "Your face, your voice, the way you move. Even the way you're sitting in that chair looking at me is different than anyone else who's ever sat in that chair looking at me before. I've been around a very long time, *belle fille*, and I've never seen anything like you."

Belle fille. Beautiful girl. It gave her a pang in the gaping hole in her chest where her heart used to be. It had been a long, long time since someone had called her beautiful.

"Is this an interrogation, or are you trying to ask me out on a date?" she said coldly.

His face hardened. He straightened and crossed his arms over his broad chest. "Interview," he said, looking down his nose at her. "It's called an interview. If this was an interrogation, there would be pain involved."

"There *is* pain involved." She leaned sideways and stuck her bandaged leg out, then bent her arms to give him a good view of the handcuffs behind her back, her wrists red and chafed inside them. Just to provoke him, she added, "And my bare behind is frozen to this chair."

Again, he didn't take the bait. His mouth just puckered as if he'd been sucking on a lemon. "You're lucky Jean-Luc gave you his shirt. I'd have hauled you in as naked as we found you, and your bare behind would have been on public display for all those reporters. Your bare behind would have made the cover of *Le Monde.*"

Eliana flushed. "Charming," she muttered. She sat upright and adjusted herself in the chair so her tailbone wasn't flush against the cold seat. Her entire rear end was numb. And her leg *throbbed.* When she saw Caesar again, she was going to kill him.

"You're the one who likes being naked so much. And I may be rude, but I'm not stupid," he rejoined. Something odd had crept into his voice, and she glanced up to find him still staring.

"I know who you are, *belle fille*," he said, eyes glittering. "I know how you think. I've been studying *La Chatte* for years. I'll admit you became something of an obsession for me. A thief who evaded all security systems, who never triggered a single alarm, who drifted in and out of locked buildings and rooms and vaults like…a ghost? Impossible. You made us look like a bunch of incompetent fools. You made *me* look like a fool. All those rich, important people screaming for your head, and not a trace of you to be found. So I studied your pattern, the things you took, the specific times and dates and places of the crimes. And I discovered something."

Eliana waited, a growing sense of dread gnawing at her stomach.

"Even ghosts get bored."

He smiled, and the predatory curve of his lips sent fear lashing along every nerve ending.

"Every theft was a little more daring than the last, a little harder," he continued. "Either you were getting desperate, which didn't seem likely as you weren't under any heat from us, or you needed a challenge. It was me who predicted *La Chatte* would get tired of poaching from fat old goats and go for a bigger prize. I knew one day you'd hit the Louvre. And because, as you've guessed, we've never managed to capture you with normal surveillance video, I ordered a few special, very high-tech cameras designed by some old friends in the American military. Cost a pretty penny, too, and all very hush-hush top secret, but it was authorized by the prime minister himself. Because you, *belle fille*, are at the very top of his shit list."

Cameras? Special cameras? She couldn't be seen on cameras—

"He's still holding a grudge over two Picassos you stole from his house while he was sleeping," Édoard continued in a conspiratorial tone, as if they were two girlfriends talking over cocktails. "In fact, he's given us carte blanche to do whatever is necessary to get them back, along with the rest of the things you stole, some of which were from his personal friends. *Whatever* is necessary, including resorting to the interrogation you so casually mentioned before. Which, by the way, I'm particularly well qualified to do having served as an interrogator the entirety of my ten years with the counterterrorism unit of the *bérets verts.*"

An interrogator with the green berets. High-tech cameras. Several things clicked into place, and the fear simmering in her bloodstream rose to a dark, violent boil. Her stomach lurched.

As an afterthought he added, "Did you know the word torture comes from the French word meaning 'to twist'?"

His lips curved into a dark, triumphant smile, and she went ice cold.

"You're bluffing," she said, pulse racing. "You can't lay a finger on me. There are laws against that, and the entire world saw you take me in—"

"I won't go into the particulars of how photon cameras work, but the images are quite interesting, to say the least," he interrupted as if she hadn't spoken at all. He uncrossed his arms and pulled out the chair opposite hers, then sat with unhurried grace, crossed one leg over the other, and folded his hands into his lap. "Weren't you curious how, in a seventy-thousand-square-meter museum as you so helpfully pointed out, I knew exactly where to find an invisible woman?"

She didn't answer. A cold trickle of sweat rolled down the back of her neck.

"So I'll ask you again." Still smiling, he regarded her with those green, glittering eyes. "And I'll ask you nicely, one more time, before I hand you over to *un médecin.* And it won't be for your injured leg, my dear. The good doctor and I are going to conduct a few...experiments."

He emphasized carefully each next word he spoke. "What. Are. You?"

Horror tightened its sharp, freezing claws around her throat. She sat there like a statue, frozen, unable to answer, unable even to blink.

The doctor. Interrogation. Experiments.

Oh God.

EIGHT
Lock and Load

D made the thirteen-hour drive from Rome to Paris in under ten.

He'd have been even faster on the Ducati, but his plan involved heavy explosives and those took up a lot of room, especially with what he had in mind. So the motorcycle was out, left behind in its usual spot in a parking garage not too far from the sunken church and the entrance to the catacombs where he and the other members of the Roman colony lived.

Where Eliana also used to live, until everything got so turned around his eyes would cross just thinking about it.

The Range Rover he drove—pitch black and growly, like his mood—belonged to a disbanded group of *Ikati* assassins from the colony in Brazil that used to go by the name

The Syndicate. The paranoid leaders of the four colonies who comprised the Council of Alphas never left anything to chance, so as soon as The Syndicate went off-line three years ago, The Hunt went live.

Because you had to have paid killers to round up and dispose of the inevitable deserters who couldn't live by the most inviolable rule of *Ikati* Law: secrecy. Second only to allegiance, secrecy was paramount to the survival of them all. Now more than ever.

And his Eliana—in addition to being the daughter of the dead leader of the Expurgari, the *Ikati's* ancient enemy, and the assumed new boss of the organization—had violated that ironclad rule of secrecy in a truly spectacular way, making her the Council's public enemy number one.

And making him desperate with a capital D.

If The Hunt reached her before he did…

He gripped the steering wheel tighter and stomped the gas pedal to the floor. The SUV lurched forward, roaring over the empty, predawn Paris streets.

At the same moment, six men dressed exactly alike in tailored dark suits and mirrored aviators stepped off the high-speed Eurostar train at the Gare du Nord station in central Paris and without speaking to one another walked swiftly across the crowded platform and through the automatic glass doors to the pair of sleek black Audis awaiting them at the curb.

The six split into two groups of three. Two sat in the backseat of each car, one rode shotgun. The driver of each sedan said the identical thing to the new arrivals:

"Seventeen minutes. Lock and load." And jerked his head to the stainless steel case in the middle of the backseat.

Both cars had government plates and so were allowed to idle in a no-stopping zone. If any of the railway police who prowled the station had run the plates, they would have found the cars registered to one Pierre Nettoyeur, senior medical practitioner with the French Defense Health Service and personal physician to the minister of defense.

Monsieur Nettoyeur was, of course, a fiction. Like others engineered by the Council of Alphas, he existed in digital form purely for the purpose of convenience. The leadership of the *Ikati* sometimes needed to travel and was occasionally forced to do it quickly and in close proximity to the humans who remained ignorant of their existence.

Largely ignorant, that is. There had been an incident a few years back involving a disco, a territory dispute, and an eyewitness with a cell phone, but though that particular video made it to the evening news, it was roundly dismissed as fake. And all those witnesses in the club were dismissed as fame-seeking drunks.

At least publicly. There were those who did not dismiss things like that so easily.

Nettoyeur was a bit of whimsy—it meant "cleaner" in French, and "cleaner" in certain circles like the ones the eight gentlemen in the Audis moved in referred to an assassin, specifically one hired to manage a bad situation with a very permanent solution—but for this mission the fabricated profession had a much more practical purpose.

If stopped by the police, the driver would easily be able to explain why he carried such dangerous tranquilizers and weapons, and in such quantity. Monsieur Nettoyeur reported directly to the man who ran France's entire military and had all the required paperwork to prove it.

So the paperwork was in order, fake identities had been assumed, travel had been arranged, and all the plans quite carefully made. And now The Hunt had arrived in Paris.

In less than one hour, Eliana Cardinalis would be captured—or dead.

NINE
Gotcha

There was a rat inside her skull.

An angry, hungry rat, intent on devouring all the gray matter it could before she clawed her own eyes out to get at it. Eliana needed to kill it and she needed to kill it soon because the agony, oh gods, the *agony*.

"One hundred fifty thousand, Édoard," said a calm male voice, strongly accented with German. The voice drifted to her from somewhere very close but also far, far away. She heard movement, fabric rustling, shoes clicking on tile, smelled the cool tang of rain in the air from a storm that was still hours off. Somewhere in the building a window was cracked and sweet, dew-tinged air leaked in.

But not in here, wherever here was. In here the air sweltered and smelled of death.

The rat really hated it. It chewed her brain more viciously than before. Tearing, squealing, clawing, eyes small and blood-red bright.

"Canine?" said another voice, almost hopefully.

The rat lifted its head and hissed. It liked this new speaker as much as she did. Édoard, she remembered past the pain, Édoard was his name. Beautiful hair, beautiful eyes…heart like a shard of obsidian.

"Bat, actually," murmured the first voice, surprised. "Top of the auditory range. Extraordinary."

"All right, record it and shut it down. We'll do the UV next and see what we come up with. We've got to move her down the hall for that, though. And where the hell is the transfer paperwork? I needed that an hour ago." Édoard muttered the last bit, irritated.

"Patience," his friend answered calmly. "She's not going anywhere."

Then there was a small click, and all at once the rabid rat vanished, the pain in her skull subsided, and the room, spinning and white, swam into focus as she blinked open her eyes.

"Are you, *liebe*?" said a tall, white-coated, bespectacled man with ice blue eyes. He was of an indeterminate age somewhere between forty and sixty, smelled of cigarettes, and looked bland as oatmeal. He peered at her over his glasses and smiled, cheerfully benign.

The banality of evil. Eliana had heard the phrase once to describe the phenomenon whereby the most truly horrific acts were carried out not by fanatics or sociopaths, but by ordinary people socialized to accept unspeakable atrocities as "normal." The holocaust, animal testing, genocide and capital punishment and war.

Torture.

It was the man from Gregor's office, Agent Doe. The one she'd warned him was dangerous that day when she'd come with the Cézanne and he'd been entertaining the police. She *knew* he was trouble.

"I hope you burn in hell," she said to the ice-eyed doctor, her voice oddly hoarse. Then she remembered: she'd been screaming. For a long time, evidently, because her throat felt raw as ground meat.

The doctor chuckled, unimpressed with her attempt at bravado. Behind her, Édoard gave another of his now-familiar snorts. "Claws, kitty cat. Mind the claws."

He walked casually around her wheelchair—she was strapped to a wheelchair, when did that happen?—and stood next to the doctor. The table beside them held a small electronic device with wires and dials and a digital readout blinking numbers in blue against a black screen. The size of a small microwave, it must have been the source of that excruciating pain eating holes in her skull.

This was another room, clinical as the first but larger and lined with a variety of strange-looking electronic equipment in every size and variety. Testing equipment, recording equipment, some ominous stainless steel instruments laid out on a cloth on a long metal console below a video screen. It looked less like an interrogation room in a police station and more like Herr Frankenstein's lab.

Her memory was cloudy at best. She assumed she'd been injected with something because the vein in her left inner arm burned and there was a heaviness in her limbs she'd never experienced before. Vaguely, she remembered a struggle, remembered breaking someone's jaw with a vicious kick to the head and disabling two others with well-targeted groin shots before she was overpowered by half a dozen more men armed with fists and billy clubs. That was all she remembered, until now.

Édoard chuckled, an evil sound, and she glanced up at him. He stared back at her with the kind of expression usually seen on the faces of new parents and lottery winners. He looked ebullient. Exultant.

In that moment, she was more afraid than she'd ever been in her life.

"What are you going to do to me?" she demanded, masking her fear beneath an icy tone. He didn't answer, but his smile grew wider.

Just then, without warning, the room went black.

"What the…"

Édoard muttered an oath under his breath and moved to the door. With a turn of the knob, he yanked it open and walked a few steps into the dark corridor.

"Jean-Luc!" he shouted. It echoed off the bare stone walls, fading into silence. "Henri!"

Nothing. The hallway was silent as a graveyard. Though why he expected an answer at all was a mystery; the building was vast, and if they were anywhere close to the original interrogation room she'd been in, they were deep in the very bowels of it. At this hour—she sensed it was close to dawn, as she always did, even far below ground—it would likely be almost deserted.

There came a low rumble that shivered the walls, and then with a grudging *fzzzttt* the emergency lights that lined either side of the hallway flickered on. They weren't steady, though, and a few were burned out so the hallway was drenched in an eerie, flickering half-light that was extremely creepy. Inside the room, all the ominous electrical equipment had fallen dead.

"There we go," said a satisfied Édoard, walking back into the shadowed room. "Just a little hiccup. Not enough to keep us from our work, eh, kitty?" She watched as he prowled to her, smiling, and then positioned himself behind her wheelchair. With a little bump, he released the brakes and the chair started to slide forward over the floor. "Or at least, not for long. Agent Doe, lead the way," he said to the doctor, who wasted no time pulling the door wide open so the three of them could pass through.

And then, the instant they were in the hallway, she felt it.

Correction: him. She felt *him*, and the air went to fire.

Demetrius.

Burning heat and electric intensity and a crackling current of danger; she'd know him anywhere. He'd finally found her.

And now, as he had in every nightmare she'd had over the past three years, as Silas had warned her over and over again, he'd try to kill her.

Every cell in her body exploded into high, shrieking alert.

"Get me out of here!" she screamed, thrashing against the bindings at her wrists and ankles. Her heart pounded, her blood raced, every muscle clenched. She had to get out, she had to get away, now, now, now, now, *NOW*—

"Oh, that's right, you're afraid of the dark, aren't you?" said a very calm Édoard, sarcasm dripping from his voice. He didn't miss a step, just kept pushing the wheelchair at a leisurely pace down the spooky hall as she continued to buck wildly. One of the wheels hadn't been oiled and made a high-pitched squeal with each revolution that echoed off the cold stone walls and fractured to a million tiny smaller squeals, a chorus of horrible, nonhuman screams that all seemed to say, "*You're going to die! You're going to die!*"

She fought harder. Even though she was still weak and a little foggy from whatever they'd injected her with, one of the ankle straps popped its metal binding with a tinny squeal and broke free.

Behind her, Édoard cursed and snapped, "Tranq, Doe!"

But before the doctor could react, a thunderous *BOOM* shook the building to its foundations. An entire section of the plain stone wall at the far end of the cavernous hallway ahead of them exploded inward in a monstrous spray of brick and dust that carried with it a shockwave of heated air that knocked the wheelchair on its side with Eliana in it and both Édoard and the doctor off their feet.

Her head bounced against the floor.

Fireworks erupted in her vision.

She heard screaming, smelled smoke and scorched fabric, felt the ground shake as another thundering boom rattled the building, but the sound seemed to travel to her ears slowly, distorted as if from far away or underwater. In fact, everything had slowed to a crawl. She lifted her head, blinking through a murky haze of dust, and saw the doctor a few feet away, crumpled on the floor with a widening pool of liquid crimson on the white stone beneath his head. He was twitching grotesquely, mouth open in a silent scream. One eye was open, too, but from the other protruded a bent shard of metal. His broken glasses dangled from one ear.

Édoard shouted something from behind her that she couldn't make out because there was another deafening explosion, somewhere close but out of sight. With a grinding groan, a large chunk of ceiling collapsed into a pile of rubble on the floor not ten feet away and sent another choking blast of dust into her face. Her ears rang. She coughed and sputtered, struggling against her restraints, trying to push the wheelchair nearer to the wall with her one free foot. A tangle of black electrical conduit hung down from the gaping hole in the ceiling and, with a zapping crackle, began to spark and twist like a nest of angry snakes.

The emergency lights in the hallway flickered out and then came right back on, stuttering intermittently as if they might go out completely at any moment. A siren began to whine.

And through it all, the pulse of Demetrius beat like a drum against her skin, stronger every second.

Get up! she screamed silently to herself. *Get out of here or die!*

She didn't want to die. So with strength lent by fury and fear, Eliana snapped the binding around her right wrist.

Panting, she fell on the other wrist restraint and tried with trembling fingers to work open the clasp. She managed it just as a terrifying shock of electricity hit her, and she knew with sudden cold certainty that Demetrius wasn't alone. There were six—she stiffened—no, *eight* more *Ikati* with him.

She struggled to sit up sideways and worked the ankle strap open, bent almost in half at the waist, holding herself up with one elbow. Dust coated her nose and eyelashes, making it hard to breathe and see. The strap gave, and she scrambled out of the toppled wheelchair on her hands and knees, scraping her palms and kneecaps on sharp chunks of brick debris that littered the floor. She turned and saw Édoard, disoriented, staggering toward her with his hands out. He was saying something, she knew because his mouth was moving, but her ears rang so badly all she heard was a painful, high-pitched buzz that made her eyes water.

She glanced behind him, and her heart stopped dead in her chest.

There at the end of the long corridor stood a hulking dark figure, impossibly huge, face in shadow, silhouetted by a wash of weak yellow light from the emergency lamps behind him. Booted feet spread wide, hands flexed open at his sides, enormous, muscled frame almost entirely blocking the open doorway to the connecting corridor from which he'd emerged. Though wreathed in shadow and smoke, terrifying details emerged.

Shaved head. A glint of silver in one eyebrow. Black, black eyes out of which stared an even blacker soul.

Her scream was an animal that clawed its way out of her, tearing her throat, alive. On instinct, she skipped back a step, and her heel caught on a chunk of stone. She fell in slow motion, still screaming, hands flailing, and landed on her rear end with a teeth-jarring jolt that knocked the breath from her lungs.

Time and motion, slowed to a crawl only moments before, suddenly sped up, and everything seemed to happen at once.

Édoard, seeing her back away but thinking it was from him, lunged forward with an oddly animalistic snarl. Before he could lay a finger on her, he was wrenched aside from behind and flung against the wall with such force he actually bounced off it and landed, sprawling and limp, facedown on the floor where he slid until stopped by the opposite wall.

Demetrius looked down at her with such savage fury in his expression it froze her in place like a mouse staring into the jaws of a snake. He crouched as if to spring, but then his head snapped up, his eyes focused on something behind her, and a hair-raising growl rumbled through his chest.

Faster than her eyes could track, he shot past her in a black blur. She rolled to her stomach and lifted herself up on her elbows in time to see shadowy figures emerge through the settling dust at the far end of the hallway, past the snarled electrical conduit and rubble from the destroyed wall.

His team.

In one lithe, lightning-fast move, she sprang to her feet, turned, and sprinted in the opposite direction toward the open door, thinking only of escape, her blood scorching like liquid fire in her veins and her vision narrowed to the rectangle of light at the end of the hallway.

In the seconds that followed, she heard just below the whine of the alarm and the ringing in her ears the distinctive muffled pop of a semiautomatic handgun fitted with a silencer. Then another. A bullet whizzed past her head with an acrid whiff of gunpowder and ricocheted off the stone wall with a piercing twang and a puff of smoke. She feinted left, then right, desperately trying to make herself an uncertain target, but another bullet flew past, then another, and before she could twist away again one of them found the tender flesh of her hip.

Eliana crashed screaming to her knees. There was a different noise behind her now, a horrible garbled snarling, vicious and wild, like a hungry predator tearing into a meal, but she didn't turn and look and didn't give herself the option of staying still. She struggled to her feet again, pain shooting in furious sparks down her entire leg, and limped, one leg dragging, forward.

Just as she reached the end of the hallway, something heavy hit her from behind.

She staggered, but didn't fall because she was caught.

And held.

And turned around by a pair of huge, strangling tight hands wrapped around her arms.

Eliana stared up into Demetrius's eyes. Black and wild, they burned down at her with the lucid incandescence of rage, and she knew this was the end. She braced herself for it, stiffening, ready for the snap of her neck or a knife through her ribs or a gun barrel shoved into her mouth.

And then a thought flashed through her mind, horrifying in its treacherous clarity:

I remember exactly how you taste.

Then the man who murdered her father leaned in close and growled, "*Gotcha!*"

TEN
We Have a Problem

As he'd been doing for the past hour, Leander stood, unmoving and silent, gazing out the tall, lead-paned windows of the East Library. Flanked by heavy silk drapes drawn back with tasseled ties, they offered a spectacular view of the rolling green expanse of lawn, the groomed rosemary hedges, the plashing marble fountain of Triton in the middle of the manicured gardens. Far beyond the boundaries of Sommerley Manor the dark line of the forest began, rolling hills dense with hardwoods and fir that went on for miles. It was beautiful today, warm and sunny, the air scented softly with the beds of lavender and garden roses planted beneath the windows. The sky above was a perfect, cloudless blue; the white falcon stood out against it like a swiftly moving star.

She was still high, but getting closer. Impatience cramped his stomach. He checked his watch.

Ten minutes. Perhaps twenty.

Unless she changed her mind, that is. His lips lifted to a wry smile. There was always the possibility she would change her mind. He clasped his hands behind his back and looked up again, subsiding back into himself with the patience of one accustomed to waiting.

From behind him a terse voice said, "We have a problem."

Leander turned. His younger brother, Christian, stood at the open door. Second in authority only to him—the Alpha of the English colony and the head of the Council of Alphas—Christian was both brother and trusted confidant. He knew all the secrets, sat in on all the meetings, offered opinions and got things done. Over the past three years, he'd been an invaluable asset to the tribe as they struggled to adjust to the staggering shocks of discovering a new colony of their kin in Rome, discovering the leader of their ancient enemy, the Expurgari, was in fact one of their own kind, and finally discovering he'd been killed, but not before his two children had escaped with a group of rebels. Which is why most of the tribe had been moved to the colony in Brazil. It was the only colony the Expurgari still had not discovered.

Only a few were left at Sommerley. Jenna—*I'm never hiding again, Leander*—would not be moved.

Christian was known as a fixer of broken things. A problem solver. So his opening line was more than a little worrying. And so was his posture: taut as a bowstring, wound tight enough to snap.

"A problem?" repeated Leander. "Which is?"

Christian dragged a hand through his dark hair. An unconscious habit, Leander knew, and one that meant he was trying to choose his words carefully.

"Christian," Leander prompted quietly, an imperative.

"The daughter—the missing princess of the Roman colony—she's been *taken!*" he blurted.

The relief that poured through Leander was sweet and surprisingly intense. He hadn't realized until just then how much he'd been dreading this moment, when someone would come and tell him that one of the rebel children of the dead leader of the Expurgari had done something terrible, wiped out an entire colony, murdered the women and children in their sleep. He wasn't a religious man, but he almost crossed himself.

"Thank God."

He walked to the polished cherry sideboard and took up one of the heavy glasses displayed on a silver tray with cut crystal decanters filled with amber and gold liquids. He removed the round stopper and was about to pour himself a generous measure of scotch when Christian said, "No, Leander—she wasn't taken by *us.*"

Leander froze. The decanter became a sudden dead weight in his hand.

Carefully, he set it back on the silver tray along with the glass. He turned back to Christian and stared at him. Same dark hair. Same piercing green eyes. Same dusky coloring all the *Ikati* of his colony shared.

All the *Ikati* except one, that is. Jenna, his Queen, was pale as alabaster.

His first thought—always—was of her. Her safety was the only thing that mattered.

She wasn't taken by us.

"You have exactly five seconds, Christian, to tell me what the hell you're talking about."

Christian moved from the door into the ivory and gilt opulence of the library. Radiating strain, he came and stood at the end of the sideboard. Even his voice was strained when he said, "Someone else was there. The Hunt found her at the police station, but someone else got there first, set off explosives as a diversion, went in and got her out. Whoever it was killed one of the assassins. Almost killed the rest. But he got away…with the princess."

"Explosives," Leander said slowly. A terrible thought crossed his mind, but he pushed it away. It couldn't be. That would mean treason. That would mean war.

Christian shifted his weight from one foot to the other. He put his hands on his hips, looked down at the Turkish rug, then back up at Leander. "Keshav said it was one of us. A male. Big. Shaved head. Tattoos."

Keshav—recruited from the Bhaktapur colony in Nepal—was leader of The Hunt, and if he said it was an *Ikati* male that attacked them, it was. And here came that thought again, pushing back when he tried to ignore it. "Black eyes?"

Christian nodded.

"Shit," hissed Leander.

Christian blinked, shocked. Leander never swore. He hardly ever even raised his voice. He didn't need to. When he said jump, the universal response was: *How high?*

"Phone," Leander demanded, hand out.

Christian pulled one from a pocket and handed it over without a word. Leander punched in a number he'd memorized long ago and raised it to his ear. He hated the damn things, never carried one himself, but cell phones were a necessity, especially now.

All kinds of things Leander hated had recently become necessities.

He stalked back to the windows, raised his gaze to the sky, and found the falcon still high above the forest, making wide, lazy turns. He didn't take his eyes from her as the line was answered and a deep, male voice drawled in lightly accented English, "Your highness! How unexpected. This must be a dire emergency if you're calling during teatime."

Leander's jaw went so tight it popped. "Celian," he said through his clenched teeth, "I've told you not to call me that."

Celian chuckled, raising Leander's hackles even higher. "Spoken like a true dictator. Call yourself Alpha or president or whatever you like, Leander, but if you're the only one who gets a vote, you're still a dictator."

Goading him, as always. Celian had very different ideas about how best to rule his colony, ideas that included words like *democracy* and *consensus* and the ever-popular *freedom.*

Bad ideas. Ideas that could get them all killed. Or worse. He only tolerated it for the time being because there were bigger—badder—fish to fry.

"And you're a fool," said Leander very quietly, "if you think for one moment I won't wipe you and your 'democracy' off the face of this earth if you do anything to jeopardize the rest of us. Do not test me, Celian. I'm in no mood."

Silence. Loud, *gratifying* silence.

They'd only met face-to-face once, he and the leader of the newly discovered Roman *Ikati* colony, and it hadn't been pleasant. Alphas of their kind never got along, having all the territorial, animal instincts of their nature, and he and Celian were no exception. He'd managed to get Celian to agree to keep a tighter rein on his colony until the rebels were found, but fully expected him to start allowing them to come and go as they wished as soon as this crisis was over.

High in the winter sky, the falcon made a graceful, sweeping turn.

He knew what Jenna would have to say on the matter. *He's right, Leander. We all need to be free. It's time.*

He categorically disagreed. They all needed to be *safe*, and sometimes that meant restrictions on such rarefied ideals as freedom. Mainstreaming, as Jenna referred to it, was a disaster of epic proportion, just waiting to happen. Unfortunately, she was Queen, and her word held even more weight than Leander's. Her word held the heaviest weight of all.

The *Ikati*, though by nature feline, had developed over thousands of years a patriarchal, hierarchical society similar to that of a wolf pack. Each of the four confederate colonies—in Nepal, Canada, Brazil, and England—had an Alpha, the most powerful male of all the tribe, who through Bloodlines or ritual challenge and battle had proven himself the strongest. But every so often, once in a dozen generations, a female was born to the tribe who was more powerful than all the male Alphas combined. Like Marie Antoinette, the last *Ikati* Queen before her, and Cleopatra, the most infamous Queen of them all, Jenna had Gifts that made her sovereign over them all.

Because prides of cats, unlike packs of dogs, are by nature ruled by a Queen. Only in the absence of one powerful enough do the boys get to play.

He'd managed to persuade Jenna so far—war is always a convenient scapegoat for restrictions on liberty—but he knew he couldn't hold her off forever. She'd have her way whether he liked it or not.

Whether the entire tribe became extinct because of it.

Hiding is for mice, she'd say, watching him steadily with her brilliant, yellow-green eyes. *And we are not mice, my love.*

No. They weren't mice. They were beasts pretending to be people. They were animal and Vapor and stealthy, deadly predator, relics of a lost age before man ever walked the earth and magic still lived and breathed. He shuddered to think what would happen if humanity ever found out about them. Again.

"Shaved head. Tattooed. Big. Does that sound like anyone you know?" said Leander into the phone.

More silence. Then, "Excuse me?"

"One of the rebels, one of your colony who left with the daughter the night your king was killed…was he big and bald with tattoos?"

"No," said Celian, but Leander heard the slight hesitation, and his blood rose to a boil.

"Do not lie to me," he began, nearly spitting with rage, but Celian cut him off.

"That's not one of the rebels. That's Demetrius. One of my council. One of my most trusted brothers. What about him?"

"Are you trying to tell me you have no knowledge that your *trusted brother* blew up the Paris prefecture of police and took your missing princess?" said Leander, disbelief clear in his voice.

"Impossible," Celian scoffed. "Demetrius is here. He wouldn't leave without telling me…" He trailed off, thinking, and then resumed slightly less confident than before, "*Blew up* the prefecture of police?"

"So help me God, Celian, if you had any knowledge of this—"

"It must have been one of the others who ran away with her…it can't be—"

"Are there many of you that are shaved and tattooed?" Leander cut in impatiently. The falcon outside descended in a slow looping arc, heading for Sommerley and the windows by which he stood. He watched, eyes unblinking, jaw tight.

"No," admitted Celian after another pregnant pause. "But they've been gone three years; it's possible one of them decided to get inked. And shaved his head."

Without turning from the window, Leander moved the phone down to his jaw and said to Christian, "Any other details, Christian? About this male who took the princess?"

"Pierced eyebrow. Three silver rings in it," came Christian's answer from the other side of the room.

Leander lifted the phone back to his mouth. "Eyebrow pierced with silver. Ring a bell?"

He heard Celian mutter an angry, "Fuck," and then direct someone nearby to go and look for someone else. The name was garbled, but Leander guessed who it was.

"Your *brother*. Demetrius. If you don't find him there…if this was his doing—"

"If he was stupid enough to pull something like this, I'll kill him myself," Celian hissed, and Leander was satisfied by the conviction in his voice.

"See that you do," said Leander as he watched the falcon descend just a few yards above the manicured lawn outside, talons extended, wings beating noiselessly, piercing yellow-green eyes avid on his face. "Or I will."

Before Celian could reply, Leander clicked shut the phone and disconnected the call.

Outside the snowy falcon dissolved into a funnel of swirling mist and descended to the grass in a silken plume that began to coalesce into something else altogether as it touched down. Feet first, then legs, then a body—nude and breathtaking—a face that could make grown men cry for its beauty. Hair of spun gold bounced around her shoulders, cascaded in glinting waves down her chest.

Jenna. His Queen. His miracle. The only one of them who could Shift into anything she wished.

Her father's daughter, to be sure.

She quickly crossed the few feet from where she'd landed, watching him watch her as she came. Sensual and unabashed as an odalisque, she waded through the waist-high rosebushes and thick beds of lavender and stood just outside the window. She had to look up a little, her head tipped back, her shell pink lips tipped up at the corners.

He pressed his palm to the glass. She mirrored it, her fingers spread open against his on the opposite side of the window.

"Come in," he murmured, knowing she heard him clearly through the closed, double-paned window. "Jenna. Come in."

She studied his face, and her lips lost their upward curve. A little furrow appeared between her brows. How well she knew him.

"Come inside," he insisted, huskier than before.

Leander heard the door shut behind him, but he'd already altogether forgotten Christian was there.

For ten seconds in which the rage building inside him felt like he was being hollowed out with knives, Celian stood with the phone to his ear, listening to dead air.

Then, with a curse, he turned and threw it clear across the room.

It exploded against the bare rock wall with a dull metallic clatter and fell in a tinkling heap to the floor.

"Good news, I take it." Lix's dry humor, ever present, only served to enrage him even more.

"Smug son of a bitch!" Celian spat.

Lix's dark brows shot up, but Celian waved his hand dismissively, indicating he hadn't meant him. He sat down heavily into his carved wood chair, identical to the one Lix occupied across from him at the solid oak square that served as the *Bellatorum*'s version of a conference table. Like King Arthur's famed round table, this meeting place of knights had no head, no hierarchy. Everyone was on equal footing.

Everyone but D, that is, because he'd missed the morning meeting. He could only be equal if he bothered to show up.

To Celian's right sat Constantine, glowering. He even glowered prettily, which, at the moment, also pissed Celian off.

Today wasn't starting off well. He'd already lost two promising young half-Blood *Legiones* to the Transition, and five more would have their twenty-fifth birthdays within the next thirty-six hours. If they didn't make it…at this rate, they'd run out of the half-Blood caste of soldiers within a few years.

They were dying off faster than they could be replaced. Especially now since the Council of Alphas—even in his mind he said it with a sneer—had forbidden them to mix with humans under penalty of death. So breeding new half-Blood stock was out of the question.

You can't be too cautious during times of war, Leander had said, smiling his smug British smile at Celian the one and only time they'd met. He spoke slowly, with cool condescension, as if the gathered *Bellatorum* before him would have a little trouble with the big words, looked at them like they were nothing but dirty barbarians living like Neanderthals in caves. Celian had wanted to smash his face in. Only one thing stopped him.

Leander, unfortunately, was right.

The dead king Dominus had turned out to be far more treacherous than anyone had guessed, plotting to take over as dictator of all the colonies, killing his own kind if it suited his needs. Even working with humans. There was no doubt his network of paid killers and spies was still out there, waiting for the chance to pounce.

Caesar was still out there. *Silas* was still out there, and he was craftier and therefore more dangerous than the king's egotistical, Giftless son.

He didn't know what those two were planning, if anything, but Celian hated feeling like a sitting duck. And now—if it was true—D had thrown an ugly wrench into this already colossally bad situation.

"What is it?" Lix leaned his bulk over the table and propped himself up on his elbows.

"Little Lord Fauntleroy is at it again," Celian muttered, drumming his fingers on the wood.

"He's still insisting you join the Council of Alphas?" Lix asked, surprised.

In the three years since they'd met, Leander and the other three leaders who comprised the Council of Alphas had attempted to persuade him by coercion and flattery and thinly veiled threat that *not* to join was a declaration of war. But Celian had lived long enough under one dictator, and he would never trade one for four, no matter how nice they pretended to be or how many flowery promises they made. *Stronger together than apart. All for one and one for all. Duty to the tribe,* etc. etc.

He wasn't having any of it. He'd agreed to keep his people contained within the catacombs until the rebels were found, and that was enough to hold them off for now. But now this…

Celian looked at Constantine, who immediately dropped his gaze to the table and shifted his weight in the chair.

Interesting.

Celian watched him carefully as he said, "Actually, he had a bit of news about Eliana."

A muscle in Constantine's jaw twitched. He glanced up, then back down again.

"What?" exclaimed Lix, bolting upright. "Eliana? What is it? What happened? And why were you talking about D?"

Yes, that's the correct reaction, thought Celian, staring at a very still, quiet Constantine. Aloud he said, "Apparently someone who looks a lot like our beloved brother has blown up a Paris police station and stolen the missing princess."

Lix stood abruptly, shoving back the heavy wooden chair in the process. "WHAT?"

"What indeed," Celian murmured, looking at Constantine. "Anything you'd like to add to the conversation, Constantine?"

Constantine took a deep breath, spread his big hands flat on the table, exhaled, and quietly said, "I owed him one."

Lix looked at Constantine. "WHAT?" he shouted again.

The *Servorum* he'd sent looking for D chose that exact moment to burst into the room. Young and gangly, he skidded to a stop inside the arched doorway. "Gone!" he said, breathless. "He's gone! The guards at the north gate were overpowered—"

Celian lifted a hand, and the boy instantly lapsed into silence. A wave of his hand and the boy backed from the room with a bow. The entire time, Celian's gaze never left Constantine's face. "Tell me all of it now, because if I have to hear it from that fucking British peacock—"

"I was with him when we saw Eliana on TV being taken in by the French police—"

"WHAT?"

"Sit down, Lix, and shut the hell up!" Celian snapped. The long-haired warrior lowered his bulk to the chair, slowly, looking back and forth between him and Constantine with a look of horrified disbelief.

Constantine spoke, low, to his spread hands. "She was being arrested. They said on the news she was some notorious thief. They had her in handcuffs—"

"She was injured," Celian deduced instantly. She'd never have been captured otherwise.

Constantine nodded. "D just...he just went crazy. There was no stopping him. I tried to talk him out of it, but you know how he is...about her...he was totally unreasonable..." He glanced up at Celian.

It was getting very difficult to hear above the adrenaline roaring through his veins. "Keep talking," he said.

"Like I said, I owed him one." His big shoulders hunched to a shrug, and he dropped his gaze again to the tabletop.

The room was utterly silent and still. Around his ankles, one of the hundreds of feral cats that ran wild through the catacombs twined back and forth, rubbing its whiskered face against his leg. "You risked all our lives," Celian said very quietly, "you risked *war* with the other colonies because of a guilt trip."

Slowly, Constantine raised his eyes and met Celian's gaze. He shook his head. "No. I risked war with the other colonies because he's my brother and he needed my help. I would do the same for either of you."

Celian stood and began to pace over the bare rock floor. "It was hard enough convincing their *Council* that we didn't have anything to do with the Expurgari, that we didn't know what Dominus had been up to all those years. I *still* don't think they completely believe it."

Lix said to no one in particular, "Eliana is a thief?"

Celian kept talking. "And now I've got to convince them that we had nothing to do with D and this new clusterfuck—"

"A *thief?*" Lix interrupted, staring incredulously at a morose Constantine.

"Silas must have put her up to it," he muttered, nodding. "She'd never do something like that on her own. She was too..."

Sweet, he didn't say. Sweet and lovely and innocent as a fawn.

"We don't know that," said Celian, stopping in midstep beside the table. Lix and Constantine both looked up at him. "We don't know who she is anymore. Or what she's been up to the past three years since she disappeared. All we know for sure is that she saw the three of us standing over her dead father who was lying on the floor with a bullet in his head." He paused, gazing at them with a new intent. "And the male she may or may not have been in love with had a gun in his hand. How do you think that would change you?"

They didn't answer. They didn't have to. Each one of them knew they'd be changed by that experience, and not for the better.

"Is he planning on trying to bring her back here?" Lix asked Constantine, who just shook his head.

"I don't know. He didn't say. I'm not sure if he even had a plan, other than getting her away from the police."

"Okay." Celian took his seat at the table. "Any ideas where he might take her once he did that? Assuming they're not coming back here?"

"He'd need shelter, food," Constantine said slowly, thinking. "And if Eliana is injured, somewhere with medical supplies. Somewhere he could lay low until he figured out a plan."

"Somewhere like a safe house. Probably one not too far from the prison," said Lix, and they both turned to him. He looked back at them, a lock of black hair obscuring one eye, and suddenly Celian had an idea where D might have gone.

He said, "I'm going to need another phone."

ELEVEN
Cross-Dressing Pixie

A subtle hum in his blood, a thrill along the nerves in his spine; D felt it the instant Eliana awoke.

He froze, an oiled chamois cloth in one hand, the muzzle of his Glock in the other, taken completely by surprise.

That she was awake so soon, that is. The sedatives he'd given her should have been strong enough to knock out a male twice her size, for twice as long. He'd given her an extra dosage because he had to be certain she didn't wake up during the surgery to remove the bullet from her hip and sew her up, but—

A loud thump from below. Then another. D glanced at the floor beneath his feet. In one of the bedrooms one level below Eliana was awake, and judging by the sound—another ominous thump, this one accompanied by a shiver in the floorboards and the unmistakable crash of breaking glass—she was less than happy.

Damn. He really shouldn't have left that crystal vase in her room.

He'd picked flowers from the garden outside, had thought it might please her to see the pretty bouquet when she awoke, but now it seemed like a very stupid, obvious mistake. That heavy crystal vase would make an effective weapon if applied with force against the side of his head. He preferred to keep his skull intact, but if the noise coming from downstairs was any indication, she might have other plans.

He made a quick mental inventory of her room: two more vases, desk, chair, flat-screen television…all could definitely be bad for the future state of his head.

He set the gun and the cleaning cloth on the table and wiped his fingers carefully on a dish towel to rid them of the oil, trying to ignore the very slight, sudden shaking in his hands. His heartbeat had picked up, too, irregular spikes that almost painfully pounded against his ribcage. He breathed in slowly, trying to calm himself.

He'd been awaiting this moment for three years, and now that it was here, he felt like a schoolgirl—dry mouth and trembling knees and a stomach full of dancing butterflies.

"Get a grip on yourself, soldier," he muttered, throwing the towel on the table with a flick of his hand. He rose and made his way through the kitchen, the living room, the media room, everything done in masculine shades of charcoal and black and brown, Spartan as the assassins who'd previously owned this safe house liked it. They kept one just like it in every major city across the globe, for occasions such as this, and today he was thankful for it.

Slowly he went, down a set of spiral stairs to the bottom floor. The bedrooms.

He stood at the end of the carpeted hallway looking down the corridor. All the doors were open except one, at the far end, which was locked.

And vibrating. She was hitting—or kicking—it from the inside. If it hadn't been reinforced she would have easily kicked the door right out of its frame, but as it was, she was doing a fine job of trying. He wondered what the inside of the door looked like.

Not pretty, he'd bet.

"Eliana," he called. The blows on the door abruptly ceased. He took several steps forward, listening, hearing nothing but the pounding of his own pulse in his ears. "Ana, it's me." He cleared his throat, feeling suddenly like the biggest fool on the planet. *Of course she knows it's you. Nicely played, idiot!*

Ignoring that snarky little voice inside his head that never failed to demoralize him, D reached out, put his big hand on the doorknob, turned it, and pushed the door open.

It swung back on silent hinges, revealing the room in all its chaos.

She'd torn the sheets and quilted duvet from the bed and upended the mattress against the bed frame so it stood on end, a queen-size padded wall concealing the far corner of the room. All the drawers in the bureau stood open, their contents rifled through, clothing pulled out and left in piles on the floor or hanging haphazardly from the backs of chairs or over the desk, which also had all its drawers ajar, a few upside down on the floor beneath it. The two bedside lamps had been smashed, though one had survived the attack and lay on its side against a wall, uplighting the room in a wash of intermittently flickering yellow.

The crystal vase with the flowers he'd brought lay shattered at his feet, the flowers scattered over the dark rug in bright confusion, drenched and half demolished.

That actually hurt.

"I'm coming in," he warned, his voice harder than he intended because he was feeling sorry for himself about the flowers.

Silence. He took it as an affirmation and eased into the room.

His first mistake was assuming she'd hidden behind the mattress; he realized that as he saw movement from his right and heard something whizz by his head, parting the air with a sinister hiss just as he jerked out of its way. He whirled around and leapt back simultaneously, barely avoiding another slashing blow aimed at his jugular, and had exactly two seconds to appreciate the vision of Eliana—dark eyes ablaze, lovely mouth pinched in concentration—before she thrust again with the blade.

He wrenched away and got himself clear of striking distance before she could take aim again and left her standing, arm raised, dagger clenched in her fist, next to the open bedroom door.

"Hello, Demetrius," she said coldly, gazing at him with what appeared to be perfect composure. "I've been looking forward to this for a long time."

Insanely, he wanted to laugh. He was so happy he could have *danced.* She clearly hated him and wanted to kill him, but she was here and she was alive and she was all he'd wanted for so long he couldn't remember a time when he didn't, and the relief and euphoria he felt lit him up inside like a Roman candle.

His face split with a big, goofy grin, the first time he'd truly smiled in years. "Me, too," he said. "But obviously for different reasons."

Very slowly, never letting her intense gaze leave his face, she shifted from one foot to the other, repositioning her weight. He marveled at how she seemed perfectly poised and confident, totally in control, and then he noticed the throbbing pulse in the hollow of her throat that betrayed her.

Not so cool after all. Perversely, it satisfied him.

"I'm unarmed," he said as she advanced toward him with the dagger held out. He took a slow step back and held his hands up, wondering where she'd found it while at the same time cursing himself again for not clearing the room before he'd settled her in it to sleep off the anesthesia. Rookie mistake, one even a less experienced soldier in the lower class of *Legiones* would have avoided. She short-circuited his brain, as always.

"An unfortunate oversight on your part," Eliana replied, not sounding sorry for him at all, "as it's pretty idiotic to come to a knife fight without a knife."

Dressed in a black pair of men's boxer shorts rolled over at the waist so they didn't sag down her legs and a white men's undershirt she must have found in one of the dresser drawers, with her choppy blue hair sticking up in every direction and her wild, glittering eyes, she looked like an insane, cross-dressing pixie.

An insane, cross-dressing pixie with glowing skin and perfect breasts that were, unfortunately, clearly visible in all their creamy glory beneath the thin cotton undershirt. He avoided glancing at them but knew they were there, and his body responded.

Feeling that flush of heat to his groin, he smiled even wider.

Eliana turned beet red. "I'm not the innocent little princess you used to know, *Bellator*," she hissed. "She died when you killed my father!"

Then she lunged forward, dagger aimed at his heart.

He spun out of the way and she followed, thrusting, leaping forward when he danced back, slashing out with the blade, her face grim and determined. He didn't think himself in much danger—he was far stronger and had trained in all kinds of fighting since he'd been selected as a child for the king's elite guard because of the strength and purity of his Bloodlines—but he was careful not to let her see his confidence, and he kept a safe distance while letting her advance and lunge while he feinted and leapt clear.

"Stop playing with me and *fight*!" she spat as he deflected a vicious thrust with a quick turn of his wrist. He had to admire her technique, he grudgingly admitted to himself. She'd obviously trained with someone who knew what they were doing.

"We are fighting. You're lunging at me with a knife, and I'm trying not to get stuck, so it's definitely a fight. And for the record, I didn't kill your father."

In response to that, Eliana froze. He froze as well and stared at her warily as she looked back at him, her chest rising and falling erratically, that pulse still fluttering wildly in her neck.

"Right to my *face*," she muttered and shook her head.

This time when she lunged forward with a savage snarl—teeth bared, eyes alight with demonic fury—D was a little less certain he'd be getting out of the room alive.

TWELVE
A Cellular Level

Damn! Eliana barely missed D's face with a well-timed swing.

The fact that he kept looking at her like *that* wasn't helping her concentration. How he had the audacity to stare at her with such rampant glee after what he'd done—it made her even more determined to kill him. She lunged at him again.

"I'd almost forgotten how beautiful you are when you're mad," said D, feinting from her lunge so fast he was a blur. He wasn't even breathing hard, damn him, but she was sweating, her hands were clammy, and the adrenaline blasting through her veins was making her shaky. She adjusted her grip on the dagger and breathed in, trying with no success to slow her pounding heart.

This was *nothing* like fighting with Alexi.

"I don't want to hear anything you have to say," she spat. "I just want you to die!"

"Ouch." He looked pained and leapt clear as she lunged again.

She spun around and faced him. Big and brawny and utterly masculine as she remembered, he was still a masterpiece of agility, nimble and graceful with every move. He wore boots, black leathers slung low on his hips, and a half-zipped hoodie that revealed a distracting expanse of chest. Of tattooed, *corrugated* chest. His presence filled the small room, and she felt almost suffocated by the nearness of him, his size and scent. Just being close to him was overwhelming. She needed to get this over with, and quickly.

"Coward," she growled as he deftly avoided another of her swings.

"I'm not the one who ran away from home in the middle of the night," he countered. Though his tone was serious, she knew he was enjoying this, enjoying seeing her sweat and pant, trying to chase him.

Enjoying *playing* with her.

Fury blasted through her veins. He'd killed her father. He'd ruined her life. He'd taken away everything she'd ever known and used her in the worst way possible, and now he was toying with her.

She fell still and lowered the dagger to her side. D watched this with a wary expression from several feet away. "Come on then," she challenged, holding his gaze. "Come and get me if you're not a coward. That's what you want, isn't it? That's why you broke into that police station. So you could take me to some godforsaken place in the middle of nowhere," she said, gesturing to the room, "and get it out of me?"

His expression darkened. His brow crumpled to a frown. "Get *what* out of you, exactly?"

"You really think I'm that stupid?" She began to shake badly now. Emotions she'd managed to bottle up for years welled dangerously close to the surface, a tidal wave of rage and betrayal, anger and loneliness, gathering into a howling, molten core so pressurized it threatened to go supernova. "You think I don't know I'm only alive right now so you can find out where the rest of us are hiding? So you can finish what you started three years ago and kill us all?"

His nostrils flared at that. His eyes, dancing with barely repressed glee only moments before, turned murderous. "I saved your life today," he said, his voice very low in his throat. "If I wanted to see you dead, I would have left you at that prison and let The Hunt have you. And who do you think fixed those damn bullet holes in you? The tooth fairy?"

Her hand flew to the bandage on her hip, hidden beneath the boxers. The Hunt? A flicker of emotion pinched her stomach—confusion? doubt?—but it was quickly eaten by anger.

"Clever. Pretend to save me from your own gang to gain my trust, keep me alive just long enough to find out where the others are, and *then* kill me. You're even craftier than Silas said. I can't believe I ever trusted you!"

And with that, the missing puzzle piece clicked into place.

"He told you it was me," D said, incredulous. "That son of a bitch told you *I* killed your father, didn't he?"

Eliana's dark eyes flared hot, and two spots of pink appeared high on her cheeks. She sucked in a breath and then shouted, "No one had to tell me anything because I saw it with my own eyes, you bastard! You, the gun, my father lying dead on the floor with *a hole in his head!*"

She backed a step away, her breath ragged, her legs bent as if she would leap at him at any moment.

D stood ready for her move, every nerve and muscle throbbing with the effort it took to restrain himself from lunging at her, crushing her to his chest, crushing his lips to hers. "You saw nothing," he said between clenched teeth. "I was holding a gun, that was all. And then you ran away before you let me explain—"

She made the tiniest move, her muscles coiled to spring, and, tired of the cat and mouse and dagger game, he was instantly there to catch her. He reached out and grasped her wrist. With a gasp, she tried to yank free, but his grip was too strong and she dropped the blade. Struggling wildly, she ended up losing her footing and executing an ungainly back flop onto the box spring mattress, where she bounced once, then recovered her equilibrium and kicked out sharply with a leg.

But again he was too fast for her. D caught her ankle in his other hand and wrestled her, bucking and screaming, down to the mattress.

"Murderer!" Eliana shrieked in his face, all pretense of control vanished, wriggling and hissing beneath him like a snake. "Liar! Traitor!"

"Listen to me!" he shouted as she thrashed, spewing obscenities and hitting him with her free hand. She landed a hard punch to the side of his skull, and he grunted as fireworks exploded behind his eye. Damn—she was a hell of a lot stronger than she looked. And vicious as a wildcat, too; she raked her nails down his cheek, and he felt blood, hot and wet, drip from his jaw.

"I'll kill you!" she screamed. "I swear on my dead father I'll kill you!"

He dropped his full weight on her chest, pinning her, and then grabbed her other wrist and pushed both her arms to the mattress above her head.

"Dammit, *listen*!" D shouted, shoving his face right up against hers.

She shrank back into the mattress with a shocked little gasp and froze. Their noses were touching. Their bodies were pressed full together. They stared at each other, eye to eye, breathing hard, muscles rigid.

And then, oh and then…

Second by second, inch by inch, on a deep, cellular level, D became aware of Eliana.

Her breathing, ragged. Her heartbeat, pounding wildly against his chest. The blood rushing through her veins. The heat of her skin. Her body beneath him, soft and warm, overwhelming his senses.

All the little details of her—so vivid in his memory but now here, *here*—came flooding back to cripple him with a tidal wave of emotion so overpowering he momentarily lost the capacity for speech.

"It wasn't me," he finally whispered hoarsely, staring deep into her eyes. "I swear on my life, on the life of my brothers, on everything I hold sacred, it wasn't me."

"Who…who was it then?" She was whispering now, too, as though she'd felt the change in him, which she probably had. Her eyes blistered him, and he thought there might have been a tiny, tiny glimmer of hope there.

Constantine. It was on the tip of his tongue, it was right *there.* He sucked in a breath…

And couldn't say it. He simply could never turn on his brother whom he'd sworn to protect with his own life, not even to try and convince the woman he loved he wasn't the murdering bastard she thought him. Caught between love and duty, the agony of divided loyalty was crushing, and it kept him silent.

The little glimmer of hope in her eyes winked out. It was replaced by fury and withering hatred. "You better kill me now, because the minute you let me go I'm going to cut off your balls and make myself a nice new pair of earrings." She smirked at him. "A very *small* pair."

"Dick jokes? Really?" he snapped, feeling as neutered as she threatened him to be. She'd never actually seen his balls, but he didn't enjoy having his manhood called into question. Perversely, it made him want to strip just to prove her wrong.

"Get off me!"

"I'm not going anywhere until you take that back!"

"Kill me, or get off me!"

"Take it back!"

They glared at each other, neither one blinking. Fuming, she pressed her lips together and a tremor ran through her body. It took several seconds, but she seemed to garner some shred of her abandoned control. Then she said, "If your plan is to smash me to death, it's working. I can't breathe."

"You seem to be doing a fine job of breathing, Ana." D glanced down to her chest where the top of her breasts swelled invitingly over the scoop neck of her T-shirt. When he glanced back up at her, her face had gone cherry red. She turned her face aside, closed her eyes, and bit her lip.

The heat of her body against his, those beautiful breasts, her teeth sunk into that full lower lip…D couldn't help himself. An erection sprang to rock-hard life in his pants. Because their bodies were pressed together, chest to crotch, she didn't miss it.

"Unbelievable," she said, outraged. "Just…*unbelievable.*" She squirmed beneath him, trying to get away, but the friction only served to excite him further, and she gasped, feeling him grow even harder.

"You bring the animal out in me, beautiful," he said gruffly, smiling though he knew he shouldn't be, elated to be near her. "Always did."

"I'm going to throw up on you now. Get off me."

Her look was absolutely murderous—and, he decided, utterly adorable. "Not before you apologize for scratching my face and saying I have a small dick."

She growled in exasperation and said through gritted teeth, "Small. *Balls.* Now. Get. *Off!*"

"Something you need to know first, baby girl," he said, but she stiffened beneath him as if she'd been slapped.

"NO!" She stared up at him, and her dark eyes blazed cold fire. "You don't get to call me that! You don't get to call me nicknames and pretend you care and lie right to my face, not after you used me and took away everything I ever had! You took away my *entire life*! And I hate you for it! I! HATE! YOU!"

D felt his face harden. "I didn't take away anything, you *gave* it away. You ran away without a word, without so much as even a look backward, and I've spent the last three years of my life in fucking agony because of it. And your leaving like you did stirred up such an epic shit storm I don't know how it can be fixed. Maybe it can't. But I'm the one thing standing between you and certain death right now, and I'm risking my own ass to keep you safe, so you're going to be nice to me and *take it back*!"

They glared at each other, stalemate, until finally her lower lip quivered. Unbelievably, *impossibly*, her eyes filled with tears. "I wish you were dead," she whispered miserably.

D could endure physical pain of any kind. He could take blows or cuts or falls, he could even take torture. What he couldn't take was a woman's tears. Especially *his* woman's tears.

Like snow in the sun, his heart melted.

"No, baby girl, you don't," he whispered back, looking deep into her eyes. He was certain now beyond a doubt that beneath all that rage and blistering fury and wall of ice she'd erected was a tiny ember of tenderness that still burned just for him. "And I'll prove it to you."

He lowered his mouth to hers.

She gasped against his mouth, and he took the opportunity to slide his tongue between her lips. She made a little sound in her throat—horror or outrage, he couldn't tell—and stiffened to the rigidity of a wooden plank and stopped breathing.

What she didn't do was pull away.

D took that for a positive sign and deepened the kiss, still tender but seeking, tasting her, wanting her to respond instead of lie frozen, allowing him to explore her mouth with no resistance but no return, no answer to the question his lips were asking.

He pulled back and looked down at her; her eyes were squeezed shut tight. He lowered his head and gently kissed each of her eyelids, the place between her eyebrows, the tip of her nose. She made the little sound again, and this time it sounded closer to a plea. For what, he couldn't tell.

Stop? Go on? A quick, merciful death?

Her lower lip began to quiver again. She was so beautiful, so fucking *vulnerable* like this, pinned beneath him, he felt a wave of heat envelop his body, desire burning bright as the noonday sun.

Open for me, he thought, kissing first one corner of her mouth, then the other. He pressed the softest of kisses to the center of her lips, the little bow, the lower curve, a place he'd kissed in a million fevered dreams. *Open your heart for me, angel. Let me in.*

Then she sobbed.

He froze on a breath, his body burning and aching and his heart stuttering along in his chest like something half dead. She convulsed and sobbed again, turned her head to the side and started to bawl in earnest, great wracking sobs that shuddered them both and the bed beneath them.

"Baby girl," D whispered, mortified. "Ana, Eliana, stop, it's okay, I won't kiss you again, just please…stop."

He released her and sat up. She folded her arms across her chest and curled into a little, protective ball, her knees pulled to her nose, her face turned to the mattress. He didn't know what to do. He didn't know if there was anything he *could* do. Seeing her like this tore a hole in his chest big enough to drive a truck through.

"G-get out," she sobbed into the mattress. "Get away f-from me."

He reached for her, touched her shoulder, but the second his hand was on her she jerked as if electrocuted and kicked him, hard, in the stomach. "Get away from me!" she screamed as he toppled off the bed. He landed with a jarring thump on the floor, and Eliana, eyes wide, shaking violently, scrambled up against the headboard and cowered there, red-faced, staring at him but with a blank look as if she wasn't seeing *him*, but someone or something else altogether.

"Ana—"

At exactly that moment, the security alarm went off with a high, electronic shriek, piercing his eardrums. Every nerve in D's body surged into high alert.

Someone had just broken into the house.

THIRTEEN
Traitorous Assassins

Panic attack.

Eliana knew the symptoms intimately because she'd suffered from these terrifying episodes for years. Not that she'd ever told anyone. With her kind, showing weakness like that guaranteed an expedited route to the afterlife.

Survival of the fittest wasn't just an evolutionary theory. It was an actual fact of *Ikati* Law.

The first time it happened was three days after her father was killed. She and Mel and the rest of their group were still on the run from the catacombs, trying to cross the border to France on foot, not knowing if they'd be caught, not knowing where their next meal was going to come from.

One minute she'd been fine, trudging along a dry streambed in warm twilight in the forested Gran Paradiso

National Park just miles from the French border, her feet aching, her stomach growling, her mind a tangle of thoughts and memories she kept pushing aside to concentrate on the increasingly difficult task of putting one foot in front of the other. Then, suddenly, from the dry shrubbery alongside the streambed erupted a shrieking knot of kestrels, driven in terror from their hidden nests by the group of much larger predators going by.

Their terror was infectious. For a blinding moment, Eliana couldn't breathe. Her heart failed to beat. She broke out in a cold sweat, began to tremble violently, and felt tingly in all her limbs. Her chest felt like it was being squeezed by a giant, invisible hand. She thought she might be dying of a heart attack.

Which is exactly how she felt when Demetrius just kissed her.

The last year had been better; once they were settled in France—Silas had the foresight to stuff a bag full of money before they fled, not enough to last but enough to get them established—the attacks tapered off, and for the past year she hadn't suffered even one. Not when she'd been caught by the police, not when she'd been tortured by Édoard and Dr. Frankenstein, not when the police station blew up around her and she was kidnapped and awoke with two sewn-up bullet wounds, locked in a strange room in a strange house, alone.

No, it took a kiss to bring one on. A kiss from *him.*

And this was the mother of them all.

Crouched on the bed like a cornered animal, she watched with wild eyes as D leapt from the floor, his huge body coiled to spring, his face tense, a look of pure, murderous rage in his eyes, which were trained on the bedroom door. With a growled, "Stay here!" he moved silently to the door, looked out, and then disappeared though the doorway without looking back.

Once he was gone she felt a surge of relief, but she still couldn't get her gelatinous legs to move. She gulped large swallows of air, willing her heart to slow its furious beat, telling herself she wasn't dying, she was going to be fine, she just needed to *get out of this room* and away from him.

And whatever else had recently arrived.

Still shaking, she tried to step off the bed and instead fell flat on her face on the floor. She lay there panting a moment, listening hard to catch any noise above the hideous whine of the alarm, but she didn't hear anything. She finally managed to get her legs to work and crept to the doorway. From the floor she snatched the dagger D had wrestled from her hand. She reached the door and peeked out.

A long corridor lined with doors, some open, a few closed. A spiral staircase at the end, leading up to another floor.

No windows. No other way out.

She crept down the hallway, glancing into each room. All were bedrooms, none had other interior doors. She'd have to go up the stairs.

Taking each step much more carefully than the adrenaline screaming through her veins wanted, she progressed up the steps until she reached the top, then peeked over the last step: Living room. Sofas, huge flat-screen television, modern, masculine décor. No one in sight.

The alarm screamed shrilly on and on, urging her forward.

With her heart in her throat, she eased up the last few steps and ran to the opposite wall, where she flattened herself beside a tall bookcase and paused a moment to catch her breath. Her pulse throbbed through her head, pounding a staccato beat that nearly drowned out the alarm.

She heard voices. Male voices. Shouting. Her heart took off like a rocket, and her hands began to shake so badly she nearly dropped the dagger. She tiptoed across the floor to another spiral staircase that led up to who knows what, the only way out of the room.

When she reached the top of the staircase, she didn't fall apart so much as implode.

Three huge males, black-haired, strapped with weapons, larger and more menacing than any human could ever be, were wrestling Demetrius down to the floor. *Trying* to wrestle him down to the floor, without much success. They were all snarling and shouting at one another in Latin, massive arms swinging, black hair and fists flying, a heavy oak kitchen table and wooden chairs knocked aside like children's toys as they grappled with one another and staggered across the room.

D. Lix. Celian. Constantine. Her father's personal guard.

Her father's traitorous assassins.

A thermonuclear urge to kill them all with her bare hands forced blood to her face where it spread, throbbing hot, to her ears and neck. It warred with a deeply ingrained, stubborn survival instinct that screamed at her in no uncertain terms to get the hell out of there while they were busy doing whatever it was they were doing. It seemed like the other three were trying to take D down, but why, she couldn't fathom. It occurred to her that possibly D had gone rogue and killed her father himself without the knowledge of the others, but she dismissed that thought as quickly as it came, knowing the *Bellatorum* were like the musketeers—all for one and one for all and all that nonsense. If D had hatched a plot to kill her father, they were all in on it.

And this was her chance to get revenge.

Or—escape.

Which would it be? She couldn't take them all at once, she only had the dagger—but their backs were turned, they were all distracted, she had the element of surprise—

Then something strange happened. In the middle of the snarling ball of fury that was the fighting warriors, D spotted her crouched there at the top of the stairs. Over the shoulders of the others, their eyes caught and, for one infinitesimal moment, held. Then he glanced to his right and glanced back at her, a look of intense concentration on his face, as if he were trying to communicate something crucial. Eliana's gaze darted right, following his.

The sliding glass door in the family room across from them had been smashed. In its place was an enormous, ragged, gaping hole that led directly outside.

To freedom.

The bottom fell out of her stomach. She stared back at D, and he nodded once; then with a thundering bellow, he dragged all three *Bellatorum* down to the floor with him.

Eliana sprang to life.

In three long bounds she was across the room and through the smashed door, outside into a large yard of trees and grass lit ghostly blue by moonlight. She couldn't Shift, but she could still run, and run she did, like the wind, never looking back, the snarls of the fighting males she'd left behind fading as she bounded off into the moonlit night, clearing fences, climbing walls, sprinting across lawns and streets and yards, her mind a viper's nest of unanswered questions, writhing and twisting, spitting black.

D kidnapped her.

D fought his brothers.

D let her go.

What the hell was happening?

FOURTEEN
Faith

When the sharp knock came on his closed office door, Gregor didn't bother to look up from the newspaper he was reading. News of the escape of *La Chatte* from the Paris prefecture of police—accompanied by vivid Technicolor pictures of the gorgeous thief herself and the half-destroyed building—was splashed all over the cover.

"Come," he said absently, transfixed to the page.

Merck, one of the muscle-bound bouncers from the nightclub, poked his head in. "Got a problem, boss," he said in his lisping, baby-doll voice that belied the true violence of his nature. He'd spent seven years in prison for murder before Gregor hired him.

"Not the goon squad again," Gregor muttered, imagining Édoard and his minions at the door. They'd spent an entire day last week tearing up his building and had left in a snit when they hadn't found anything worthwhile.

"Not exactly." Merck's voice held a hint of a smile. Gregor looked up from the paper to find the burly, goateed man staring at him with one of his bushy eyebrows cocked. His brown eyes sparkled with laughter. "Check out camera five."

Gregor frowned and turned to the bank of video screens on the wall beside his desk. On them were displayed black-and-white images from the dozens of security cameras located all around the property, live-action feeds that showed the building in five-inch squares from every angle. Empty staircases and silent rooms, closed doors and corridors, the bobbing crowds in the nightclub…and one lonely, ill-lit back door near the Dumpsters at the loading dock, which featured the astonishing image of a drenched, shivering, half-naked woman, arms wrapped around her chest, wet hair plastered to her head, huge, dark eyes staring up beseechingly at the camera.

With his heart like a jackhammer in his chest, Gregor shot to his feet.

"Wouldn't take no for an answer when we told her to piss off. Says she knows you." Merck's voice was carefully neutral. He never asked questions, passed judgment, or got involved in Gregor's business, which was one of the many reasons he made an excellent employee.

"Christ! Jesus Christ! Take me to her!" Gregor barked, red-faced. Merck just nodded and stepped aside, swinging the door open with one arm as Gregor barreled through it.

One elevator ride, two flights of stairs, and three near heart attacks later, Gregor threw open the loading dock door, and a wet and weeping Eliana collapsed into his arms.

"Found me—kidnapped—ran—ran all the way here—" she choked off with a sob.

"Easy, lass," he murmured, equally stunned by this new, vulnerable Eliana and by her almost nude body plastered against him. Barefoot, wearing what looked to be boxer shorts and a man's T-shirt gone translucent with the water that soaked it, she was shaking, panting, clinging to him like a buoy in a storm-tossed ocean. He wrapped his arms around her, pulled her close, and murmured soothingly, "You're all right now. You're safe here, little *chatte*. Come inside. Come inside with me and let me get you dry."

He glanced up at the stars twinkling in the mirror-clear night sky, frowned, and then pulled her inside. With her leaning heavily on his arm, Gregor made his way back through the darkened dock toward the stairs.

Gregor took her to a room buried somewhere deep in the building that was decorated with ivory carpets and silk-paneled walls and lit a fire in the cavernous marble hearth. He settled her into the comforting embrace of an overstuffed armchair near the fire and sent Merck for fresh towels. When they arrived and Merck had been dismissed after receiving quiet instructions to bring some dry clothes from Céline's closet, Gregor spent several wordless minutes drying her carefully and methodically as one would a child from a bath, tousling her hair, wiping her arms and legs and feet, gentle and affectionate yet utterly chaste.

Just that simple courtesy filled her with gratitude.

When he was done, he tossed the towels on the end of the king-size, pillow-strewn bed. Eliana eyed the bed—and the large mirror mounted on the ceiling above it, and the nightstand beside the bed with a discreet gold plaque that read "treasure chest"—and tried not to think about what that was all about. He wound a plush cashmere throw around her shoulders, gazed down at her a moment, then settled his bulk in the armchair opposite hers, steepled his fingers under his chin, and said, "So."

Eliana bowed her head and closed her eyes.

She'd imagined this moment for years, though of course never dreamed of quite these circumstances. Various scenarios had been considered and disregarded, and the longer she knew him the more she trusted him and wanted to tell him…but could she trust him with this?

So guess what? I'm a shape-shifter exiled from my colony of shape-shifters who live hidden in the catacombs beneath the Vatican. Oh, and there's several more colonies of us hidden throughout the world. I'm not human, you see. Isn't that great? Let's have a drink!

Somehow she didn't think it would go over.

But she'd come here. *Here,* not to the old abbey and catacombs with the rest of her exiled kin. Here, to the safety offered by a human who'd never denied her anything and had accepted all her secrets and strange comings and goings without even a question. She didn't try and fool herself that it was because Gregor's building was closer, though it undoubtedly was. Once she found a main road that led away from the house she'd escaped from in the suburbs and had her bearings, she just ran straight here, though only a few miles more and she'd have been home.

Home, she thought with a sharp pang in her chest. Would she ever really have a home again?

She glanced up to find Gregor considering her carefully, his eyes warm but very shrewd.

"Those feet need looking after." His gaze dropped to her bare feet, resting gingerly on a tufted stool. The soles were cut and torn from running so far, something she never did in human form. They hurt like hell, but she'd suffered worse, and said so.

"Worse than shredded feet?" he mused, brows lifted.

Try a shredded heart, she thought, then slammed that thought back into the little dungeon in her mind where she kept errant demons. She was calmer than when she first arrived, more clear-headed, but still in a state of shock, and if she let herself think…

Demetrius. The *Bellatorum.* Her father. Édoard and the German. Silas. Caesar. It all swirled around in one howling, teeth-gnashing twister inside her brain, pulling her down, down—

"How do you know who to trust, Gregor? You're a businessman, a man of the world. You've seen and done almost everything, I'll bet. How do you decide when it's time to give someone your trust?"

He gave her a knowing little half smile. "Someone?"

Her heart banged against her ribcage. "You," she finally said, bluntly. "How do I know I can trust you?"

"You don't, princess," he replied softly, holding her gaze. "You just close your eyes and let yourself fall, and see if I'm there to catch you. That's why it's called *trust.* It's a little like faith, only you don't have to wait until you're dead to see if it's real."

She didn't smile at his joke. "There are too many lives at stake for me to indulge in a luxury like trust without some kind of guarantee it won't be broken."

He huffed a breath through his nose. "There are no guarantees in life. Without risk, there's no reward, and trust is a big risk, I'll grant you that." His voice gentled. "But you already know I'd do anything for you, don't you? You already have your proof. You're just gettin' the feel of the wind on your face before you jump off the roof."

Eliana furrowed her brow at him. "Is that a Scotsman's version of a pep talk? Because it's awful. By the way, I could really use a drink. Whiskey if you've got it."

He gave her a look. "Alcohol doesn't solve any problems."

"Yes, Mother, but neither does milk."

Gregor gazed at her for a beat, then rose from his chair and crossed to a sideboard laden with bottles of whiskey, port, vodka, and gin. He poured a stiff measure of amber liquid into two glasses and handed her one, then quaffed his in one long swallow. He settled himself back in the chair while she gazed down at the glass in her hand.

After a moment of silence he said, "Why don't you just tell me a story, Eliana."

Wary, she glanced up at him. "A story?"

He slowly nodded, his warm hazel eyes trapping hers. In the fireplace, the wood snapped and settled with a muffled *thunk* into the grate, sending a spray of orange ash floating up into the chimney. "A story. It doesn't have to necessarily be true, you see, we can just be two friends sharing a story over a fine glass of single malt. Something unbelievable and fantastic, you know, like, 'Once upon a time, there was a mysterious woman who could appear out of thin air, and just as quickly, disappear. Just like the Cheshire cat from *Alice in Wonderland*, she flitted in and out of locked buildings like a ghost…" His voice turned gently ironic. "A ghost who needed semiautomatic weapons and land mines and showed up soaking wet and terrified in the middle of the night after being sprung from jail by a gang of ninja munitions experts."

She passed a hand over her face and pinched the bridge of her nose between two fingers. "My story is a very boring one, Gregor. There's really not much to tell."

He leaned forward in his chair and propped his elbows on his massive thighs, looking at her with clear-eyed intensity. Barrel-chested and ginger-haired, with a three-day growth of beard and a piratical smile, he claimed to be a direct descendant of the Scottish outlaw Rob Roy. She believed it, too; it was easy to imagine him leading a charge of ten thousand screaming, kilt-wearing, sword-wielding warriors. Very quietly, he said, "Don't bullshit a bullshitter, luv. I'll bet your story is fucking priceless."

She stiffened. The hand she had clutched around the cashmere throw went white-knuckled. Gregor saw the change in her, and his face softened.

"No. Don't go there, princess. Whatever's happened to you, you're safe now. You're with a friend who isn't going to judge you or hurt you. I'll do anything in my power to help you, always, you know that. You *should* know that. Whoever else might be against you, I'm on your side." He hesitated and his expression grew serious. "You promised me you would come to me if you were ever in trouble, and you did. And now I need to know exactly what kind of trouble you're in so I can help you."

"No one can help me. Especially no one like…no one like…"

"Me?" said Gregor, guessing correctly. All the softness went out of his face. "No one like me, you mean?"

She nodded, and his eyes went flat. "Gregor, no," she said softly, seeing his misunderstanding. "Not because you're you, because of what you do." She gestured at the room, the mirrored bed, the chest of playthings beside it.

"Then what?" His voice had gone as cold as his eyes.

He didn't believe her. And she'd hurt him. He'd helped her and she'd hurt him. By withholding, she'd hurt one of the only people she might actually be able to trust.

Just close your eyes and let yourself fall.

Would she? *Could* she? Eliana inhaled a long, slow breath, debating.

Her heartbeat picked up. Gregor stared at her, angry, intent. Every aspect of the room grew sharper, the muttering fire grew louder, the light grew almost unbearably bright.

Then, with the sensation of stepping off a very high cliff and dropping down into a pit of permanent blackness, she said, "Because you're human, Gregor. And I'm not."

After a silent moment so long and painfully tense she felt as if her body were a wire pulled close to breaking in two, Gregor made a noise in his throat, low and contemplative. He leaned back in his chair. He rubbed a finger over his lips and let his gaze drift over her face, her body, her bare legs and torn feet. His jaw worked. Then in a very quiet, rough voice, he said, "When I was a wee lad, my grandmother used to tell me stories of the *aos si.* Heard of them?"

Dumfounded by his reaction—or lack thereof—Eliana slowly shook her head.

"They were the spirits of nature, she said, gods and goddesses that exist in an invisible world that coexists with the world of humans." His gaze, piercing now, traveled back to her face and pinned her with its raw, intelligent power. "They were stunningly beautiful and equally fierce, gifted in ways we humans could never understand. The *bean sidhe* announced a coming death by wailing, the *bean nighe* washed the clothing of a person doomed to die, the *leanan sidhe* was a fairy lover or muse who sought the love of mortals…and the *cat sidhe* could transform into a cat and steal your soul."

He stared at her, and Eliana, wide-eyed and breathless, felt a rash of goose bumps rise on her arms.

"My grandmother was a crazy old woman, princess. She was from the oldest part of an old country, steeped in folklore and the ways of ancient magic. I was a city boy, never believed a word she said." His voice dropped an octave. "Until I met you. Until, maybe, right now. So I'll say it again, princess, and I hope you'll indulge an old friend. *Tell me a story.*"

Eliana's lips parted. Everything inside of her burned and trembled. She felt electrocuted. She felt terrified. She felt alive.

She'd told someone. A human.

He knew.

He *believed.*

Flushed, nearly euphoric with a heady mixture of hope and fear, she stared at him.

"Once upon a time," he softly prompted.

"Once…" When she faltered, Gregor nodded reassuringly, as if to say, *Go ahead.* Unable to bear his keen gaze any longer, she turned her face to the fire and stared into the crackling flames. She moistened her lips and began again.

"Once upon a time, in a kingdom of magic and mystery and permanent darkness, there lived a princess. She was powerless and overprotected and also, as fairytale princesses are, incredibly naïve. She didn't know not to trust strangers. She didn't know how to properly choose friends. She didn't know, unfortunately, that behind the most beautiful smiles sometimes lurk the ugliest, most dangerous lies."

She closed her eyes, remembering, the ache of betrayal still so deep after all these years.

"Born to a family of great wealth and a people of great—and unusual—Gifts, the princess only knew that though her world was privileged and she was pampered, another world lay beyond the confines of her gilded cage. A world of adventure and possibility. A world of *what if.* The human world. The world to which she did not belong, yet yearned to see with every fiber of her being."

She glanced at Gregor, and he nodded again, encouraging, so she took a breath and continued.

"But because she was the daughter of a great and powerful king descended from an ancient line of great and powerful kings who had learned to survive the human world by hiding from it, the princess was not allowed to dip her toes into the forbidden waters of humanity's enticing delights. She was kept under lock and key in her sumptuous underground palace and satisfied her craving for adventure with books and movies and daydreams about what could never be." Her voice dropped to a whisper. "One day, however, fate intervened."

The fire mesmerized her, orange flickering wraiths that danced and spun and drew her back, back, into the past, into the bittersweet memory of the time before she split into two people. Eliana *Before* and Eliana *After*, one happy and blissfully ignorant, one frozen forever, encased in a coffin of ice.

"The king was murdered. Like the human king Caesar Augustus who once hunted their kind near to extinction, he was betrayed by those closest to him. The kingdom was stolen, and the princess…the princess fled, never to return."

Her throat tightened. The flames wavered and swam in her vision. Gregor hadn't moved, and she didn't look at him. She was afraid if she did she'd dissolve into tears.

He murmured, "What happened to her?"

"She...she changed. She learned the ways of the world. She began to steal." Her gaze flickered to Gregor's. "To survive. For money. And for...other things. Things she needed." She looked back at the fire.

"And these other things she needed," Gregor murmured, "were they for protection from whoever killed her father?"

Eliana closed her eyes and felt a lone tear track down her cheek. Silas's voice whispered in her head, *There is a war coming,* principessa. *Survival of the fittest is the only thing that matters now.* "That's only part of it," she whispered, drawing the cashmere closer around her shoulders. Suddenly she felt very cold.

"And the rest? What's the rest for?"

"Revenge."

The word hung there in the air between them, simple and sinister. Gregor regarded her gravely, weighing it. "That's an awful lot of burners for revenge."

"It's more complicated than that."

A slight shake of his head and Eliana knew he didn't fully understand and wanted her to explain. Because she was feeling like she was having an out-of-body experience anyway, she went ahead and said, "Every country derives power in a myriad of ways, from population size to natural resources to financial stability. Without those things, power is impossible. *Freedom* is impossible. But there is one thing that can even the playing field so that even the weakest David can trump the strongest Goliath." She glanced at him, and he was staring back at her, rapt. "Weapons."

Gregor started, understanding dawning on his face. "You're building an army," he accused.

He was quick, she had to give him that. "I'm just telling a story, remember?" She swiped at her face with the back of her hand and refused to look at him.

He sat stiffly forward in his chair. "So I'm helping you stockpile weapons so you can, in turn, do what? Kill people—humans?"

Shocked, she stiffened. "No! Of course not! We merely have to protect ourselves! We want to come out of the shadows and coexist peacefully, but we have enemies—"

Gregor stood and glared down at her, radiating tension. "Protect yourselves with automatic weapons? With *land mines*?"

"Gregor," she said, hard. "Sit *down*."

He must have seen something in her face because he complied, begrudgingly. He folded his arms across his chest and gazed unblinking at her, all the softness from before gone.

She downed the rest of the whiskey and set the glass on the low table beside her chair with a sharp *clink*. "We have a lot of enemies, and they're very nasty, Gregor. This isn't about hurting people, this is about protecting ourselves from those who want to hurt us."

He looked dubious, so she said, "Do you remember the man who was in your office that day I came with the Cézanne? The one who was with the police—the German with a shard of ice where his heart is supposed to be?"

Lips as tight as his jaw, Gregor gave a curt nod.

"When I was taken to the police station, he tortured me."

It was as if he was an overfilled balloon that had been pricked with a pin. He visibly deflated. Weakly, his face paling, he said, "What?"

"They know, somehow, about us. They were"—she grimaced, then went on, determined—"experimenting on me. Running tests, seeing how I reacted to different stimuli, that sort of thing. They know about us, but they don't *know,* and we have to protect ourselves if we're going to take the risk to be out. Maybe it started with that video a few years ago," she muttered, "stupid Constantine and his stupid disco fight—"

"Wait. Wait." Gregor sat forward in the chair again, hands spread wide. "The infamous video in the disco in Rome? With the…the uh…" He trailed off into silence, unable to say it himself.

Eliana gazed at him from beneath her lashes. "Panthers. Yes."

He visibly blanched. She saw him replay it in his mind, the grainy cell-phone video caught by a bystander at a popular nightclub that showed the bizarre sight of six impossibly huge black panthers engaged in snarling, bloody battle on a dance floor before the police had shot one and captured two others. She'd seen it herself because it had received a lot of air time before being roundly dismissed by the authorities as fake. At least publicly.

"Huh. Huh," he said, turning it over in his mind, wrapping his head around it. He leaned back in his chair and exhaled a long, quiet breath. "*Cat sidhe* after all, eh?"

"Every culture has their shape-shifter myths," Eliana said gently. "Some of them are just closer to the truth than others."

He sat on that for a minute, recalibrating, and Eliana waited, watching his expression flit from one emotion to another, her heart in her throat.

Had she done something very, very stupid?

After a while, his lips quirked. "Should have known when you stole my soul," he murmured.

Relief coursed through her, and she let out the breath she didn't even know she'd been holding. "Silver-tongued devil."

"Thieving feline."

She grinned at him, and he leaned over and grasped her hands, suddenly grave again. Vehemently he said, "Promise me you're not going to pull a Montecore on me. Or anyone else for that matter."

"Montecore?" She was confused. "What's a Montecore?"

Utterly serious, firelight shining red and gold off his ginger hair, Gregor stared at her and said, "The white tiger that ate that fruit loop Las Vegas magician. Roy what's-his-name. You know, in the show at the Mirage hotel."

She laughed weakly and leaned over and pressed her hot forehead to their joined hands. His fingers against her flushed skin were ice, ice cold, and she guessed he wasn't nearly as composed as he was pretending to be. With a low, rumbling laugh tinged with the merest hint of entreaty, he said, "Because I fancy keepin' my head attached to my body, lass, if you don't mind."

"I promise I will not eat you," she said solemnly. "But that little dog of yours..."

Gregor gasped in mock outrage, and she lifted her gaze to his face. His hazel eyes sparkled down at her. "Although you might be doing me a wee favor there."

Eliana shook her head, overwhelmed by gratitude and the dawning realization that her father's dream of living in the open—the dream she was working toward—might actually be plausible. If one human could accept her, why not ten? Why not a hundred?

Why not *all* of them?

"Well, then, let's see what you can do, princess. Go ahead and show me." He made a gesture with one hand, encouraging, but she shook her head.

"I can't," she said, knowing what he wanted. "I can't Shift when I'm hurt."

He snorted in disbelief. "Oh, how convenient! A few little scratches on the soles of her feet and the great shadow cat is spayed!"

She sighed and shrugged her shoulders beneath the throw. "That would have done it, yes, but the bullet holes didn't help, either."

His merriment instantly fled, and his voice dropped low and menacing. "*Bullet* holes." His gaze swept her and settled on the bandage on her lower leg. He hadn't mentioned it earlier, and now she didn't respond to the question in his eyes. After a moment he said in that same low voice, "So the king's assassins have caught up with the runaway princess."

"It would seem so."

Tension radiated from his body as if a switch had been thrown. He stiffened, looking around the sumptuous boudoir as if expecting to find them hiding behind the curtains. "Can they all do the vanishing Cheshire cat bit?"

Demetrius could. As for the rest of his new gang, The Hunt, whatever he'd called them, she didn't know for sure, but if they were on his team, she had to guess yes. Miserable again, she nodded. "But they didn't follow me here. I'm sure of it. I wouldn't have put you in danger that way. And I disguised my scent so they wouldn't be able to track me like that."

When his brows pulled together in confusion she explained, "Water dampens our scent. I ran through every damn sprinkler, fountain, and wading pool in the city on my way here."

"Jesus, Mary, and Joseph," he muttered, staring at her in dismay.

"Tell me about it."

A knock on the door produced Merck, returning with a dry set of clothes purloined from Céline's closet. They both rose, and Gregor took the proffered items—gauzy loungewear, gossamer thin, and a drapey silk knit sweater in the palest pearl gray, things she would never choose for herself—and set them on the bed. Merck excused himself, and Gregor turned to her.

"You're staying here tonight. I'll call the doctor, but it might take an hour or so before he gets here, so get some sleep in the meantime."

"The doctor?" she said, alarmed, remembering the German from the police station.

"For the bullet holes," he explained gently, glancing at her bandaged leg. His gaze traveled up her body, searching for the others.

"Hip. But it's already stitched up, the wounds are clean. I'll be healed in a day."

"From a bullet wound?" His face remained neutral, but his tone was clearly disbelieving. She only nodded. He accepted that with a shake of his head and then said, "You stitched your own bullet wounds? I've known hardened mercenaries who weren't able to do that."

She faltered. "I…no. It's, um, complicated."

His brows slowly lifted. He said, "Go to a veterinarian?"

She rolled her eyes. "If you must know, the same person who shot me and broke me out of jail was the person who stitched me up."

He stared at her, nonplussed. "Walk me through this, princess. Someone who wanted you dead took the time to *blow up* the largest jail in France to spring you, then shot you—more than once—then took you somewhere safe, removed the bullets, and sewed you up?"

Put like that, it sounded less than reasonable. Eliana chewed her lip. "He only did that because he was trying to get information out of me. About the rest of us. Where we are. Where we're staying. So then he could—"

"Assassins generally don't have to perform surgery in order to get their marks to divulge information," he interrupted, reasonable. "A pair of pliers would be sufficient. If this guy worked for me, he'd be fired."

Eliana opened her mouth to say something, but found she had no reply.

"And you escaped from this do-gooder assassin…how?"

"He…well, he let me go. When his friends showed up. The other assassins."

Of all the unbelievable things she'd told him in the last few minutes, this was the one with which Gregor chose to find issue. His face assumed an expression of extreme incredulity, as if he'd walked into his bedroom to see a unicorn reclining with a yeti on the bed. "Ah-ha. And he would do that because…"

Her lips twisted. "Like I said, it's complicated."

"That's not complicated, Eliana. That's nonsensical."

"Well," she said, defensive, "that's what happened! Who knows why Demetrius does *anything*—"

"Ah," he said, and folded his arms across his chest.

She stared at him. "What, *ah*? What does that mean?"

He raised his brows and shrugged. "Judging by the way you say his name, I'm guessing you and this Demetrius have some history."

In a wave, heat rose up her neck, spread over her cheeks, her ears, her brow.

Gregor snorted, examining her face. "Some *major* history."

"Yes, we do," she said, her voice gone small. Her eyes filled with that traitorous moisture, and she didn't even bother to blink it away. "I—I was in love with him, and he killed my father."

Gregor's arms fell to his sides. His face softened. "Oh, princess—"

He took a step toward her, and at that exact moment an extremely agitated Merck crashed back through the bedroom door.

"Got some bad company, boss!" he shouted, red-faced and sweating. "Sky out!"

He disappeared through the door without another word, leaving Eliana with a skyrocketing heartbeat and a grim-faced Gregor, who answered her question before she could get it out of her mouth.

"It means *run*," he hissed, grabbing Eliana by the arm.

FIFTEEN
Off the Reservation

They'd had a hell of a time subduing D; it was only the tranquilizer Constantine had been smart enough to snatch from the infirmary before they'd left Rome that had finally done the trick.

"He's going to have one mother of a headache when he wakes up," Lix said as he watched D's enormous, slumbering form on the couch where they'd deposited him. They were gathered in the living room at the safe house where they'd found D...but no Eliana.

She'd been here, though. Celian, Constantine, and Lix could all smell her, faint traces of clover and roses diffused in the air, stronger downstairs, strongest of all in one of the bedrooms that looked as if a tornado had passed through. Lix had forgotten how amazing she smelled. An unmated, incredibly powerful, full-Blood female in her lush, exquisite prime…there was nothing on Earth to equal it.

No wonder D had been practically impossible to put down.

"He deserves a damn headache," muttered Celian from his position in the doorway across the room. He leaned against the doorjamb—the largest of the group at almost six foot eight, his head was one inch from the top—and folded his arms across his broad chest. He sent an ominous glower toward the unconscious warrior sprawled on the couch. "Stubborn, pigheaded, rebellious bastard."

Lix inspected his forearm and winced. A perfect outline of D's teeth was embedded in his skin. "Since when is he a *biter*?"

"Since he fell head over balls for Eliana, that's when. Which is exactly the same time he lost his damn mind."

A low groan from the direction of the couch snapped all their heads around. Lix rose, Celian straightened from the doorway, and Constantine—pacing back and forth in taut silence on the other side of the room—stopped short. D's head rolled first one way, then the other. One of his big hands twitched.

Sounding worried, Lix said, "Should we restrain him?"

"That will only piss him off." Celian shot a glance at Constantine, who still hadn't moved. "Let's give him a minute, see what he does. Keep that syringe ready, though."

One eye cracked open, then the other. D blinked up at the ceiling. The hand that had just twitched flexed open, then curled to a fist. Then in one blinding fast movement he shot from the couch as if someone had electrocuted him and sank to a reflexive fighting stance, fists raised, knees bent, legs spread apart. A wicked snarl ripped from his lips.

"Easy, brother," said Celian, low. D looked over at him, black eyes unfocused, and wavered on his feet. "It's only us. We had to put you down for a minute. That tranquilizer you've got in your system is going to make you a little wobbly—"

As if to prove his point, D staggered sideways and crashed into a wooden side table that promptly splintered to pieces. He regained his balance, shook his head like a dog, and growled, "What the *fuck*?"

"Excellent question," said Celian dryly, "and one I was hoping *you* could answer for *me*."

"How the hell did you find me?" D reached out and spread his hand against the wall for balance.

"It wasn't exactly rocket science," Lix answered in a neutral tone. "Xander was more than happy to tell us the location—"

"Son of a—"

"—of The Syndicate's old Paris safe house. It was only a matter of putting two and two together."

D spat, "I knew I should have killed him when I had the chance!"

"Where is she, D?" said Constantine from the other side of the room. "Where's Eliana?"

At the mention of her name, D drew himself up to his full, bristling height and glared daggers at all three of his brothers. He didn't say another word.

Celian's voice was brusque when he said, "Okay. Here's how this is going to go. You're going to tell us what happened here, what you know, and what—if anything—she said that might help us determine the location of their new colony. And then we're going to decide what the next play is—"

"The next play is my fist down your throat." D uttered this with so much cold, savage fury it actually gave Celian pause, which was a feat in and of itself.

"I told you," Constantine said to Lix and Celian, his voice defeated. "He's gone totally off the reservation."

"Maybe we can use that to our advantage." Celian seemed almost distracted as he said this, contemplative in a way that had Lix and Constantine sharing a look. "For a while, at least."

With D watching him with wild eyes, Celian casually crossed to a table set against the wall and seated himself. He stretched his long legs out, crossed them at the ankle, pursed his lips, and began to slowly trace an invisible pattern on the tabletop with his finger.

"Let's say, for example, you are beyond reasoning with. *For the time being*," he emphasized, glancing up at D, then back down. "Let's say we report back to the Council of Alphas that we did indeed catch up with our love-crazed brother"—D hissed a low warning at that, but Celian went on, unperturbed—"but unfortunately he escaped from us before we could get any information from him about the whereabouts of the missing princess, who he so inconveniently sprung from jail, and her tribe."

D's growl tapered to silence. A shade of hostility faded from his posture, but he continued to watch Celian in narrow-eyed, wary belligerence.

"And let's say we request more time to bring him in, because only we can do it and only we can get any information from him which he may—or may not—have about said princess."

D understood that Celian had already talked to the Council, had probably been threatened with bodily injury and a war…and still wanted to buy him some time to find Eliana. The anger drained from his body and was replaced by an even deeper respect than he already had for the leader of the *Bellatorum.* This was a risk, and a big one. He said, "They'll never agree to it."

To which Celian quietly replied, "They will if I tell them the Roman colony will join the tribal confederacy and I'll serve on the Council of Alphas if they do."

This pronouncement was met with shocked silence. Everyone in the room knew how much Celian had resisted joining the confederacy, how much he hated the idea of subjecting his own people to outside laws. Foreign laws. Joining the Council would mean big changes, less control, and definitely less freedom. Plus a lot more contact with one Leander McLoughlin, Alpha of Sommerley, whom he openly loathed.

"Hardly a fair trade," said Lix, his voice tight, watching D.

He had a point. "If they agree to it at all, you'll only get a few days. Maybe not even that. It's not worth it."

Celian gazed at D in steady calm, ignoring the others. "It is if you tell me it is. And then the three of us will vote on it."

Instantly, Constantine said, "I'm in."

"Great," Lix muttered. "Guess we don't need to vote, then."

D folded his arms across his chest. After a silent stare-off with Celian that lasted several long moments, he said, "Silas is behind it. He told her I killed her father, and I got the distinct impression he's been leading them all to believe the four of us planned a coup…and that she's got a bull's-eye on her back."

Celian's brows rose. "She thinks you want to kill her?"

"She thinks I want to kill them *all.*" Disbelief, anger, and pain rang in his voice. He ran a hand over his head and held it there, briefly closing his eyes.

"It does look like she's pretty mad at you." Constantine eyed the fresh red gouges on D's cheek.

"Mad doesn't even begin to cover it," D muttered. He touched a hand to his face and winced. "She went ballistic."

"I'd have paid good money to see that." Celian's voice was mild, but there was a hint of laughter behind it. "Our little *principessa,* angry enough to take *you* on."

"She's angry all right." But even worse than the anger was the terrible sadness he'd witnessed in a woman he remembered as ebulliently happy and alive. D's chest constricted at the memory of her tears, the memory of that bottomless well of sorrow he'd glimpsed in her eyes, pain that—wrongly or not—she thought was caused by him. He felt the sudden, violent urge to wring that lying Silas's neck until it snapped. He slowly walked back to the couch and sat with his arms hanging off his knees.

"The police know what she looks like now," said Constantine quietly. "They'll be looking for her." He looked at D. "And you. It'll be a lot harder for you to track her now."

"What did you hear about it on television? Did they report any bodies the police were unable to identify?" D was looking at the floor, hunched over and lost in thought, all the anger from moments before drained from his posture.

"No." Celian sat forward in his chair. "You hit someone?"

D nodded. "One of The Hunt. They got there the same time I did. If I'd been a few minutes later..." He looked up at Celian, and his eyes burned. "They're still out there, looking for her." Then his jaw worked and his voice was shaded with venom. "Seven of the eight, anyway."

Celian frowned. "The television reports only mentioned that the chief's right-hand man was slightly injured in the bombing. Apparently there were no other injuries—"

"There was another injured man," D interrupted. "Human. Injured pretty badly from what I could tell. Glasses. White coat. Looked like a doctor type."

Celian shook his head. "No mention of him, no mention of any unidentifiable bodies. Leander didn't mention it, either."

D's lips peeled back in an ugly snarl over his teeth, and he sat up, ramrod straight, radiating violence. He growled, "Tell him, from me, that I am going to personally tear off the heads of every one of his little group of assassins—"

"Probably not helpful to the cause at hand," interrupted Celian.

"—and if any of them harm *a single hair on her head*, I'll come after him and his entire colony myself! I'll go Old Testament biblical on them. I'll rain fire and brimstone on that mother—"

"Again," Celian said, louder, harder, "not helpful. Our objective is to buy you more time to find Eliana and bring her in, not start a tribal war!"

D ground his teeth, stood, and began to pace back and forth in taut, smoldering menace in front of Celian's table. He flexed his hands open and closed, itching to get them around someone's neck. "She's just going to keep running from me. She thinks I want her and the others dead. She thinks I killed her father—"

"You didn't tell her?" From across the room, Constantine's voice was low and shocked, and his expression was shocked, too. "You didn't tell her what happened? That it was me who pulled the trigger?"

D kept right on pacing. "That's your story to tell, brother, not mine."

Moving slowly, Constantine walked to the table where Celian sat and sank into the opposite chair. He ran a hand through his thick, black hair, blew out a breath, and shook his head in wonder, watching D pace.

"There's got to be a way for me to prove to her that whatever Silas told her about us, it's all lies."

"Except for the killing her father part." Constantine dropped his gaze to the table. "That part's actually true."

"He was going to kill me, Trollboy." D used the nickname he hadn't used since they were both children, teasing each other about everything from girls to their looks. Constantine was Trollboy because he was anything but, and, accordingly, D had been dubbed Chatterbox. "He was a batshit crazy bastard who terrorized our entire colony and sunk a knife in my chest when he found out I went on a date with his daughter. You just had my back." D slowed his pacing and lifted his head to look at Constantine. "Guess I never said thanks for that."

"No," said Constantine, "you didn't."

"Well...thanks for that."

With those few words, Constantine knew that the rancor between them from the last three years had been forgiven. D held his gaze for a beat, nodded, and then resumed his restless pacing.

"So my problem is, unless I have some kind of proof that Silas is no good, Eliana will just keep running forever."

"Like, written proof?" Lix piped in. Three pairs of questioning eyes turned to look at him, and he stared back at them, waiting for them to guess. When they didn't he rolled his eyes and said, "The journal, geniuses. Her father's journal. We still have it."

The air went electric.

The journal of the mad King Dominus had been found after he'd been killed and the princess and her retinue had fled the catacombs of Rome that night three years ago. It outlined—in meticulous detail—his plan to take over the other colonies, his genocide against his own people, the genetic testing he'd commissioned, which resulted in a serum that allowed human and *Ikati* blood to be compatible. Like all sadistic megalomaniacs, his ultimate goal had been world domination. He was going to put the *Ikati* back at the top of the food chain, using human DNA and fertility to do it.

And then he was going to wipe them off the face of the earth.

Silas—his trusted servant, equally sadistic and power-hungry—had been assisting him with all of that.

D looked at Celian. "How soon can you—"

"Twenty-four hours, maybe sooner if we leave right now."

"You'll call Leander on the way?"

Celian nodded, rising from the table. "I can't guarantee he'll call The Hunt off Eliana's trail, but I'll get *you* a few more days. We'll figure it out from there. You better work fast, though."

Constantine rose as well. "Do you have any idea where she might have gone from here? How are you going to track her?"

D smiled, and it was almost gleeful, the happiest any of them had seen him in years. "While I was taking a little nap thanks to your tranquilizer, I had a dream, brother." He tapped his temple. "I had a dream."

SIXTEEN
School for the Blind

The first bullet screamed by Eliana's right ear, and the second embedded itself into the wall next to her head at eye level with an ominous *thunk* that dislodged a puff of smoke and spat razor-fine chunks of drywall right into her face. Clutching Gregor's hand, she threw up an arm and twisted away, cursing.

"How many of these bastards *are* there?" Gregor shouted, barreling down the stairs three at a time, dragging Eliana along like a sack of rocks behind him.

Just before the third shot rang out—another near miss that ricocheted off the metal handrail with a high-pitched, ringing *twang*—Eliana shouted back, "Seven!"

The ferocity of their pursuit made it seem more like seventy. She felt each one of them as separate, stinging waves of heat across the surface of her skin, their silent intent to kill her as clear as if they'd screamed it. Four *Ikati* assassins behind and three more somewhere nearby, unseen beyond the walls, moving fast on different floors of the building.

Probably, like them, headed for the exits.

They were in a narrow stairwell, racing down in headlong, dizzying spirals. Gregor's footsteps clattered loudly off the unpainted walls and metal steps, and the torn soles of Eliana's bare feet left little bloody prints like a trail of crimson breadcrumbs. She didn't know how they'd found her, she'd been so careful to disguise her scent, but somehow she'd led the assassins right to Gregor's building, right into the very *heart* of her friend's business—and life.

If they survived the next few minutes, she was resolved to kill them all.

Then she'd get on her knees and beg his forgiveness.

Gregor crashed through an unmarked door on one of the stairwell landings, and suddenly they were in a parking garage, dim and silent except for the ominous sound of the steel door slamming shut behind them with cold, unnerving finality, grim as the lid on a crypt.

Eliana gazed around at the long lines of cars, their dark windshields like rows of blank eyes, reflecting back nothing. She muttered, "This is always the scene in a movie where someone dies."

Gregor ignored her and yanked her forward over the cracked cement, heading directly for a sleek, two-tone gunmetal-and-black Ferrari parked two aisles down at the end of the row. It only took a few seconds to get there, get the doors unlocked, and start the engine.

But it was long enough.

Just as they tore out of the parking spot—engine roaring, tires squealing and sending up plumes of acrid white smoke, a deep, rumbling vibration rising up through the leather seat to set her teeth a-clatter—the door they'd entered the garage through flew open to reveal the tall, straight figure of a man in a tailored dark suit and white dress shirt, gripping an enormous silver gun in each raised hand. The guns were leveled directly at the Ferrari.

"Oh shit," said Gregor, stomping his foot on the gas pedal.

The only way out was *toward* the assassin, unfortunately, and they took four bullets to the windshield as they raced down the aisle. Swerving wildly, they ducked and screamed as the glass splintered into a spider's web confusion of tiny cracks that surrounded four perfect holes, but didn't shatter. Around a corner shots rang out again, but everything was a flying muddle of noise and motion in Eliana's brain. All she could do was dig her heels into the floor mat, clutch the molded leather of the seat, and hang on.

With rubber laid on the cement in two long, black, wavering lines, they left that level of the parking garage—and the shooter—behind them. Inside Eliana flared a brilliant white hope, clear and crackling like a firework: *They'd escaped!*

Oh, so wrong. Laughably wrong. Hope, she quickly discovered, was not particularly helpful when there were over half a dozen trained killers gunning for one's head.

Around two sharp turns they entered a double helix exit ramp collared by thick cement columns. Both sides of the ramp yawned open between parking levels, and like swiftly descending spiders, a trio of men scuttled with effortless leaps from level to level beside them, clinging briefly to the cement columns before pushing off, heading down.

"You've gotta be kidding me!" shouted Gregor, apoplectic. "Seriously! You've *got to* be kidding!"

"Watch out!" screamed Eliana as one of the suited spiders dropped to the ramp directly in front of them and raised his weapon. She sank down in the seat and threw her arms over her face, but then there was a bump and a sickening sort of crunch, and the gun-wielding assassin disappeared under the car.

"That's right, asshole!" shouted Gregor gleefully, pounding his big fist on the steering wheel. "Suck on *that!*"

Eliana turned and through the rear window saw a crumpled figure tumbling lifelessly down the ramp behind them, arms and legs akimbo, limbs bent at awkward, unnatural angles.

They hit the bottom level of the garage in a sliding sideways spin, fishtailing as Gregor struggled to keep control of the wheel.

"There!" Eliana shouted over the squealing tires, pointing to a small neon exit sign that hung on the opposite side of the level.

Gregor tightened his hands on the wheel, the Ferrari leapt forward with a near-deafening roar, and Eliana was slammed back into her seat with the sudden propulsion. As they rounded the final corner, she was horrified to see not one but *two* assassins standing with spread legs and raised guns directly in front of the metal gate that led to the exit.

The *closed* metal gate.

"Glove compartment!" shouted Gregor. "Gun!"

"*Now* you tell me!"

With the press of a button, the compartment lid *snicked* open, and Eliana snatched up the gun. It was heavy and cold in her hand, sleek and utilitarian, and at that moment she thought it was the most beautiful thing she'd ever seen in her life.

Gregor rolled the window down, and Eliana leaned out, aimed, squeezed the trigger, and fired off four rounds…and the assassins didn't even twitch.

"Where'd you learn to shoot a gun, the goddamn school for the blind?" Gregor screamed.

But then one of them sagged to one knee, lowered his weapon, and looked down, surprised, at the front of his white shirt, where a dark liquid stain had begun to spread.

The other one, luminous green gaze canny and unwavering, leveled his gun at Gregor in the driver's seat and fired. Just from that single look—murderous, *certain*—Eliana knew even before Gregor jerked back and hollered that the bullet would hit its intended target.

A spray of blood misted the dashboard. The Ferrari barreled ahead. Gregor's hands slid from the wheel.

They crashed into the metal access gate at full speed with Eliana twisted sideways, gripping the steering wheel, screaming at the top of her lungs. The assassin leapt clear at the last moment, still shooting, but everything had taken on a dreamlike unreality, color and lights flashing by at hyper-speed, sound warped slow and strange as if it traveled underwater.

The beating of her heart seemed like cannon on a battlefield. The coppery smell of blood hung penny bright and thick in the air.

The gate tore from its hinges with a violent, ear-splitting screech, and they blasted through it in a shower of orange sparks. It flew away overhead like a huge, warped bird, and jagged chunks of metal and plastic from the damaged hood and both shattered headlights followed it. Something heavy caught on the undercarriage and dragged beneath them, setting off an unearthly clamor as they hit the pavement again, breaking free of the garage, and careened down the deserted collector road that ran alongside the building.

"Gregor!" she shouted, frantic. "*Gregor!*"

Slumped motionless in the seat, he didn't respond.

Eliana glanced in the rearview mirror just in time to see four more assassins appear in the quickly receding rectangle of the garage door, which glowed a ghostly white against the dark building and the night. Gregor's foot was still pressed against the accelerator; she yanked hard on the wheel, and they spun around a corner onto a side street at breakneck speed, narrowly missing getting wrapped around a streetlamp.

Right before the building they'd left behind disappeared from sight, she saw all five dark figures in the rectangle of light transform in a violent eruption of black fur and sharp fangs and sleek, sinewy muscle that shredded their tailored clothing into a spray of black-and-white confetti that hung suspended for a moment before drifting slowly to the ground.

With savage roars she heard even above the strung-out whine of the engine, five impossibly huge black panthers leapt forward from powerful hind legs and took off after the car at a flat-out run.

It was five o'clock in the morning in England, the palest blush of dawn beginning to spread pink and lavender over the smoke-dark hills. Thrushes and sparrows had begun to stir in the dewed branches of trees and sing their first, tentative songs of the morning, and the fog that curled in thick fingers around trunks of pines and elms had begun to lift. All the little creatures of the woods were still abed, but in the village of Sommerley—quaint as a postcard, tucked back against the New Forest in a lush, green valley far away from the prying eyes of civilization—one creature was wide, wide awake.

She was pearl pale and feminine, a poet's muse of golden hair and Mona Lisa smiles and quiet, effortless grace. Born a commoner, she was now a Queen, the most Gifted and powerful Queen her kind had seen in centuries. She could read a mind with a touch of her hand, she could change from woman to mist to lethal, cunning predator, among other things. She could even, when the mood struck, change into something that quite shocked and offended all her predator kin, and made her happy precisely because it did.

Cats thought birds were lesser creatures, *silly* creatures, good for only one thing: snacks.

But for the moment she was only a woman, sitting upright and breathless in bed, listening to the low, rumbling voice on the other end of the telephone.

"...and if you grant me this, I will agree to join the confederacy. I'll agree to...your terms."

Jenna had never met the man on the other end of the phone, but she knew him regardless. Celian, leader of the Roman colony, gave her husband fits.

She glanced over at that beloved husband now, sleeping on his back with one heavy arm thrown over his face, his muscular chest bare and gleaming in the pale morning light. His other arm was still wrapped around her naked waist; he hadn't moved, even when the shrill ring of the phone broke the stillness of dawn.

Leander always slept like the dead after a long night of loving. Which meant he almost always slept like the dead.

"Tell me, Celian," Jenna said, tracing a light finger down her husband's chest. At her touch, he stirred and made a low sound in his throat, then sank back into slumber. "Why would this Demetrius—your brother, you call him—take it upon himself to do what he did? He must have known what the consequences of his actions would be. Help me understand why he would risk so much, for what appears to be so little."

There was a pause, a cleared throat, another pause that felt pregnant. Then Celian said simply, "Love."

Jenna's hand stilled. "He fights for love?" she whispered, arrested.

She heard the long exhale from so many miles away, heavy with a hundred unnamed things. "Are our ways so different, Jenna?" He refused to call her Queen as steadfastly as he'd so far refused to join the Council of Alphas, which she didn't hold against him; in his place, she'd feel exactly the same way about both. This also gave Leander fits. "Where you're from, will a man not forsake everything he has for the woman that he loves? Even, if necessary, his life?"

Her eyes found Leander's sleeping form again. No, their ways were not so different. They were not different at all. She murmured, "Even if the woman he loves is the new leader of the group that's been trying to kill us for centuries?"

Silence. Sudden, crackling anger she felt like a hand around her throat. "Eliana is not her father—"

"No," Jenna agreed, "she's not. But she *is* the daughter of the madman who left my sister-in-law maimed for life, who tortured and killed many of my kin, who kept the heads of his enemies like trophies, and who," her voice lowered to steel, "had *me* tortured and beaten near to death."

Celian had no answer to that. Jenna went on, "Blood follows Blood, Celian. It's the way of our kind. What proof do you have that she—or her brother—hasn't followed in her father's footsteps?"

"I can't speak for her brother," he replied, his voice tight, "but Demetrius believes Eliana is innocent, therefore so do I."

It wasn't enough; the Council of Alphas would say it wasn't nearly enough to grant the favor he asked, even with his willing capitulation to join them and bow to their will. Demetrius had broken ranks and gone against orders, and that made him dangerous to them all. No matter how much Celian believed in him.

And yet…and yet…

Outside a bird began to sing, a high, trilling warble in the stillness of the pink-lit dawn. Jenna glanced at the expanse of lead-paned windows that ran along the east wall of their bedchamber and saw beyond the sill a tiny white butterfly bobbing above the planted flowerbeds with bumpy grace, settling finally on the open bloom of a rose. The flower didn't even tremble under its weight.

Life is pain and everyone dies, but true love lives forever.

Her mother's words. They came back to haunt her at odd moments like these. She'd died years and years ago, but Jenna often wondered if she was still out there somewhere, watching over her.

Reminding her.

Jenna herself was the product of such desperate love and granite loyalty, a child of two star-crossed lovers who paid the ultimate price for their dreams. She knew what it meant to risk everything, to gamble on love, to lose in the end but never regret one brilliant, doomed moment because what was gained was worth every sacrifice, even death.

Perhaps Demetrius would come to regret following his heart. Perhaps he would be lucky enough to find true love, or cursed enough to lose it—only Fate could tell. But Fate was burdened with the minutia of the universe, and sometimes she needed a little helping hand.

Jenna sat a moment longer, thinking, then came to a decision in her usual way: she went with her gut.

"I'd like to meet this Demetrius of yours, Celian," she said softly. "And you, too. I admire that kind of loyalty. It's very rare. And I'm sorry…that we all got off on the wrong foot. The last thing I want is more fighting. More bloodshed. We've all had too many years of that." She paused a moment, allowing the silence between them to deepen. On the other end of the phone, Celian waited, his attention honed sharp as the tip of a knife. Firmer, she said, "I'd like to see you join the confederacy, Celian, but I won't force you to, even under the circumstances. If we're going to work together, it has to be on equal footing. You have to *want* to join us. I know all too well what our laws are like." She smiled, a wry twist of her lips. "Fortunately, I'm above them. So you have your two days. Make them count."

There was a beat of astonished silence before she heard Celian's low, amused chuckle. She imagined him shaking his head. "Well, for all the ways your husband and I disagree, at least we can both agree on his taste in women."

"I'll tell him you said so." Jenna glanced back at Leander. Without another word, she ended the call.

She made another call—quick and to the point—and then set the phone back in its cradle on the nightstand beside the bed and snuggled into the space between Leander's strong arm and warm body, the safest spot in the world.

He turned his head and mumbled something incoherent into her hair. "Sleep, love," she whispered, closing her eyes and tightening her arms around him. "Go back to sleep."

They had hours yet before the sun would crest the mountains and he and the Council would discover what she'd done. They might as well both be rested for what lay ahead.

SEVENTEEN
Sinuous as Smoke

Belief in Fate, like belief in God, requires a certain suspension of *dis*belief, the ability to accept without physical proof that there is something larger than yourself operating behind the scenes in the universe, there is a Plan that's being followed and your own small life is a part of it.

That was a concept so foreign to Keshav it was rendered not only unimaginable, but entirely ridiculous.

An assassin by trade and by nature, Keshav believed not in Fate but in Chance, Fate's blind, gleefully chaotic sibling who had no long-term Plan but wreaked havoc on hearts and lives just because he could. Keshav had seen and done too many horrible things to harbor any tender notions of a benevolent God. He knew God was a concept humans had created back in the days when they'd first crawled from the mud, gasping air with amphibious lungs. God's primary function was simply to help soothe the primal, animal terror of death.

The primary function of Chance, on the other hand, was to really screw with you.

Perfect example: his current situation.

Chance had not been on their side at the police station. A few moments more and they'd have had their target firmly in hand. But Chance had decided her erstwhile lover would get there first. Fine, Keshav could deal with that, and he did. They swiftly and silently removed the body of their fallen comrade from the wreckage of the building, and then they retreated, they regrouped. They decided on the best spot for a temporary grave—he'd be reburied later in his home soil because it was an abomination for any of their kind to molder in an unnamed grave in a foreign land—and discussed their next move.

Then Chance lobbed them a lovely golden apple: driving from the burial site, the girl ran across their path. Literally, right across it. They were at a stoplight on the outskirts of the city, waiting for the light to change, and she'd sprinted across the street in a blur of raven blue hair and long legs and disappeared over a fence into a quiet neighborhood backyard.

Keshav looked at the other members of The Hunt. They looked back at him. Then, without uttering a word, they abandoned the car right in the middle of the street and took off on foot after her.

Then Chance had found it amusing to equip her with a gun and a human sidekick with a sports car.

As the taillights of the Ferrari faded into the distance down the Rue de l'Arbalete, the five remaining members of The Hunt slowed from a sprint to a trot, and finally to a standstill. In flashes of swirling gray Vapor, they Shifted back to human form and stood naked in the middle of the empty road, watching.

"Couldn't have been driving a Fiat," commented Calder beside him. Originally from the Quebec colony, he was lean and rangy, with a thick scar that ran in a wavering line from his jaw all the way up to his hairline, bisecting one eyebrow. He never said how he'd gotten it, and none of the others had asked.

"Zero to a hundred kilometers per hour in three seconds," answered Ang, a member of the Nepal colony who had a fetish for expensive cars. He collected and restored them in his spare time. When he wasn't killing things. "Top speed over three hundred twenty-five kilometers per hour… We're fast, but not even we can beat that."

"All right," said Keshav, cool. He knew Chance wasn't done with them yet. "Let's clean up and call it in."

Clean up was assassin parlance for *get rid of the bodies.* Two of the team were still back at the building, one felled by bullets, the other flattened by over a ton of metal. The bullets he understood; travelling at over a thousand miles per hour, a bullet headed in your direction affords only milliseconds to react before you're dead. A car, on the other hand—why that idiot hadn't just Shifted to Vapor was beyond Keshav's comprehension. He deserved to get run over.

One by one, the five assassins now did exactly that. Five glittering gray plumes of mist gathered sinuous as smoke, surged up into the cool weight of the night sky, and headed back the way they'd come.

Laurent had worked for nineteen years as the head of the emergency medicine department at the Centre Hospitalier Sainte-Anne, one of the oldest and most prestigious hospitals in Paris. He'd seen nearly every trauma and injury in his long career, and it had been many years since he'd been surprised by what occurred in hospitals, by what people did to one another in anger or to themselves in despair.

But tonight had proven he still had the capacity to be shocked.

He *heard* their approach first. He'd been standing at the nurse's station near the sliding doors to the entrance of the ER, flicking through the admitting form for a patient with a severe head cold who was convinced she was dying of plague, when from somewhere down the street outside came the distinct sound of a car screeching to a protracted halt, its brakes locked and screaming in protest. Whatever the driver of the car had been trying to avoid, he failed spectacularly because the car in question came flying into the hospital parking lot and collided with half a dozen parked cars as it careened to and fro like a pinball in an arcade game, and then as Laurent and the night nurse at the desk watched in openmouthed horror, it made a beeline for the sliding glass emergency room doors.

At full speed.

He leapt over the desk, grabbed the frozen nurse by her fleshy white bicep, and ran.

At the last second the driver gained a measure of control over the car. And by measure, Laurent would later tell his wife, I mean *une petit quantité*. A smidge. A squealing sideways slide slowed it down enough so that when the low-slung sports car finally made impact with the building, it only destroyed the row of groomed rosemary bushes along the front walk, the wrought iron railing beside them, and a portion of the low brick wall where he sat contemplating his sins during his smoke breaks. A rather substantial portion, but it could have been much worse.

When the smoke had cleared and the flying bricks and shrubbery had settled and the only noise was the angry hiss of a fractured radiator releasing pressurized steam, Laurent emerged from his hiding place behind the tiled column near the staff elevators just in time to see a woman—young, indigo-haired, half-dressed in men's underclothing—tear off the driver's door of a mostly demolished Ferrari, toss it aside like it weighed no more than a feather, and lift an unconscious, bleeding man twice her size in her arms.

His first thought was *PCP*.

Long out of fashion but still available, the hallucinogenic drug phencyclidine tended to imbue users with superhuman strength. When it wasn't making them schizophrenic. His second thought as the duo entered through the sliding doors and the woman pierced him with her eyes—silvery-black and glittering, like coins at the bottom of a wishing well—was *Dieu aidez-moi!*

God help me.

She was supernaturally stunning, with an abstract face and courtesan's body Picasso would have swooned over. She possessed a weird species of beauty, the type average people have no words or use for, alien and compelling, all lips and eyes and smoldering stare. Seeing her, Laurent thought for a moment he was having a heart attack. She literally took his breath away.

"You!" she growled, freezing him in place with those ferocious inkwell eyes. "Help me!"

Her French was nearly perfect, but not completely so; obviously, she wasn't a native speaker. Perhaps she hailed from Mars.

"*Now!*" she said as he remained rooted to the linoleum. The word was hard as two fingers snapping, and it jolted Laurent into action.

"In there." He pointed to an exam room just behind her, watching as she shouldered through the door and gently deposited the man she carried on the white-sheeted hospital bed. A quick glance over his shoulder and a mouthed instruction to Michelle, the night nurse—*Call the police*—and he followed her in.

"He's been shot." The alien beauty stepped back to allow Laurent to move closer.

He took his glasses from the pocket of his white lab coat and donned them, snapped on a pair of thin nitrile gloves, and did a quick, cursory examination of the victim. Blood had spread in an erratic circle over the front of his button-down dress shirt, and Laurent ripped it open with a yank that sent buttons flying. There it was—a perfect, round hole four inches below the burly man's collarbone. Just above—or in—his heart.

"Will he be all right?" The woman stood almost too close, watching intently as he examined the wound.

"He's lost a lot of blood. There's no exit wound, which means the bullet is embedded. We need to prep him for surgery."

He straightened, faced her, and made a swift, visual assessment of her condition. No pupil dilation. No nervous twitching or shaking. No obvious signs of drug intoxication. She was, oddly, barefoot, even more oddly wearing men's boxer briefs and an undershirt gone slightly translucent with perspiration that made it cling to her beautiful breasts in a most distracting, enticing way—

She stepped closer, took his elbow in an iron grip, and said, very quietly, "He lives, or you die. Understood?"

Laurent had heard this on more than one occasion from distraught family members. Threats to his life or safety were not so uncommon, but something about the way this woman shaped the words, the cold, cold intent in her dark eyes, truly frightened him. He chose not to antagonize her and instead simply said, "You're family? We'll need to get some information for treatment. And for the police."

At the word *police*, she released his arm as if she'd been burned and stepped back with a low, spine-tingling growl that reverberated through the room, animal, chilling. It was like nothing he'd ever heard before. Slowly, she backed away to the door.

She was going to run. He'd seen this before, too.

"Madam," he said, holding out a hand, but she cut him off with a savage snarl that froze him in place and had his bowels threatening to spill themselves.

"He lives or you die," she reiterated, deadly soft, vibrating menace. She glanced at the cursive stitching on the front pocket of his lab coat. "*Laurent.*"

The high, wailing scream of sirens underscored his hissed name. Wild, she glanced over her shoulder at the ER doors and then back at him. For a moment he imagined her eyes changed, something about the pupils...Had they elongated? To slits?

But then she was gone. Like a gazelle she bounded away and disappeared through the glass doors into the night, just as three blue-and-white police cars with sirens wailing and lights flashing blazed into the parking lot.

EIGHTEEN
Diversion

Eliana limped into the catacombs just before dawn, exhausted as she'd never been, every muscle aching, every step burning sharp with pain.

The pain of heartache. The pain of confusion. The intense, stabbing pain of guilt.

If Gregor died, she'd never, ever forgive herself.

It took nearly an hour of navigating the silent, twisting passageways before she came upon the rusted metal stepladder hidden around a black corner deep in the belly of the catacombs. The ladder, drilled right into the rock, led up three stories through a ragged fissure in the limestone to the basement of the abbey. She climbed slowly, dazed, the chilled air doing little to soothe her abraded skin.

She needed a bath, and sleep, and to talk to Mel about everything that had happened. Not necessarily in that order.

The old wooden trapdoor was much heavier than usual to push open, but she did it, emerging into the frigid darkness of the basement—

When suddenly, a strong hand reached out, lightning-fast, and painfully fisted itself in her hair.

"You stupid fucking bitch!" Caesar hissed in her ear. Viciously, he yanked her head back and she lost her footing on the stepladder, twisting away from him. Pulling her by the hair, he dragged her clear of the tunnel and slammed her down to the dusty stone floor.

Before she could rise, he kicked her hard in the ribs. Twice.

Eliana heard Mel's scream, and she heard another voice she recognized as Silas's, but mainly she heard the furious snarls of Caesar as he beat her with iron fists and booted feet and called her every filthy name she'd ever heard, and many she hadn't. She doubled over, too stunned to comprehend what was happening, too exhausted to do more than twist and roll on the hard floor, covering her head to avoid the more violent of his blows.

"Stop!" Silas shouted, dragging Caesar away. "My lord, *stop!*"

White dots danced in her vision. It had suddenly become very hard to breathe.

Mel's face swam into view, hovering above her, pale and horrified. "Ana! Ana, can you talk? How badly are you hurt?"

Eliana inhaled a breath that felt like fire, and she coughed. Pain shot up her right side where Caesar had kicked her, and she moaned.

"So help me, Caesar," Mel hissed, staring at him, still restrained in the circle of Silas's arms, "one of these days—"

"One more word and you're *both* dead!" Caesar shrieked, veins popping out on his neck. He twisted and fought Silas's hold, kicking, but the older man was stronger and taller and held him fast, murmuring soothing words into his ear. Caesar settled after a few moments, and Silas allowed him to shake free, bristling but no longer spitting in rage.

"You ruined everything! You led them right to us! Now everyone knows we're in France, in Paris. We'll have to move before we're ready. We'll have to change all our plans—"

He shouted on and on, pacing back and forth over the stone floor, wild-eyed, red-faced, held back from attacking her again only by the outstretched hand of Silas, who seemed able to dissuade him with only that.

Mel helped her to a sitting position, her hands firm around her back while she gulped in lungfuls of dank air.

"My lord," interrupted Silas smoothly, still with that outstretched hand, "perhaps you could allow your sister a moment to collect herself so we can find out exactly what happened." He glanced at Eliana and Mel, still crouched together on the floor, and then turned his gaze back to Caesar. "I would be happy to speak with her and report back to you as quickly as possible." His voice, still soothing, turned velvet. "In the interim, I'll arrange for a girl to be sent over. Your favorite, perhaps? The blonde?"

Still breathing hard, Caesar stopped pacing and shot a black glance at Silas. After a moment, he nodded curtly and then looked back at Eliana. His upper lip curled. "You're lucky he's here, *sister*." He spat the word as if it tasted evil in his mouth. "If he wasn't, you wouldn't be breathing right now."

He turned and strode from the room, and as soon as he was out of sight Silas swept over and knelt down beside her.

"I'm sorry," he murmured, gently touching her shoulder. "He felt your approach. It was all I could do to keep him from bringing his gun."

Their eyes met. She saw the genuine concern, the sincerity of his apology, and she also saw the unspoken *I told you.*

"You were right." She tried not to inhale too deeply because it caused too much pain. "I didn't believe you, but you were right."

"Right about what?" Mel asked as she and Silas gently helped her to her feet.

Silas gave her a look—probing, intense—and Eliana glanced away.

"Let's get you cleaned up and we'll talk," he murmured, allowing her to lean on his arm as he led her toward the door. She felt his penetrating gaze slant down to her. His voice dropped even lower. "Thank Horus you're back. When I heard you'd been captured by the police, then the explosion at the station, I felt…" He left it unsaid, the thought unfinished, and it hung there between them, louder than any spoken word. His voice turned harder. "And don't worry about your brother. I won't let this happen again."

Neither will I, Eliana thought bitterly, but she only nodded and allowed herself to be led away.

Silas knew she was lying. What he didn't know was *why*, or what exactly about.

Eliana had rested and bathed and dressed, and now she stood staring at a crumbling eighteenth-century headstone, the winged angel perched atop, mossy and blackened with age. They stood in the little decrepit cemetery beside the old abbey, its rows of leaning headstones with faded inscriptions ringed by gnarled plum trees who decades ago had stopped bearing fruit. It was late afternoon; the sun was slung low in the sky and cast long, sinister shadows that crawled hungrily over the dead grass and up their legs.

He thought it best to be outdoors, away from any interested ears, so they could speak openly.

"...so I hid in a drainpipe until I was sure they were long gone." Eliana's voice was utterly emotionless.

Silas studied her. Clad in her usual black leather ensemble, she looked even more somber than usual. There were faint blue smudges beneath her eyes, her lips held a downward curve, and every once in a while she would give a small, unconscious shake of her head, as if she were answering the same unasked question, over and over again.

"And you didn't know these men..." he prompted.

"No. They weren't from the Roman colony. It wasn't the *Legiones,* or"—she hesitated for an infinitesimal second—"the *Bellatorum.* They were obviously sent by one of the other colonies. Or all of them, I suppose."

Silas narrowed his eyes. The way she'd hesitated was worrying. Very worrying indeed. But why would she withhold anything? What could she gain? Or lose?

"You were in that drainpipe a very long time. It must have been awful." He watched her hawkishly, scanning her solemn face for any hint of what she might be hiding, but she gave nothing away.

She didn't even blink when she murmured, "You have no idea."

"And you're certain you weren't followed here?"

"If they knew where I was now, we'd have already seen them. I'd already be dead."

Hmm. He believed her sincerity about that; her voice was hard with conviction. But something was most definitely off. He decided to push her a bit and see how she'd react. In a sympathetic, thoughtful voice he asked, "Why do you think they bothered to blow up the police station? It seems a bit…*loud* for a group of assassins. At least, I always imagined assassins to be more of a stealthy group."

Her face changed, a flash of unidentifiable emotion, here then gone. "Diversion, maybe. I don't know."

She turned her head and he couldn't see her expression, so he slowly walked around behind her with his hands clasped behind his back, contemplative, patient. When they were shoulder to shoulder, he set his gaze in the middle distance so he could see her in his peripheral vision. "You're probably right. Killers seem to enjoy creating diversions. Your father's killers, for instance—they certainly knew how to divert you. Getting Demetrius to woo you so you wouldn't suspect his real motives was, in its own way, a stroke of genius."

It was nothing, it was *less* than nothing, but his hawk eyes detected it and recognized it for what it was: a tell. A tiny muscle beneath her left eye twitched. Once. Otherwise, her face and body remained entirely impassive. Her breathing didn't even change.

But now he knew. Whatever she was hiding, it had to do with Demetrius.

His mind leapt far, far ahead, calculating possibilities, creating, examining, and discarding hypotheses, working with the swift, cold precision of a well-oiled machine.

Perhaps there had been no assassins. Perhaps instead of an attempt to end her life, the bombing had been more of an attempt…to win her heart. She'd returned here, so the attempt had obviously not been successful, but perhaps something had been planted.

Perhaps a seed of doubt had been sown.

"Yes," she agreed, her voice steady and cool, "it was genius." She turned her head and looked him full in the face, her eyes flat, revealing nothing. "Ingenious, rather. One wonders how a group of males with room-temperature IQs normally preoccupied with nothing more than screwing and fighting could be quite so cunning."

Ah. A challenge. He'd been prepared for it for years. What actually surprised him was that it had taken this long.

He returned her gaze with a steady, open one of his own. "Hatred is a powerful motivator, *principessa.*"

"Hatred?" she repeated, incredulous, and turned to him. "What reason would they have to hate me?"

"Not you," he said with a gentle shake of his head. "Your father."

She stared at him, revealing nothing. "Go on."

Silas let his gaze drift away, lingering over the forlorn headstones. A raven caught his eye, and he followed its flight from the branches of a leafless tree until it disappeared into the winter sky beyond the pitched roof of the abbey. "Children can never truly know their parents," he murmured sorrowfully. "Love and loyalty conspire to blind them to certain distasteful truths."

Without looking he felt the change in her; the stiffening, the flash of heat. "Don't talk to me in riddles, Silas. Say what you mean to say."

He took pains to ensure his expression was exactly the right combination of angst, caring, and sincerity when he turned to face her. "Your father was a brilliant man, Eliana.

I served him for most of my life. I know his intentions were good—"

"Silas," she warned, moving closer.

"But he wasn't always the kindest man. In fact, he could be...unspeakably cruel."

He let it hang there between them, enticing as a windfall plum. Eliana said nothing for long moments, and Silas guessed she was searching her memory banks for corroborating evidence. She was silent just long enough to make him think she'd found it.

"Kings are known to be heavy-handed," she said stiffly. "The burden of rule rests on their shoulders. They can't afford to be...soft."

"There is heavy-handed, Eliana, and then there is bloodthirsty. Tyrannical. Ruthless." His voice dropped. "Mad."

She barked a disbelieving laugh. "Mad? My father, mad? You yourself said he was brilliant—"

"Genius and madness often go hand in hand—"

"What proof do you have?" She was livid now, breathing hard, eyes flashing cold fire. She stepped even closer, and he took in a deep, intoxicating breath of her scent, not perfume but something richer, darker, decadent. "What evidence can you produce? My father worked his entire life to find the solution to the problem of our infertility and the curse of the Transition that's plagued us since the beginning of time. And he found it! He actually did it! What kind of brutal madman would want us to survive, to join Bloodlines with humans and live in peace—"

"Your brother shares a portion of your father's particular brand of madness," Silas interrupted, very quietly. She blanched, her lips flattened in disgust. "But none of his genius and none of his foresight. Caesar is warped in ways your father wasn't, but, my dear, your father was warped in ways only the devil himself could conjure. Ask, if you don't believe me." He gestured toward the abbey. "Ask your friend Mel. Ask any of the rest of them. Your father had a side so dark it puts the blackest pits of hell to shame."

She flinched. All the color had drained from her face.

"I'm sorry. Truly I am. I only say this to you now to help you understand why the *Bellatorum* conspired to kill your father and take the kingdom for themselves. They found out about the serum somehow—I assume it was from reading your father's journal, or from Demetrius's Gift of Foresight—and they knew it would put their own status in jeopardy if all the half-Blood caste of *Legiones* could survive the Transition. They'd no longer be one-of-a-kind warriors—they'd be one of hundreds upon hundreds upon hundreds. How special would they be then? They used you as a pawn in their game of domination, and I believe, I have always believed, that their ultimate goal is nothing less than domination of the world itself. They'll move first on the other colonies, kill the Alphas and their families, just like in Rome, and then they'll turn their sights on the world at large. These are killers, Eliana. Killers who are tired of answering to *anyone*. Killers who will not hesitate to take what they want, by any means possible."

He stepped closer, his voice beseeching, his brows drawn together. "This is why it's so important the serum doesn't fall into their hands. Why it's so important we continue to fortify ourselves with weapons and keep hidden for now, until we have the stronghold built and we can invite the members of the other colonies who are tired of their own tyrants to join us. Then we can take revenge for what the *Bellatorum* took from us." He lifted his hand, brushing his knuckles across her heated cheek. "What they took from *you.*"

She swallowed hard. Her lashes lowered, and a slight breeze blew a stray tendril of hair across her cheek. Was it his imagination, or had she leaned into his hand? A surge of heat pulsed through his veins, victorious. Then her lashes lifted and she pinned him in her gaze, clear and cold as a dragon's.

"I definitely plan on taking revenge, Silas. On all my enemies, whoever they might be."

His hand on her face stilled, and he gazed back at her in arrested silence. Was she agreeing with him? Or was that a threat? She confused him even more with what she said next.

"Thank you for what you did with Caesar this morning. He might have killed me. It kills me to admit it, but…you were right about him."

Now she sounded truly grateful, indebted even. "Eliana," he murmured.

"And you're also right about children being blind. But I'm not a child anymore. Whatever the truth is, I'll find it. Because real power doesn't come from hatred. It comes from truth."

Silas almost laughed out loud at that. He had to bite his tongue to silence it.

Power didn't come from truth. Power came from the ability to manipulate outcomes to one's own favor. Just as he had now done.

She'd find out the truth about her father, and though she wouldn't like it, he'd gain even more of her trust. Yes, killers did enjoy creating diversions. They did indeed.

Poor, sweet Eliana. Like a lamb to the slaughter.

He nodded solemnly, allowing his hand to fall from her face. Without another word she turned and walked slowly away, winding through the graves, dry leaves crunching like broken bones beneath her feet.

It was something Mel said earlier that day that had done it. A simple story, awful but undoubtedly true, had made a tiny grain of doubt take root and push up an evil leaf.

They were in the room where she slept—she didn't refer to it as her bedroom, though there was a cot; it was more like a hotel room in purgatory, anonymous and cold—and Mel had been helping her into a new set of clothes after her bath. She'd napped for a while, but she was still exhausted, and her body was sore all over. Her ribs, they'd determined, weren't broken from Caesar's kicks, merely bruised. The bullet wounds on her hip and leg had already begun to heal.

Eliana had recounted in unwavering detail all that had happened from the moment she was shot in the museum, and Mel had listened, unusually silent. When she'd finished with her story and sat staring at the old stone wall across from the cot on which they sat side by side, the last thing she'd said had been, "I keep coming back to something Gregor said, before we had to escape from his building."

"Which is?"

"Assassins generally don't have to perform surgery in order to get their marks to divulge information." Eliana glanced at Mel. "Why would Demetrius take the time to do that? And why, when the rest of the *Bellatorum* showed up, did he let me go?"

It was a long, long time before Mel answered. In the dim blue shadows of the room—there was no electricity in the building—her elfin face was very serious, almost austere. Finally she let out a small sigh, as if she'd come to some bleak, unwanted conclusion.

"Do you remember the day we met?"

This startled Eliana, it was so out of left field. She tried to think back, but couldn't precisely recall. "Um…"

"It was two days after the Christmas *Purgare,*" Mel continued, gazing around the room. "My twenty-first birthday."

"Birthday? I…I didn't know it was your birthday."

She shrugged. "Why would you? You were the king's daughter. I was a servant. A lowly handmaiden. It wasn't important."

They sat in silence for a moment, both feeling the resounding truth of that simple statement. *It wasn't important.* How things had changed.

"I was terrified." Mel laughed softly. "You were like this alien creature, so perfect and pampered"—she shot Ana an apologetic look—"and unlike anyone I knew. Six years apart in age, and worlds apart in every other way."

"You were very skinny," Eliana gently teased, poking a finger into the firm, well-developed muscles of Mel's thigh. "All knees and elbows."

"We were both skinny," she agreed, nodding. "Skinny and innocent. Little skinny ducklings with our heads shoved so far up our asses we thought our shit was the stars."

Eliana laughed, a sound that seemed jarring in the cold, dusty room. "You really have a way with words, Mel."

She smiled. "It's a gift." She glanced sideways at Eliana, and her face grew serious again. "But I remember that day more for something else."

"What?"

Mel looked at Eliana for a long, searching moment and then turned away, swallowing. She took a breath and in a low voice said, "It was the day my husband died."

Eliana started, shocked. "*Husband?* What—Mel, I never knew you were married! Why didn't you ever tell me—"

"No one knew. He was a half-Blood. Handsome as hell, with a great laugh and dimples you could get lost in. We weren't supposed to be together, of course. I was a servant, and he was one of the best of the *Legiones*, being personally groomed by your father to enter the *Bellatorum* if he survived..." She trailed off into silence.

"Oh no," said Eliana quietly. "Oh, Mel. I'm so sorry."

"We had the same birthday. We never talked about it, the fact that I was full-Blooded and didn't have to worry about the Transition, and he had a gnat's chance in hell of making it through. We went ahead and got secretly married, both of us knowing we didn't have long." Melliane looked down at her lap. "I prayed so hard my Fever would come so I might get pregnant. So I'd have something to remember him by..." She swallowed and bit her lower lip. "But it never happened. At least we were together at the end, though. He said he wanted me to be holding his hand when...when..."

She suddenly covered her face with both hands, and Eliana wrapped her arms around her shoulders. They sat like that for a moment, silent, still.

"I never knew," whispered Eliana. "You were so...composed when we met. You didn't even cry. I never guessed you were going through that." After a moment, Mel sat straighter and swiped at her eyes while Eliana crossed her arms over her chest and stared at her. "Why didn't you ever tell me?"

Her face, always so lovely, hardened. She looked away. “Because your father ordered me not to.”

Eliana gaped at her, astonished, but Mel just went on in this dead tone, avoiding her eyes. “He found out we’d gotten married. Of course he would, wouldn’t he? Never missed a thing, your father.” An edge of bitterness snuck into her voice, which Eliana didn’t miss. “He found me with Emil—that was his name, Emiliano—and made us swear to never tell a soul. He said we could stay together until… until the day came when Fate would decide if we should stay together or not. Afterward, only one thing kept me from killing myself.”

Eliana’s voice trembled. “What?”

Mel turned and regarded Eliana with haunted eyes. “Demetrius.”

The blood drained from her face. She stood abruptly from the bed.

“Not like that,” said Mel, guessing what her shocked expression meant; D was known to be a womanizer of the first order. Back in their old colony, he’d chewed through women like a termite chews through wood: relentlessly. “We were only ever friends. I know Emil never told anyone we’d gotten married because he knew the trouble it would cause, but somehow Demetrius got wind of it, or figured it out…I really don’t know. But after Emil died, he came to me every single day and held me while I cried. Just… held me. He never said a word the entire time, but knowing someone else knew how I’d felt about Emil helped in a way I can’t explain. He’d come to my chamber, and I’d cry on his shoulder, and when I calmed down a little, he’d leave. After weeks and weeks of that, I began to feel like I owed it to him to keep on living, like he’d invested so much time and effort in me it would be the lowest kind of selfishness if I repaid his kindness by slitting my wrists.

"So I lived. And once he saw I was past the worst of it, Demetrius stopped his visits and never said a word about any of it, just nodded as he passed me in the corridors, like nothing had ever happened. But every year on the anniversary of Emil's death I'd find a single white rose on my pillow, and I knew it was from him."

Eliana shook her head slowly back and forth. There seemed to be a weight on her chest, crushing her lungs, stealing her breath.

"What I'm trying to tell you, Ana, is that man who handled me with such care, that man I barely knew who sat with me so patiently, that man who gave me so much comfort at the worst hour of my life is not the kind of man who would plot to kill the father of the woman he loved."

"He didn't love me," said Eliana instantly. "He *used* me. And you weren't there. I saw him with the gun in his hand, Mel. I *saw* him."

"You saw him shoot your father?" Mel said quietly, looking up at her.

Eliana's jaw clenched. "I didn't have to see that." Color came flooding back to stain her cheeks. "I'm perfectly capable of putting two and two together when I see a…a body on the floor and someone holding a smoking gun. And don't forget, Silas discovered his plot to take over my father's reign—"

"Yes," said Mel bitingly. "Silas. That paragon of virtue."

"I know you've never liked him, but he's been nothing but helpful, supportive. Even if he is a little"—she paused, remembering his calculated marriage proposal, the way he'd argued for her hand, all logic and no love—"astringent."

Mel shrugged, but her face was hard as granite. "Maybe you're right. I don't know. I do know how he helps your brother with his little...*problems,* though. And I do know how he looks at you, E."

Eliana stared at her.

"Like you're dinner," she said darkly. "A roasted pig, all trussed up and ready to eat."

Eliana's skin crawled. Something about that sounded just right. She walked slowly back to the bed, sat down beside Mel once more, and leaned into her shoulder. Looking at the worn stone floor, the bare, shadowed walls, she said, "Why didn't you tell me any of this before? Why tell me now?"

Mel's sigh was heavy. "Because you'd never have believed me, and I didn't want it to come between us. What difference would it have made, anyway? Dredging up the past when nothing could change it? You and I have always been so good at leaving the past behind. But," her voice faltered, and she glanced at Eliana, "now the past is catching up with us, and I think you should consider, really *consider,* the possibility that nothing is what it seems. And make your choices going forward accordingly."

Mel had left her after that, sitting alone in the middle of the empty room with memory and confusion a pair of snarling dark monsters inside her skull, one thing repeating itself over and over, relentlessly.

Nothing is what it seems.

To Eliana, that was the most frightening possibility of them all.

NINETEEN
Rematch

This can't be the right place, thought D, staring at his final destination from across the tree-lined boulevard. *It can't be.*

But, according to the dream he'd had, it was.

The gothic Montmartre Cemetery, famous for being the final resting place of such luminaries as Degas, Nijinsky, and Zola, was built below street level in the hollow of an old quarry. The gated entrance to its sprawling twenty-five acres of tended gardens and tombs was on the quiet Avenue Rachel under the overpass of Rue Caulaincourt, where he now stood well hidden from the soft yellow glow of the streetlights in the shadows of a weeping willow. Perplexed, he looked up and down the street, hoping for more clues.

The dream had shown the number two Métro stop at Place Blanche, the peep show hawkers outside the Moulin

Rouge, the tiny guard shack beside the cemetery gate where visitors paid an entry fee of six euros to tour the narrow, cobblestoned walkways, gawking at the crypts and carved obelisks and blank-eyed marble statues and elaborate, crumbling monuments to the uncaring dead. In the deepening twilight of the hour past closing time, the guard shack was dark and deserted, the rusted iron gates locked.

It had been just like this in the dream, down to every detail—him standing here under this tree with his hands shoved in his pockets, thin coils of fog snaking around his ankles, the sound of music and laughter from a bistro half a block away warming the quiet cool of the evening. But now that he was here, D had no idea what to do next.

Accustomed to the capricious nature of this particular Gift of his, D decided to wait.

He didn't wait long.

From down the street rumbled an ancient green Peugeot, belching smoke from its muffler in feathery blue plumes, one headlight flickering sporadically as if signaling in code. It neared and D stepped behind the gnarled trunk of the elm, watching. The car jerked and rattled to a stop at the curb and disgorged four young men, laughing and ribbing each other in expletive-laced French. They carried a strange collection of items: compasses, rubber boots, lumpy backpacks, flashlights, and a map they unfolded on the hood of the car that they began to peruse, arguing in a friendly way about some bet they had going.

"I'm telling you there's no *way* you'll win, dude. You'll just end up getting bitch-slapped and wetting your frilly pink panties."

A derisive snort. "Right, like I'm gonna let a *girl* beat me."

"That's what Jules here thought, and he was limping for a week afterward."

A round of raucous laughter, to which the offended Jules responded, "I did not!"

"Dude, you were totally hobbled."

"I tripped on a rock!"

"Really? Was that before or after the Butterfly kicked your leg out from under you and slammed you on your ass?"

"That was just a lucky hit."

"Yeah, she's pretty lucky that way all right. You guys got your money?"

Murmurs of assent were heard, boots and backpacks were donned, and the map was folded and put away. The men kept chiding one another as they locked the car and headed toward the cemetery, flashlights raking the ground in shaky yellow swaths. One by one, they leapt the low gate and were soon swallowed by darkness.

"Well," murmured D as he stepped off the curb and followed, "this should be interesting."

Friday night was fight night in the catacombs, and Eliana wasn't about to let a little thing like bullet wounds, bruised ribs, and a rapidly deteriorating sense of reality deter her from participating.

After all, she was the star attraction. And she really needed an outlet for the nuclear rage that had been building inside her all day.

She hadn't been able to find Mel after leaving Silas in the afternoon. The need to discuss what he'd said about her father was overwhelming, a gnawing compulsion that had her heart thrashing like a shark on a chum line inside her chest. Several things Mel had said—and her voice, eyes, and posture when she'd said them—had stuck with her also, irritating as a splinter under skin.

Never missed a thing, your father.

Because he ordered me not to.

Made us swear to never tell a soul.

Why? Eliana circled back to that one question, over and over. Why?

Why had her father insisted Mel keep her marriage a secret?

Why would Demetrius go out of his way to clean and stitch her wounds?

Why were those assassins—who she'd honestly told Silas were not of the *Legiones* or the *Bellatorum*—trying to kill her?

Could what Silas said about her father actually be true?

Nothing added up. None of it. Uncertainty slithered, cold and reptilian, under her skin.

By the time she entered the heated, cavernous enclave of New Harmony, she'd worked herself into an epic lather.

The crowd was huge tonight. Bodies pressed against the bare stone walls, against one another, nearly everyone with a drink in hand, many laughing, dancing, shouting to be heard above the thumping bass and electronica music of a DJ who had set up a mobile turntable and speakers in one candlelit corner. It was nights like these—drinking and talking and *being* with humans—that made her believe all she and her father had dreamed was possible. No, they didn't know the truth of who and what she was, the gritty *details,* but most of them seemed to know on some animal, primal level that she was different. That she was Other. They watched her, they moved aside to let her pass, they glanced away when her dark gaze met theirs.

And still they came.

They came to have fun and be entertained and escape the drudgery of daily lives spent at desks, in cubicles, behind windowless office walls. They came to lose themselves in darkness and adventure and the camaraderie of the underground. They came to fight. They came to dance. They came to play and drink and love.

They came to live. And tonight, more than ever before, Eliana needed to live, too.

A roar went up as she was spotted. She strode from the shadows of the connecting tunnel, her black trench billowing out behind her, a small, satisfied smile on her face. This was her home, and these were her people—related or not—and she loved it. She loved them all.

"Butterfly!" someone shouted from the back of the crowd, and hundreds of voices took it up in a chant that swelled and crested like a wave. *Butterfly! Butterfly! Butterfly!*

Always a chilly fifty-five degrees, the air in the catacombs took on a decidedly electric vibe.

She prowled to the middle of the grotto and paused. She shrugged off her coat, handed it to an anonymous person who darted forward from the crowd to take it, and let her gaze drift over the sea of bodies. She knew what the cataphiles saw when they looked back at her: choppy blue hair and tight black leather, motorcycle boots and a cinched bustier that left her arms and shoulders bare, the butterfly between her shoulder blades exposed and strangely animated as the shadows played over her skin. For the first time in a long time she'd worn makeup, smoky eye shadow and eyeliner drawn out past the corners of her eyes to accentuate their catlike tilt. Her lips were a curving slash of vermilion.

"Who wants to go first?" she shouted above the noise.

A group of four men, money held aloft in fists, pushed to the front of the crowd. One of them—the biggest one, blocky and grinning, with ham-hock hands and the cauliflower ears of a professional boxer—peeled off his shirt, dropped it to the ground, lifted his hand, and pointed a stubby finger at his chest.

Eliana smiled and thought, *The bigger they are, the harder they—*

"I'll go first," boomed a deep, masculine voice from the shadows along the back wall, a voice every cell in her body recognized, and every head in the crowd craned around to see.

They didn't have to try very hard. He stood head and shoulders above everyone else. He stepped forward from the shadows, and one by one, mouths hanging open, every person shrank back as he passed.

Demetrius.

Here.

Here!

The music died. Hushed whispers ran through the gathering. A palpable crackle of excitement leapt from person to person, viral, infectious.

He prowled toward her, exuding a raw current of danger, feral and heated, his eyes locked on hers. When he reached the edge of the crowd he paused. Deliberately, holding her gaze, he slowly unzipped the black hoodie he was wearing, shrugged it off, and let it fall to his feet.

That was when the air actually turned to fire.

Audible gasps went up through the crowd. The ham-hock hands of the man who'd just been ready to fight her trembled. Someone whispered an astonished, *Merde!*

And beyond her thundering heart and frozen muscles and horror, Eliana could appreciate why.

Huge, bare-chested, and leonine, D stood exposed, chin lifted, eyes hooded, shoulders thrown back. His body was carved and corded with muscle, a sculptor's imagination gone wild. From the V-shaped muscles that rose from the waistline of his low-slung leathers to the articulated corrugation of his rock-hard abs to the bulging biceps of his arms and the flare of heavy lats on his back that tapered down to his narrow waist in an inverted triangle, he was magnificent. Breathtaking. Hercules, Adonis, Samson, and Tarzan, all rolled into one.

He had multiple, elaborate tattoos: the stylized Eye of Horus on his left shoulder, thick black tribal symbols tracked down the length of his right arm, an enormous cobra that snaked its way down from his neck, around his back, and up to his chest, where it coiled, sinuous. In the center of one loop of scales right over his heart there was inked a name in cursive letters with thorny vines and flowers patterned around.

The letters spelled out *Eliana.*

Astonished, she glanced back up at his face, noting the scratches she'd given him had already healed. He was smiling at her, a slow, seductive curve of his lips. "How 'bout a rematch?" he said in a low, amused rumble. "Five hundred says I win this time, too."

Son of a bitch.

The crowd exploded into a frenzy. Bets were placed, money changed hands, and shouting and shoving and chaos ensued. From one corner of her eye she noticed Alexi standing with arms crossed, glaring back and forth between the two of them. The flabbergasted blonde beside him couldn't tear her wide-eyed gaze from Demetrius's naked chest.

He took a step forward. She took a step back. They began to circle each other slowly, warily, their gazes locked together. All the noise and movement faded to the background as her focus honed on his face. His movements. His breath.

Her own breath was ragged, her pulse a thunderstorm inside her skull.

"If you think I'm going to lead to you to the others, you're wrong," she said, low enough she knew only his ears would be able to hear. Over four hundred miles of hiding spaces in the catacombs; he'd have to search for days to find them, and by then they'd be long gone.

He cocked an eyebrow. The silver rings in it glinted in the light. "Not here for them, baby girl. I'm here for you."

If he meant to anger her with his endearment, it worked. "Nice tattoo, by the way," she snapped, glancing at his chest. "I'll be carving that off your dead body later."

He tutted. "You'll have to kill me first. Good luck with that."

Then he lunged forward in a blur of bronzed skin and leather and grabbed her.

She twisted out of his grasp, using all her strength to tear free. But he had her again in an instant and pinned her arms behind her back. Heady and warm and masculine, the scent of his skin flamed hot in her nose as he leaned down and whispered into her ear, "You're not trying very hard. You need to give the crowd their money's worth. *Butterfly*." She felt the fleet brush of his lips across the flesh of her shoulder, and then he released her and sprang away.

She whirled around with a savage snarl. He was on the other side of the space cleared by the circle of bodies, hands on his hips, staring at her with a heated expression somewhere between amusement and anticipation. He stretched a hand out and crooked two fingers at her, a silent command.

Come.

Oh no. Oh no he *didn't.*

Fury blinded her, and she went on pure instinct, striking out, hitting, kicking. The next few moments were a blur. There was the sensation flying, of falling, of gravity spinning away. Her hands were around his throat, his hands came around her waist, and suddenly she was flat on her back in the center of the fighting ring with Demetrius straddling her body, his hands pinning her wrists to the ground above her head.

The roar of the crowd was deafening.

He grinned down at her, victorious, and then, before she could scream the curse that was on the tip of her tongue, his mouth was on hers.

Ache and salt and softness, the ground cold and hard against her back, Demetrius warm and hard against her chest, pulling greedily at her lips, drinking deep…the sharp edges of her fury began, awfully, to melt.

He pulled away first, panting, flipped her over, and in one horrifying, fluid movement, flung her over his bent knee so she was staring in shock at the dusty, scuffed ground.

And then—horror of all horrors—he spanked her.

In front of everyone.

Three times.

Hard.

The crowd went absolutely insane.

"That's for every year you were gone," D growled, bending near her ear. She kicked and screamed, fighting him, but he held her fast, immovable and ironfisted, trapping both her hands in one of his, leaning his weight onto her back with his forearm.

Then he spanked her another three times. Her scream of outrage was drowned by the delighted, uproarious cheers of the spectators.

"That's for calling me a liar, a murderer, and a traitor."

Her cheeks burned molten hot. She couldn't get *away*, she was at his complete *mercy*—

He spanked her again, three more hard, humiliating times, then lifted her up, took her in his arms, and said, "And that's for the next three things you're going to do that will annoy the hell out of me."

Then he pulled her against him and kissed her again, in full view of everyone, his hands in her hair and his mouth hot on hers and a low purr of pleasure rumbling deep in his chest.

"Not cool," Alexi said from somewhere nearby. "So *not* cool."

She came to her senses and shoved him away just as the crowd broke suddenly apart and began a wild, careening stampede toward the numerous shadowed tunnels that led out of New Harmony.

"Cataflics!" someone shouted, pushing by.

Police.

Eliana leapt to her feet and bounded away, flashing through the crowd, using the chaos to her advantage to duck into a low access tunnel that was rarely used because of the treacherous, unmarked pits that would suddenly appear in the uneven floor, plunging down into darkness.

She knew without looking that Demetrius followed not far behind.

TWENTY

Devils Are Everywhere

The prostitute was a blonde, as Silas promised, but not his favorite blonde, the one who screamed with such beautiful abandon, the one whose milky pale skin welted to the perfect berry pink, bruised to the most gorgeous mottled purple.

She wasn't his favorite, no. She wasn't young, or pretty, or thin.

She wasn't moving at the moment, either.

Standing at the end of the bed fully dressed, Caesar regarded her in the bleak fluorescent light of the bedside lamp. She lay facedown on the stained and rumpled coverlet, spread-eagle, naked.

He cocked his head, inspecting her with the cold, clinical calculation of a collector, of a connoisseur. There was good naked and bad naked and everything in between, but the worst was *ugly* naked, the kind where even a hospital nurse, used to seeing people steeped in shit and blood and vomit, would recoil.

This bitch was definitely ugly naked.

Angry red ligature marks marred her wrists and her ankles from where he'd bound her, and a splatter of blood decorated the fleshy, dimpled arch of her hip. Her back was dusted with freckles, soft as a sifting of cinnamon against her pasty skin. Her lank yellow hair—thin, he *hated* thin hair—lay in limp strands across the pillow and her face, hiding her eyes. Open? Closed? It didn't matter. He didn't want to see her eyes, anyway. He always liked to cover their eyes; it was only their screams he wanted.

This thin-haired whore had given those to him in spades. The plastic ball gag he'd cinched around her mouth and neck had done little to muffle them.

The hotel room was in the red-light district on the outskirts of Montmartre, seedy and glum, visited by a certain caliber of men who moved furtively through shadows, scurrying like rats. It reeked of sweat and piss and cigarette smoke, of pain and desperation. It was all Caesar could do to block it out. At times like these he cursed his heightened senses, one of the few differences between himself and those ratlike men.

Perhaps the only difference, if truth be told.

He lifted his foot and gave the lumpy mattress a sharp kick. The whore didn't react, didn't make a sound, just rolled slightly with the bed and then settled back a little too quickly to heavy, unnatural stillness. Her skin was beginning to show the faintest tinge of gray. Outside in the parking lot, unseen beyond the drawn drapes, someone screamed something unintelligible and slammed a car door. Off in the distance, a dog barked three times.

Yellow hair. Gods, he hated her hair.

Folded on an old rattan chair against a wall stained and peeling was a blanket, threadbare, patchy, and plain. Caesar spied it and allowed his gaze to linger, arrested, appreciating the only thing of beauty in the room. The color of it. The beautiful, saturated hue.

Indigo. He'd never really realized how beautiful that particular shade of blue was before.

His mouth watered. Another erection—much firmer than the one he'd inflicted on the whore—stirred to life in his pants.

Slowly, enjoying the anticipation, lust and rage simmering in his blood like a rising fever, Caesar crossed from the bed to the chair against the wall. He took up the blanket in his hands. He pressed it to his nose, his lips. He moved to the bed, where he stood over the dead prostitute and looked down at her, repulsed. But once he'd carefully arranged the blanket over her head—blocking out her face, her eyes, her ugly yellow hair, everything personal about her—he felt better.

He felt *right.*

He returned to his place at the foot of the bed and admired his handiwork.

He imagined the blue blanket wasn't a blanket at all, but hair. Hair so thick and dark and lovely it could never be rendered plain by an indifferent cut, an inexperienced dye job.

Hair so midnight blue it mimicked the heavens and should be crowned with stars.

Hair like…his sister's.

Mouth watering, heart pounding in his chest, Caesar began, slowly, to work open the buckle of his belt.

"Everything is arranged for the meeting?"

The man in the fedora inclined his head, murmured respectfully, "*Ita, domine meus.*"

Yes, my lord. How Silas loved the unchanging ways of the Church. Everyone spoke Latin, no one questioned authority, underlings knew their place. He'd refused to speak Latin since he'd left the Roman catacombs, but he supposed he could bend that rule today, this being a special occasion.

After all, it wasn't every day you arranged to meet the pope.

"*Excellens,*" he answered, and the man in the fedora smiled.

Their meeting place was a tiny café with strong espresso, surly waitstaff, and an excellent view of the Place du Tertre, a cobblestoned square ringed by small shops topped with tidy red awnings. Strung through the bare branches of trees all around were tiny blue lights, and sparkling white along curbs and windowsills was a confectioner's dusting of snow. In spite of the hour and the dropping temperature, the square still buzzed with shoppers and diners and row after row of artists with easels, hawking portraits to all the tourists. This close to Christmas everything stayed open late.

To the slight, smiling man in the fedora and cloak sitting across from him at the scrolled iron café table, Silas said, "The timing is very important. Just before his Christmas morning speech would be ideal. We won't keep His Holiness long, of course. He has so many important matters to attend to that day."

Silas sent a little nudge along with these words, a hint of agreeability that had the man nodding.

"*Il papa* is eager to meet you, *domine meus.* He had only the highest respect for your predecessor, and he knows the work you do is necessary to our Mother the Church. To keep her safe from the evil that would prevail were we not so vigilant." His face darkened. "These devils are everywhere these days."

Oh, he really had no idea. Silas had to work hard to keep a straight face. "Give the cardinal my warm regards, will you? Please thank him for arranging the meeting and for his service. He will be rewarded handsomely for his loyalty. As will you all."

Again the respectful incline of the head. They exchanged a few more words, particulars of timing and travel, until Silas discreetly looked at his watch. Without needing to be told, the man knew the meeting was over and rose from his chair.

"*Ire cum Deus,*" he murmured as a farewell. He lifted his hand to tip his hat, and Silas saw the small, black tattoo on his inner wrist, a tattoo all his kind shared: a headless panther run through with a spear. The man turned and made his way across the busy square, and Silas watched him go until he slipped into the shadows between two buildings and was lost from sight.

Go with God. It had been their motto since time immemorial, three words spoken as a blessing or farewell or any number of things in between. Strange how fanatics always needed some kind of slogan. Silas played along with it, as had Dominus before him, as had all the nonhuman leaders of this decidedly human group of hunters.

Expurgari, they called themselves. The purifiers. What a laugh. Almost a thousand years since the Inquisition began and their little troupe of Church-sanctioned killers formed, and they still had no idea what kind of monsters really pulled their strings.

Soon, though. Very soon they'd find out.

He tossed a few coins to the table and rose, smiling languidly at the girl who rushed over to clear his plate. Plain as vanilla pudding, she blushed and looked down. Tempting, but he had no time to dally this evening. He had more important matters to attend.

He had a murder to plan, a revolution to lead, an empire to overthrow.

He was much too busy to get sidetracked now.

TWENTY-ONE
The Only Thing That Matters

It was the strangest place D had ever seen.

Vast and dark and cavernous, it was some kind of underground cathedral, a monument erected to exalt the talent of anonymous street artists and remember the long-forgotten dead. Graffiti, vivid as nightmares, was everywhere. Splashed over the rock walls in lurid swaths of purple and black and red, yellow flowers painted on towering columns, a swirl of kaleidoscope color on the rounded cavern ceiling far above his head. There were flying gold dragons and mincing white geisha and snarling pale ghouls with clawed hands reaching out. There were enormous letters in some forgotten alphabet and an eight-foot-tall depiction of a nude woman with one arm draped over her head.

But the bones were far more bizarre than the artwork.

Rising all the way to the ceiling along one long, curving wall was displayed an artfully arranged array of human bones. Countless bones, possibly thousands, femurs and ribs and skulls stacked with careful, almost reverent precision. It was an ossuary, ghoulish in its grandeur, made all the more eerie by the hundreds of candles that glowed along its walls.

And somewhere in this empire of paint and bones, Eliana was hiding.

He couldn't see her but he *felt* her, that frisson that tingled over every inch of his skin like thunderclouds just before they disgorged a bolt of lightning. He took another step forward into the cool, echoing space, his gaze searching every shadowed corner, every crevice, every hiding place.

She was nowhere to be seen.

"I'm not here to hurt you, Eliana." His voice carried through the quiet space, echoing softly and then dying to silence. The naked graffiti woman seemed to mock him with her sly, painted smile. "I only want to talk. I'll say what I have to say, and then I'll leave. You have my word."

The sound of dripping water. A candle in a niche in the wall behind him sputtered out. Then a disembodied voice from somewhere in front of him said with gentle sarcasm, "Your *word*? Well, how reassuring."

He froze. The voice, he was sure of it, came from the deepest shadow of the room, a hollow created by the intersection of two massive, perpendicular slabs of limestone. He narrowed his eyes, stretched his senses, and allowed every bit of ambient light to enter his swiftly dilating pupils. Beneath the veil of shadows where he was certain the voice originated lurked only painted mushrooms that sprouted wild from the cavern floor, foresting the two walls of rock with slender stalks and spreading caps that loomed cartoonishly large.

She wasn't there.

He took a step forward, then another. Hoping to get her to speak again and get a better lead on her location, he said, "Tell me what would convince you, then. Tell me and I'll do it."

The rueful, answering snort came from that empty corner, he knew it did. But how? He took another step forward, carefully, then inhaled and opened all his senses to let the relentless drone of his surroundings sink in.

A pair of mice, scurrying along a ledge somewhere above his head. That dripping water, falling through caverns before it hit a body of standing water, far, far below. Rock dust and bone dust, both fine as silt, suspended and diffused as atoms in the air. A pulse of heat ahead of him, the scent of her bright in his nose. He took another sure step toward that sultry scent, and she said abruptly, "Stop."

He did. He put both hands up in a posture of surrender. The air, cool and damp, felt delicious against his heated skin.

"I can kill you now and you won't even see it coming. Stay where you are or I'll spill your guts all over the floor. Understood?"

Considering the fact that he somehow couldn't see her now but the last time he had she'd been quite handy with a dagger, D thought it prudent to nod.

He sensed movement without seeing its source, felt the pulse of her body heat move slowly around to his left. Nonchalant, feigning boredom, he lowered his gaze to the ground and then slid it left, following that delicious, satiny heat. There in the pale sifting of dust that covered the ground was a trail of footsteps, unremarkable in themselves, but astonishing for the fact that they appeared as they did, one in front of the other, right before his eyes.

Damn, he thought, floored by the sheer impossibility of it.

Eliana was invisible. How the hell had she managed that?

"I don't feel the other *Bellatorum* nearby. Or your new team. So I have to assume you've come to kill me on your own this time."

Instantly he said, "You don't believe that. You know I'd never hurt you."

"Do I?" she murmured in response, her voice now directly behind him. It took every ounce of willpower he had not to whirl around, but he held himself immobile, his limbs and posture and breathing nonthreatening and relaxed.

"Yes. And the team you mentioned isn't mine. As I told you before, they're called The Hunt. They're assassins from the confederate colonies."

The movement behind him ceased. He imagined he felt her glaring at the back of his head, willing it to explode.

"Do tell," she invited, not cold but not particularly warm, either.

His hands were still lifted in the air, and he itched to lower them, but instead he turned his head and said over his shoulder, "They think you're the new leader of the Expurgari."

She spoke Latin as well as he did. So her voice was a little more heated when she said, "Purifiers? What is that supposed to mean? Why would they think that?"

Careful, he'd have to be very, very careful now. "I'd like to say this to your face, if you don't mind," he murmured. "Can I turn around?"

"No," came the instant reply. Something sharp and cold pressed against the space between his shoulder blades: a knife. "And you have about ten seconds left to tell your story, so make them count."

He accepted both the verbal threat and the more immediate one of the weapon with the tranquility of someone long used to facing death as a matter of course in his daily life. A soldier through and through, his self-preservation instinct had been deadened in infancy, when he'd been taken from the nursery and began his training as a warrior. He protected a colony of supernatural creatures, he protected their genocidal leader, he'd long ago come to peace with the simple fact that in all likelihood, his life would be short and violent. There were no grandchildren in his future; that was for sure.

"They think you're the new leader of the Expurgari because your father was the old one."

A quarter turn of the blade against his back. A slight hesitation, then, very quietly, "And what is it that these purifiers purify?"

He inhaled. He exhaled. "Us."

"That makes no sense," came the instant response. The knife pressed deeper into the flesh of his back. He felt it like an exclamation point on the end of a sentence, emphatic.

"It's complicated."

"Nine." She sounded as if she'd like to shove the blade through his spine even sooner.

"They're a militant branch of the Church, trained assassins—"

"More assassins!"

"Who've been led since the Inquisition by an *Ikati* disguised as a human—"

"Eight."

"Which was a very ingenious way, if you think about it, to use humans to kill their own kind without drawing attention to the real culprit—"

"To what end? For what reason?"

"Vengeance, Eliana. Vengeance."

"Seven." Her voice, hard as granite.

"Why do you think your father was so devoted to Horus? God of vengeance, god of war…ring a bell? He used humans as a spy network to gain information about the other colonies so he could overthrow them, all the while disguising himself as a devout disciple of the Church, a spiritual warrior against evil. Against human heretics and that nonhuman scourge, that abomination against God and nature… *shifters.*"

"Six, five, four—"

"I have proof," he said abruptly, and he felt the knife at his back give a little jerk.

"What proof can a liar give?" Her voice was bitter.

"Written proof. Straight from the horse's mouth."

The point of the knife drew away. He sensed movement, and then from around his left shoulder, he saw it and caught his breath.

She was there, but only just, beginning to take shape against the darkness behind her with little crystalline sparkles of light like motes suspended in a sunbeam. Her face appeared first, ghostly pale, and then her body began to take form, a growing mass that gathered around a core of shifting particles, ethereal as smoke. From one heartbeat to the next she became fully realized—flesh and bone and clothing—and began to move, slowly, carefully, watching him with eyes intense and unblinking.

"Ana," he breathed, "that's incredible. That's so beauti—"

She said, "Which horse?"

It wasn't a knife she'd been holding, he saw now as she paused and stood just beyond arm's length with the weapon held out, leveled at his heart. It was a sword. A short sword, elegant and curved with a bone hilt banded in silk cord and a tapered carbon steel blade. It looked vaguely Asian. And deadly.

He drew in a lungful of the cool cavern air and replied, "Your father's. We have your father's journal. You left it behind."

He saw the way she faltered, just the tiniest furrow drawn between her arching dark brows before it was erased. Before she could respond, he said, "You'll recognize the binding, you know his hand. It will answer all your questions."

"Where is it?" she whispered, staring at him. "Give it to me."

He shook his head, once, and slowly lowered his hands to his sides. "It's not here. I'll bring it tomorrow. I'll bring it here—"

"No," she insisted vehemently. "Not here. Somewhere else. Somewhere public."

He studied her face. Drawn and pale, she looked suddenly terrified, but not of him. No, of something she was thinking. Of what she imagined inside that journal.

"The Eiffel Tower."

Her brows flew up.

"Second-floor observation deck. Meet me there at sunset tomorrow. I'll be alone."

"I'll know it if you're not," she warned. She still hadn't lowered the sword. "I'll know if it's a trick."

"I know," he agreed softly. "I know you will. It's not a trick."

"And if you try and search for any of my—"

"I told you, baby girl. I don't want them. I came for you. It's only you. It's always been only you."

Her eyes closed for just longer than a blink. Before she could speak, he murmured, "Don't you know?" He stepped forward, slowly, until the blade of her outstretched sword rested against his chest, cold and sharp against the flesh over his heart, the flesh tattooed with her name. Her nostrils flared with her inhalation, but she didn't retreat or move.

Looking deep into her eyes he said, "*Ego mori tibi.*"

I would die for you.

Latin, because that's how they were both born and raised. Catacombs, darkness, secrets, and dead languages, apart from the rest of the world.

Eliana twitched and exhaled a little, stunned breath. Her eyes were very dark and wide.

Still in Latin, still fierce, he continued, "I would kill for you. I would tear out my own heart with my bare hands if that's what you asked, because your pleasure is my reward and a smile from you is worth more to me than gold. I've searched for you every second of every minute of every day since you disappeared, and all I want now is for you to be safe from the others who are searching for you, too—others who want to see you dead. I won't let them hurt you, and though you don't believe me, I won't hurt you, either. Ever." His voice grew even deeper, huskier, and he swallowed. "Because I'm in love with you, baby girl, and I have been for as long as I can remember. You're the one ray of sunshine in the total darkness of my life. You're the only thing that matters."

She made a low, anguished sound in the back of her throat. He saw her grip tighten on the hilt of the sword, saw her fingers go white with how hard they squeezed, saw her intention to run him through right where he stood.

Just before she lunged forward, D Shifted to Vapor, and Eliana's thrust was met with empty air.

TWENTY-TWO
Invisible Flame

The first thing Gregor heard was the beeping.

Loud and insistent, the electronic noise was so irritating it had worked itself into his dream. He'd been having the most wonderful dream, distinct as daylight, in which he was visited by someone vaguely familiar. A woman, standing at the end of his bed. But she was more specter than flesh, scented of nighttime and the outdoors, silent as that damned beeping was not. She'd drifted to the beside, surrounded him in calming, cool mist, murmured his name into his ear, then other things. Lovely things.

"Rest, old friend. Heal. We'll see each other again soon."

But the beeping wouldn't let up, and finally the beautiful vision had disappeared, only to be replaced by the sight of a room, eye-wateringly bright when he opened his eyes. He squinted against the glare, disoriented, saw white walls and a fabric curtain hung from a track on the ceiling, smelled the sharp, chemical bite of disinfectant and the more subtle, homey scent of freshly laundered cotton.

When he turned his head left he spied the source of that infernal noise: a heart monitor, rectangular green, on rolling metal legs next to his bed.

His bed. In the hospital.

With a jerk he sat up, and pain, searing hot, tore through his chest.

A murmur of disapproval came from his other side, and Gregor, growling his displeasure and gritting his teeth against the pain, allowed a pair of gentle hands to push him back against the mattress. The nurse leaned over him, smoothed down the neck of the pastel flowered gown that covered his chest and body, and inspected a square of white bandages taped to his chest.

"Try not to tear your stitches, Mr. MacGregor," she admonished in a husky, accented voice. She was fortyish, dishy, with a cap of shiny dark hair that accentuated a pair of cheekbones so chiseled they could cut glass. She turned smiling, warm brown eyes to his. "We don't want you staying here any longer than necessary, now do we?"

He hated it when people asked rhetorical questions. But in the dishy nurse's case, he figured he'd let it slide. "How long have I been here?" He let her plump the pillow beneath his head, fuss over his blankets. She lifted a plastic cup to his mouth and helped him sip water from a bendy straw, all the while making little noises of encouragement. He began to like her more and more.

"Two days," was the answer as she watched him drink. When he finished, she set the cup back on the small table beside the bed. "And they've been a royal pain, if you know what I mean, the whole time."

His brows pulled together. "They?"

She darted a sour glance toward the door of the room. Beyond the narrow strip of glass inset beside it Gregor saw a trio of men, two uniformed gendarmes flirting with an unseen woman at the nurses' station, standing with their backs to him, and one seated man in a plain black suit with spectacles and a patch over one eye. He was looking away so Gregor saw him only in profile, but he knew exactly who it was.

As if he felt him watching, Agent Doe looked over. Their eyes met through the glass.

"Say what they want?" he muttered, holding Doe's icy blue gaze.

"Well, *mon amie*," said the pretty nurse with a wry little smile, "you made quite an entrance when you checked in. The damage to the front of the hospital was extensive. And your girlfriend scared the *merde* out of one of our senior doctors. He took a few days' personal time after your surgery. I'm not sure if he'll ever come back."

Gregor's hand flew to his bandaged chest. Surgery. He'd been shot. Eliana—

"What happened to the woman—the woman who brought me in?" He caught the nurse by the wrist. "Where is she? Is she hurt?"

With the slow, nonthreatening movements of one trained to deal with irrational people, the nurse removed her wrist from his grip and then patted his hand. "She walked out of the emergency room on her own two feet, Mr. MacGregor. From what I understand, she was not injured. You're lucky she got you here so quickly, though. You nearly bled to death on the way over."

Gregor slumped back against the pillows, clammy with relief. She wasn't hurt. But where was she now?

"The car you arrived in, on the other hand, was not so lucky." She chuckled and moved around to the other side of the bed to check the readouts on the heart monitor and the amount of pale liquid left in a plastic bag hanging from a hook on a rolling pole. There was a length of clear tubing from the bag to his arm, a piece of white tape over the vein on the back of his hand where the tubing was attached with a needle. "Antibiotics," she said, seeing his look. "Just to make sure you don't get any infection from the wound."

The door swung open. He and the nurse turned to watch Agent Doe, leaning on a cane, enter the room, followed by the two uniformed officers. The three of them sent him baleful glares.

"Well." The nurse shot Gregor a meaningful glance. "My name is Lily. I'm on until nine o'clock. If you need anything, just push that red button on the remote beside the bed and I'll be in momentarily." She brushed past the men and let herself out, closing the door behind her.

Gregor said into the following silence, "Agent Doe. We meet again." He glanced at the two unsmiling gendarmes. "Where's my good friend Édoard? Our little reunion won't be the same without him."

Agent Doe's knuckles were white around the curved handle of the cane. His jaw worked, but his cold, cold eye revealed nothing. "He's at your building as we speak."

There was a lump in the mattress the size of a cat that was pinching a nerve in his lower back, but Gregor refused to shift his weight to relieve the discomfort. "Oh?"

Doe grew a smile that would have looked at home on Hannibal Lecter. "Do you have any idea how long the prison term is for operating a bordello?"

So they'd found it. Gregor said flatly, "Five years to life. Or so I'm told."

"Ah, but you are correct! Your lawyer must be very intelligent. Though not intelligent enough to dissuade you from engaging in such a reprehensible activity. Pity."

Gregor did have an intelligent lawyer. A genius lawyer, in fact, who charged fifteen hundred dollars an hour and had drilled into his brain never, *never* to admit anything, even if caught standing over a decapitated body with a bloody machete in one hand and a severed head in the other. Which in Gregor's case was not entirely outside the realm of possibility.

"Actually, I only know that from television. It's amazing what you can learn from those—"

"—crime shows," Doe finished for him. "Yes, you said so before." His ugly smile grew mocking. "You certainly do watch a lot of television."

The two officers snickered. Gregor and Doe stared at one another, deadlocked in silent animosity, until Gregor made a motion with his hand.

"What happened to your eye?"

Doe stiffened. The smile leached from his face, and he shifted his weight from one foot to the other. "I am not after you, MacGregor, you should know that up front so you can make your decisions going forward accordingly." In answer to Gregor's plain expression of disbelief, he said, "I am after far bigger fish, and if you assist me in that regard, all charges against you will be dropped."

"I thought you weren't with the police. How can you have the authority to do that?"

Ominously, he said, "My organization is above the police."

Gregor's interest was piqued. "Is it now? And here I thought no one was above the law."

"Enough money can put you above anything, even God Himself."

Without explaining further and apparently tired of standing, Doe snapped his fingers and one of the officers brought him a chair from the corner of the room. He settled himself into it—lips pinched, legs stiff—and then waved a hand, dismissing them. They looked at one another for a moment before leaving the way they'd come. Gregor saw them take up position outside his door, noticed they both wore sidearms.

The police were acting as his very own armed guards. Even more interesting.

"Speaking of God, are you a religious man, MacGregor?"

Gregor blinked over at him and watched as Doe withdrew a cigarette from his inner coat pocket, lit it, and drew the tip into flame. His deep, satisfied exhalation sent out a cloud of smoke.

"I assume there's a point you're trying to make, Doe. Make it."

Doe chuckled. "Neither am I, as it happens. But there are things we don't understand in this world, wouldn't you agree? Things beyond our comprehension? Things…you may have even seen yourself. In the very flesh."

Gregor stared at him, giving nothing away.

"Have you seen the video of your quite spectacular arrival at the hospital? No? Hmm. Well, it's actually not that interesting"—his one good eye, icy blue, peering at him from behind round spectacles, grew positively arctic—"when you compare it to the video we retrieved from the security cameras at your building. Amazing system you have there. State of the art, I'm told."

"Doe—"

He leaned forward in the chair, suddenly intent, all humor vanished. "Did you know what she was all along? Did you have any idea what you were really dealing with?"

Gregor leaned back into the pillow, silent, and Doe struggled to his feet. From another pocket he removed a cell phone and held it up between two fingers. "A copy of the feed. It's been edited. I thought you might enjoy the highlights."

He touched a button and then edged nearer to Gregor, holding the phone out. He took it, gazed down at the small square screen, and found he could not look away.

In all his life, he'd never seen anything move like they did. They'd crawled up the building's exterior glass walls—literally crawled, like lizards—and entered from the roof. From a dozen different perspectives he saw the assassins running, jumping, bounding, all so quickly their movements were just an on-screen blur. He saw himself and Eliana in the stairwells, the chase in the parking garage, the horrifying impact with the metal door. He saw the Ferrari vanish into the distance out of camera range, but not before he saw, edited from a dozen different angles, five grown men morph into snarling animals and give chase.

Panthers. They turned into panthers, impossibly huge and black.

His skin crawled.

Doe removed the camera from his cold fingers and smiled at the look on Gregor's face. "Exactly my reaction. I think we're going to have to build a lot more zoos."

He returned to his chair and finished his cigarette in silence while Gregor lay back against the pillow, suddenly exhausted. He stared at the ceiling, his brain on an endless replay loop. Men with guns; panthers. Men with guns; *panthers.*

"As I said before," Doe murmured, stubbing out the cigarette on the plastic arm of the chair, "it's not you we want. We want her. We want *them.* Tell us everything you know, and all charges against you will be dropped. And you won't receive any more visits from the police, I can guarantee it."

She'd been right about having many enemies, Gregor thought as he watched a fly march across the ceiling tiles above. Her own kind wanted to see her dead, this crazy German bastard wanted to stick her in a zoo…she was going to need more guns.

Gregor turned his attention back to Agent Doe. He smiled, humorless. "I think I just realized I have a terrible case of amnesia. Who are you again?"

Doe shook his head, disappointed. "Why would you protect them? Why would you risk imprisonment? They're only animals, MacGregor." He said the word *animals* with a sneer and a delicate shudder that wiped the smile right off Gregor's face.

"So are we," he said, his voice hard. "So are we, Doe, but some of us are better animals than others. She told me what you did to her. She told me about the tests, about the torture. So what does that make *you*?"

Doe stared at him for a long, long, moment, scrutinizing Gregor's face from his one visible eye. "I am a patriot," he finally said. "A protector of our way of life and of our race."

"Hitler thought the same thing."

There was another silence, long and cavernous, broken only by the beeping of Gregor's heart monitor, now wildly erratic.

"Lay down with dogs and you get up with fleas, MacGregor," Doe said softly, one hand wrapped in a death grip around his cane. He stood slowly, in obvious pain, favoring one leg and leaning heavily on the cane. "This is not over. This is only the beginning. Do you think these creatures will be content to live forever in the shadows? Our information indicates there are hundreds of them, possibly thousands. Maybe more; there's no way to be sure. But consider what will happen if they one day decide humans have been at the top of the food chain too long. You've seen what they can do." He patted the pocket of his suit jacket where he'd stashed the phone. "And that is only the tip of the iceberg, as they say. They're killers, MacGregor. They're monsters. Their potential to cause harm to the human race is unlimited. Consider that carefully when you think of the reasons you are protecting your lady friend."

He moved slowly to the door. One of the gendarmes saw his approach through the glass and swung the door open for him, holding it as he drew near. He paused in the doorway and looked back at Gregor over his shoulder. His gaze was ghostly pale and eerie as it rested on him.

"You will have plenty of time to ponder all that in prison, I'm sure."

The hospital door was the kind that had a magnet on it, so when pushed against a wall with another magnet, it stuck and held. Agent Doe passed through the door, but because the gendarme had pushed it all the way open it stayed that way, and Gregor was able to overhear a few words as he made a phone call from his cell phone, walking slowly away from his room and down the hall.

"Thirteen here. Section Thirty. Put me through to the chairman. Yes, I'll hold."

He rounded a corner and limped out of sight.

Crouched in the same spot she'd been hunkered down in for the past six hours, Eliana's legs were numb.

The tall, turreted red brick structure long ago used as a furnace and chimney to burn waste during construction of the Eiffel Tower was dwarfed by the tower itself, but on its little grassy hill directly beside it, provided a perfect, unobstructed view of the surrounding area. She'd be able to see D's approach from any direction.

She'd be able to see if he brought anyone else with him.

Twilight conspired to paint Paris in a romantic glow perfectly unsuited to her mood. It was cold but lovely; light snowfall tinted the sky all silver and haze and muffled the roar of the cars and buses on the Avenue Gustave Eiffel to the south. The lights from the port on the river Seine snaking by to her north sparkled in long, winking waves off the dark water. The tower itself was awash in gold light from the thousands of lamps that illumed it, a spear of brilliance that rose straight up to the heavens from the heart of the greatest city in the world. Everything was beautiful.

Everything was awful.

She hadn't been able to string together a single coherent thought all day. After the catacomb police—a separate division of the force tasked with clearing out the cataphiles on a regular basis—had finally left and the dark corridors were once again silent, Eliana had gone aboveground and wandered the streets for nearly a full day, blank-eyed and hollow. She didn't see the pedestrians Christmas shopping who thronged the quaint, cobblestone lanes and chic boulevards; she didn't care when she bumped into them and they skittered away, frightened by whatever look must have been on her face.

She could guess it wasn't friendly. Or particularly sane.

Curiously, she couldn't feel it. She wasn't feeling much of anything at all, except a tightness in her chest that wouldn't go away and a growing tension in her muscles that felt like a winch, constricting. There was a black cloud over her head, descending, engulfing her in darkness.

A tingle of recognition snapped her head around and pulled her out of the morass she'd been lingering in with an abrupt jolt, as if she'd been plucked from quicksand. Her heart began to pound. Her hands began to shake.

Because there he was. Walking slowly toward the ticket booth at the south foot of the tower marked *pilier sud*, queuing up like a regular person with all the other tourists, there he was, dressed identically to her in boots and black leather, a long coat with the collar turned up against the wind.

He stood out like a lion in a flock of dozing lambs.

A lion that carried, in one large hand, a small parcel wrapped in butcher paper.

Instead of the elevators with most of the tourists who preferred to avoid exposure to the cold, Demetrius took the narrow stairs in the south leg of the tower to the second floor. She watched him as he ascended through the open latticed network of iron until he reached the wide platform. Moving with slow deliberation, shouldering through the thinning crowd who darted aside to let him pass like a school of minnows fleeing from a shark, he went to the railing and looked out. He closed his eyes and stayed that way for several moments, unmoving, his coat flapping and billowing around his spread legs, while Eliana watched from her hidden perch, feeling as if her heart would claw itself out of her chest.

Then he turned his head, and across the distance his eyes found hers, as if he knew where she'd been hiding all along. As if he'd felt her watching.

She stood. She stared back at him. Even with the distance, everything was between them, palpable as rain, bright as summer sunlight. His gaze was heat across her face, his dark eyes burned, just staring at her, not a muscle moving, searing intensity and the crackle of invisible flame. She felt pinned by that look, the stark longing in it, the hunger, raw and real. She felt powerless against it, and suddenly a wave of anguish rose up in her, a longing to match his own, and she had to look away.

She turned to the stairs of the old chimney and began the winding descent down.

When she finally stood beside him on the second-floor observation deck and looked out over the vast, sparkling majesty of Paris on a winter evening, she had herself a little bit more under control.

D didn't turn to look at her. He acknowledged her presence with a slight bow of his head, but that was all. They stood silently for a while, shoulder width apart, listening to people chatter in a dozen different languages, feeling the wind on their faces. Up here it was colder, the flakes of snow more biting than below.

"I have this memory of you," he said in a low, solemn voice, still looking out over the city. She kept her own eyes on the view as well as he continued to speak. "You were sixteen, maybe seventeen. It was the winter solstice, and everyone had gathered in the great room after the ceremony in the temple for the feast of Horus."

Eliana closed her eyes, remembering the cavernous great room they used on festival days, the smell of hot beeswax and incense, the glow of a thousand candles in iron braziers and chandeliers, the shouting and laughter, the heat of so many bodies pressed close together at long wooden tables as they feasted on suckling pig and roasted beef and delicacies from all over the world, brought in to celebrate the birthday of their patron god.

"You were sitting with your father and brother at the main table. I was standing behind you, against the wall, on duty as always. The *Bellatorum* had drawn straws to see who would stand guard during the feast, and I was the one who drew the short straw. It didn't matter anyway; the rest of them had women they wanted to go to, but I had no one, so I didn't mind.

"But you kept glancing back at me, with this worried look on your face. I didn't dare look at you, but I couldn't figure out why the king's daughter, the precious *spem futuri*, would be paying the slightest attention to me."

Hope for the future: that's what the elders had called her, though she never knew exactly why. He went on and his voice grew softer, tinged with something close to awe.

"Then when your father was distracted by someone who'd come to speak with him, you called one of the servants to you and passed her something. You whispered something to her, and I could tell she was trying to talk you out of whatever you'd said. She looked very angry, but you insisted, and eventually she made some pretense to walk by me and hand me what you had given her."

D glanced down at her. "An apple. You gave her an apple to give to me."

"You looked hungry," Eliana whispered. "You looked miserable, standing there alone. I thought you might like something to eat."

"You kept sending her back, every chance you could, too, didn't you? Pieces of fruit and cheese, bread, candy."

"You wouldn't eat any of it. I had to keep trying until I found something you liked."

He turned to her, staring down at her with all the intensity from before still burning in his eyes. "I liked *all* of it. I couldn't eat it because I was on duty, but I liked all of it. You were the only person in that room of thousands who gave a damn about me, the one person with the least reason to. You were kind to me. You noticed me. You *looked* at me, when everyone else went to great lengths to avoid doing that. Everyone else was terrified of me, and yet you never were. You smiled at me whenever we passed. You said hello." His voice dropped. "You said my name. Said it like you liked it… like you liked *me*. That was the beginning for me. Just like that apple, you were this perfect, delicious thing I hungered for with every cell in my body, but was forbidden to eat."

"Stop," she whispered, frozen in place. "Please. Stop."

They stood like that, not moving, a foot apart, his gaze searing, hers trained on some spot in the distance because she couldn't bear to look at him.

Finally, around the lump in her throat, she said, "You brought it?"

From the corner of her eye she saw him nod. She held out her hand. He placed the paper-wrapped bundle in it, and she closed her fingers around it, hard. "I'm leaving now."

"If—afterward—I'll be at the same place I brought you after the police station. The safe house. You remember where it is?"

She glanced at him, her eyes as freezing as the wind. "I won't come. Don't wait."

He said nothing, just looked at her. She slowly backed away, clutching the parcel to her chest. "I won't come," she said again, but he didn't even nod.

Eliana turned and fled.

TWENTY-THREE
Yes

D did wait, though. His heart gave him no other choice.

He managed to convince Celian and Lix and Constantine that it was best if they left the safe house and returned to Rome. She'd mistake their presence if she did show up, and leaving the Roman colony unprotected for longer than absolutely necessary at a time like this was unthinkable. Celian had brought the journal and gotten him the few days' reprieve from the confederate colonies that he'd petitioned for, and all he had left to do was see if she would come to him. In only a few hours, his reprieve would expire.

If Eliana didn't come, he would turn himself in to the Council and let Fate have its way with him. If she didn't come, nothing mattered anyway. Let them do their worst.

In the meantime, he'd have to find some other way to convince them she was innocent of her father's treachery. Because he knew she was. He knew it to the marrow of his bones.

He was pondering that, lying on the couch in the dark subterranean living room of the safe house with his hands behind his head, staring at the ceiling, when he heard a noise.

The sound of knocking, angry and loud.

Two stories above, in the furnished and unused house that hid three levels of secrets below, someone was pounding on the front door.

With his heart in his throat, he leapt to his feet, took the stairs four at a time, and ran, literally flat-out *ran* to the door. He didn't even bother looking through the peephole to see who was there—he didn't need to. Now he smelled her, he *felt* her, and his blood scorched through his veins like liquid fire.

He threw the door open, and a shock of cold night air, sucked in from outside, hit him in the face.

Then a fist hit him in the face.

"You knew!" Eliana shrieked, loud as a banshee. "You knew and you never told me! *How could you not tell me?*"

She'd caught him square in the jaw with the punch. It snapped his head around but didn't budge him, but now she gave him a shove with both hands on his chest that actually set him back on his heels. He stepped back to regain his balance, and she was on him before he could, another fist in his face, wild swinging punches that were all fury and no control, snarling like a lion sprung from a cage.

He spun away and managed to kick the front door shut before she was on him again, pummeling him, cursing him.

He thought she might actually cause more damage to herself than to him, so he grabbed both her wrists and pinned them behind her back.

"Settle!" he growled, having to use a surprising amount of his strength to keep her contained as she twisted and fought him. He pulled her up hard against his body and said it again, into her ear. After a second, she did settle, though her breathing remained wild, her heartbeat loud enough for him to hear in the silence of the room. She leaned her head against his shoulder.

"You knew," she panted, halfway between a whisper and a sob. "You knew all along what he was really like, and I…I… God, I was so blind. I was so *stupid!*"

He let go of her wrists and crushed her to him. Her body shook against his. "You weren't stupid. He didn't let you see. He controlled all of us. There was no way you could have known—"

"But you did!" Her voice rose to a near-hysterical pitch. "And you didn't tell me! I went around in ignorance for my entire life, and you knew he was a monster, and I'll never forgive you for that, never, never, *never!*"

She broke away from him and began stalking around the room, wild-eyed and enraged. She tore a picture from the wall and threw it with a scream across the living room. A lamp met her wrath next, destroyed in an explosion of flying ceramic and splintered wood as it was slammed against a desk.

"Everything was lies! My entire life—*lies!*"

She was beyond herself, beyond rational thought, beautiful and violent like an avenging angel, a whirlwind of destruction. D watched her tear through the room with a calm that didn't match the circumstances, because he knew on some basic level that this was exactly what she needed at this moment. She needed to get it out. All that rage and betrayal and pain needed to come out.

He'd fix the house later.

She swung around and faced him, breathing raggedly, fixing her livid black gaze for the first time on his face. "Did you kill him?"

His answer was swift and emphatic. "No."

She took a step closer, eyes unblinking. "Did you and the others plan to take over the colony?"

"No."

Her lips twisted. She took another step closer. "Did you make fun of me, behind my back? Knowing what I fool I was?"

He took a step toward her, and his voice grew dark. "No, Eliana. No."

"How can I believe you? How can I believe anything? I can't trust anyone—I can't even trust myself. I can't trust my own judgment!"

She was distraught, working herself up again, her voice rising where only moments before it had fallen. He closed the distance between them, took her roughly by the arms, gazed deep into her eyes, and said, "You can trust this."

And he kissed her.

She didn't fight him as he expected. She melted against him with a low sound in her throat and her mouth soft and warm against his. Her arms came up around his neck, and his arms wound around her body, and they stood there like that, tasting each other, fused together in the darkness of the ruined living room, wreckage all around them. It went on and on until his breath was short and his body was hot and inflamed. His fingers dug into her hips, her waist, her bottom. Beneath the cold leather she wore, her flesh was soft and yielding, and imagining it beneath his fingers, beneath his tongue, made him moan into her mouth and kiss her even harder.

She broke away with a horrified look. Then she slapped him, hard and stinging, her palm open against his face.

He sent her a ruthless smile that drained the color from her cheeks. He said, "You know what you need, baby girl?"

She stared at him, breathing erratically, her dark eyes huge.

His smile grew darker. "You need to fuck it out."

She blinked, huffed a little astonished breath, and said, "I really hate you, you know that?"

"You hate me because I'm right." He fisted a hand into her hair at the base of her neck and pulled her back to him. He kissed her again but she struggled, she pushed against his chest. He ignored it and deepened the kiss. It was hard and rough and greedy, their teeth clashing. She bit him on the lip, and he tasted the salty tang of his own blood.

"That's it," he whispered against her mouth, and kissed her again, deep and demanding.

She pulled back and stared at him for a beat, panting, a strand of blue-black hair caught at one corner of her mouth, a smear of his blood across her full lower lip.

Then she leapt on him.

He caught her around the waist as she locked her thighs and arms around him, kissing him with an unchecked hunger that took his breath away. He staggered, knocked into a table, the desk she'd broken the lamp over, until finally one leg hit the couch set in the nook of the bay window and he dropped them both to it.

She rolled on top of him, tore off her leather jacket, tore off his shirt, tossing it all to the floor in between frantic kisses. She was as starved as he was, heat and shadow above him, their ragged breathing matched. He shoved a hand beneath her shirt and cupped one breast in his hand, pinched her hard nipple, and thought he would come when she moaned into his mouth and rocked her pelvis against his. She sat up and moonlight from the paned window above them painted her ghostly pale, banded in checkerboard shadow. She looked down at him, her cheeks flushed, her lips red with his blood and swollen from his kisses, and his breath caught in his throat.

He'd never seen anything so lovely.

She lifted her arms and pulled her shirt over her head, dropping it to the floor. She wore a black lacy bra, delicate and feminine, which ripped apart like tissue paper when he took it between his teeth. He cupped her breasts in his hands and nuzzled them, reveling in her little mewls of pleasure as his lips closed over one nipple and he drew it into his mouth.

He was rock hard, throbbing, and she ground against him, her hips rocking in a rhythm that had his heart pounding. She bent down and took his earlobe between her teeth, and he thought his heart might fail when he heard the words he'd longed for so many years to hear.

"Yes," she whispered, her lips against his ear. "Demetrius, *yes.*"

He flipped her over so her back was on the couch and she was stretched out beneath him, squirming. He shucked off her boots and peeled her out of her pants and then she was naked, gloriously naked except for a pair of panties. He leaned down and kissed her again, sucking on her lips, running his hands all over her heated skin. She felt like silk and velvet and nothing else he'd ever touched, and he was so greedy for her he didn't know if he was bruising her or hurting her, and he couldn't stop himself in any case.

He was on fire. Every cell, every muscle, every nerve. Every breath he took was fire.

He kissed her breasts, drew his tongue down to her stomach, bit her there because she was so tender, her flesh so soft. She shivered and arched against him, her hands at his shoulders, nails clawing into his skin. He put his face between her legs and inhaled deeply and she gasped, shocked.

She gasped even louder when he shoved aside her panties and slid his tongue inside her.

Musk and salt and woman, already soaking wet, she tasted incredible. They moaned at the same time. His erection twitched in his pants, aching to be set free.

He pressed her thighs apart and began to stroke her with his tongue, licking and sucking greedily, swallowing her taste, learning what made her twitch and what made her moan. He slid two fingers inside her, and she arched sharply against the couch and cried out.

"Not yet, baby girl," he whispered, stroking his thumb where his tongue had just been. "You don't get to come yet. Not until I say so."

"No, no, no." She squirmed beneath him, and he put his forearm over her stomach and pressed down. He lowered his mouth to her sex again and began, slowly, rhythmically, to lick her. He slid his fingers in and out, and his other hand fondled her breasts, pinched her nipples.

"Please, oh, please," she gasped, arching. Her hands clutched at the couch, the back of his head.

He drew back and blew a breath over her swollen lips, smiling when she shuddered and called him a dirty name.

He freed himself from his pants and rose above her with his leathers falling open to his hips, balancing his weight on an elbow. He leaned down and kissed her, hard, letting her taste herself on his lips, teasing her with the head of his shaft which he held in one hand, stroking himself back and forth across the wet entrance to her sex. When he ignored the demands her hips were making, she reached down and grasped him herself.

He gasped, stilled, closed his eyes at the feel of her hand on him.

"You're huge," she breathed, running her thumb over his head. The shaft pulsed and strained in her hand. He leaned down and suckled her breast again, nudged himself against her, groaned when he felt her heat and tantalizing wetness against the most sensitive part of his body.

"Oh, baby girl, flattery will get you everywhere," he whispered, and shoved inside her.

He did it hard and he did it fast because he wanted to shock her out of her head, he wanted her to forget, to focus only on him. She cried out and arched against him, her breasts crushed against his chest, her body a taut bow from the couch to his. Before she could recover from that, he began to thrust, long, slow rolls of his pelvis that sank him deep inside her, stretched her wide.

She moaned his name, guttural, her thighs tightening around his waist. He lowered his head again and bit her on the neck, drowning in the feel of her, his beautiful rebel bare and wild beneath him. Her hips met his every thrust. Her nails dug into his lower back.

He growled something in Latin, he didn't know what, his immersion in her was so total.

"Please, please, please, oh, please," she begged in a broken whisper, nearly sobbing.

He stilled, framed her face in his hands. "Not yet." He was panting, biting her lips, her jaw, her throat, little nips that left a trail of pink behind on her skin. Her shoulder was a delicious heat against his tongue. "Not yet."

She writhed beneath him, demanding, clawing at his back, but he put a hand on her hip to still her. "Open your eyes," he whispered. "Look at me."

She did as he commanded, and they lay like that for a moment that spun on and on, breathless, beautiful, their eyes locked together, noses inches apart, the only sound their labored breathing, their bodies drenched in moonlight.

He flexed his pelvis, once, and her lids fluttered. "Open," he softly warned and ran his thumb across her lower lip. "Keep them open for me." He reached down and hooked his thumb around the back of her knee, slid her leg up around his waist, and then thrust deep into her again, watching her face. She made a sound, a low moan of pleasure, and slid her hands up his back, but she kept her eyes trained on his, unwavering.

"Yes," he whispered. "Like that, baby girl. Keep your eyes on me."

She nodded and bit her lower lip as he thrust again, slow and deep, burying himself to the hilt. Still buried deep inside, he made a slow circle, grinding against her pelvic bone, and she gasped, then moved with him, matching his slow, small motions with her own, building the pleasure to a gathering, exquisite peak.

Looking into his eyes, she whispered his name. Her fingers dug into his shoulders.

He slowly righted himself to his knees, pulling her along by her hips, and then he took the leg hooked around his waist and slid it up over his shoulder. She opened to him even more, and he took advantage of it by sliding partly out of her and then slowly all the way back in; he could not go any deeper.

On the very edge of orgasm, she shuddered. Her chest rose and fell in short, uneven bursts.

He stilled because he knew how close she was, and he didn't want this to end. Not yet. He knew as soon as she went over, he'd go over with her. So he ran his hands over her breasts, her hips, turned his face to her leg and kissed a trail up her calf to her ankle, resting against his shoulder, and all the while she kept her gaze on his, half-lidded and shining with heat.

He reached down and stroked her, just above where they were joined, the nub of her sex wet and swollen beneath his thumb. Her mouth opened but no sound came out. Her hips jerked.

"No," he warned, and she answered with a groan of objection. She made a move as if she was going to push out from under him, but he captured her wrists in his hands and pinned them over her head, pushing them down into the cushion. She protested, but he crushed his lips against hers and thrust hard and she moaned, bucking beneath him, biting his lip. Panting, his threadbare control unraveling with every movement of his body, he pulled away to look at her and found her staring right back at him, her brows drawn together, her face contorted in something like agony.

"*Please.*" So urgent it was nearly a plea, she said it in a hoarse, broken whisper, and it unwound the very last shred of his will.

He took both her wrists in one of his hands and cupped her face in the other. He let his hips take over, a primal thrusting that had her moaning her approval beneath him, but he never took his gaze from hers.

"Yes, Ana. *Now.*"

And because her eyes were open he saw the exact moment it happened, when she tipped over the edge and went spinning beyond pleasure into ecstasy, even before her body clenched and arched beneath him. Even before her eyes slid shut and her moans formed the shape of his name.

"Baby girl," he whispered, fierce, fire licking along every nerve ending, electricity snapping up his spine. "My beautiful girl…"

When it hit it stole his breath and sent shockwaves through his body. Pleasure, so acute it was almost pain, rocketed through him, and he jerked, spilling himself into her, growling and grunting like some kind of wild animal, his face against her neck, the beast inside him screaming, *Yes yes yes yes yes! Mine! All mine!*

Her nails in his back. Her heart against his chest, pounding wildly. Her body, plush and warm beneath him. The moonlight sketching shadows on the walls and the leafless winter tree in the yard and the car passing by, unseen, somewhere far off in the night. Every little detail of the moment seared itself into his memory like a brand so that even beyond his shaking and hoarse panting and the roaring in his ears, he was aware on some level that this moment would stay with him for the rest of his life.

Sometime later, when their breathing had slowed and their heartbeats returned to normal, she murmured his name. Dazed, he raised his head and blinked at her, and she stroked his face, smiling.

"This doesn't change anything," she whispered, her eyes soft. "I still hate you."

And he had to laugh. Weakly, his forehead pressed against her chest, he laughed.

TWENTY-FOUR
Holocaust

It was a long, long while before they spoke again.

At some point in the night he'd carried her to the bedroom, but she wasn't awake for that. She wasn't awake when he tucked her into his side and pulled the blankets over them both, his arm around her, holding her close. His body was heat and muscle at her back, his legs drawn up behind hers. She came awake only when she became aware of his deep voice at her ear, murmuring something that ended with "…forever."

"What?" She blinked into the unfamiliar room. A candle in a little saucer on a dresser across the room sent up a merry flame that flickered and spun, a warm yellow spot of light in the darkness.

He pressed his lips to the back of her neck. "Nothing. Go back to sleep."

But she couldn't, now that she was awake and the ice storm was howling inside her head again.

He was right, before. His crass way of informing her exactly how she needed to "work" things out had been successful. He had taken the sharp edge of her anguish and dulled it with his body. And for that she was profoundly grateful, because she wasn't sure she would have survived the night without it.

The pain of betrayal is a physical thing, a deep, hollow ache in the pit of the stomach that spreads to every organ, corrosive and black. If it spreads to the brain it might even cause insanity, and Eliana was convinced she was halfway there already, but she couldn't possibly care less.

Her father had been her idol. She knew on some level he was damaged—she'd seen the way her kin sometimes shrank away from him, blanched and trembling; she'd seen the dark, dangerous light that sometimes crept into his eyes—but she also knew he was gentle and good to her, and though he was within his rights by law to put Caesar to death because he was unGifted, he'd spared his only son. From all accounts, he'd loved her mother and treated her well, he protected the colony, he gave them whatever they needed in order to survive, to thrive.

But he was a monster. Dominus might even have been the devil himself.

What she experienced reading the pages of his journal was a terrifying descent into the mind of a brilliant, evil creature, a creature with no soul and no conscience but with a very healthy appetite for vengeance and an iron resolve to turn the planet into his own personal playground. The serum she thought he'd created only to help half-Bloods survive the Transition had a far more sinister application.

Holocaust.

He was going to use it to wipe out the human race. Their dream of peaceful coexistence had been a lie written in the sand, meant to pacify her until the tide turned and reality washed all those dreams of peace away in a tsunami of blood and tears.

Oh, there would be a few left. Enough for slaves who would cook and clean and breed the next generation into servitude. But their entire gene pool would be wiped out within a few generations.

She realized then what the elders meant when they called her *spem futuri*, hope for the future. She realized with sudden, horrible clarity what he'd meant when he'd told her the night he died, "Your young will rule the earth."

She was the last of Dominus's Bloodline, a line that had sired kings for a thousand generations while humans were still busy making cave paintings. A line that until the failure of Caesar had produced males far more Gifted than any of their kind. A line that would go extinct without new heirs to continue it.

Her heirs. Her and her brother's.

Her father had planned to breed them together.

That's why he never insisted she marry though all of their kind married young. That's why he didn't kill Caesar when it was discovered he was unGifted. Dominus didn't believe a female could rule, and the colony would never accept an unGifted Alpha, so the crown would skip a generation and go to the male child she would produce with her brother. An heir and a spare, because Dominus intended to ensure there would be more than one male offspring from the joining of his two children.

He intended to be there. He intended to *watch.*

The horror of it, the horror of all of it, had made her literally sick. She retched in a corner of her room at the abbey until there was nothing left for her stomach to eject except bile.

And Silas, trusted family servant before her father died, trusted friend after, had known about all of it.

His guilt was implicit. Promised a special place in the new world kingdom imagined by her father, Silas had improvised quite ingeniously when her father had been killed. He'd used her Gifts to get the money to develop the serum and stockpile weapons, used her ignorance to keep her under control.

One cold, undeniable fact remained, however; it was Demetrius she'd found standing over her father's dead body, not Silas. Demetrius who'd been holding the gun.

Demetrius who claimed he didn't kill Dominus but refused to say who did.

And something else left her feeling as if her blood had turned to ice water. There was still the possibility, however small, that Silas had told her the truth about the *Bellatorum.* That Demetrius not only killed her father but knew of his plans for the serum beforehand and saw an opportunity to seize power far greater than just assuming control of a single colony. He somehow knew about Mel and her husband. What if he knew other things?

What if he knew everything?

What if, as Silas had said, D's Gift of Foresight had shown him a future in which *he* ruled the world?

It couldn't be discounted, no matter how much it sickened her.

She didn't want to believe it. She wanted to believe what her body told her, what her heart told her. She wanted to melt into his arms and let his heat surround her until she spiraled down into forgetting, into not caring what the truth might be.

But she wasn't that girl. She cared about the truth. The *Truth,* capital T. And she was going to get it, even if it killed her.

"You're not going back to sleep," D gently accused, stroking a hand up her arm. She made a noncommittal noise and then sighed.

He seemed to sense her inner turmoil, because his hand drifted over her shoulder, and he spread his palm flat over her chest, feeling for her heartbeat. It thudded against her breastbone, fast and erratic. She could almost hear him thinking.

But he stayed away from anything too dangerous and said with a hint of a smile in his voice, "So you're the invisible girl now. Pretty impressive, I gotta say. How'd that happen?"

"By accident, I guess. I mean, living underground in permanent shadow all my life I never really had the need to hide from anything..." She faltered, and D's arm tightened around her. Eliana guessed they were both thinking of what she had to hide from now. "Anyway, the first time I saw the sun was the day we left Rome. We were walking through an olive tree grove in Mazzalupeto when the sun rose over the horizon, and I was so scared I hid in this ruin of an old barn, in a horse stall. When Mel came to look for me, she couldn't see me, even though I was standing right there, not three feet away." She closed her eyes, remembering Mel's panic and her own. "It took awhile to learn to control it. At first, I had to be scared

in a bed in which they'd slept after making love. She still felt like killing someone, only now she wasn't sure if it was him, herself, or the next person she laid eyes on. Maybe all of the above.

Irritated now, she said, "How did you find me? At the catacombs?"

Another low chuckle. "Dreamt it."

Her heartbeat accelerated—did that mean he knew exactly where the rest of them were? About the abbey, the entrance from the catacombs?

D stirred behind her, nuzzling his face into her hair. "Followed a bunch of guys into the catacombs from a manhole cover hidden behind a crypt in the Montmartre Cemetery. Had no idea where I was going, just got a starting point, and then they showed up."

To hide her sigh of relief, she pretended to yawn. "And those assassins that are after me…who sent them?"

"I told you, they're a group assembled from the other four colonies—"

"But who sent them, exactly?"

There was a pause, and then D said, "The Queen."

"Queen?" whispered Eliana, astonished. "They let a woman lead?"

"There have been others before," he murmured, tightening his arms around her. "Marie Antoinette, Cleopatra—"

"No!"

"It's rare, but when it happens, an *Ikati* Queen is far more powerful than any male Alpha. They say this English Queen can Shift to anything she likes, not just panther—"

"No!" Eliana sat up in bed, the sheets rucked around her waist, and stared down at him. He stared back, shadowed eyes and corded muscle, heat rising from his naked body in delicious, heady waves. He reached up and swept his thumb, very lightly, across the apple of her cheek.

"Whether they realize it or not," he murmured, gazing into her eyes, "women are always more powerful than men. The only reason males are bigger, physically stronger, is because we're made to protect and serve the more valuable sex: females. Nature bestowed on them the ability to conceive and give birth. Only females grow life inside their bodies. Only females bring it forth. They're made to create and nurture life. There's nothing more powerful, more *necessary*, than that."

Heat suffused her cheeks. When his look became too intense, too probing, she dropped her gaze to the covers. *We're made to protect and serve.*

"And now this powerful, can-shift-into-anything Queen wants me dead."

"They haven't read your father's journal. They don't even know it exists, so what you read is for your eyes only. But they know he was the leader of the Expurgari, and they believe you—or your brother—have taken his place. They've been hunted by this group for hundreds of years, their leaders have been killed, their people tortured. She herself was apparently tortured. You know now what Dominus planned to do…we've been on the brink of war with them since you left. They don't fully believe none of us knew what your father was doing, but we've given them enough concessions to hold them off. For now."

So because of her, the entire Roman colony was in danger. But why, if the *Bellatorum* wanted to keep peace with the other colonies, hadn't they let the Queen read her father's journal, thereby proving Dominus's guilt and their own innocence?

The serum, a little voice inside her head whispered. *They want it for themselves.*

A chill ran over her skin. She pushed the thought aside, but it kept swimming back in front of her eyes, resolute, damning. She watched D's face carefully as she asked, "Do they know about the serum?"

His expression did not change. His voice remained neutral. "No. As I said, they never read your father's journal, and as far as the *Bellatorum* know he never developed it, just tested it successfully." His eyes narrowed. "Why do you ask?"

She stared at him for a long moment, her stomach in knots, her heart beating frantically against her breastbone once again. "Why wouldn't you show them the journal, Demetrius? If it could prove you'd done nothing wrong?"

His head tilted to one side on the pillow. Something changed in his face. A hardening, a slight closure that indicated an awareness of her distrust, perhaps, she couldn't be sure. There was a new hollowness in his voice when he spoke, a new tightness around his mouth.

"I've read that journal, Eliana. Over and over and over, searching for some kind of clue as to where you might have gone when you left. There wasn't any, of course, but what your father planned for you...your brother...all the terrible things he did and wanted to do...that's not something I would ever let anyone read. That's not for anyone else's eyes. Especially *theirs.* The other colonies can take their threats and go straight to hell—I'd never let you be humiliated like that. Never." His voice darkened. "There are some secrets we should take with us to the grave."

Oh, what those words did to her. If she was conflicted and confused before, this was the cherry that topped her triple-scoop ice cream sundae of confusion. The words seemed sincere, but the tone he spoke them in and the look on his face seemed…what? Odd, if nothing else. Protection is the motivation he claimed, *her* protection, and she might have believed it, but for that final sentence that held a strange ring of prophecy. *There are some secrets we should take with us to the grave.* And for that oddness in his manner, which might have been hurt at her disbelief.

Or might have been *fake* hurt, intended as a diversion.

Killers enjoy creating diversions, Eliana.

Even now, Silas's voice echoed in her head.

She slowly lay down and pressed her back against the hard expanse of D's chest, avoiding his eyes, avoiding the sudden tangle of flying chicken feathers that were her thoughts. "I see," she whispered, not really seeing anything at all.

He lay behind her, tense and silent, until he let out a breath and dragged the blankets up around them and pulled her tight against his chest once more. They lay like that for a long time, until she felt his breathing grow more regular, his heartbeat more slow. When she was certain he was almost asleep, she whispered into the dark, "Do you really believe males are made to protect and serve females, or is that just pillow talk?"

He mumbled something, and she turned her head to hear him better. "If you hadn't already worn me out, woman, I'd serve you right now." He chuckled softly. "But it'll have to wait 'til morning. I'll show you exactly how a male should protect and serve his female in the morning."

But when morning came and D stretched and opened his eyes, the bed was empty, the sheets beside him cold.

Eliana was already gone.

TWENTY-FIVE

Crazy Person

Mel awoke with a start to the feel of a hand clamped over her mouth.

She bolted upright in bed, a scream strangled in her throat, but let out a huge sigh of relief when she saw it was only Eliana, crouched beside her bed in the dark, pale and wild-eyed with a finger to her lips like some kind of mute, blue-haired ghost.

"What are you doing, crazy person?" Mel hissed. "You scared the hell out of me!"

"Get dressed," came the urgent, whispered response. "Wake up the others and go down to the Tabernacle and wait for me. I'm going to go see Alexi—"

"Alexi? What? You *are* crazy, E, it's the middle of the night—"

"We need to get everyone out of here, and Alexi's place is big enough for all of us." Her voice darkened. "Most of us."

Mel stared at her, long and hard, through the shadows of the room. She smelled Eliana's fear and rage like the sour tang of food left out too long in the sun, and something else that surprised and pleased her in equal measure: the dark, spiced musk and masculine power that could only be Demetrius.

"Tell me what's happened. I know you saw Demetrius."

Eliana started like she'd just jumped from behind a door and yelled, *Boo!* Mel said, "I spent a lot of time crying on his shoulder, sweetie. I remember exactly what he smells like. Spill it."

Resigned to the fact that Mel wasn't going to budge until she knew what was going on, Eliana let out a frustrated sigh and dragged her hands through her hair. She sat beside her on the bed and closed her eyes. "He brought me my father's journal. I read it, and it was…bad." Though a whisper, her voice grew hard, harder than Mel had ever heard it. "It was worse than bad. Your hunch was right, Mel. Nothing is what it seems."

Mel didn't know what to say. The way she was talking, just the way her lips shaped the words, gave her pause. "And… and Demetrius? What about him?"

Even in the dark, Mel could see the heat suffuse Eliana's face. She chewed on her lower lip, then, in a motion so out of character it spoke volumes, hid her face in her hands.

Mel clapped her own hands together silently in a pantomime of glee and bounced up and down on the mattress. "Oh my God, you *did it!* Tell me *everything!*"

From behind her hands Eliana scoffed, "What are you, twelve?"

Mel was too busy swooning to care about the acid in her tone. "Was he gentle? Was he rough? Was it over too fast? Oh my God, I hope it wasn't over too fast, he's soooooo hot—"

"He told me he loved me."

This was said with so much pathos, such bleak hopelessness, she might as well have just said, *He told me to burn in hell.* She stared at Eliana, who had dropped her hands to her lap and was staring at them as if she'd never seen them before, as if her own ten fingers were strangers, not to be trusted. Something huge and ugly seemed to be growing in her, an evil, cancerous blossom of rage or despair, flowering slowly to life.

"Why is that bad? What exactly happened?"

Weary, weary, Eliana answered, "He's lying about something, Mel. I don't know if it's that, or if it's about what really happened the night my father died or what, but he's hiding something." She paused, said more softly, "They know about the serum. I can't help thinking…"

"No," was Mel's instant reply. "Not him."

Eliana turned her head and looked at her with the kind of glassy eyes you see on victims of natural disasters or wars—shell-shocked, darting. Haunted.

"That's what I thought about my father. That's what I thought about Silas, and my brother, too. Apparently being a good judge of character is not one of my Gifts. In fact, I think we can safely say I suck at it."

Mel took her friend's cold, cold hand and squeezed it in her own. "I can assure you *my* perceived awesomeness is bona fide, however, so you're not totally hopeless." The ghost of a smile was her only answer before Eliana looked away. "What did you find out about Silas?"

Eliana's face hardened again. The expression reappeared too quickly and easily, as if it were a default setting and every other look that crossed it just a transient visitor. It was eerie, and Mel didn't like it at all.

"He's a traitor and a liar, and very soon he's going to become well acquainted with the edge of my sword." She hissed a breath through her teeth, then stood and looked down at her with those glassy, shell-shocked eyes. Only now they burned. "That's why we have to get you and the others out of here, quickly and quietly. Don't take anything, just get everyone rounded up as fast as you can."

"A traitor?" Mel whispered, hand at her throat. She stood, the bare stone floor a jolt of cold against her bare feet. "What has he done?"

Eliana stood and went to the wooden chest at the end of the bed where Mel kept her clothes and began rifling through it. She pulled out a jacket, pants, shirt, boots, and threw it all on the bed. "What *hasn't* he done, is the real question. If you looked up the definition of evil incarnate in the dictionary, his picture would be next to it. Right next to my father's. Get dressed."

Mel pulled on the clothes as fast as she could, her heart pounding like a hammer. "So what are you going to do?"

"We're going to get you all someplace safe, and then Silas and I are going to have a little *talk*."

"Or," said a voice from the doorway, "we could talk right now."

Eliana and Mel spun around in unison, and horror descended on her, thick and hot, like a blanket dropped over her head.

In the darkened doorway stood Silas, robed in black. Radiating menace, he looked back and forth between them with a little unnerving smile, fingering the gun in his hand.

The gun he now raised and pointed directly at Eliana.

TWENTY-SIX
A Yearning So Sharp

This is what love was to the warrior Demetrius:

Years long as lifetimes of yearning, a yearning so sharp and terrible and unrelieved it was like a sword of heated steel permanently embedded in his chest. Love was stolen glances and smothered hopes and vivid, illicit dreams that taunted him upon waking and the cold, unrelenting fear of discovery that followed him, sly and clinging like a shadow, during all his days and nights. Because if, somehow, the love that burned inside him like a swallowed sun was discovered by the wrong person, his life would be ended as swiftly as two hands clapping, and the flame that had sustained him for as long as he could remember would be snuffed out like a wick between wetted fingers.

That was bad but bearable. He was a soldier, after all, born and bred for battle. His life was not expected to be long, and, forbidden from taking a wife, it was also expected to be loveless. Even any children he sired from the anonymous encounters with the *Electi* or *Servorum* or random human women would never know him as a father; he was a sperm donor, nothing more.

He knew it. He'd hardened himself to stark reality long ago.

What was not bearable: If somehow, against all odds, his feelings were returned…his beloved would die, too. Only it would not be swift. It would be gruesome. It would be used as a lesson to all, an assertion of power so blatant its meaning could not be misunderstood. A spectacle that would make even the most fearsome of warriors tremble in dread as they watched.

Disobedience equaled death. Taking a woman above his own caste equaled death. Taking the king's *daughter*—slow, torturous, *epic* death. There was no other way for a soldier of his station and hadn't been in millennia.

So love—aside from being pointless—was agony. Love was a soul-eating demon. Love was the most terrible feeling in the world.

A close runner-up: despair.

He was filled with that now. Dead cold where love was red hot, despair clogged his throat and choked him as if he'd swallowed handfuls of crematory ash.

She'd come to him and they'd fought and made love and even slept together—simple things, *normal* things he'd wanted for years—and yet he'd awoken alone, and the simple fact of the silent room and the empty bed beside him filled him with such despair he wondered for a breathless, bottomless moment if this is what hell might be like. Not flames and screams and lakes of fire, but anguish and hopelessness and misery wound together like a wretched braid, cinched tight around his neck in an invisible noose from which he would hang for all eternity, alone.

D had no Foresight to anticipate this. His sleep had been deep and silent.

Slowly, painfully, he rose from the bed he and Eliana had shared together, his heart like a wild thing in his chest, refusing to settle. He'd told her the truth last night; he had no idea where her colony was, he'd just followed those laughing men through a silent graveyard and then into the winding bowels of the earth. He could go back there, he supposed, but what hope did he have to find her in the same place? If she wanted to be lost to him, she would be. She wouldn't go back to the same place. She might already be on another continent.

Or captured by The Hunt.

The thought sent an electric jolt of fear through his body, which was swallowed quickly by fury. *Damn* her. Damn her stubborn pigheadedness, damn her refusal to believe him when he said it wasn't him who shot her father. Okay, he'd concede it didn't look good, him standing over Dominus's corpse with a gun, but she should *know* that his word was his *oath*—

He stiffened. The hair rose on the back of his neck. He looked around the darkened room, listening hard into the silence.

Was that a scream?

He held still, breathless for a long moment, every nerve alert, every pore attuned to any noise, until—

No. It wasn't a scream. It was a *pulse*, an invisible push, palpable as a hand reaching out to shove him, which sent a shockwave of recognition through his body. It came again, fainter than before, but unmistakable.

D never dressed so fast in his life. Shirt, pants, boots, and blades, all of it donned without thinking, both ears attuned to the feeling that might come again at any moment, the vibration that would show him the way to find her.

Because it was her. He didn't know how, but he knew it was Eliana, and she was in trouble, and she needed him.

And because she was his life, his heart—his soul—he would find her. He *would.*

It thrummed through him like the bloodlust he sometimes felt after a kill, bright and blinding. In the sharing of their bodies, their breath, in the consummation of a love so long unrequited, his soul had fused to hers the way a grain of sand accretes to the nacre of a shell, and something else had been born between them. Passion had always existed, but tonight a pearl of something deeper had formed, permanent and unbreakable.

Possession.

She belonged to him now. He'd find her.

Not even death could keep him away.

TWENTY-SEVEN

Sock Puppet

"Demetrius," said Silas with a sneer, his handsome face contorted with anger. "Always this obsession with Demetrius. It's beneath you, my dear. He's nothing but the help."

Eliana felt frozen to the floor. She didn't have to look over at Mel to see she was frozen as well, her face reading white against the dark stone wall behind her, eyes wide and staring at the gun in Silas's hand.

"So are you," Eliana said calmly in spite of the blood roaring through her veins.

He clucked, disapproving, but it didn't faze him. Silas smiled, a malicious specimen that pulled his lips flat over his teeth, and took a slow step into the room. "Probably not smart to antagonize the man holding the gun. However, you are incorrect. I *was* a servant—and a loyal one, at that—but now I'm something a bit more elevated, wouldn't you agree? Your father's death created a vacuum, my dear, and as we all know, nature abhors a vacuum."

"My brother—"

"Your brother is a sock puppet." It was hard, abrupt, and possibly louder than he intended, because his glance flickered to the doorway behind him before it settled back on her. "Not only is he unGifted, he's a fool, unworthy of his position. Not even worthy of his *name.* Caesar, indeed. What a bit of wishful thinking that was! Didn't it ever bother you, Eliana, that you were the one in the family with the brains but you were never allowed to be...*anything*...because you were a woman?"

He took another step forward, and she and Mel took corresponding steps back. He seemed to be enjoying this, their shock and patently obvious fear. His smile grew wider and more excited by the second.

"I would have changed all that, you know. I would have let you lead beside me. We could have made a glorious team, you and I." His voice grew soft, while his eyes, ever dark and glittering, grew heated. "Unfortunately, I don't team up with *whores.*"

He'd heard everything, then. It didn't sting, him calling her a whore; it hardly even registered because she was too intent on formulating a plan for getting out of this that didn't include getting shot.

She backed away another step as he moved closer. "What are you going to do?"

"I?" he replied with feigned innocence. "I'm not going to do anything. You, however, are going to kill your best friend."

What?

She wasn't sure if she spoke it aloud or not, but Silas answered as if she had, smiling his chilling, rabid smile all the while.

"Terrible how you just couldn't adjust to our new life here. You never really got over the sudden death of your father, did you, my dear? Everyone could see how much it affected you. How depressed you'd grown. It won't be much of a surprise when you finally go over the edge and kill your best friend, and then yourself. So tragic, really. Such a waste of life when we were on the verge of such momentous things."

It hit her with sudden clarity, and she knew he'd be able to pull it off because he had a way of making people believe him. Mel's dead body, her own beside it, his gun in her hand…she saw it with the detail of a photograph. How her kin would react with shock, how Silas would comfort them, how he'd use their grief to his own advantage and make them rely on him even more. He would kill the two of them, and no one would be the wiser to his treachery.

His callousness, his cunning, sent a surge of rage unlike anything she'd ever known singing through her body. There was a thrum of light and noise inside her, a sound like a thousand wing beats, a gathering that incinerated her fear and honed everything to a pure, crystalline sharpness.

Then Silas changed his aim and pointed the gun at Mel.

TWENTY-EIGHT
Katachi

Literally translated, *budō* means "way of the warrior". It is more than a fighting system, though it is certainly that. An ancient samurai practice from Japan, *budō* is a way of life, a philosophy. It is an art.

The art of killing.

As with all art, there is beauty in it.

Eliana had practiced ritual katas at dawn for years. It was a way of assimilating herself to a new life, and a way of acquainting herself with the sun. For a girl born and raised underground who'd never glimpsed the sky until she was twenty-three years old, the sun had been a terrifying thing to her, a monster of heat and light suspended against a canvas of blue so vast it had no edges but bled off into infinity. She cried the first time she saw the night sky, but the first time she saw the sun, she cowered in terror.

She was a child of darkness. For her, daylight was where the bogeymen lurked, not in the cool, comforting arms of the night.

So she practiced in the garden of the ruined abbey at dawn, the rhythmic, calming flow of steps and turns and sweeping moves with her sword, until the rising sun was no longer a source of fear and her mind had sharpened, her spirit deepened, her muscles hardened from the girlish softness they once held. She practiced with a *budō* master who challenged her concentration and her form, and she became his best student. She never achieved katachi, however, that state when the repetitive mold-making of katas becomes perfection of shape and all training is aligned so you arrive at the calm center of yourself, weightless and magical, where movement is effortless, everything is slowed and crystallized, and you see with perfect vision what is all around you.

In this heightened state, even the intentions of others become visible. Their light moves ahead of them just before they do, and you can see what they are about to do.

In the hairbreadth of a second just before Silas turned his gun toward Mel, Eliana, at long last, achieved katachi.

It was instantaneous and unthinking. From one heartbeat to the next, she *became.*

A surge of energy crackled over her skin, and a wave of power, huge and pulsing, lit through her like dry kindling bursting into flame. Her sword was at her side, sheathed in its leather scabbard and hidden beneath her long coat, and then it was in her hand, sweeping up in a long, perfect arc with no more effort or concentration than it takes to inhale.

There was no conscious decision; there was only action and reaction. The clarity of her vision supplied her muscles and nerves with everything they needed to move lightning-fast, invisible.

She lunged forward, and her feet never even touched the ground.

In a single, clean stroke, she lopped off Silas's hand at the wrist.

Still clutching the gun, it went flying into the air in a spray of crimson and landed with the flat thud of meat against the wall. It fell to the floor, and the gun popped out from between the lifeless fingers and clattered against the bare stone.

He staggered back, stunned, mouth gaping, as blood from his severed hand began to run from the wound in a trickle, then a pulse, then a flood. He clutched his wrist with his other hand and backed away, then turned and ran, trailing blood in a long, dark smear behind him.

Then as quickly as she became, Eliana *un*became, and all the light and magic drained out of her as if a switch had been flipped.

She sagged against the doorway Silas had just been standing in and let out her breath in a gust. There followed a silence so profound it seemed as if the Earth itself might have stopped spinning on its axis and everything on it—every person and bird and insect, lacking gravity—had been flung out into the far reaches of space.

Then an odd sound, liquid and gurgling, broke the unnatural stillness.

Choking.

She whirled around and—no. *No!*

Mel was lying on her back on the stone floor, coughing up blood.

The bottom fell out of the world. Eliana dropped her sword and dropped to her knees beside Mel, her hands fluttering over the spreading stain in the middle of her shirt. It couldn't be, it couldn't be, she hadn't heard the gunshot, she hadn't seen the flash of light, it *couldn't be*—

But then she smelled the sharp, lingering scent of gunpowder in the air, registered the swiftly widening pool of red around Mel's shoulders, and she knew that it could.

"Ana." Mel's eyes were wild, rolling, one hand clutched at the front of her coat. "Ana." It was almost lost beneath the horrid burble of the crimson tide that spilled from her mouth and bubbled from her nose. Her lung must have been punctured. She was drowning in her own blood.

"Help!" Eliana screamed, turning to the door. "Someone help us!"

There was the sound of fleet footsteps and murmuring voices, and then faces appeared in the doorway, blinking away sleep. One of them rushed forward—Bettina, gray-haired and nimble-fingered, she'd been the midwife back at home. She'd helped to bring Eliana into the world long ago, had been her mother's devoted friend and something like a mother figure after she died. She'd refused to stay behind when they'd fled the catacombs, insisting her place was at Eliana's side.

"Sweet goddess Nephthys," she whispered, bending over to inspect Mel, "don't take her yet." She tore open Mel's shirt to reveal a gaping wound in the center of her breastbone, pulsing blood. She cursed in Latin, tore a strip of the sheets from the bed, and pressed it to Mel's chest.

Mel's head lolled to the side. She coughed, and a spray of blood splattered Eliana.

"What happened?" It was Aldo, one of Caesar's most devoted followers, a young male with wide shoulders and a brash, in-your-face attitude that had rubbed her the wrong way for years. He followed Caesar like a dog follows a trainer with bacon in his pocket.

"Silas shot her!"

Aldo recoiled in disbelief. "Why? What's going on? What did she do?"

Eliana wanted to kill him for that. "We have to get her to a hospital!" she shouted, her control beginning to crack. Everything was beginning to slip sideways, and the shape of the room was beginning, just slightly, to blur. She bit down hard on her tongue to focus herself and tasted blood, but she blinked back into control.

If she had a panic attack now, she'd be utterly useless. And Mel might die. And Mel *could not* die.

"No hospitals, Eliana, you know that," replied Bettina, very softly. She met the woman's gentle black eyes. "We can't take the risk."

She read it in Bettina's eyes. It wasn't only the risk, it was the way of their kind since time immemorial. Survival of the fittest meant exactly that; all who were no longer fit due to age, injury, or infirmity were left to die. It was a hard, cold truth they all lived with, a law of nature that until now had seemed brutal but just. Necessary, even. Strength was their one advantage over all the other species. Only the *Bellatorum*, who were too valuable to her father to be discarded if injured, were given medical attention, trained to do it themselves. Everyone else was SOL.

Shit out of luck.

Her face hardened. No. Not this time. She would do whatever it took to keep Mel alive.

Mel writhed on the floor between them, wracked with a spasm of pain. Her mouth was working, and Eliana leaned down to hear her. "Mel," she whispered, "Mel, you're going to be okay, we're going to figure something out—"

"Demetrius." Mel choked it out, the veins on her neck straining. "Take me to Demetrius. He'll know what to do."

At the mention of his name, Bettina drew back, horrified, and there were more murmurs of shock from the doorway where more of the others had gathered. She noticed that Aldo had disappeared.

"What is she saying? *Demetrius?*" hissed Bettina. "Why does she mention the King Slayer?"

That's what he was to all of them now, the King Slayer, the one who'd plotted to kill Dominus and take over the kingdom for himself. Better the devil you know than the one you don't, and Silas had done a wonderful job of convincing them all that Demetrius wouldn't hesitate to slay them all if he ever found them, or if they ever returned to the catacombs.

He'd convinced her best of all.

"Help me lift her," she said to Bettina, ignoring the question, and then she turned to the gathered group, gray-faced and wide-eyed in the faint light that was just beginning to show through the cracked window. "Geo." She looked at a tall, young male standing near the door who had a talent for hot-wiring anything electrical. "Find a car. Fast. Bring it to the south entrance. We'll meet you there."

Geovanni nodded and disappeared.

From the others that were left, there were murmurs of confusion, Silas's name repeated in shocked whispers, the shuffling uncertainty that accompanies a scene of such jarring unreality. No one knew exactly how to react or what to believe.

"Silas is a traitor." Eliana, voice throbbing, looked at each of the gathered group in turn. "He's a liar and a murderer and cannot be trusted. He shot Mel and would have shot me, too, if I hadn't stopped him."

Eliana jerked her head toward the corner, to the bloodied stump of Silas's hand lying still near the gun it had been grasping, and some of the shocked whispers turned to cries of disgust. "Everyone go to the Tabernacle and wait for me until I get back. Has anyone seen my brother?"

"He went out, my lady," came a small voice from the back of the gathered group.

They turned aside and Lina stepped forward, the youngest of them all, a girl with glossy black bangs and a shy smile who'd fled with them from the catacombs because her highborn father had informed her that very night she'd be wed to the son of another highborn family the day she turned fifteen. That boy had been known to enjoy torturing stray dogs he captured by taping their muzzles shut until they suffocated to death.

"I saw him leave, and he hasn't come back; I've been up since he left."

"All right. Never mind. Get to the Tabernacle as quickly as you can and wait for me there, all of you. I'm going to get Melliane some help, and then I'll come back for you. We can't stay here anymore."

More shocked whispers and shuffling, but no one challenged her openly. In the absence of Caesar or Silas, she was the temporary head of the colony and they had to do what she said…at least until one of them came back.

"Bettina, please, help me." Eliana slid her arms gently beneath Mel, who sagged against her, heavy, but then someone stepped forward. Fabrizio—universally called Fabi—was a gentle giant, one of the *Castratus* charged with guarding the harem in his former life, now charged with doing all the cooking for the tiny new colony; it was his eggs she took such pains to avoid eating every morning. How she wished that was the least of her problems now.

"I've got her," Fabi rumbled, his deep voice like a balm on her shredded nerves. He lifted Mel easily in his arms as if she were a child and cradled her body against his chest. Mel moaned, her eyes shut, her lips a terrifying shade of pale blue. The pulse at the base of her throat had grown faint.

"Hurry. *Hurry,*" Eliana urged, moving to the door and waving him along. The gathered group parted to let them pass, and Bettina followed close on her heels, pressing the bloodied remnant of sheet against Mel's chest to try and stanch the bleeding as they quickly made their way through the echoing, arch-ceilinged common room toward the back of the abbey. Behind them, the whispering crowd began to split apart into smaller groups, conferring.

Eliana didn't give herself time to wonder how many of them would actually be waiting for her when she got back. She had her own loyalists, but so did Caesar.

So did Silas.

To get to the back of the abbey where the main gates opened to the only access to a road, they had to pass through the old church, dusty and gloomy in the half-light of dawn that spilled down from the windows carved into the white-pink stone far above. There was an iron door set into the east wall in a niche adjacent to the altar. It was rusted and padlocked, but Eliana gave it a vicious kick and the lock and chain crumbled. The door swung open with an eerie groan, and they pushed through, heading for the weed-choked gravel driveway.

And Geo was already driving up.

Relief surged through Eliana, and she ran toward the black SUV, waving frantically, her boots crunching over the gravel. The headlights blinded her for a brief moment, and she lifted a hand, shading her eyes against the glare, and then pulled up short as her vision adjusted and her heart threatened to crawl right out of her throat.

It wasn't Geo behind the wheel of the SUV.

It was Demetrius.

He wasn't smiling.

TWENTY-NINE
A Hollow Platitude

D wasn't surprised to see the look of stunned horror on Eliana's face when he drove into the tree-lined gravel drive of the abandoned abbey. He wasn't surprised the pulse had led him here. He'd long ago learned to trust his instincts, and the instinct had led him directly to this shadowed, abandoned place near the Sacré-Coeur as certainly as a homing beacon or the rays of a lighthouse cutting through fog.

What he was surprised about was Melliane. A bloody, unconscious Melliane, cradled limp in the arms of the *Castratus.*

He slammed the Range Rover into park and jumped out. "What happened?" he barked, staring hard at the *Castratus.* Fabi—he remembered past his shock. The man's name was Fabi.

It quickly became apparent Fabi remembered him, too.

He snarled, "One more step, King Slayer, and your head will be auditioning for a spot on a new body!"

Fabi glared at him with open hostility. He was big and solid, and D thought he'd give him a run for his money if he tried to get to Eliana, who Fabi had edged in front of in a display of protectiveness that had D clenching both his fists and jaw. The midwife Bettina, beside him, was even more openly antagonistic. She hissed a warning through her teeth the minute he stepped from the car and hadn't let up since.

"I didn't kill Dominus," he said flatly, looking only at Bettina and Fabi. Eliana, he saw from his peripheral vision, was trying to decide what to do. She was fingering something under her long coat that he suspected was a sheathed sword. He put up his hands in a show of surrender and lowered his voice, letting the tension ease out of his stance. "I'm no danger to any of you, but I can help Melliane—"

"You won't *touch* her!" Bettina stepped forward, hands curled into fists, hissing like a snake. "And if you think for one second we believe anything you have to say—"

"It's not me that's been lying to you—"

"So says the King Slayer, a man of his word, no doubt!"

"Now is not the time to argue about this—"

"Go back to whatever rock you crawled out from under—"

"Bettina—"

"Don't you *dare* speak my name!"

D was beginning to lose his patience. He watched a rivulet of blood roll down Melliane's bare arm, gather at the tip of one finger, and then fall and land with a soft *plash* to the gravel at Fabi's feet. "I'm not here to hurt you—"

"No, you're just here to kill us!"

D shouted, "If I wanted you dead you'd already be dead, woman!"

Bettina's jaw closed with a *snap.* Eliana stepped forward, put a hand on her arm, and stared at D with a strange look, dark and unfathomable.

"He's right, Bettina, Fabi. If he wanted us dead, we already would be."

Bettina shoved back a stray tendril of gray hair that had escaped from her bun and wrapped her arms around herself, glaring murderously at him. "Why are you here then, if not to kill us? What do you want?"

Instantly, D's eyes cut to Eliana.

She stared back at him with that odd look, one hand flexed open at her side, the other wrapped around the hilt of the sword she'd been fingering moments before. It pierced him, seeing the defensiveness in her stance, that hand on her weapon. It cut him to the bone. Their eyes held, and though her face did not change, he thought he sensed a great tumult inside of her, a silent battle she waged against herself.

"Fabi," Eliana said finally, very soft, her gaze level with his, "put Mel in the back of the car."

Bettina gasped and Fabi took a step back. Still soft, still watching him, Eliana said, "He knows how to remove bullets, I can vouch for that. Mel trusts him. And we can't take her to a hospital. So he's our only option."

She sounded as if she wished she had another option—*any* other option—and the knife in D's heart sliced deeper. *Mel trusts him.*

Not her. She didn't trust him. She wouldn't defend him against their accusations.

Why should she? he reminded himself. She didn't know the truth because he hadn't told her the truth. He *couldn't* tell her, because he swore a Blood oath to defend his brother Constantine to the death, which—very, very unfortunately—included tragic misconceptions, present circumstances included.

Like truth, honor is only a hollow platitude if it can be discarded when personally inconvenient.

Or soul-killing, heartbreaking, I'd-rather-die-than-have-to-do-this *hard.*

"Put her in the back of the car, Fabi," Eliana said again, still with that terrible softness, that eerie look on her face. She said it again, sharper, when Fabi didn't move, and the big male finally drew in a breath and relented. He stepped forward, bristling, the cords in his neck standing out, his eyes flinty cold.

"I swear on Amun-Ra, Ma'at, and Sekhmet, if any harm comes to her while under your protection, I will dedicate my life to killing you. I will hunt you down like a dog, and you will die like one, too, with my sword buried in your gut and your lying tongue torn out and flung to the buzzards. Your name will be cursed for a thousand generations, and your soul will writhe on the end of Osiris's spear for all eternity."

He spit on the ground to seal the curse and then turned his black glare back to D, whose brows had risen.

To hide his anger and gripping indignation at the sheer crookedness of the entire situation, D lightly said, "Very elaborate, Fabi. Well done." He gave a short, mocking bow and then rose and pursed his lips. "Do they even have buzzards in France?"

Fabi growled, and Eliana pushed past him to open the rear door of the SUV. She jerked her head—inside, *now*—and Fabi gently laid Mel on the backseat, murmuring to her when she moaned as he adjusted her legs.

When it was done Eliana turned and gave Fabi and Bettina swift, hard hugs. "Gather the rest, as many as will come, and take them to the Tabernacle," she murmured. "I'm going to send Alexi for you. You can trust him. Follow him and wait for me." Her gaze flickered to D. "You'll get word from me within a few hours. If for any reason you don't hear from me, assume the worst. Take all precautions. *Evanesco,* like we planned, but find a new place. Someplace Silas—or anyone else—won't think to look."

Evanesco. Vanish. D stood there, his heart like a stone in his chest, listening while his beloved gave instructions on what to do in case she disappeared, never to return.

In case *he* disappeared her.

Sick. He felt sick. He felt like breaking something. He felt like *dying.*

They murmured together for a few more minutes, plans and assurances and parting instructions. Then with a final glare from Fabi and a teeth-baring snarl from Bettina, the two of them moved off the way they'd come, back toward the stone bulk of the old church, hulking and silent in the hush of early morning. Eliana watched them for a moment, worry pinching her face, and then she turned and looked at him, grim and resolute as if she were going off to face a firing squad.

"Let's go."

Then she opened the passenger door to the SUV and jumped inside.

Moving slowly, feeling a little shell-shocked, D got behind the wheel and shifted the car into reverse. As they backed down the gravel drive, he said through clenched teeth, "You should know by now I'm not going to hurt you, Ana."

She stared out the window into the rising light of morning. She exhaled slowly through her nose. She muttered, "Demetrius, just looking at you hurts me."

After that, he didn't much feel like talking.

Alexi answered on the first ring. His "What?" was an annoyed, sleepy mumble.

"I need your help." Eliana tried to ignore the murderous glare D shot at her from the driver's seat.

There was a moment of silence followed by the rustle of fabric. She imagined Alexi sitting up in bed, sending a look to the unmoving bump beside him that would be his latest conquest. "Anything," he said, low. "What do you need?"

A sigh of relief escaped her. She hadn't been entirely sure of him, but Alexi sounded instantly alert and sincere. Thank God for trustworthy ex-boyfriends. "I need a safe place to stay."

"Eliana," he breathed, "yes. You can always stay with me."

"It's not only me," she equivocated. "There are a few people I have to…hide. Just for a few days until I can make other arrangements."

She heard his confusion in his voice. "What, like your family? What happened? Is everything all right?"

"No," she answered honestly. "Everything is the opposite of all right." She swallowed, suddenly hoarse. "Mel's been shot," she whispered.

"Shot!" he exclaimed. In the background, she heard another sleepy mumble, this one female. He covered the phone with his hand and muttered something sharp, then got back on the line. "What's going on, Butterfly? Where are you?"

Eliana cleared her throat. "I need you to go to the Tabernacle, Alexi. There will be people waiting there for you, ten, no more than fifteen—"

"Fifteen people! What the—"

"Just get there as fast as you can and bring them back to your place and try not to let anyone else see you. I've got to get Mel some help, but I'll come as soon as I can, and I'll explain everything then. Okay?"

Another silence, this one weighty, then the sound of Alexi exhaling through his nose. "Okay. But this isn't going to be like the usual Eliana where you come and go like the weather and I'm left wishing I had a barometer. I'll go get your people, and you can stay with me as long as you need to, but as soon as you get here you're going to have to level with me. You'll have to tell me what's going on, Eliana. And I want the truth. Deal?"

"Deal," she whispered miserably, because she really had no other option. She hung up after saying good-bye and looked back at Mel, white and silent on the backseat of the car. She reached over and took her hand, feeling for a pulse. It was there, but weak.

"How far?" she asked D without looking at him.

"Close." It was clipped and hard. She glanced over to find him staring in cold fury at the windshield. They were going so fast the streetlights flashed by in a near-solid blur, headed back to the safe house where D had medical supplies and anesthesia.

"Who is he?"

Eliana let out a breath. She knew D would have easily been able to hear the entire conversation, sitting so close with his stupid, heightened hearing. He'd have heard the inflection in Alexi's voice. The emotion...the *intimacy*.

"He's a friend."

"What kind of friend?" he growled. His fingers wrapped around the steering wheel so hard they turned white.

"The *best* kind—one I can trust," she shot back, because who the hell was he to interrogate her? Mister I won't answer your questions, but you have to answer mine? Mister no, of course I didn't kill your father the crazy lunatic, but oops, yeah, I was kind of standing over him with that pesky smoking gun?

He didn't speak again, but his rage was palpable. The final minutes to their destination seemed interminable, but they finally pulled into the driveway and a garage door slid open and shut behind them on silent, well-oiled automatic tracks.

D burst from the car as if it had coughed him out, opened the rear door, and gently picked up Mel in his arms. She was deathly pale and limp, blood soaked through her shirt and splattered all over her neck and arms. Without looking in her direction, he snapped, "Hot water. Fresh towels—you'll find them in the bathroom on the second level. Bring both to the third level bedrooms. Then stay the hell out of my way."

He disappeared through the garage door into the house, leaving Eliana standing alone beside the car, shaking, blinking back tears, and swallowing the sob that was caught in her throat.

THIRTY
Stop the Bleeding

Aldo knew where Caesar was even if the others had no clue. Their lord and master was where he always was when he went missing—with some degenerate whore.

This time it was two.

Though it was well after sunrise when most people were getting ready for work or making breakfast for their families or doing one of a million everyday things one does in the early morning, Caesar's whoring adhered to no particular schedule. Neither did his drinking, or his predilection for unprovoked cruelty. One of the women lay stunned on the bed, bleeding profusely from the nose, the other cowered in a corner of the room, sobbing, and Caesar himself was standing in the open doorway, naked, reeking of alcohol fumes.

"You *dare* disturb me?" he said imperiously, glaring in black-eyed, thin-lipped displeasure at the sight of Aldo, who'd knocked on the door of room 9 where the terrified clerk had told him Caesar checked into when Aldo had snarled a warning right into his face. He'd gone to Caesar's other favorite haunt first, a seedy hotel a few miles from this one, but that place had been closed due to a murder a few nights before that the police were still investigating.

Caesar drew himself up to his full, imposing height. "What the hell do you want?"

He wasn't quite slurring. Not quite. Aldo wished he would cover himself; it was unnerving to be standing so close to a naked man. Especially a drunken, naked *king*. He could reach out and tap him on the breastbone if he wanted.

"Your sister, my lord. She's told the colony Silas is a traitor and a liar. She's rounding them up and preparing to leave for—somewhere. I don't know where. I thought you'd want to know."

Aldo had never seen anyone sober so quickly. Caesar's eyes, slightly glazed only seconds before, sharpened and took on a sinister, predatory edge. He stiffened, hissed in a breath.

"Where's Silas?"

"I don't know, my lord. I didn't see him, but your sister… it appears your sister has cut off one of his *hands*."

Caesar recoiled with a gasped exhalation. He recovered, muttered, "That bitch," then snapped, "Wait for me," and slammed the door in Aldo's face.

It wasn't two minutes before he reemerged, dressed and radiating anger, his eyes a deadly, flat black Aldo had seen on many, many occasions, right before something terrible happened.

Caesar said, "Let's go."

They found Silas in one of the old outlying buildings on the abbey property, a crumbling, mossy stone structure that had once been used as an infirmary. Seated on an upended milk crate next to a small fire he'd built in the middle of the bare floor, he was shirtless, sweating profusely, and pale as a sheet. On the arm missing a hand, he'd tightly tied a strip of fabric—torn from the discarded shirt that lay at his feet—just above the elbow as a tourniquet. How the hell he'd managed to tie a tourniquet with one hand was a mystery Caesar had no intention of unraveling.

Below the tourniquet the flesh had turned a waxen, lifeless gray. There was a trail of blood from the door to where he was sitting, and a crazy splattered pattern of crimson drops zigzagged back and forth across the bare room, a visual map of where he'd been since he arrived. Smoke from the little fire gathered against the vaulted wood ceiling was funneled off toward rotted gaps in the boards in long white fangs.

In Silas's one remaining hand, he gripped a dagger.

"My lord," he greeted him, stronger than Caesar would have thought for someone missing an important body part. But Caesar couldn't look at Silas's face, because the bloody stump of his missing hand held a hypnotic, almost sensual appeal. He couldn't wait to get a better look at it. He and Aldo moved closer.

"Your sister," Silas began, but Caesar interrupted him.

"Yes, I know." He finally met Silas's eyes. "She's always been unreasonable."

Silas exhaled, strangely relieved. "She's seen Demetrius—"

"Demetrius!"

"She slept with him, my lord. I overheard her talking with Melliane—"

"*Slept with him!*" Caesar screeched, eyes bulging. The world ground to a halt.

"He's somehow convinced her I've been lying to her, to all of you—"

"*SLEPT WITH HIM!*"

Caesar felt as if a bomb had detonated inside his body. He couldn't see. He couldn't speak. He couldn't move. He was frozen with horror and a fury so gargantuan it felt nuclear. She'd slept with the vermin who'd murdered their father. Slept with him. *Slept with him.* It kept slapping against the inside of his skull like a trapped bird.

"Kill her," he choked out. Silas and Aldo stared at him. The fire crackled merrily, sending up feathers of glowing ash and whorls of smoke. "We have to kill her! She's a traitor! She's—she's a *whore*!"

Slowly, Silas smiled. It was more of a grimace the way his lips peeled back over his teeth, but the blood was pounding through Caesar's veins and there was a booming in his head and he couldn't see much of anything anymore because the room had started to spin.

Slept with him. Slept with him.

He imagined it in stunning, Technicolor detail, their naked bodies pressed together, the warrior's big hands all over her bare flesh, her wanton moans and their sweat and the squeaking of a mattress beneath them—

Aldo caught him as he staggered sideways. Caesar shoved him away and began pacing to and fro with his hands clenched in his hair to manage his sudden dizziness, the acid burning his lungs. Hatred glittered through him, consuming, and Caesar had never wanted to kill something—*hurt* something—so much in his entire life.

He swung around and spied the dagger in Silas's hand. "What are you doing with that dagger, Silas?" he hissed, prowling forward.

Silas's face hardened. Sweat dripped from his chin. "I have to stop the bleeding, my lord."

Caesar looked at the dagger, at the fire, and understood in a flash that was like a thunderbolt. He yanked the dagger from Silas's hand, held it over the fire until the tip glowed white hot and his own fingers were blistering, and then spat at Aldo, "Hold him." He looked back at Silas, and his smile was like an animal's, rabid and wild. "This is going to hurt."

A man walking his dog down a quiet residential street six blocks away heard the screams. He stopped and crossed himself, peering up. A mother walking her two children to school heard it, too, and so did the fruit vendor and his wife setting up their stall on the Rue de Marquet. Many more heard it as well, the long, eerie shriek that seemed to descend from the sky itself, echoing off walls and trees and buildings before being cut off abruptly, leaving all to wonder just what had caused such a terrible noise.

Or who.

THIRTY-ONE
It's Only Food

Eliana had no idea how much time had passed. It might have been minutes, it might have been hours. It might have even been centuries for all her dead heart could tell.

She was slumped against the wall in the long corridor on the level of the bedrooms, her arms resting on her bent knees, staring down at the fibers of the black carpet, seeing nothing. Demetrius had been inside the room with Mel since they arrived. She'd brought him hot water in pans and all the towels she could find, then left him alone as he'd asked. Her last sight of Mel had been of her still, pale body lying on the bed, Demetrius leaning over her with a scalpel in one hand.

She would die. Eliana was sure of it. She'd lost too much blood. She would die.

Her fault. Her fault. So much blood and chaos and the unending, nearly unendurable agony of living with half-truths and twisted lies that passed for their sad reality. And what was the point of it all, really? More and more and more years of living on the run and hiding from still more people she once thought were her friends and family. More dragging days and endless nights, hoping for a future that would probably never come, more betrayal, more assassins, a future of living in the open with another species that seemed to prefer her dead, or—worse—caged?

The answer was: there was no point. It had all been a pipe dream, a castle built in the sand. Emptied of the dreams that had sustained her for so long, she felt gutted. She felt hollowed out.

The door cracked open. Eliana's head snapped around. She staggered to her feet.

"Well?"

Demetrius looked as if he'd gone down to hell to do battle with demons, and lost. His face was strained, his shoulders were hunched forward in an attitude of defeat, and there were dark smudges of blue under his eyes which, to her great horror, reflected the defeat in his posture. The utter lack of hope.

"You should sit with her," was his cryptic response, and then he brushed past her and walked slowly up the twisting stairs to the level above.

No. Her heart began to pound it out like a drumbeat in her chest. *No. No. No. No.*

She went into the room and had to bite her lip to keep from sobbing.

There was a pile of bloody towels in one corner, gruesomely vivid, pans full of now cold water that had all turned red pushed against the baseboards along one wall. A tray of bloodied instruments lay on a dresser near the door, and Mel's ruined shirt hung from the back of a chair, tossed there in an obvious rush. And Mel was on the bed, still, silent as a corpse.

D had cleaned her and washed the blood from her face and arms, and he'd covered her up to her neck with a sheet and folded her hands over her chest. She was peaceful and ghostly pale, and if she wasn't already dead, she looked as if she soon would be.

On the white sheet just at the center of her chest was a tiny spot of red.

She sank down beside the bed and took Mel's icy hand in her own. "I'm sorry," she whispered. "I'm so sorry."

Mel didn't answer. She didn't move. The long dark plait of her hair had come undone and lay bedraggled on the pillow, wisps like eiderdown from the softest underbelly of a black swan. With shaking hands, Eliana unwound the braid and ran her fingers through the strands, tidying them, brushing them smooth over the pillow until they lay in a glossy fan all around her head. She was barely holding herself together, and only because she thought Mel would be horrified if she could see her face, all screwed up and red with the effort not to cry. She knew she'd tell her to snap out of it and grow a pair, and then she'd laugh her wonderful, witchy laugh at what a sissy she'd turned out to be after all.

Eliana thought maybe she should pray, but all that came out of her mouth was a plea instead. "Please. Please, Mel. Don't leave me. Don't die. Please don't die."

But Mel's pale lips formed no encouraging words, and her bluish lids stayed closed, and finally the dam broke and Eliana dissolved into tears. Her body was wracked with sobs, and she gave herself over to it, kneeling at the bedside with her face pressed to the mattress, Mel's hand beneath her forehead, her cold, cold fingers getting wet with tears.

Time passed. Her tears slowed, then stopped. Her legs went numb. She slid from her knees and sagged against the bed, still clinging to Mel's hand, unwilling to let go. Her lids grew heavy and she let herself drift, and finally she fell asleep in the same spot, still holding Mel's hand.

And that's exactly how D found the two of them when he returned hours later.

He stood in the doorway a long, silent moment, watching with a heavy heart. He thought it might only be moments now; in fact, he was surprised Mel hadn't already passed into the arms of Anubis, god of the afterlife. He'd seen much stronger men than she bleed out and die from lesser wounds.

She was a fighter, but she wasn't immortal. There was only so much trauma a body could take. He'd done what he could—stopped the bleeding, repaired the ruptured artery and the torn flesh around the wound—but she'd lost too much blood, and he didn't have the tools to do a transfusion. What was left of his hope was quickly fading.

His gaze rested on Eliana. In sleep she looked younger and vulnerable as she never did when awake. Her face had lost all its hard edges, and her generous mouth was slack. She looked almost as peaceful as Mel did, except for the little line between the dark crescents of her brows. Slumped on the floor against the bed, her head bowed and her knees drawn up to her chest, she also looked cramped and uncomfortable, and he couldn't bear to see her like that. D drew a breath and moved forward.

He picked her up as gently as he could without waking her and disentangled her hand from Mel's. She made a little protesting noise but didn't open her eyes, and when he lifted her she rested her head against his chest and sighed like a child. When she wound her arms around his neck, he had to swallow around the tightness in his throat.

He carried her to the bedroom he thought of as theirs, though there was certainly no *they*, she'd made that perfectly clear. He laid her down, gently removed her boots, and unclipped her sword from her belt, putting it aside on the table beside the bed so she could see it as soon as she opened her eyes and know he hadn't tried to disarm her. He leaned down to pull the sheet over her, and when he straightened she was awake, watching him.

"Thank you," she whispered, eyes shining. "I know you did all you could. So…thank you."

He nodded. His heart did a strange, painful flip-flop inside his chest. He turned to go, but she sat up and caught him by the hand, and he looked back at her, arrested.

"Please. I…"

She seemed unable to go on. Her throat worked, and her face held the expression of someone entirely lost, or surrendered. Their eyes held, and hers were wet, beseeching. Her voice breaking, she said, "Demetrius."

She said his name like it meant something else, like it meant something *to her*, and he had to gather every ounce of his will not to fall at her feet, had to physically force himself to stand there with his face wiped clean of emotion because that's the way she wanted it between them, that's what she'd proven by leaving him in the middle of the night and putting her hand on her sword at the abbey and with the phone call to Alexi, whoever the hell that bastard was. And he knew, he knew on some level *exactly* who Alexi was, but he wanted to *un*know it. He wanted to burn it out of his mind.

But he couldn't. He wouldn't. Lying to himself was never his strong suit.

"You should get some rest," he said quietly. "I'll go in. I'll wake you in case…I'll wake you in a little while, and we can sit together with her. There's nothing else we can do tonight."

Her look was pure torture. He couldn't remember ever seeing such anguish on someone's face, and the fact that it was *her* face—her beloved, beautiful face—made it all the more terrible. He looked away, drew his hand away, but she tightened her fingers around his and used his hand to pull herself up so she stood in front of him, just inches away, staring up into his face. She was shaking, shaking and breathing as if she'd just run from across the city and looking *into* him as if she was trying to find some kind of answer to a question she hadn't asked.

What he saw when he looked back at her was someone whose soul was in cinders.

"I don't know how to love you," she whispered. "I don't even know if I can. I've spent years cursing your name, wishing you dead, and years before that infatuated with you and I hardly even knew you and almost just as soon as I began to get to know you, we—you—it was over and I was here and you were there and everything was so wrong—so wrong and I thought it could never be fixed but now I don't know what to think—I don't know what to do—I don't—I don't know anything…"

She blurted it out in one long, run-on sentence, breathless and broken and stammering her way through it until she petered out to silence at the end and stared at him, eyes huge and dark and haunted. D stood there in shock, stomping down his heart when it wanted to soar out of his chest, smothering the heat and the passion that rose in him like magic conjured from a sorcerer's spell, and he felt bathed in drenching golden sunlight, his arms longing to crush her to him, a sharp, sweet thrill running through him as if he were a live wire, conducting electricity through his veins.

Then he thought of Alexi, of her face when she'd called him, her palpable relief, and the sweet thrill turned sour. She might not know how to love *him*, but it certainly seemed like she knew how to love someone else.

Bitterly, hating himself because jealousy was a pettiness he'd once thought beneath him, he said, "It must be easier, having the kind of heart that lets you choose what you want. Unfortunately, I don't have that problem."

And he turned around and walked out of the room without looking back, each step fresh misery, every beat of his heart a shrill, clanging din in his ears.

That day spun by like a dream, shifting and hazy. Eliana slept, but when she awoke after dark she was still exhausted, staggering when she stood from the bed. Her body felt bruised and broken, and her heart felt like a little cold lump of coal inside her chest.

She went to Mel first, but she remained unchanged from when she'd last seen her hours before—pale skin and a faint heartbeat and almost imperceptible breathing. It was a miracle she was still hanging on, but life clung to her like a lover clings to a parting beloved, returning again and again for one final kiss before leaving for good.

She called Alexi; her people were safe. Bettina and Fabi had led seventeen to the Tabernacle; the rest had sided with Silas and stayed.

Seventeen of twenty-four. Better than she dared hope. Good thing Alexi's place was big.

She told him she'd see him soon and then rang off and sat staring at the wall, at a loss what to do next. Eat, she supposed, though she had no appetite. Food seemed like an unnecessary luxury somehow, and eating selfish. How could she eat now? How could she eat ever again?

Then she was ashamed for feeling sorry for herself. She had people who were relying on her. She had to be strong for them. She *would* be.

She dragged herself out of the room and down the hallway. At the top of the stairs she found a room obviously decorated by a man. The size of the television alone would have been enough proof, but everything else was utterly masculine, too. Angular leather furniture, a glass and metal coffee table, no plants or bric-a-brac a woman might have used to soften the starkness of all that charcoal gray and black of the chairs and sofas and walls. At the far end of the long room was an open door to a kitchen, with a dining room beyond.

And in a chair in the dining room sat Demetrius, perfectly still, staring down at a cell phone that lay on the table in front of him between his spread hands.

She swallowed, steadying herself, and stood straight. She took a step forward into the room, and at that moment, the cell phone in front of him rang.

But he'd noticed her movement. A fleeting look crossed his face, pain or something darker, she couldn't tell because it was quickly extinguished as he abruptly stood, ignoring the shrilly ringing phone and focusing all his attention on her.

A flash of déjà vu jolted through her. She saw him in a million fleeting memories, doing this exact thing. No matter what he'd been doing, no matter with whom, he always stood whenever she entered a room. Always. The realization made her chest constrict.

The phone continued to ring. Neither one of them made another move.

Whoever was calling was persistent, because her nerves were pulled to near-breaking when the ringing finally stopped. The sudden silence was deafening.

"You look tired," he finally said. His gaze moved over her face to her hair, which she hadn't bothered to comb and stuck up in crazy tufts over her head.

She didn't have the energy to feel defensive. "I slept."

His look narrowed. "When was the last time you ate?"

She thought about it and then shrugged. "Don't know."

He pointed to the chair across from him. "Sit."

"Demetrius—"

"Eliana," he said in a tone that indicated he wasn't tolerating any lip, "*sit.*"

She sat.

"Good. Now stay."

Her lips tightened. Stay? Like a dog? But she kept her mouth shut.

Cabinets opened and closed, the refrigerator opened and closed, the microwave hummed and chimed, liquid was poured into a glass. She didn't see any of it because she didn't turn around to look because she was *stay*ing—as instructed—put.

When he gently set the plate in front of her and she looked down, all her irritation vanished and she felt...she felt...gratitude. And wonder. Roasted chicken, garlic mashed potatoes, buttered green beans—she'd been expecting a frozen dinner, a few pieces of meat slapped between slices of bread.

"What's this?"

She looked up at him, but he'd turned away so she couldn't see his face. "There wasn't any food here. Had to go out and get some."

She looked back at the plate, perplexed. "You...cooked?"

His low chuckle drew her eyes to him again. He was leaning against the kitchen counter, arms crossed over his chest, one corner of his mouth quirked up in amusement. "You sound surprised."

"I *am* surprised. Since when do you cook?"

His face darkened. He glanced away. "Since I needed a hobby. To keep me from—to pass the time."

There was so much more to that, she felt it all underneath the simple words. But he glanced back at her, and his face had cleared.

"You should taste my sweet potato pie. It's killer."

Her mouth opened. It closed. It opened again and she said, with feeling, "Wow."

He gave her a true smile then, one that lit his face and his eyes and brought out a dimple in his cheek. She had to look away because she thought she'd never seen him look so beautiful. Tattoos and piercings and acres of muscles and a glower able to freeze lava that he wore more often than not and still he was always the most beautiful thing to her, masculine and strong and *real.*

She looked at the plate and was appalled to find it swimming in the moisture that had gathered in her eyes. He set silverware down and a glass of white wine and then sat beside her. She knew without looking his eyes were on her, intent.

"Eat," he said softly.

It's a terrible feeling, trying not to cry, pretending everything is okay and getting your face and body to cooperate. She almost had it together, too. Her hands were steady when she reached for the glass and her face was composed, but there was too much damn water in her eyes and a single tear spilled over and tracked down her cheek. She swallowed the wine she'd poured into her mouth anyway and set the glass back down, pretending like that bastard tear hadn't escaped, but of course he saw it. Of course he did. He was right *there.*

His voice so, so gentle, D said, "It's only food."

"No, it's not," she whispered. She didn't dare look at him. "You cooked for me." She said it again, emphasizing each word. "You. Cooked. For me."

"Well," he murmured, laughter in his voice, "had I known this would be your reaction, I would have done it years ago." He reached out and brushed his thumb over her cheek, wiping away the tear she'd tried so hard not to let fall.

She looked up at him then, and let everything go. It all showed on her face, everything she felt for him, all the anguish and confusion and pain and longing, and she knew he saw every nuance, every spark and hope and the bottomless depth of her despair because his breath caught and his smile vanished and when he looked back at her it was with sudden fierce intensity burning in his eyes.

"I…I…" She couldn't get it out, but it didn't matter.

"I know," he whispered, vehemently. "I already know."

"I'm so sorry." Her voice was barely audible, and his face was so close and she thought he might kiss her. And she wanted it, she could die with how much she wanted it, but he exhaled, a heavy, doleful expulsion of air, and she knew he wouldn't.

He withdrew. He stood up. He walked to the doorway and paused, then said quietly, "Eat."

He watched her until she took the first few bites. Then, satisfied, he turned and moved away, and it was all she could do not to throw the plate of food against the wall in frustration.

But she didn't, because as it turned out, she was really hungry.

And damn, but the man could cook.

THIRTY-TWO

Wily Old Dog

Money—a lot of it—is bulky.

Only so many stacks of bills can fit into suitcases, and only so many suitcases can fit in the back of a truck. Right about now, Caesar was wishing they'd rented a bigger truck.

Or opened a bank account.

Obviously they couldn't have, however, because large cash deposits tend to invite the curiosity of certain legal entities, whose curiosities they could not afford to pique, so they'd been forced to stash it all in the catacombs, like rats plumping a nest. Eliana had been almost too efficient in her moneymaking endeavors, because moving all this cash quickly was proving to be an unforeseen problem.

Stupid bitch.

He sighed, watching Aldo and one of the others who'd stayed behind—men, all of them, because only a moron… or a neutered male in Fabi's case, which didn't count… would follow a woman—try to shove one final black leather case into the back of the rental van. They succeeded against all odds, and Aldo drew down the rolling metal door and latched it.

"Good," said Caesar with a nod. "Now all we have to worry about is moving the weapons."

"They're in shipping containers," said Silas from his right.

Surprised, he turned and looked at Silas, who stood rigidly to the side of the gravel drive with his arm in a makeshift sling and pain etched on his face. Caesar was frankly shocked he was standing at all. He'd passed out cold when they cauterized his amputation with the heated dagger, and the pungent stench of charred meat still lingered in his nose, gamy and sweet. But he'd awoken within minutes, sucked down half a bottle of whiskey, and that was that. Not a single murmur of pain, not one complaint; only the sweat on his brow and his expression gave him away, and Caesar could tell he was trying his damnedest to quell even that.

He had to hand it to him, Silas was one tough bastard. No wonder his father trusted him so much. Perhaps he'd underestimated him. Caesar would have appreciated a few more of those lovely screams of his, but you can't have everything.

Besides, when he got his hands on Eliana, she'd make up for it in spades.

"I moved all the weapons to the docks at Le Havre so she wouldn't have access to it without my—your—knowledge, my lord, and the inspectors were paid handsomely to overlook the lack of proper paperwork and ensure the freight is forwarded without incident. We can have the containers ready to be shipped to wherever you like within eight hours."

And when had he been planning on telling him about *that*? "Why, Silas," Caesar drawled, his eyes narrowed, "you wily old dog, you. You're proving to be even more resourceful than I thought."

Silas inclined his head, the picture of deference, but suddenly Caesar found himself not only convinced he'd underestimated him, but wondering by exactly how much.

"If you like, we can load the money onto the containers as well, ship it all together."

His voice was mild, entirely without guile, but Caesar realized that a man who could be stoic when a limb was chopped off could certainly manage to conceal a great many other things, without much effort.

He smiled cheerfully. "No, Silas, thank you, but I'll make arrangements for the money to be sent to our final destination."

A flicker of annoyance crossed his face, there then gone, and then Silas said, "As you wish, my lord. Shall we begin the taping?"

"Ah!" At once, Caesar forgot his suspicions. He clapped, and Aldo jumped down from the lift gate of the truck and snapped to attention in front of him. "Is it ready?"

"Yes, sire, the camera and lights have all been set up!" Aldo sounded nearly as excited as he felt; this little endeavor was, against all odds, proving to be *fun.*

"Well, then, hup to!"

Aldo and the five others scattered like ants, heading toward the shack at the end of the driveway. It was a ramshackle mess of a place that he guessed used to be a gamekeeper's shed or kennel, with a caved-in ceiling and one wall missing. They'd draped a sheet across one of the standing walls and had set a wooden chair in front of it.

Opposite the chair was a video camera on a tripod, and to another tripod in the corner was affixed a light.

"My lord." Aldo gestured to the chair and positioned himself behind the camera. He flipped a switch, and a little red light at the front of the camera blinked on. "We're recording."

Caesar seated himself in the chair, smoothed a hand over his hair, and smiled. Into the unblinking eye of the video camera he said, "Merry Christmas, humans, and allow me to introduce myself." His smile grew wider. "I'm your new God."

The taping had, of course, been Silas's idea.

He watched Caesar smile and preen and posture, reciting the words he'd written himself, and in spite of the pain searing white pathways down every nerve ending in his body, he felt deep, deep satisfaction.

Caesar would be the one the humans blamed. It would be Caesar's name they cursed, his likeness they remembered. Silas would be free to operate behind the scenes as he always had, planning and scheming without the burdens notoriety inevitably brought.

No matter what happened now, his days of servitude were over.

Because when Caesar's part had been played, he would have to die.

Remembering the look on Caesar's face when he'd pressed the heated steel against the raw, bleeding stump of his wrist, Silas smiled. Yes, Caesar would have to die. By his hands. *Hand,* he mentally corrected himself. By his hand.

He was really looking forward to that.

Three hundred and fifty miles away across the English Channel, the Queen of the *Ikati* was once again sitting up in bed in the pale pink rays of early dawn. She sat peering around the opulence of her bedchamber for a moment, listening hard into the silence, her heart thundering inside her chest.

It wasn't a phone call that had awoken her this time, but a dream. She dreamt of a comet streaking across the night sky, trailing fire in a long, flared tail of orange. The comet had illuminated a dark landscape below, an ancient, hilly city with miles of twisting streets and red-roofed houses and a river winding through all of it, slow and serpentine.

There was a familiar dome in the center of the city, an enormous white dome that glittered atop an even more enormous cathedral, which was built atop the bones of the most famous saint in all the world. In all of *history.*

Beneath the fiery glow of the comet, St. Peter's Basilica and Vatican City looked bathed in red.

They looked bathed in blood.

With a glance at the slumbering form of her husband beside her, Jenna slid from beneath the warmth of the goose down duvet and crossed the room on silent feet to stand at the lead-paned window. She pushed aside one heavy velvet drape and gazed up at the heavens, a sense of dread gnawing at her like swarming insects.

Her father had once told her the ancients believed comets were a sign of ill repute, an omen of terrible things to come. Famine and earthquakes and floods, destruction and death and crops lost to frost.

Plague. Pestilence.

War.

The last time she ever saw her father, when she was ten years old, a comet had blazed a brilliant trail across the night sky. A comet with a tail of fiery orange, just like the one in her dream.

She shivered, suddenly ice cold, cold straight down to her bones, as if a ghostly wind sliced right through her.

"What is it?"

The voice was smooth and masculine, carrying that wary weight she'd come to know so well. Jenna turned from the window to see Leander sitting up on his side of the massive, four-poster bed, staring at her through the silvered half-light. He was alert and on edge; she felt the tension in him even from all the way across the room. As he must have felt her thundering heart. Her pulse like a kettledrum beating a dire warning through her veins.

"Wake the others," she said into the hush. "Wake everyone. Something is going to happen. Something very bad."

"He's not answering the damn phone." Celian's voice was tight, darker and more tense than either Lix or Constantine had ever heard it, and that was saying something.

"Can't you leave a message?" asked Lix.

"The fool doesn't have voice mail set up."

Lix snorted, his usual response to something he found ridiculous. "Leave it to D. That would require *speaking*."

"It's not funny," Celian snapped, pulling up short from the pacing he'd been doing for the last several minutes, long, agitated strides that took him back and forth over the blood-red woven rug in the candlelit opulence of what had once been the king's personal library, but now was open to anyone in the colony who desired it. "We haven't heard from him in days, and his time is up and so is Eliana's, and our *good friend* Leander has his panties in a twist over this entire situation, not the least of which is because *I* managed to talk his wife into allowing something *he* never would have allowed in the first place, which didn't pan out and made me look like I can't be trusted, in addition to making me look like a total *ass*."

He dragged a hand through his dark hair, cursed, and started pacing again.

Lix and Constantine shared a look; Celian rarely lost his temper. He was the rational one, the controlled one, the one with an iron will and a stare that could make men shrivel like testicles exposed to cold. In opposition to Lix's lighthearted good humor and Constantine's sensitivity—which he took great pains to hide—Celian had no soft spots or sentimentality. He was pragmatic and nearly always stone-cold calm, which made him a strong leader and an even stronger warrior, and his agitation was a good indicator of just how bad this situation was.

"That Queen of theirs…I had a chance, at least, with her. She's the only one in that entire colony who seems reasonable." His voice dropped. "But now all bets are off. D's been formally declared a deserter and a traitor, and our colony has been declared *persona non grata.* Unless we hand D over to them, of course. Otherwise, we're essentially at war." He paused and his face grew grim. "Which means they could invade at any time."

In stereo, Lix and Constantine gasped.

"Yeah. Welcome to the party."

Constantine leapt to his feet and Lix followed, the two of them flexing and snarling like the animals they were. They'd been lounging on a velvet sofa watching as Celian spoke on the phone with Leander before trying, in vain, to reach D, but their quiet repose had been replaced instantaneously with fierce readiness, and the willingness to rip out the throat of an enemy and lay down their own lives in order to protect their colony.

Celian turned and stared at them. "Get the *Legiones* ready. Call the elders to order and make sure everyone knows what's at stake. Get the women and children to the Domitilla; the sunken church is the farthest outpost, and they can escape easily from there if worse comes to worst. And then join me in the armory. We're going to lay some traps for these rats."

He smiled, mirthless, his lips curving cold red.

"There's a thousand secret passageways in these catacombs, a million black, dead-end corridors to get lost in. If they do invade, that British peacock and his friends won't be getting out of here alive."

THIRTY-THREE
Love Like Drowning

"We can't stay here long."

D was turned away from her with his hands on his hips. His voice was low and solemn.

She'd found him this way, staring out the curved bay window in the living room into the pale, shifting light of dawn. She'd eaten, checked on Mel—no change—and then wandered around the safe house aimlessly, not realizing until she found herself at the top of the stairs of the main level that she'd been looking for him.

"Why not?" She thought of his ringing cell phone from before, and her heart fluttered in panic. "You've had news?"

A nod of his head, almost imperceptible. His shoulders were stiff, pulled back in a way that accentuated their breadth and belied his inner tension. He seemed to be scanning the street outside, looking for something. Or someone.

"They'll be checking everywhere now. This place isn't safe anymore."

Eliana swallowed. "*They?*"

He turned and looked at her. His face was set in a grim mask, and his eyes were dark and fathomless. "Mel has to be moved. This Alexi"—his voice took on a dangerous edge when he said his name—"his place is secure?"

With that question, Eliana understood with perfect, terrible clarity that there was a choice to be made, a choice between her nemesis, Faith, and her old, comfortable friend, Doubt.

She would need his help to safely move Mel. And where else could Mel be moved but to Alexi's, where she could be given care and watched over? But then *he* would know where Alexi's was, and all the other members of the colony who'd fled there. She had few options, little time, and no money on hand to secure them other lodgings, and only his word that he would never hurt her to go on. His word and the look in his eyes when he said it, which had almost, *almost* made her believe.

If she took him to Alexi's, there would be no more hiding. There would be no more secrets. There would be nothing but hope and desperate, blind Faith.

She was going to have to trust him or stay here and risk death for herself and Mel. Either way, she suddenly realized, their lives were already in his hands.

And he hadn't let her down yet.

He watched her face as these thoughts crowded her mind, watched her silently and unmoving, until finally she drew in a slow breath and chose.

She nodded. "Yes. It's secure. I'll give you directions in the car."

Let the chips fall where they may, she thought, turning away. *I can always kill him later.*

Alexi's place turned out to be far more than a mere *place.* It was practically its own postal code.

Six stories tall, nearly as wide as a city block, the modest, classic stone exterior hid a lavishly opulent interior of cream silk furnishings, polished marble floors and antiques, and a collection of modern art to rival that of the finest museums, which hung in vivid pops of color from walls painted delicate eggshell white. Located on the Avenue du Président Kennedy directly across from the Eiffel Tower, it also sported a rather awe-inspiring view of the Seine.

"Let me guess. Rich parents? Trust fund?" D said sourly to Eliana as he stood beneath an elaborate chandelier in the grand foyer that threw sparkling prisms of color in rainbow radiance around the room.

She shook her head. "He's self-made. Came from nothing. Hard work and talent got him where he is. He's a genius, really." Her lips lifted to a faint, fond smile. "I wouldn't be surprised if someday he rules the world."

D began to hate this rich, genius Alexi with an almost biblical wrath. He hadn't made an appearance yet; they'd been admitted to the foyer by an arch, elderly butler in a tuxedo who took one look at the two of them and pursed his lips, then glided away to inform the master of the house more "guests" had arrived.

"Does he know what you are?"

Eliana contemplated that for a moment, staring at a crystal Lalique figurine on a nearby table of a couple entwined in an embrace, and then murmured, "He knows what I'm not."

"Which means?"

She slid him an indecipherable, sideways glance. "He's doing me an incredible favor, Demetrius, letting us stay here. Please don't antagonize him."

D ground his teeth together, and all the broken things inside him ground together, too. He said between clenched teeth, "He should take care not to antagonize *me*, Ana. I suddenly feel like ripping someone's head off."

"Which won't help anything—"

"No, but it would make me feel a hell of a lot better—"

"Demetrius, please—"

"You can't expect dogs and cats to play nice together—"

"Alexi is not a dog!"

D smirked, and Eliana glared back at him. "He's a dog, all right. I noticed him at the catacombs, Ana. He's a pedigreed, pampered little yipper who likes to bury his bone all over town."

Eliana's mouth dropped open. Her face went pale and then flushed red. She opened her mouth to, no doubt, excoriate him, but at that moment the little yipper decided to show up.

He burst through a set of etched glass doors at the opposite end of the glistening foyer with his arms held out, worry lines bunching his golden brow. Blond and tanned and fit, he was one of those men who managed to look well groomed and wealthy even in bare feet, torn jeans, and a tight Rolling Stones T-shirt, which served double duty as an "I'm-too-rich-to-be-bothered" fashion statement and a showcase for his gym-hardened physique.

Without a glance in D's direction, Alexi enveloped Eliana in a tight, possessive embrace.

D's hate ratcheted up to a thermonuclear malignity. He *did* want to see this poser's head torn from his body—torn from his body and impaled on a post. A growl, low and threatening, rumbled through his chest, and he stepped forward, bristling.

Eliana broke away from Alexi and angled her body between them. Alexi looked at D, and to his credit, he didn't balk. He gave him a swift, disdainful once-over, as if just noticing his presence, and then said, "Ah. You."

"The feeling is mutual, pretty boy," D snarled, curling his hands into fists.

Without looking back at him, Eliana reached out and laid her hand flat on his chest. It had the intended effect. D stopped dead in his tracks, distracted—*disabled*—by her touch.

"What he meant to say was thank you," Eliana said smoothly, "for what you've done. We're in your debt."

He'd be damned before he'd be indebted to this smug, priggish dilettante, but Alexi reacted as if he'd been stroked on his head. He purred his pleasure in lilting, flowery French.

"*Bien sûr. Quelque chose pour toi.*"

Anything for you. He'd said the same thing to her on the phone, and from the tone of his voice and the look on his face, D had no doubt it was true. Eliana sensed his growing fury and stepped back toward him, still with her hand on his chest, which Alexi noted with flattened lips and a fleeting glance at him that telegraphed, *This means war.* His gaze settled back on Eliana, and it softened.

"Your family is upstairs resting comfortably. I've prepared a bedroom for you, as well. You can stay as long as you like, of course—"

"Mel can take my bedroom. She's downstairs in the car. We'll bring her in now."

"Mel!" he exclaimed, eyes widening. "Wait—you said she was *shot*."

Silent, Eliana slowly nodded.

Alexi threw his hands in the air. "Why isn't she in the hospital?"

"We can't...we can't go to hospitals," she said lamely.

Alexi looked at her with narrowed eyes for a beat and made a little noise of disbelief or disapproval in his throat. Then—apparently accustomed to this kind of thing from her—he rolled his eyes and sighed. "I'll phone my private physician. He gets paid enough to be on call. He should be able to be here within the hour."

"A doctor?" Eliana whispered with something odd in her voice.

Through the fabric of his shirt, D felt her fingers tremble. He reached up and placed his hand over hers, an action not meant as anything but comfort, but Alexi took note of it, his mouth puckering as if someone had just stuck a lemon in it.

"Yes, a doctor, Butterfly," he said sourly. "That is who normal people go to see when they've been shot. Right before they go to see their lawyer."

Eliana said, "Lawyer. Um..."

Alexi crossed his arms over his chest and went into problem-solving mode. "What's her condition now? Is she stable, conscious? Where exactly was she injured?"

"She was shot in the chest, and she's still not conscious, but she's stable, she's been…operated on…"

Alexi's golden brow crumpled to a frown. "I don't understand. You said she hadn't been to a hospital."

"Er, no…"

"Field surgery," D cut in abruptly. "I did what I could with what I had on hand."

Alexi regarded him with new interest, his expression bordering on incredulous, his eyes keen. "Well. This just keeps getting better." His gaze flickered over D's shaved head and pierced eyebrow, the tattoos peeking out above the neck of his black shirt, his long black coat, and his boots and leather pants. "Let me guess—Harvard School of Medicine?"

D smiled. He withdrew the Glock from the waistband of his pants, pointed it in the general direction of Alexi's crotch, and calmly said, "Harvard School of Another Word and I'll Turn You from a Rooster to a Hen with One Shot, motherfucker."

"Demetrius!" Eliana hissed. She snatched her hand from his chest and looked at him, a plea in her eyes.

Don't antagonize her human boy toy. Right.

In what was maybe the third-hardest thing he'd ever done, D stepped away and stuck the gun back in the waistband of his pants.

Alexi, again to his credit and surprisingly, hadn't twitched a muscle. D guessed it wasn't the first time he'd been threatened with grievous bodily harm; the man really had a way of irritating people. But Alexi looked back and forth between D and Eliana twice before he spoke.

"Bring her in. I'll call the doctor. And afterward, you and I, we'll talk."

He made the word *talk* sound like something they'd do in bed.

To Alexi he sent a look that said, *I've got your number; touch her again and it's up*. To Eliana, D said, "I'll get her." Then he left the two of them standing in the silent opulence of Alexi's grand foyer and headed for the SUV in the parking garage below.

"So are you going to talk to me or just keep staring out the window?"

This was said without rancor in that gently teasing way Alexi had that used to make her smile, but now it only made her head hurt. More than it already did.

They were in a room next to the one Mel had been ensconced in, some kind of sitting room on the top floor outfitted all in white with mod furnishings and a shaggy rug and a view of the city through the glass windows along the east wall. She'd made sure Mel was taken care of, spoken with Bettina and Fabi, and then allowed herself to be led here, though she wouldn't take the hand Alexi had offered on the way.

The sun was rising, painting the city in shifting tones of lavender and blue and gold, and with every degree it rose in the sky, she felt it like an opposing weight in her body. She could not recall the last time she'd had a good night's sleep.

"Have I said thank you yet?"

She turned to look at him. He was seated beside her in a chair identical to her own, an egg-shaped, plastic affair that might have been designed as a torture device for all the comfort it gave. She didn't understand how something with no sharp corners could be so damn...pinchy. But that was Alexi. Form over function any day of the week. "If I haven't—thank you. I'll start by saying that."

"You're welcome." He regarded her very seriously, though she knew he was pleased to have her here. Happy, even. It radiated from him in waves, thick as honey. As if to prove it, he said, "It's nice to have company. I should have bought something smaller. This place is really too cavernous and lonely, even with Smithers."

Smithers. The dour British butler who always pretended not to remember Eliana's name. She'd been here dozens upon dozens of times when she and Alexi were an item, but he remained aloof, with an air of vague disapproval, though in all honesty the poor man must have quite the challenge, what with the revolving door of women Alexi presented him. At the moment he was in the kitchen, preparing breakfast for his bevy of unexpected, hungry guests.

"I'd almost forgotten how relentlessly unflappable you are," she mused. "Over a dozen bedraggled, semi-hostile strangers in your house, including one with a gunshot wound, and you act like it's an impromptu cocktail party."

Now he did smile, widely. "Relentlessly unflappable? You make it sound like a personality defect. I'm *positive,* Butterfly." He tapped his temple. "Secret to my success."

"Really? That actually works?"

"You should try it sometime." His voice was droll, his look pointed, and suddenly she felt defensive.

"I'm positive," she protested, which was met with soft, mocking laughter.

Alexi raked a hand through his hair, thick strands of golden brown and honey that glinted in the rising light, and shook his head. "You're many wonderful things, Eliana, but positive, I'm sorry to say, isn't one of them."

Now she was more than defensive. She was outright offended. "In what way am I not positive, exactly?"

"Well, let's see." He looked at the ceiling and, in irritatingly quick succession, ticked a list off his fingers. "You don't trust anyone, you don't let anyone in, you assume the worst in every situation, you think people are guilty until proven innocent, you wield sarcasm like a weapon—which technically you don't need since you always have a sword strapped to your waist in case you need to cut someone down to size—and you have some really bad anger management issues. Oh, and you *like to fight.*" He looked back at her. "Did I forget anything?"

"Yes," she said, her voice flinty. "I hold grudges. Like, forever."

He dissolved into laughter, which, if she wasn't so mad, would have been charming. She stood stiffly from the chair and went to stand in front of the windows. "I don't see what's so funny," she muttered acidly to the breathtaking view, her arms crossed over her chest.

When his laughter finally died, he came up behind her and laid a hand on her shoulder. Only because he was helping her family, she didn't bite it off.

"You're also loyal and strong and brave," he said, very softly, the laughter gone from his voice. "You put other people's needs ahead of your own. You're disciplined, self-reliant, smarter than you give yourself credit for, and you're the only beautiful woman I've ever met who isn't vain."

"Hmpf." She lifted her chin and stared at the tall, sweeping form of the Eiffel Tower and thought about standing there with Demetrius on the platform overlooking the city, what seemed like a lifetime ago.

Alexi's voice grew even softer. "When you're not being evasive, you're honest, though I suspect your evasion has less to do with wanting to deceive and more to do with wanting to protect something. And now that I've met your family—who I never knew existed, aside from Mel, before your phone call—I think that something is *them.* Which makes me think that in addition to being mysterious and sexy as hell...you're honorable."

Honorable. If there was one thing she truly wished to be, it was honorable. She wasn't, but just hearing him say it made all her righteous indignation drain away as if a plug had been pulled. She shivered, and the sunlight reflected from a building across the river almost blinded her eyes. "Honor among thieves," she murmured, "isn't quite the same thing as Honor, capital H."

"It says nothing against the ripeness of a spirit that it has a few worms."

She turned and looked at him, brows lifted, and he shrugged. "Okay, I stole that from Nietzsche. But it's true."

"So now I have worms?"

His brown eyes were warm and soft as they gazed down at her. "You have *wounds,* but you don't let them get in the way of doing what you think is right. I've been with a lot of women, Eliana, but you're the only one I've ever admired. So, no, you're not exactly the most positive person in the world, but you're light years ahead of most everyone else I know in terms of character. Myself included."

She blinked at him. She swallowed. She said, "You sure know how to pay a girl a compliment, slick."

One golden brow cocked. "Really? Am I better at it than, say, your charmer Goth Godzilla Romeo who's waiting downstairs in my garage to slit my throat even as we speak?"

Her face reddened. She wouldn't even try to deny it; she knew D was lurking in the garage, where she'd sent him in an effort to calm him down and hopefully distract him from the mayhem plain on his face when he looked at Alexi.

"Is that why you didn't want to see me anymore? Because of him?"

"No," she admitted truthfully. "We weren't together then."

"But you are now," he persisted.

She was taken aback. "No."

He was clearly dubious at her refusal. "You sure you don't want to think about that before you answer?"

"We're not together. What would make you think that?"

"Because, mysterious, blue-haired, sword-wielding Butterfly," he said gently, "you're in love. It's all over you both."

She blanched, stiffened, and sucked in a breath, all at once. *In love?*

He said sourly, "Try not to look so hopeful—you're giving me a complex, here."

She sputtered, "I'm not—I'm not hopeful—I'm not—not *anything*—"

"Oh," he interrupted flatly, "I did forget something. You have a tendency to reject the obvious even when it's smacking you upside the head with a two-by-four. Also, you're a terrible liar."

"I'm not lying!"

"Okay then. Look me in the eyes and tell me you're not in love with him."

She was horrified. This was ridiculous. "Alexi!"

"If it's true, it'll be easy. Just do it." He folded his arms across his chest and stared at her, waiting, not angry but not happy, either, just…patient.

"This is stupid."

"No, this is my price for letting you stay here."

"What!"

He lifted his shoulders.

"Alexi," she said through gritted teeth, "don't make me kick your ass all over this room."

One corner of his mouth lifted. "Yeah. That's what I thought."

He gave her a swift kiss on the forehead, turned, and made his way to the door. Over his shoulder he said, "Think about this, Butterfly; Godzilla Romeo spanked you in front of a few hundred people *and you let him live.* If I'd have done that, I'd be lying in a shallow grave somewhere." He paused just outside the doorway and looked back at her. "Right?"

"You suck."

He laughed. "What are friends for, if they can't call you out on your shit?"

"Lucky for me, I don't have many friends," she muttered, and his face grew soft.

"You don't need a lot. Just a few really good ones."

They stared at each other for a few seconds, and then she said, "You are a good friend, Alexi. This is"—she made a gesture to the room—"above and beyond. Thank you for what you're doing."

He smiled, devilishly charming. "I told you when you broke up with me that you'd come crawling back."

"You did. Yes. And then you flaunted half the women in Paris in my face, which didn't much make me feel like crawling."

He had the decency to look chagrined. "Well, this is me trying to make amends here, lady, take it easy on me. And for the record, this wasn't exactly how I pictured it, but for what it's worth…I'm glad you're here. You and all your crazy, black-eyed family. Who, incidentally, all speak *Latin*. What's up with that?"

"Oh," she said, smiling darkly, "that's the least of it, slick. Do yourself a favor and don't try and sneak up on any of them. You might wind up missing a limb or two."

He shook his head slowly, amazed or bemused, she couldn't tell.

"You're going to tell me all about it later. Don't think I've forgotten our deal." His devilish smile made a reappearance. "And don't think just because I'm playing nice and you're in love with a seven-foot-tall, tattooed gorilla who wants to kill me that I'm going to give up trying to get you into bed."

She pressed her lips together to hide her smile. "No, I didn't think that."

He nodded, satisfied. "Good. Your room's across the hall. Take a shower, if you want, clean up. Then come downstairs; Smithers makes a mean holiday crepe."

"Holiday? What holiday is it?"

"It's Christmas, Butterfly. Don't they have Christmas on your planet?"

Then with a mischievous wink, he was gone.

The shower turned out to be the best advice she'd had in ages.

She stood under the hot spray, letting the water relax the knotted muscles in her shoulders, letting the steam do its best to try to lull her worries away.

Not that it worked. No amount of hot water could wash away her kind of worries; no amount of scrubbing could get them unstuck.

Where was Silas right now? Where was her brother? What were the few who refused to leave the catacombs doing in her absence?

Was Demetrius, right at this moment, telling the *Bellatorum* where they were?

She pushed that thought aside, surprising herself at the vehemence with which her mind shouted a resounding *No!* Stupid. Stupid. Anything was possible, everything was, and to try to deny it was just stupid…but what Alexi had said kept echoing in her head, over and over.

You're in love. It's all over you both.

Because she'd grown to understand that life was as strange as it was unpredictable, it didn't really surprise her when she heard the door to the bathroom open a few minutes later and close and a deep, tense voice growl, "The little yipper said you needed to see me, right away. Said it was important."

Her disbelieving laugh was drowned out by the running water. She rested her forehead against the smooth tile, relieved and terrified in equal measure, both cursing Alexi and wanting to give him a hug of gratitude.

Just when you thought you had people figured out, pegged as petty or selfish or shallow, they went ahead and did something like this. Something *huge* like this.

Sweet Isis, maybe there was hope after all.

Thinking that, feeling that possibility, that little bud of hope, made her heart soar.

"What's wrong? Are you all right?" When she didn't answer, D stepped closer to the shower door and his voice grew louder, more urgent, impatience mixed with sharp concern. "Eliana. Answer me!"

The glassed shower door was fogged with steam, so she couldn't see his face. And she suddenly, very badly, needed to see his face. She pushed away from the tile as if in a daydream, swung open the door, and stood there naked in the spray, staring at him as if she'd never seen him before. Which, maybe, she really hadn't.

He dwarfed the genteel, luxurious room and frankly upstaged it. His bulk, masculinity, and sheer, unstudied elegance rendered all the expensive trimmings around him—gilded mirrors and gold fixtures and polished marble—effete and superficial, and she wondered why she hadn't noticed it before, the way his presence made other things pale in comparison. The way he made everything else seem figuratively and literally *small*.

He stared back at her, lips parted, his face transforming from worry to shock to molten heat as his gaze traveled over her wet, naked body. When his dark eyes found hers again, they were on fire.

"No, Demetrius," she said simply, "I'm not all right. I've never been less *all right* in my life."

He took a step forward, his eyes searing hers. "I'll kill him. I'll kill that bastard if he laid a finger on you—"

"He did something worse. He said we were in love, you and I."

He froze. His nostrils flared. His jaw went tight, and his hands, hanging at his sides, clenched into fists. Steam swirled around them, hot and billowing, brushed over her naked skin like a million fairy fingertips, raising goose bumps in their wake.

"Is that what this is?" His voice was hoarse. "Love? Because it feels more like ongoing electrocution."

She nodded, agreeing. "Or being burned at the stake."

Slowly, heart pounding, breath growing short, she stepped forward to the edge of the large glass and tile enclosure. He watched her every move with avid, devouring eyes, his expression wary and yearning and hot.

And tortured. How tortured he looked, how wretched, like a prisoner of war—*their* war, the bloody battle that had been slowly killing them both for years. It pierced her, that look. It almost made her want to cry.

He said, "Run over by a truck and dragged along a thousand miles of bad road."

She reached out, touched a hand to the flexing muscle in his jaw, and gently stroked her fingers across it until she found his lips, and then she traced those. "Drawn and quartered."

"Swallowing battery acid." His voice had dropped to near a whisper, grown gravelly, unsteady. His hands reached for her, finding her waist, encircling it. His face tilted down to hers, and he looked a little dazed, the heat and the thrill she felt being near him reflected back in his eyes, the raggedness of his breathing.

"Devoured by a shark—"

"Buried alive—"

"Drowning—"

"*Drowning*, yes, it's just like drowning," he whispered vehemently, gazing into her eyes, his voice broken, his face full of misery and desire. "Except you never die, and you never surface, and the suffering never goes away, it just goes on and on and on. For fucking *ever*."

He pulled her up against him and crushed his lips to hers.

And then it was nothing but hunger, savage and raw, both of them drowning in each other.

It was effortless for him to pick her up in his arms and balance her weight as she wrapped her arms and legs around him, effortless to carry her into the shower without breaking his stride or breaking their kiss, effortless to press her against the tile and make her cry out when he took her nipple in his mouth and sucked, hard. They were both half in and half out of the spray, and he was getting soaking wet, still in his boots and pants and shirt, and she clawed his wet shirt from his back and ran her hands over him, heat and muscle and slick skin, his arms around her strong and deliciously possessive.

He kissed her ravenously with one hand fisted in her wet hair and the other digging into her bottom. She kissed him back, their teeth clashing, her breasts pressed against his chest, aching nipples slipping against his wet skin. He panted her name, fumbled with his zipper. When the long, hard length of him sprang free and pressed hot against her belly she was ready; she reached between them and grasped him, reveling in the husky greed in his answering moan.

"Maybe this *is* what love is, Demetrius," she whispered hoarsely into his ear. "This is what love is for us—torture and suffering and pain. And this."

She sank down on top of him with a swift, fluid motion of her hips.

He arched back and shuddered, clenching her to him, his body straining against hers. Then he held her up against the wet tile and thrust into her again and again, relentlessly, hard and unforgiving, as she pressed her heels to his spine and rode him, hearing the slap of their flesh and his erotic, low groans and the sound of her own blood roaring in her ears.

Pleasure gathered to a bright, electric peak inside her body. She moaned his name, drunk with him, teetering on the very precipice of release…

And then—bastard that he was—he fell still.

Her eyes flew open. Breathing hard, he was staring back at her, a wicked grin on his face.

"Oh no. Oh no you don't," she said, sudden cold realization dawning over her.

But he did, he was, and his next slow, seductively spoken words proved it.

"Not yet."

"You son of a bitch!" she hissed, stiffening. "Not *this* again!"

He flexed his hips and pressed deep into her and she was so, so full—her anger turned liquid along with her limbs. She groaned and shuddered, and he laughed darkly against her neck, triumphant.

"Demetrius," she whimpered, "please."

"Begging won't help you, baby girl," he teased gruffly, flexing into her again, somehow knowing exactly how much pressure and speed would take her over the edge and how much would keep her hanging on it. "You have to let go and trust me."

"I will kill you." Her voice was hoarse and, even to her own ears, utterly lacking conviction. "I swear I will kill you."

He flexed into her again, with a little twist of his pelvis to top it off, and this time she gasped. He put his lips against her ear and murmured, "Let go. Trust me. Just once. Just this *once.*"

Oh, slippery, slippery slope, this. She'd already trusted him once, more than once, but she couldn't think with him buried inside her, she could barely even breathe, and for some ridiculous reason all she wanted to do was give him what he wanted. Whatever he wanted.

She turned her head, looked up at him, and whispered, "Okay."

He wasn't expecting it, she could tell by the way he froze and looked down at her, startled. She bit her lip and nodded, just to make sure he knew she was coherent, and relaxed in the circle of his arms. "Okay."

"Ana," he breathed in wonder, "you never cease to amaze me."

She smiled, feeling almost shy. "Don't screw it up."

"Oh?" His brows rose. He leaned down and brushed his lips across her cheek, his own rough and shadowed with a growth of day-old beard. "Interesting choice of words, considering…"

He slowly sank into her again, and she tightened her arms around his neck.

She whispered his name as her eyes slid shut and her head fell back against the tile, whispered it again, broken, when he cupped her breast and bent his head and suckled her. The drawing of his tongue and lips sent spikes of pleasure/pain straight to her core, and though she wanted to writhe against him, she held still, allowing him to hold her up and caress her and control her body, allowing him to bring her back up to that edge again, with his lips and his beautiful, hard body filling hers.

He began to thrust again, slowly, brought her face to his with his fingers on her chin. She knew he'd want her eyes open, so she kept them that way and gazed at him, noticing every detail of his face, strong jaw and full lips and the thicket of dark lashes around his eyes. His breathing was ragged. His hands dug into her bottom.

She began to lose herself to sensation. He was everywhere, filling her in every way, his scent in her nose and his tongue in her mouth and his need for her like another skin wrapped around her body. She was burning, she was flying, and with every single thrust she was falling and letting herself fall, glad of it. Glad to finally let go, if even for only a while.

"That's right," he murmured, watching her with half-lidded eyes when she moaned and shivered against him. "That's my girl."

She was so close now; every nerve ending was firing, and her entire body was shaking. She felt as if she would crack wide open and die from pleasure, or be devoured by this thing between them that felt like a monster in the room, an entity, primal and hungry and animal.

She cupped his face in her hands and looked deep into his eyes, letting him see everything. Asking permission.

His arms were crushing. His eyes, wild. "Like drowning," he groaned.

"Like dying," she agreed in a harsh whisper as she rode the crest of the wave and felt something vast and dark rushing at her, inescapable as death.

D began to thrust hard, letting himself go. "Yes, Ana," he panted. "Come for me, baby. *Now.*"

Love like drowning, love like burning, a million different ways to die—

She exploded, supernova, the world went white and then black. Her body bowed, and she sobbed his name, clenching around him, racked with tremors, pleasure so acute it almost hurt.

It did hurt. It burned.

Maybe this is what love is for us…unending, unendurable pain.

She buried her face in his neck to hide her wet eyes.

"*Tu mea es!*" D groaned suddenly, fiercely. He pulled her head back with a hand in her hair and stared into her eyes, and his look was animal, agonized and intense. "*Tu mea es.*"

You are mine.

He bared his teeth and came inside her, shuddering, his eyes rapt and locked on hers. She cried out as she felt him spilling inside her, saw his face through a prism of tears.

"*Tu mea es.*"

He whispered it over and over again as he held her up against the tile shower wall, whispered it against her lips, her neck, her breasts, and the words swirled around like the eddies of steam, dizzying, disorienting, echoing, piercing down to the very corners of her soul.

You.

Are.

Mine.

THIRTY-FOUR

An Honest Answer

The wide marble steps that led to the Apostolic Palace at the Vatican were designed by Bernini, and the entrance was flanked by a cadre of armed Swiss Guards. Silas, Caesar, and Aldo were ushered past the guards by their escort, a slight man in a fedora and black cape, and ascended the staircase in silence.

It was ten forty-five in the morning. In precisely thirty minutes, the pope would give his Christmas morning address to the world from the balcony of his private study in the papal apartments, overlooking St. Peter's Square.

And then the course of history would be changed forever.

The drive from Paris had taken all night, but Silas wasn't tired. Quite the opposite. Filled with an almost excruciating anticipation, he was finding it hard to keep a straight face. Years and years and years of servitude, of bowing and biting his tongue and being told what to do, all leading up to this moment.

It wasn't supposed to have happened exactly like this—he was missing a hand, after all, and he couldn't Shift because of it—but if nothing else, Silas was a master of adaptation, and this was just one more thing he'd adapted to.

Hence, the inclusion of Aldo.

Aldo could Shift, whereas Silas couldn't at the moment, and Caesar had never been able to. And that was precisely the point, really, getting that particular Gift on film for all the world to see. He couldn't exactly establish the kind of fear and awe he wanted to inspire in humans just by offing the leader of their most powerful church, for goodness' sake. No—they had to be shown what it was the *Ikati* could do. They had to be *humbled.* There had been one or two instances where they'd been caught on film, but those were accidental, small scale, easily dismissed.

It would not be so easy to dismiss the sight of the pope being slaughtered on live television broadcast all over the world in front of thousands upon thousands of eyewitnesses.

And then, oh, and then they would reign supreme. While the walls between two worlds crumbled and the humans who had persecuted them for eons fell into terrified chaos, he would unite the scattered clans, distribute the serum, and wring his hands—hand—in glee.

Right after he killed Caesar.

Though he was technically Alpha of their little colony because he was the eldest son of the last Alpha, Caesar's lack of Gifts meant his hold on the title was tenuous at best. Strength always had to be proven, even for an Alpha, and

Silas was a little surprised none of the others had formally challenged him yet. He certainly would have lost, which would have deposed him, but no matter, his time left as Alpha was short.

And after the spectacular coup Silas had orchestrated, no one would dare question *his* supremacy, his right to claim the title as his own.

Caesar hadn't questioned how Silas had been able to gain access to the pope's inner circle. He hadn't questioned how or when Silas had come up with such a monumental scheme. He hadn't questioned anything, really, he'd simply accepted that he'd be present at this little coming-out party of theirs, taking all the glory for himself.

He'd always been a selfish, small-minded little prick.

They reached the top of the sweeping staircase and paused before a set of towering, carved wooden doors. The man in the fedora murmured in Latin, "This way," nodding to the two guards posted on either side, who opened the doors and stepped back.

With a deferential nod and an outstretched hand, Silas ushered Caesar and Aldo in before him.

"You look like shit."

This pronouncement was whispered with barely any strength behind it, but it made Eliana so happy she almost cried. She had the fleeting thought that she must have been storing up a huge cache of tears over the past few years, because recently it seemed like they threatened to leak out at every occasion.

"You give the best compliments, Mel."

She squeezed her hand, and Mel, weakly, squeezed back. Her eyes drifted around the room. "Where the hell am I? Rich people's heaven?"

"Oh, this?" Eliana looked at the ridiculous, opulent room. There was a marble fireplace, tall windows flanked with silk curtains, a flat-screen television on the opposite wall, and a chandelier hanging over the bed. The very big, Thai-silk-covered bed. "This is nothing. Wait 'til you see the billiard room. And the rooftop pool. And the gym."

She managed a wan smile. "The gym. Oh, goodie. I could really use a workout right now."

"Shut up, sickie."

"You first."

They shared a smile and a moment of profoundly relieved silence.

Eliana had crept into the room only moments before to find Melliane awake, trying to sit up in bed, her face pale and sweaty with the effort it took just to move. She'd gently pushed her back against the pillows and sat down, scolding, beside her.

"We're at Alexi's."

Mel's dark brows rose into twin quirks. She sniffed, a delicate flare of her nostrils, and looked Eliana up and down before giving her a faint, smug smile. "And Demetrius is here, too."

Eliana flushed. "Can I just say that's really annoying? And vaguely creepy?"

"Spill it."

"It's a long story."

"Should be an interesting one."

"You have no idea."

Mel's smile faded, and she regarded her very seriously. "You'd tell me if I was going to die, right? Because it feels like I am. My chest feels like there's a really fat guy sitting on it, and the rest of me feels like I got hit by a truck."

"You are *not* going to die," Eliana enunciated, leaning closer. "I won't let you. And neither will Demetrius." Just saying his name made her feel funny inside, like a million tiny butterflies had opened their wings and started to dance. Her voice softened as her gaze dropped to the white bandage that was peeking out of the neck of Mel's top. "He's the one who fixed you up."

An odd look crept over Mel's face. "He's good at that." There was a little hitch in her voice. "Has he fixed *you* up yet?"

Eliana chewed her lip. "Insert another word that begins with an *f* into that sentence and you'll get the general idea."

Mel's look became dire. "Details. I want details."

Eliana tried not to smile and instead tried to look very stern and intimidating. "I think I might have liked you better when you were unconscious."

Her attempt at intimidation failed. Mel said, "Don't pretend you wouldn't have made a little shrine for me with incense and candles and my picture—a good one, I hope—and cried over it all the time and prayed to it like one of those Buddhist nuns if I never woke up. You so totally would have."

She brushed a stray wisp of black hair from her friend's forehead, feeling her heart squeeze to a knot inside her chest. She would have done more than built a little shrine. She would have built a monument, adorned by stone angels with vast wings and fierce eyes, and there would have been wreaths of holly and inscriptions in marble and candles that never burned out.

Eliana shrugged, keeping her voice nonchalant. "I don't have any pictures of you. I'd make some kind of crude drawing, where you'd be a tiny stick figure with a huge mouth and big scary teeth. I might light one candle. A little one. If I could find any laying around."

Mel grinned.

There was a soft rap on the door, and then Alexi stuck his head in. "Doctor's here. Is she—"

He caught sight of Mel awake in bed and broke into a smile. He swung the door open and entered. "Yes, she is. Welcome back to the land of the living, tiny, ferocious one."

"The land of the extravagantly wealthy living," Mel said, eying him. "How come I never knew you were rich before?"

"Why, do you like me better now?"

Her lips pursed, considering, and then she nodded. "It helps." When he beamed she amended, "A little."

Alexi walked toward them, still smiling, looking more like he'd just been handed a challenge instead of an insult. "What if I bring you breakfast in bed? Crepes with fresh cream and raspberries?"

"Oh," she whispered, very serious, eyes wide, "you evil, evil man."

"That's a yes, she'll like you more," said Eliana. "She's very easily swayed by food, in case you couldn't tell. If you bring her chocolate, watch out."

"Ah, an easy woman." Alexi's smile grew wider. "My absolute favorite."

"I think the entire world is well aware of your fondness for easy women, Alexi," Mel said dryly.

"On that note, I'm leaving," said Eliana, rising from the bed. She looked to Alexi. "Where's—"

"Godzilla Romeo is on the phone with someone downstairs, Butterfly."

"How did you know I wasn't asking about the doctor?"

He cut his gaze to hers, and his smile grew ironic. "Please. I didn't get where I am in life by being clueless. But speaking of the doctor, will you send him in if you're going? He's just outside the door."

She nodded, thought it best not to respond, and then blew Mel a kiss and walked to the door.

"Godzilla Romeo?" she heard Mel repeat as she left the room.

To which Alexi sighed and replied, "I know. There's really no accounting for some people's taste."

She found Demetrius looking out a window in the vast, empty dining room on the main floor, gazing in silence at the spectacular view of the city beyond the glass. When she entered, he turned and looked at her.

And his face transformed.

It made her feel lighter, seeing the way his hard, sensuous mouth softened and curved, the way his eyes, settling on her face, lit up. His entire aspect changed as if he were bathed in sudden starlight, and his look of such obvious *hope* made her feel like she might float right out of her shoes. She wanted to curl up in that look and bask in it, like a cat in the sun.

To manage it, she bit the inside of her mouth.

Orgasms do not equal trust, Eliana. Don't be a fool.

"Interesting outfit."

She regarded the white silk robe he wore that was at least three sizes too small for him. It barely reached his knees, just barely managed to stay closed in front with a tie that was a little too strained, threatening to give at any moment and burst wide open, letting Demetrius in all his naked glory spill out.

"Clothes were wet. They're in the dryer." His smile turned into a smirk. "Pretty boy didn't have anything that would fit me, so he gave me this."

"Oh? No spare sets of giant black clothing hanging around in his closet? Strange." She walked closer, slowly, a lifetime's worth of ambivalence in every step.

He grinned. "No size seventeen shoes, either."

She rolled her eyes. But now she was within arm's reach, and he took advantage of it. He stretched out one long arm, caught hers, and pulled her against his body. He pressed his face to her neck, and they stood there like that for a moment, feeling each other's heartbeats, their arms wrapped around one another, silent and still.

In another life, she thought, heart clenching, *how I could have loved you. How beautiful it all could have been.*

He murmured, "Tell me what you're thinking."

"I'm thinking…" She sighed. No. Not going to go there. "Mel's awake. She insulted me right off the bat, so I think she's going to be okay."

She felt his smile against her neck. "That's good. And you? How are you?"

Confused. Conflicted. Worried. Unsettled. *Unhinged.*

She sighed again and pulled away. "I'm fine. But I have to go out for a while. There's someone I have to go visit."

He stiffened. He pulled back to stare at her, and his eyes, so soft and open only moments before, grew wary. "Someone? Who? Where? I'm coming with you."

"No, you're not. He's a friend—"

"Another *friend.*" His voice had dropped dangerously low.

"Not like that, Demetrius. He helped me escape from the assassins—"

"What!" D hissed, suddenly livid and terrifying, even in the silly white robe. He gripped her upper arms. "When did that happen? Why didn't you tell me?"

"We haven't exactly been doing much *talking,*" she said sarcastically, but he cut her off.

"You can't seriously think I'm letting you leave this house while they're still out there. We haven't figured out what we're going to do yet—"

She yanked away from him. Anger blazed to life inside her, and the confusion she'd felt only moments before turned to hot, crackling indignation.

"*We?* There is no we, Demetrius. Just because we—" she waved her hand in the air, skipping the obvious, "doesn't mean I have to ask your permission to do anything."

His face hardened. A low, sinister growl rumbled through his chest. And just like that, they were back to where they'd been for years: enemies.

She scowled at him. "Don't think you're going to growl me into submission, either. I don't belong to you—"

"*Yes, you do!*"

Suddenly, he was in her face. His arms wrapped around her, pinning hers behind her back. His hands encircled her wrists, hard. He stared down at her, enormous and frightening, his eyes burning with a dark, savage fury. "You *do* belong to me. You are mine and I am yours, and there is nothing on this Earth that can ever change that! Stop fighting it!"

"Let me go!" She trembled with fury and tried to break away, but there was no release from the iron bands of his arms.

"We're bonded, baby girl, whether you like it or not, so you better get used to the idea."

Her breath huffed out like she'd been punched in the stomach. "Bonded! You're taking a hell of a lot for granted, *Bellator!*"

He put his mouth next to her ear and said deliberately, "Don't make me put you over my knee."

Because she hated, absolutely hated what the thought of that did to her, what his voice and strength and heat did to her, how *weak* he made her feel, she froze. Very, very quietly, she said, "And don't make me remind you why we are in this situation in the first place."

He jerked.

Still with that deadly softness, she said, "If you think we're past the fact that I found you standing over my dead father with a gun, you're wrong. If you think that just because we had sex I've forgotten the past three years and everything my people have been through, you're wrong. And if you think that I would allow myself to trust someone who won't even give me the courtesy of an explanation, you are very, very wrong."

A tremor ran through him. His hands around her wrists loosened, and she broke away and stared at him. He was frozen, staring back at her without expression. All emotion had drained from his face, his eyes. He looked dead. When he spoke his voice was clipped, hard.

"You read your father's journal. You know what Silas is—"

"Yes, I do. But what are you? Let's just get it all out now, Demetrius, why don't we?" Trying to speak over the fierce booming of her heartbeat, she hurried on. "Because I for one am sick of secrets. I'm sick of lies. I'm sick of not knowing the truth. You've helped me, you've helped Mel, but what about the rest of it? How do I really know what your endgame is, if there is one? If you won't tell me the truth, *how can I ever trust you?*"

He stood there staring at her in silence for what felt like forever, his face flat, an icy stillness growing between them that felt like being slowly submerged in a sea of inky black water. Her body and blood were freezing from the feet up.

Finally, in Latin, slowly and deliberately, gazing into her eyes, he said, "Your life before mine. Your needs before mine. Your desires and hopes and dreams before mine. I pledge you my life, and upon my death I pledge the service of my everlasting soul. There shall be no others before you, now, until the end of all time. On my honor, I swear it."

Her mouth fell open. She stared at him, stunned.

Ritual words. Bonding words. Words she'd only ever heard spoken in a ceremony that involved hands painted with henna and fastened together with silk ties, crowns of rosemary and candles and the exchange of rings.

And his face still so flat, but his voice now was pure agony, reverberating with everything he wouldn't allow his face to reveal. It was awful, almost too painful to hear.

But he wasn't finished yet. He said, "You evidently are not bonded to me, but I am bonded to you. That is permanent. That is forever. I have no endgame except to love you, Eliana. And protect you, and keep you safe. It's up to you if you believe that or not, but the truth of it remains."

She swallowed, feeling like something very large and heavy had fallen on her head. Her heart didn't know whether to stop or pound or explode, so it settled on a horrible kind of twisting that felt like an animal in death throes trapped inside her chest.

"Tell me what really happened that night," she demanded, her voice harsh. "If you love me like you say you do, tell me what happened and let's be done with it, once and for all."

Eerie, the look he gave her then. His flat expression contorted into something truly dreadful to behold, something she knew all too well from years of avoiding it on her own face in the mirror: desolation.

She waited, she held her breath, and it felt like the air all around them held its breath, too, everything suspended like motes in the sunlight. Like her heartbeat.

But he didn't speak. He held his silence and the raw, barren look on his face didn't change, but no sound came out of his mouth and that was almost too much for her to bear. In that moment, she felt like something inside of her died.

She took a step back. Another.

He said, "I've never lied to you. Give me your trust and I can prove it."

Her laugh was a bitter, ugly thing that she might have been ashamed of if she weren't so choked with the ashes of her hope. "If you were in my shoes—if the roles were reversed—would *you* trust you?"

He stared at her, unmoving, miserable. His mouth twisted. He whispered, "No."

She closed her eyes and briefly wondered how long it would take before her ravaged heart just decided to stop beating, bereft as it was of any reason to keep on.

"Finally." She opened her eyes and looked at him. "Finally an honest answer."

Then she Shifted to Vapor and left her clothes in a pile at his feet, leaking air.

THIRTY-FIVE
Overripe Fruit

The problem with Shifting to Vapor and leaving all your clothes in a heap on the floor is what happens when you Shift *back.*

In other words, if you're anywhere except a nude beach or alone, people are going to stare.

Eliana crept, as slowly as she could without being noticed, over the smooth plaster ceiling of the hospital corridor. Nurses and doctors passed unawares beneath her as she flowed silently forth, navigating around buzzing light fixtures, trying to be as unobtrusive as a small cloud of mist slinking along a rough ceiling possibly can. She passed the visitors' area and the information desk and swept into an elevator with a hugely pregnant woman holding the hand of a small boy.

Stretched thin as a breath of air, she hovered against the metal fixture on the roof of the car that held a row of florescent lights. The boy—towheaded, barely a toddler—looked up and smiled. To her horror, he pointed and said to his mother, "Thmoke."

"There's no smoke, honey." The mother didn't even look up. The elevator doors slid shut, and the car began a smooth climb. But the child would not be dissuaded.

"Thmoke!" he insisted, and stomped a foot. "*Thmoke!*"

Eliana shrank slowly to one corner.

The mother sighed—the heavy, defeated, I-never-signed-up-for-this-shit sigh of motherhood—dug through a large handbag slung over her shoulder, and produced a set of brightly colored plastic rings on a chain with bells. She dangled it over the boy's head.

"Here, sweetie. Play with this."

When the child snatched the rings from her hand and began to chew on them, instantly forgetting his fascination with the cloud of mist that was Eliana, she relaxed, profoundly grateful for short attention spans. The doors opened on the fourth floor, and mother and child disappeared down an empty corridor.

She took form for a millisecond as woman and pressed the button for floor six, then Shifted back to Vapor, drifted back up against the ceiling, and rode the rest of the way alone.

Once on Gregor's floor, she found the nurses' break room without too much trouble, and luck, for once, was on her side. Someone had left their uniform in a plastic dry cleaning bag slung over a chair.

Eliana smiled. She wouldn't have to visit Gregor naked after all.

"Time for your sponge bath, Mr. MacGregor."

Gregor opened his eyes, saw a somber Eliana in a nurse's uniform and white hat perched on the metal rail at the foot of his bed, and wondered how a man of thirty-eight could survive a bullet to the chest but later die of heart failure from the simple pleasure of seeing a sexy woman in tight, fantasy-inducing clothing, mere feet away.

"Sweet Jesus," he muttered, eyeing her. "Saint Nick was feeling generous this year."

She tugged on the collar of the uniform, which appeared to be a size too small; she was bursting out in all the right places. "Better than a lump of coal in your stocking?"

He grinned. "I've got a lump all right—but sweetheart, it's not in my stocking."

This earned him a smile, small and wry. She slid off the railing and took a seat in the ugly green chair next to his bed. She had her hair tucked up under the hat, but a few messy strands escaped, blue-black and telling. He glanced at the door, at the two armed police officers still stationed outside.

"Not safe," he murmured, and then glanced back at her. "Probably not too smart, either."

"How could I stay away? You underestimate the power of your charm, Gregor. Also, you overestimate the intelligence of our friends, there." She shot a dour look to the door. "They didn't even look at my face when I came in."

Gregor dropped his gaze to the low V of the white uniform, perusing the lush landscape of cleavage presented therein. "Can you blame the poor bastards?"

She sighed, but somehow it seemed unrelated to him.

"A nice rack can topple empires, princess. It's just the way we're built."

Her look was one of pained disbelief. She said simply, "Men."

He held his hand out. She took it. They looked at each other for a moment in silence while the television droned on softly in the background. It hung on the wall opposite his bed, and he used it as white noise to block all the sounds of sick people coughing and crying and calling for the nurses, for more morphine and better food. A hospital seemed to him one of the most depressing places imaginable. He hated it, but prison—he knew as a fact—would be even worse, so he was milking his stay for all it was worth.

"How are you?" Her gaze dropped to his chest, to the bandage visible above the neck of his blue gown which was changed every twelve hours by the lovely Lily.

"Been better," he said matter-of-factly. "I'd forgotten how much gunshot wounds hurt."

Her brows rose. "Forgotten? Am I taking that to mean you've been shot *before*?"

He made a dismissive noise and waved his free hand. "In my line of work, it's par for the course. Your little friends, though—that was a new one. Can't say I'd like to see them again anytime soon."

"I'm sorry." Her mouth twisted. "Had I known it would all turn out like this—"

"No apologies, princess. My life's been a wild ride, and one I wouldn't change a minute of. Including knowing *you.*" He reconsidered a moment. "Although if you want to buy me a new Ferrari, I wouldn't object." His voice soured. "Not that I'll be needing it in prison."

"Prison?"

At her look of confusion, he said, "Agent Doe. The German. He came to see me."

Her fingers beneath his tensed. She whispered, "He's not dead?"

"He is very much *un*dead," Gregor confirmed.

"And?"

"And you were right. They know about you. About your kind."

Her black eyes burned. "How much?"

He considered that. "Enough to be problematic."

"What did he say? What did he want?"

"He wanted me to fill in the holes in their information. He offered me a deal: squeal and stay out of jail."

She dropped his hand and sat up rigidly in the chair, which he took to mean she assumed he *had* filled in the holes in their information. He glowered at her. "Seriously, princess—that's insulting."

She stood and began to pace, chewing her thumbnail, throwing worried looks at the door. She pulled the fabric curtain that hung from a rod on the ceiling around his bed, blocking the view of the door. "Tell me. Tell me everything."

"Come here," he ordered, pointing at the bed. "Pacing women make me nervous."

Surprisingly, she complied without comment. Once perched on the edge of the bed, she took his offered hand and stared down at it.

He said quietly, "He—his organization—wants to round you up, confine you. The word *zoos* was mentioned."

Her head snapped up with a gasp. Her eyes were wide and horrified. If they grew any larger, they would devour her face.

"He said his organization was above the police, and I heard him call someone. He asked for the chairman, identified himself as Thirteen, of Section Thirty. Does that mean anything to you?"

Pale and trembling, she shook her head.

He squeezed her hand. "I should have given you more guns. I have a feeling you'll be needing them."

It took her a long time to answer him. When she finally did speak, her voice was uneven and low. She spoke to their joined hands without looking at him. "Tell them to look in the catacombs. Tell them that's where I said we lived—in the catacombs and the old abbey near the Sacré-Coeur in Montmartre—the DuMarne. We're gone now, so it won't matter, but there will be evidence we were there. It should be enough to keep you out of jail, make them think you're cooperating. And I think…" She lifted her gaze to his, and it was utterly without hope. "I think this will be the last time we'll see each other."

Gregor glowered at her. "Don't be stupid, princess! I'm not letting you—"

He broke off because out of the corner of his eye, he saw the picture on the television change to a scene in St. Peter's Square, at the Vatican.

Chaos.

Thousands of people screaming, pushing, trampling one another. Wobbly video of blood-splattered cobblestones and toppled wooden barriers and scores of frantic police trying to direct and control the plainly terrified, surging crowd. A long, grainy shot of a balcony draped in crimson bunting, an empty window with a long streak of blood dripping down the panes.

The caption read, "Christmas Day Slaughter at St. Peter's Basilica—Pope Injured, Feared Dead."

When the picture cut to a replay of the earlier live broadcast of the pope's speech, Gregor—a man who had seen many grisly, ungodly things, who had himself *done* many grisly, ungodly things—thought he might lose his bland hospital breakfast.

Blood. So much blood. Great, arcing sprays of blood, almost comical in the sheer, unlikely volume of gore, like something from a Tarantino movie. A blur of black fur and claws and muscled sleek bodies, whiskered snouts with long, sharp white fangs tearing viciously into vulnerable human necks.

Into arms. Into legs. All of which split apart in lurid bursts of meat and juice like overripe fruit, squeezed hard.

Half a dozen black panthers had attacked the crowd at the Vatican during the pope's morning address, and another had attacked the pope himself.

Right there on camera. For all the world to see.

He had Eliana's hand in his; he gripped it so hard she said, "Ow, Gregor!" and tried to pull away. But it was as if his muscles had hardened to stone—he simply could not let go.

She turned her head and followed his gaze. There was a beat before she recognized what she was seeing, and then, with a sound of strangled horror, Eliana leapt from the bed, tore her hand from his, and covered her open mouth.

Gregor's eyes followed hers and, in following, stuck. The expression on her face was indescribable—fear mixed with panic mixed with despair and revulsion—her features screwed into a grimace of such pure, animal horror she was almost unrecognizable.

"No. No. No, no, no, no, no. Please, please *no!*"

She whispered it over and over in low, choked shock, her face white, hands trembling violently, still covering her mouth. The whites of her eyes showed all around her black irises. Then Eliana reacted as if an invisible fist had swung hard and connected with her stomach. All the breath left her body in a startling, harsh *whoosh,* and she collapsed into the chair beside the bed like a discarded ragdoll. A sob that sounded like she was dying slipped from her lips.

He looked back at the television. The image had changed to one of a handsome, dark-haired man, black-eyed and confident, smiling the most chilling smile Gregor had ever seen. He was odd and otherworldly in the same way as Eliana, and the fervor that burned in his eyes made Agent Doe look like a Girl Scout.

The news announcer said, "The news media has received this prerecorded video from the unknown terrorist group claiming responsibility for the attack," and the handsome man began—cheerfully, with veneration and pomp, as if delivering the commencement to a graduating class—to speak.

"Merry Christmas, humans, and allow me to introduce myself. I'm your new God…"

All the world fell away, and instant, encompassing agony arose to take its place.

Eliana felt as if her skin had been peeled off with one sharp, violent tug and she was standing there raw and exposed, muscle and tendon and bone. Pain seared bright and blistering through her as if she were one giant nerve, scraped raw.

The knowledge of what had been done and what would surely follow was instantaneous.

Her people: hunted.

Her colony: killed.

Her dreams: dead.

In one fell stroke, Caesar had sealed all their fates. There would never be recompense for this. There would never be forgiveness. There would be war everlasting.

There would be extinction.

The magnitude of it was breath-stealingly *astonishing.*

A sound drew her attention away from the television, where Caesar was still speaking. It was Gregor, cursing, his face ashen, his gaze on the opposite side of the room, where a hand had appeared, curled around the fabric curtain. The curtain was whisked briskly aside.

"Oh dear." Agent Doe looked between the two of them. His one blue eye burned. "Am I interrupting?"

He stepped forward with a leer, two armed officers behind him, and every ugly, dark, wounded thing inside Eliana exploded to hideous life.

THIRTY-SIX
Good-Bye

Shifting is an elemental thing.

Transforming matter—teeth to fangs, face to muzzle, legs to haunches—is a primal process that is acutely, fleetingly painful. It is real in a physical sense, but it is also a form of magic. And like all magic, it creates energy.

Energy that can be *felt.*

The moment the assassin Keshav felt the girl Shift to panther, he was leaning against the wall beside a vending machine in the hospital hallway, holding a cup of coffee to his lips. He and two of his team had stayed at the hospital, lurking in the background, prowling the halls, and the other two had staked out Gregor's building. The assumption/hope that she would return to see her injured friend was all they had to go on because she'd disappeared completely once again.

He was just about to take a sip of his coffee when the first shockwave hit him. He crushed the Styrofoam cup in his hand, spraying hot coffee all over his face and chest.

A pulse of heat. A vibration. A *release,* like a spring coiled tight and then loosed, or a door blown open in a sudden wind. It was both shocking and exhilarating—she was so powerful it sent a surge of electricity crackling over his skin.

He looked up at the ceiling—sixth floor, northwest corner—and then bolted toward the elevators in a flat-out run.

"Don't shoot! Don't shoot!"

Gregor screamed it, upright and red-faced in bed, his hands held stiffly out toward the two officers who had drawn their guns and were pointing them at the surreal scene in front of him.

Agent Doe, flat against the wall, arms up, face contorted in a grimace of terror. The enormous black animal who had him pinned with heavy paws on his chest had its ears flattened, snout peeled back over glistening sharp fangs, and was snarling down at him.

And it was definitely *down.* On her hind legs, in panther form, Eliana towered above him like Goliath to a one-eyed, whimpering David.

The officers were shouting something, too, screaming in French for her to stand down while Gregor was screaming in English and French and every other language he knew for them to hold their fire.

With the screaming and the television and the vicious snarl of the panther, no one heard the door open until it was too late.

Whump. Whump. Both officers jerked, then silently crumpled to the floor. A man in a tailored black suit stepped forward over their bodies, holding a sleek black gun in front of him, fitted with a long, cylindrical silencer.

"Shift back or die," he said very quietly to the snarling panther. "Choose. Now."

The panther hissed savagely, digging its claws into Doe's white shirt. Eight pinpoints of blood appeared, flowering out from where the tips of razor-sharp claws pressed through fabric into skin, and Doe let out a pitiful, choked sob.

Gregor whispered, "Eliana."

The man with the gun put his finger on the trigger.

Then the panther shimmered, losing shape, and turned to mist. Floating and ethereal, ruffling in a pale gray plume in the air, the cloud of Vapor hung there a moment too long for the man with the gun.

His face never losing its cold concentration, the tone of his voice still so quiet and controlled, he pointed the weapon at Gregor and said, "Choose again."

Gregor's heart screeched to a stop.

This time there was no hesitation. The cloud of Vapor coalesced, contracting on itself, gathering and thickening until it took shape as the form of Eliana, completely nude. Voice throbbing, she said, "Don't hurt him," and stepped around the bed, her hands held up in surrender. "Please. I'll do whatever you want. Just don't hurt him."

The assassin's cold gaze flickered over her. A muscle in his jaw twitched. Still with the weapon pointed at Gregor, he took something out of his coat pocket that glinted metallic silver. He held it out. "Put it on."

With shaking hands, Eliana reached out and took it, held it up. With the musical *chink* of metal sliding on metal, it spun in the light for a moment, twisting from her fingers.

"Around your neck," the assassin instructed with a jerk of his chin. Eliana complied, then folded her arms over her bare chest and stood before him with her chin up, waiting.

Behind her, against the wall, a paralyzed Agent Doe lost his battle with gravity and slid silently to his knees.

The assassin shoved the gun into the waistband of his pants, removed his coat jacket, thrust it at Eliana, and motioned for her to put it on. To Gregor he sent a glance that said, *Move and you're dead.*

When Eliana was covered, the assassin said, "The collar will prevent you from Shifting. Any attempt to escape and we'll kill him, and you. Understood?"

She nodded silently. The assassin grabbed her arm and yanked her forward, pushing her over the bodies on the floor.

"Eliana!" Gregor's voice cracked. His heart started up again with a painful throb.

He couldn't see her face, but as she was shoved out the door he heard her whisper, "Good-bye, old friend."

For a long moment, there was nothing but the sound of the television. His own breathing was a booming racket in his ears. Then, slowly and deliberately, Agent Doe leaned over and retched, gagging up a stream of yellow vomit onto the floor.

THIRTY-SEVEN
Oops

Everything had gone perfectly.

Getting in: perfect. The timing: perfect. Meeting alone in the pope's personal study, just moments prior to his television broadcast: perfect.

It had all gone so well…until it all collapsed into chaos in a horrible, unforeseeable turn of events that made Silas's head swim with the improbability of it.

It was he and Caesar and Aldo, Ottavio the Expurgari minion in the fedora and cape who'd arranged it all, bowing the introductions in hushed reverence to the Holy Father. The human pope was much more frail than Silas had anticipated—papery skin and a soft, rasping voice, spotted hands that shook more than slightly with age.

His outfit was something, though. Silas had never seen a hat quite so elaborate, or ridiculous.

He'd thanked them for their service to the church, thanked them for their years of dedication and sacrifice, assured Caesar that his father had been a holy warrior in the fight against evil, to which Caesar appeared confused, not knowing his father actually had anything to do with anything involving the church.

Dolt.

More energetic than he looked, the pope prattled on and on in his raspy voice, amusing Silas with his outpouring of thanks. Then even more amusing: a blessing, waved over their heads.

How he wanted to laugh then. How he wanted to clutch his stomach and howl with unmitigated glee.

But of course he did not. He only smiled and nodded, knowing that very shortly those benign, impotent blessings would be forever silenced when Aldo ripped off his face.

They said their farewells and were ushered to an antechamber, where Silas neatly slit Ottavio's throat. He died quietly gurgling, choking on his own blood with a very surprised expression that brought another smile to Silas's face.

Even though they know it's eventually coming, death always seems to take people by surprise.

The three of them waited until the pope's address started moments later—broadcast live on television, it was also piped in over speakers throughout the papal apartments and the Vatican—and then they simply walked back into the room and began.

There were no guards this deep in the inner sanctum. There was no need. Access from *outside* was carefully monitored and protected, but as honored guests, they had been ushered right in. So there was no one to give warning, save the two black-robed priests, assistants who repeated the prayer verses into microphones stationed just behind the window where the pope himself stood, overlooking the vast, gathered crowd, reading the opening blessing into his own microphone.

They died first.

Silas didn't bother having Aldo Shift for that—the two assistants got the same, swift treatment as Ottavio had.

It was only when the pope turned slowly away from the Plexiglas podium, turned and looked behind him in evident confusion when the assistants failed to respond to his verbal prompts, that Silas gave Aldo the go-ahead.

He really wished he'd brought a camera then, because the pope's expression—seeing a man he'd just blessed and thanked minutes before morph into a huge, snarling predator—was *priceless.*

It took only seconds, but Aldo knew precisely what to do. He'd been well prepared.

He leapt on the elderly pontiff, dragged him right to the edge of the balcony with his mouth closed over the scruff of his neck as if he were prey—which he was—knocked aside the Plexiglas podium with one sweep of a powerful paw, and dangled him half over the edge.

His voluminous white robes, real gold thread glinting in the bright morning sunlight, fluttered in the cool morning breeze. The tall, elaborate hat toppled from his head and sailed down toward the crowd. Their gasp was collective.

Then Aldo bit down and the gasps turned to screams.

Caesar, standing beside him, laughed at the extravagant spray of blood. Silas turned his head and looked at him, said, "It really *is* funny, isn't it?" and then plunged his knife straight through the back of Caesar's neck. The tip emerged through his open mouth, slick and red.

Caesar didn't even make a noise. He just jerked, once, and then when Silas yanked the blade out—with the wet suck of raw meat and a grinding of bone against steel—he fell to the floor, dead.

Aldo was preoccupied; it was almost too easy to drive his blade down, two-handed, through the top of his skull. He released his prey with a strangled cry, and both Aldo and the pope slid, limp and bloody, to the stone balcony floor. Then Silas sheathed his knife and backed away, careful not to show his face in the open window. From what he could see of the crowd below, they were in full panic mode, scared witless not only by what had just occurred in the window, but by the coordinated attacks going on down below.

He turned around and let out a startled scream.

There in the middle of the floor, awash in his own blood, sat Caesar.

Staring at him.

Frowning.

He put his hand to the back of his neck, feeling around while Silas gaped at him in stunned incomprehension. He shook his head as if to clear it, spat to clear the blood from his mouth, and then, unbelievably—*impossibly*—climbed to his feet.

The clamor of shouting and booted feet stomping down the corridor in a rush distracted Caesar, who turned his head toward the noise, but not Silas, who was unable to move a muscle to save his life. A million different explanations flashed through his mind at the speed of light, a million different questions, and always the answer flashing back huge and electric like a Las Vegas neon sign:

No. No. No.

A cadre of armed Swiss Guards burst through the antechamber door. Caesar was the first one they saw, standing in a pool of blood in the center of the room, the bodies of the dead priests at his feet, eyes and slit throats gaping. Silas was still by the balcony window, partially out of their line of vision, but Caesar might as well have had a bull's-eye on his bloody shirt, the way the guards reacted.

They lit into him with a unified roar.

Showered in a hail of bullets, Caesar twitched and staggered back as the flying shards of metal bit into his flesh, ripped open his shirt, tore through his body. Blood sprayed from a hundred ragged wounds, and almost in slow motion he fell, arms flailing, a cry of anguish on his lips. He crumpled to the floor and lay unmoving.

In the aftermath: Hush. A lone ambulance siren, far out. The sting and gray haze of gunpowder in the air.

Then the unbelievable and the impossible took on the distinct taint of the *insane* when Caesar's eyes, once again, blinked open.

He sat up abruptly, tore open his bloodied, ruined shirt, and watched in fascination—along with everyone else in the room—as dozens upon dozens of bullets appeared on the surface of his chest and abdomen, squeezed out of the wounds in his skin like seeds from the pulp of a lemon. One by one, they dropped to the floor with little *plunks* like the sound of pennies tossed into a wishing well, where they rolled, compacted and bloody, in little wobbly circles until falling still.

Caesar looked back up at the guards, several of whom had dropped their weapons and were crossing themselves in horror. He smiled. He said, "Oops. Bet you weren't expecting that."

Then Silas sank to his knees on the hard wooden floor of the pope's private study, and, for the first time in his entire life, he wept.

Demetrius knew even before the phone rang that something terrible had happened.

He just didn't know how bad it would turn out to be.

As he stared down at the ringing cell phone in his palm, a premonition of disaster turned his blood cold. It was Celian calling, he knew from the number, and something made him hesitate before he put it to his ear and said tersely, "What's happened?"

A moment of silence. Then, "You haven't been near a television."

The premonition turned into a cold and vile surety that felt like a hungry reptile slithering around in the pit of his stomach. "No."

Celian said, "There's been an attack. On the pope, and the people in St. Peter's Square, during his Christmas morning—"

"An attack? What does that have to do with us?"

"It was *by* us."

Demetrius stood there by the windows where Eliana had left him not fifteen minutes prior, stunned into momentary silence. "Us?"

"*Ikati.*" Celian's voice grew hard. "Caesar."

With the phone still pressed to his ear, Demetrius ran down the hallway from the dining room at Alexi's house, bolted into a bedroom, and slammed his hand against the power button of the television mounted above a dresser. The screen flickered to life, and it was on every channel, the gory details on instant replay, expert discussions and hysterical eyewitness testimony and outraged religious leaders and politicians screaming for someone's head.

And Caesar, smiling and laying out his plan for world domination.

He'd always known Caesar was craven, but to see it made so clear was another thing. He made a wordless noise of horror that encapsulated both his disgust and his perfect understanding of what this would mean for all of them.

"That's not the worst of it, brother."

Every cell in D's body froze, and he knew, he *knew*, even before Celian said it. He whispered, "Eliana."

"The Hunt's got her. Leander called me just now—they're taking her to Sommerley. They assume she and Caesar—"

"*No!*" he hissed, flooded with fury, with anger at himself for letting her go and not following, with her for being so recklessly stubborn and blindly loyal, risking her life to see a "friend."

"I told him that. And he told me in no uncertain terms that I should kiss my colony good-bye. They're going to make an example of us for any of the other colonies that feel like stepping out of line, and then they're going to close ranks and go underground." His voice darkened. "But not before she's made to pay for the sins of her brother."

Demetrius gripped the phone so tightly the plastic case shattered and snapped in two with a *crack*. "I'm going to go get her."

In the background, he heard Constantine say, "Told you."

Celian breathed a long, protracted sigh. "Yeah. Thought you were going to say that. Which is why we're on our way."

D realized he was on speakerphone; he heard road noise in the background, along with the low, somber voices of Lix and Constantine. Something had entered his bloodstream and was boiling up inside him, curdling him from the inside. "You won't get here fast enough. It's a thirteen-hour drive here from Rome, but only a few hours from Paris to Sommerley via the train. It'll be too late by then."

Celian said, "They're not taking the train from Paris, D. They're flying. Leander sent his private jet. She'll be there in just a few hours. Maybe less."

His private jet. Of course. Of *course* the Earl of Sommerley would have a private jet.

Which meant that D had no other choice but to fly, too.

With fury steeling his voice, he said into the phone, "Well, then, I'll have to beat them there, won't I?"

Without waiting for an answer, he Shifted to Vapor and surged toward the open mouth of the fireplace on the other side of the room, letting the cracked phone fall with a tinkle of broken plastic to the floor.

Alexi's too-small white silk robe floated in a sideways drift down beside it.

THIRTY-EIGHT
Truth Is an Absolute

It was an uncomfortable feeling, but it paled in comparison to the other feelings Eliana had dealt with over the last few hours.

With cold pressure against her skin and an electric hum that sent a thrill of pain surging down her spine whenever she pushed it too far, the metal links of the collar fastened around her throat held her just at the brink of the turn, primed but unable to Shift. The heated charge would build, and the flare that caught and sparked like gunpowder, and then the scent of smoke and honey that signaled the final moment just before transformation. But the charge faltered and then faded, leaving a hollow ache in its wake.

No use. She was trapped.

In more ways than one.

The plane ride had been beyond grim. Ensconced in the burl wood and leather luxury of the private plane of the man responsible for her imminent death wasn't the way Eliana had envisioned the last few hours of her life. Not that she'd spent much time envisioning it prior to today, but there you go. She was dressed in handcuffs and a single article of men's clothing—again. She was surrounded by enemies and unable to Shift.

Again.

Three of the sleek assassins in suits had accompanied her on the trip. The one who'd captured her at the hospital—tall and stone-faced with a cool, shark-like beauty—and two more who'd met them in front of the hospital, waiting in a black sedan with tinted windows. They were at total odds with the camaraderie and code of honor of the *Bellatorum*.

This obviously wasn't a band of brothers. This was a hired group of killers, cold and unencumbered by ties like brotherhood.

They didn't look at her. They didn't speak to her, or to one another, and their silence was more ominous than any threats or thrown insults would have been.

Eliana was sick with fear with what was about to happen.

She knew it wouldn't be quick, and it wouldn't be painless. If the laws of this British colony were anything like the laws of her own, she'd be made an example. A traitor was the worst thing a tribe member could be, and the execution of one was savored. They would gather 'round and watch for as long as it took—hours, at the very least—until their sense of justice had been served or she died, whichever came first. And because she knew they would employ the most barbarous of torture techniques in order to elicit information, she'd been trying to steel her nerves by imagining the worst they could do.

She would never tell them where the others were. Never.

But they would surely have terrible ways of trying to make her.

Suicide was the better option, but there had been no opportunity. And she knew that if she were somehow able to kill herself, Gregor would be made to pay in her stead.

There was no way out. She was going to die—very soon.

Sweet Isis, please give me strength, she prayed to the goddess of slaves, sinners, and the downtrodden. *Let me not dishonor myself. Let me not beg.*

She looked out the window of the limousine that had arrived at Heathrow to collect them and watched as the landscape slid by, emerald rolling hills bisected with low stone walls and dotted with black-faced sheep, thatched-roof cottages and thickets of ancient trees spreading their boughs over arched bridges, everything green and glistening with the gray, misty rainfall that had tapered off only minutes before. She'd never been to England, and she'd never been this far out in the countryside, and the thought that her bones would be buried so far away from home brought a sheen of tears to her eyes.

She wasn't allowing herself to think about Demetrius. She knew that would start a waterfall of tears that could never be stopped.

"We're here," said the driver from the front seat, and the air inside the car electrified.

The car pulled to a stop outside a massive, scrolled iron gate. The gate was flanked on either side with roughhewn stone walls—ten feet high and topped with barbed wire—which stretched as far as the eye could see in either direction. The driver rolled down his window, waved a hand at the stone gatehouse, and after a slight hesitation, the scrolled iron gates began a slow, outward swing.

And Eliana's heart began a frantic, hummingbird beat.

Let me not beg.

Upon seeing the traitor, Christian's first thought was, *Blue hair?*

As she was hauled out of the car by Keshav and shoved forward in bare feet over the groomed white gravel of the circular drive, hands cuffed behind her back, long legs bare, his second thought was, *Is she* naked *under that coat?*

His third thought wasn't actually a thought at all. It was more of a garbled impression of several things at once, all rendered unintelligible by the fact of his utter astonishment.

She had her head down, eyes trained on the ground, but as she rounded the back of the car she lifted her head and looked straight at him, and Christian felt as if he would be knocked back off his feet.

Her face—lovely, arresting—held an expression of such bottomless desolation it was like a hand had reached out and seized his heart. There was misery and grief but also an awful sort of steely resignation, and beneath it all, a beautiful, haunting pride. It was clear she knew she was being led to her death, knew it would not be an easy one…and she was determined to face it with dignity.

Admiration blossomed inside him.

And the first, tiny pinpricks of doubt.

Keshav yanked her to a stop with one hand curled hard around her upper arm. She stumbled and gasped, then bit the gasp back and straightened her spine. She lifted her gaze to his, and he was pinned by the force of it, by her air of magnificent doom, both heroic and tragic. He had the fleeting thought she could be the inspiration for an epic Greek poem about battle and betrayal and love. Chary and intense, she looked like someone who had spent years wandering the darkest depths of hell, met all its inhabitants, and been given a job counting the incoming dead.

In a husky, accented voice, she said, "Are you the one who'll do it?"

Keshav made a move to drag her back, but Christian stopped him with a curt, "Wait."

She didn't take her gaze from his. He'd never, ever seen eyes so black.

"No," he said. "My brother, Leander. The Alpha."

Something flickered in her black eyes at that, there and then quickly gone. It didn't seem like fear...perhaps it was anger? Contempt?

"Too bad," she said. "You have a kind face. I'm guessing your brother the Alpha will really make a meal of it." Her voice grew bitter. "They're always the worst."

He wondered at her composure. In her shoes, he wasn't sure he'd be quite so self-contained. "You're not scared," he said, and she blinked at him, surprised.

Her composure slipped. She swallowed, a flush crept over her cheeks, and her eyes grew fierce with unshed tears. "Yes, I am," she whispered. "But only of being weak. I can't stand the thought of...breaking."

It moved him, this irrational admission of hers. This honesty. He fought the sudden urge to comfort her with some kind of platitude, but he knew it was useless.

She would break. They all did, sooner or later.

And—he sternly reminded himself, trying to push his doubts aside—she was a savage. They'd all seen the evidence of what she and her brother had done. They'd all seen the carnage, along with the rest of the world.

He motioned with his chin for Keshav to take her inside the manor, and she was jerked away and led up the marble steps toward the iron-studded doors twice the size of a man. They swung open, and Christian turned and followed them inside.

The air this high in the atmosphere was thin and cold, filled with ice crystals that bit at him and the occasional crosswind that blew him off course and threatened to tear him apart completely, but raw, ragged fear kept D going.

Fear that he'd be too late.

He'd found a fast-flowing, narrow air current that swept him over the English Channel in good time, but then it turned sharply east, when he needed to go west. He dropped out of it, lower, surging over steaming fields and rolling moors and small townships and villages, all of it a painted blur of green and purple and brown far, far below. He didn't know his exact velocity, but he knew he'd never be as fast as a plane, and he hoped against hope that when he found her she wouldn't be—

No. He wouldn't allow himself to consider the possibility. He was going to find her alive, that was all there was to it.

Or God help them. He'd slaughter them all.

The manor was vast and luxurious, a labyrinth of drawing rooms and music rooms and sitting rooms, everything lavished in silks and velvets and gilt. Eliana was led down corridor after corridor, past a dual staircase that wound up to the second floor, her bare feet touching cool, polished wood between the soft pile of the Turkish rugs placed everywhere, until finally she arrived at the entrance to a grand, gilded room. It was cavernous, outfitted with even more attention to finery than the rest of the place.

And something else quite unique from the other rooms she'd passed: thrones.

A matched set of them, two glossy, elaborately carved mahogany thrones with cushioned seats, set on a dais at the far side of the room.

Her lips twisted ruefully. Back in the catacombs beneath Rome, her father had sat on one almost identical.

The thrones were empty, but the long tables that flanked them were not. A group of men sat facing her in substantial wooden chairs of their own, arms crossed over cashmere sweaters or silk jackets, or hands spread on the fine linen cloth of the table or clenched into fists at their sides, each one with a face that didn't bode well for the state of her health. Their expressions were uniformly hard, hostile, and grim.

One at the end—a younger one, boyish and bookish with a lock of dark hair flopped over one eye, glasses he kept pushing up the bridge of his nose—looked a little green around the gills.

Must be his first execution.

They didn't stand as she was brought forward, only watched her approach with eerie, vivid yellow-green eyes, lucent and piercing in the wan sunlight that slanted through the far windows of the chamber. They were the same eyes as the one she'd met outside, the brother of the Alpha, and they chilled her in exactly the same way.

Her people's eyes were the color of a tropical midnight, or the richest, loamy earth—dark but warm and full of life. *These* people's eyes were clear and glacial, and they sliced through her like gusts of killing cold wind.

They were wealthy and elegant and refined, but beneath all of that, they were killers, to a one.

She lifted her chin. *I am Eliana, daughter of the House of Cardinalis. The women of my lineage are lionhearted; I won't be intimidated. I won't let them see me beg.*

In a bone-jarring move that snapped her teeth together and elicited an instinctive snarl from her lips, Keshav shoved her to her knees in front of the men.

"Silence!" one of the men at the table commanded. Older, gray-haired, and pompous in formal, outdated clothing that included a brocade vest and cravat, he stood, and Eliana let her snarl subside to a low, warning grumble in her chest.

The one who'd stood glanced at Keshav behind her and nodded. Without warning, pain speared through her and her breath was knocked from her lungs as he kicked her, hard, in the kidney.

She fell forward, gasping, tears of anger and humiliation burning her eyes. She rested her forehead on the cool wood floor for a moment to regain her balance. The air was frigid on the backs of her bare legs.

I won't beg. I will not.

The pompous one spoke, and his British accent somehow managed to make him seem even more arrogant than his posture and expression attested.

"I am Viscount Weymouth, Keeper of the Bloodlines. I will be in charge of these proceedings, and if at any time your answers do not satisfy me, I will order Mr. Keshav to administer another motivational little prompt, and another, until they do."

There was a pause. "Do you understand?"

Eliana said to the glossy parquet floor, "No. I thought I was supposed to be silent. How can I answer your questions if I'm supposed to be—"

There came another kick, this one more vicious, to the ribs.

She moaned with the pain and would have curled into a little ball around it, but she was roughly dragged back to her knees by a hand fisted in her hair. She couldn't right herself, though, because pain had absconded with her motor skills—and her ability to breathe. She gulped hoarse, hacking breaths, waves of agony radiating through her like fire. The only thing that held her upright was the fist in her hair.

She tried to go to the place of peace and relaxation in her mind where she went when she did her daily katas, but it was no use. Adrenaline and fear lashed her with the crack of a bullwhip, and it was no use.

"Attempts at humor," intoned Viscount Weymouth, "will not be tolerated."

Eliana heard Mel's snarky reply in her head: *Evidently.*

"What the bloody hell is *this*?"

Eliana looked toward the shocked voice. From the door beside the end of the table, the Alpha's brother had appeared, and he now stood staring at the viscount in livid, unblinking outrage.

Unapologetic, the viscount looked at him down the end of a long, aquiline nose. "It was agreed that I would oversee—"

"You weren't granted permission to begin without us—and you weren't granted permission to *touch* her!"

They started going back and forth, the brother outraged and Weymouth sputtering indignantly, the other men at the table throwing one another restless looks, deciding, it seemed, whose side to take.

Gods, how she loathed politics. She'd seen it since she was a little girl, the posturing, the pandering, the currying of favor done at court. There was always an intrigue and a scandal, a secret to be kept, a deal to be made. There was always a bully, always someone who felt loftier than their station, and always—like Weymouth—a climber in the bunch.

Finally, apparently sick of the discussion, the brother turned his attention to Keshav and spat, "Unhand her! *Now!*"

Perversely, that made her want to smile. She'd forgotten there was always a courtly knight, too. Then she felt another pang of regret that he wasn't the Alpha. She'd bet anything his brother wasn't half as knightly as he.

Keshav released her as if she burned. She fell forward again, but this time the brother was there to catch her. He steadied her, let her rock back onto her heels, and when she was ready, gently pulled her to her feet. He kept his hand, warm and steady, under her arm.

"A chair," he directed to Keshav, between gritted teeth.

A chair was produced posthaste, and she sank into it with a whispered word of thanks.

Then the air in the room seemed to shift, a swift, snapping-to of attention that swept toward the door the brother had appeared through. Fighting a wave of nausea from the acute pain in her back and side, Eliana glanced up and froze.

The Alpha. It had to be him.

Dressed in the palest pearl gray button-down shirt and black slacks that showcased the lines of his lean, muscled physique, he might have been anyone, except for this:

He was ferociously beautiful.

Shining black hair that brushed wide shoulders, classical features, a mouth that seemed a little too sensual for a man. Piercing yellow-green eyes like the others, dusky skin like them, too, and there was something else that set him apart, something about his posture that screamed *power*. Even just standing still in the doorway he exuded a rapacious energy, violent and wild, that pulsed outward from him like a bubble, encompassing everything around him.

This was no commoner. This wasn't even a lord, though undoubtedly he was titled, landed aristocracy of the Empire.

This was a king, through and through.

Effortlessly, he commanded all their attention and held it as he silently surveyed the scene. Eliana felt the fleeting, electric brush of his gaze as it rested on her, then profound relief when it passed.

Her father—her mad, evil, genius father—had the same kind of presence. The same kind of easy, elemental power. Eliana briefly wondered if this king was insane, too, but that thought was obliterated by who appeared next.

The Alpha took a slow step away from the door and held out a hand. A long, white arm appeared from the shadows of the door as if in a stage drama, its wrist and hand bent in a motion of fluid, feminine grace. The pale hand rested in the Alpha's, and then the woman attached to that gracefully curving arm stepped over the threshold and into the light.

And all Eliana's pain and fear simply vanished.

It was instant and total, the feeling of kinship. Of *kindred*. It was also colossally stupid, because she knew nothing of this woman or this king or this land, but just looking at her face imbued Eliana with a feeling so warm and relieved and profound it could only be called homecoming.

Or maybe insanity.

The woman paused a moment, studying her. Garbed in the plainest gray wool dress, without cosmetics or jewelry or a single ounce of apparent effort, she was easily the most stunning woman Eliana had ever seen. Her face and figure, her skin, the loose, golden hair that cascaded over her shoulders to her waist—everything was perfect and utterly unblemished, like some kind of master artist's representation of an angel, of ideal, feminine beauty.

Picasso would have killed to paint your portrait, she thought. *Michelangelo would have sold his soul.*

It brought a faint smile to her lips. Seeing it, the Queen looked momentarily bemused. Then, impossibly, her own lips curved, a slight, upward tilt that her formidable husband didn't miss.

He looked back and forth between the two of them. Sharply, he directed, "Viscount. Carry on."

The warm feeling of homecoming was snuffed out, replaced by a very non-warm feeling of dread.

The viscount shot the Alpha's brother a smug, victorious look, but it turned sour when the Queen spoke.

"Why is she half naked?"

Everyone froze. Her husband drew in a breath, his lips flattened.

"And handcuffed?" She turned to the viscount. "Weymouth?"

Her voice—the unembellished American accent startling in the midst of all this English regalia—was exquisitely neutral.

The viscount shifted his weight from one foot to another. "She was brought in with handcuffs, Your Majesty, and it would be prudent to keep her in them—"

"Surely all you men could manage to control one *collared* woman?"

There was faint mockery in her voice, and Eliana sensed a lifetime of anger behind it.

Weymouth's face turned a mottled shade of red. "She is a traitor—"

"That remains to be seen."

"Of the worst kind—"

"I didn't realize there were degrees."

Weymouth's voice rose. "Who is the *daughter* of a traitor—"

At that, the Queen's voice lost all its light neutrality and hardened to a knife-blade coldness that had everyone in the room sitting a little straighter in their seats.

"As am *I*. Or had you forgotten?"

The Queen's gaze, flinty now, rested on the viscount. He fidgeted under it, lips twitching in outrage, but she kept her frozen gaze on him, a dare or a warning, and apparently he thought better of arguing. He looked at Keshav and gave a quick jerk of his head.

The handcuffs were unlocked, removed. Eliana's arms slid forward, and she had to bite back the moan of pain when feeling came flooding back into her numb arms.

"Thank you, Viscount," said the Queen, neutral once more. "You're always so accommodating."

If her words or her tone held no offense, the slight curl of her lips belied her opinion of the pompous viscount.

Weymouth's nostrils flared, his face went from red to purple, and he looked to be physically biting his tongue.

The other men at the table didn't even dare to look at him, or the Queen. Everyone kept their eyes down or on her, the lone traitor in a chair set across from them.

And this was absolutely fascinating to Eliana. Even when the Queen's voice had hardened, she hadn't raised it, and if she'd had any doubts before how a woman could be allowed to lead they were summarily extinguished.

This elegant, angelic-looking woman had them all—even her fierce, powerful husband—under complete control.

Instantly, Eliana knew that whatever decision was made about her fate, whatever punishment would be applied, it would be the Queen's doing, and no one else's. She might let them have their clown court, but the ultimate say would be hers.

In light of that, Eliana addressed her statement directly to her.

"I know there's no way for me to prove my innocence, and if I were you I probably wouldn't believe anything I'm about to say. All I can do is tell you the truth—if you want to hear it—and let you decide for yourself."

This little speech was met with arched brows from the Queen, a scoff from the viscount, and a few chuckles from the other men at the table.

The Alpha, however, did not look amused. He escorted his wife up the dais. "Truth is a highly subjective thing." His voice was as elegant and masculine as the rest of him, a resonant tenor that, combined with his British accent, she imagined was devastating to all but the most frigid of females.

Or the ones he was about to condemn to death.

"You're wrong," she said forcefully. This elicited a round of little gasps from the men. "Truth is an absolute, and one of the only things that really matter."

Horribly, horribly, because she was going to die and pain was burning through her and the full weight of the realization that she might never see Demetrius again finally sank in, her eyes filled with tears. "And love." Her voice broke over the word. "That's the other thing. Lose either one and life becomes meaningless."

The Queen, seated now, froze in her elaborate throne. She stared at Eliana long and hard, then quietly said, "I couldn't agree more."

With thinned lips and a long, sideways glance in her direction, the Alpha sat beside her and then turned his gaze back to Eliana. "You expect us to believe you had no knowledge of what happened? That you and your brother were not partners in this?"

"I don't expect you to believe anything I say. But the truth is, I knew nothing of it."

The viscount added flatly, "None of us will ever believe that."

Eliana swallowed around the lump in her throat, big as a fist, and repeated a quote she'd once read, attributed to Gandhi. "Even if you are a minority of one, the truth is still the truth."

"Your father," the viscount went on, his voice acid, "was a mass murderer. Would you have us believe you knew nothing of that, as well?"

Eliana closed her eyes for a moment. Shame. Shame so hot and rancid and total it was like being submerged in a lake of vomit. Like a full-body tattoo, she would never be free of it.

"Yes. I—know. Now. I'm sorry." She opened her eyes and looked at the Queen. "I don't share his…ideas. I wanted to live *with* humans, not—"

"Live with humans?" The Queen jerked forward in her throne, her hands wrapped tightly around its carved arms.

Her expression was incredulous. "You believe we can live together with humans, openly?"

It was evident from her reaction, from the restless shifting and blanched faces of the others, that this was a topic of monumental importance. She knew nothing of their ways, if they interacted with humans in the same way as they had in the Roman colony, some allowed to come and go, some—like her—confined, but judging by what little she'd seen so far, she'd bet they weren't exactly revolutionaries, espousing equality and the abolition of segregation.

Would this be the truth that would get her killed?

She stared at the Queen and decided she'd rather die from this truth than from all the lies they'd accused her of. At least—here at the very end of things—she could be brave.

"Yes," she said simply. "In fact, some of my best friends are human."

More gasps from the gathered men, these louder than before. She'd never heard so many gasping ninnies in her entire life, and she wondered if they might suck all the oxygen out of the air and she'd suffocate to death.

But the Alpha wasn't gasping. He wasn't even moving. He was just inspecting her with a pair of glittering, malice-filled eyes. His voice came low, and very dark. "You've *already* been living together with them."

It wasn't a question, it was a statement, vibrating with menace.

I will not be intimidated. She lifted her chin. "We're no better than them. And they're no better than us. There's no reason we shouldn't live together."

A look passed between the Alpha and his Queen.

"No more hiding, is that what you propose? No matter the consequences?" The expression on the Queen's face was indecipherable.

Gathering her courage like armor, Eliana said quietly, "Hiding is for mice. And we are not mice." She looked at the viscount. "At least, I'm not."

The Alpha's mouth fell wide open. The Queen gave a small, astonished laugh.

"This is ridiculous!" the viscount shouted. "Why are we listening to this nonsense? Just this admission is enough to confirm her guilt! My lord," he entreated the Alpha, "please! Can we not move on?" And he pointed to something Eliana had not noticed before in her pain and her panic, something large and bulky in the corner of the room, partially hidden beneath a drape of black fabric.

A machine. Some kind of tall, wooden machine—with blades.

But it wasn't the Alpha who answered, it was the Queen, and her green eyes burned.

"Yes. Let's get this over with."

With hard fingers digging into her arm, Keshav yanked Eliana to her feet.

THIRTY-NINE
Shield

But she wasn't taken to the draped machine, as she'd assumed. The Queen ordered, "Bring her to me," and Eliana was led across the cold floor and up the steps of the dais, then forced to kneel before the Queen's throne.

The Queen proffered her hand.

Eliana stared at it, confused. What did this mean? What was expected?

"Take it," the Queen said. "If you are innocent as you claim, take it."

She lifted her gaze and stared into her brilliant, searching eyes.

"Or let them have their way with you," the Queen murmured with a glance at the viscount, the machine. "You decide."

So Eliana did as she was told and slid her hand into the cool, soft hand of the Queen.

There was a silence, breathless and pregnant. Then she frowned.

"Jenna?" The Alpha jerked forward, radiating violence, his hand gripped around the carved wooden arm of his throne so hard his fingers turned white.

"She's…she's…" She trailed off, wondering, and the sense of anticipation in the room ratcheted higher. Her lashes lifted, and she met Eliana's gaze with her own. Astonishment was there, along with uncertainty. "She's a Shield."

"What?"

"A Gift," the Queen mused, staring into her eyes. She seemed strangely impressed.

"What does it mean?"

"It means I can't See in unless she lets me. Her mind is impenetrable."

The room went utterly still. Wound tight enough to snap, the Alpha looked back and forth between them. "That's why I was never able to locate them. That's why it seemed as if they'd disappeared altogether. She was Shielding them."

Locate them? Eliana was struck with horror and sudden comprehension. This woman could *find* them, over vast distances, with just her mind? Panic lit through her like kindling touched with a match. Everyone at Alexi's—

Watching her carefully, the Queen said, "I don't think she even knows she was doing it."

"The Blessing," Eliana blurted. "That's what I called it. My father—he couldn't—"

"Read your mind," the Queen finished, with distaste. "I'd heard he was quite good at that. Among other things."

"But to hide *all* of them?" said Leander incredulously.

The Queen nodded. "It's remarkable." She cocked her head, lips quirked, and murmured, "Always the females..."

The mood in the room had grown restless, and Eliana's panic began to spread. If she couldn't prove her innocence with words or by allowing the Queen access to her mind, what would become of the Roman colony? Of her kin at Alexi's?

Of Demetrius?

"Tell me how to let you in—how can I do it?" Suddenly desperate, her commitment to not be intimidated vanished, Eliana gripped the Queen's hand harder, but at that moment her head snapped up and she examined the high, frescoed ceiling above with narrowed eyes.

Beside her, the Alpha hissed, "What is it?"

To which the Queen replied, "We have company." The men around the tables leapt to their feet, as did the Alpha, everyone on instant, crackling high alert.

"How many?" Leander snarled.

"Only one." The Queen dropped her gaze back to Eliana and pulled her hand free. "And he's moving fast."

FORTY
Proper Punishment

D didn't bother to try to disguise himself, to slink in through a chimney or a back door or a crack in a windowpane. He simply flew straight down and landed without ceremony in the center of the circular drive, Shifted to panther, and bounded toward the tall iron-studded doors of the entry to the mansion, spraying gravel in his wake.

He crashed through the doors, and splinters of wood went flying.

Once inside, he used his nose to guide him, and he ran, snarling murderously, past room after empty, lavish room, seeing none of it, running on pure instinct, the scent of Eliana's fear pulling him onward like a hook, like the gravitational force of a collapsing star.

She was in pain. He felt it, and thought, *I will slaughter them all.*

With a terrifying roar, Demetrius blew through the open doors at the far end of the throne room. As soon as he passed the threshold, every one of the men behind the tables on either side of the thrones with the exception of Leander and the viscount Shifted to panther as well, in a unified burst of power that sent a shock wave like a bomb detonation ripping through the room.

Her heart stopped. In a flash, Eliana saw what would happen.

There were over a dozen of them, maybe twenty, and only one of Demetrius.

It would be a bloodbath.

Without thinking, she seized the Queen's hand and screamed, "*No!*"

Instant, electrifying connection, like a plug into a socket.

All the air sucked out of the room, gravity ceased to exist, and she was hurtling through space at a thousand miles per hour, mute, blind, paralyzed. The sense of invasion was acute, as was the nausea that roiled her stomach. Bile rose into her throat.

And then the memories came, hard and fast and nearly indecipherable from one another, flashes of color and voices and sounds and smells, violently drawn out of her by an invisible force, like starlight sucked into the vast, inescapable vacuum of a black hole. She was being inhaled, she was being *emptied*, and the worst part was that she was as helpless as a kitten against it.

As abruptly as it started, it stopped. She was released, gasping and reeling, and fell to the floor.

Beside her, in a clear, commanding voice, the Queen said, "Stop!"

And everyone—everything—did.

Eliana raised her spinning head, too weak to stand, not too blind to see but not quite understanding what she was seeing. In a circle around Demetrius were a dozen or more glossy, muscular animals, hundreds of pounds each, spitting and hissing and bristling, fangs bared, long tails twitching menacingly back and forth. Demetrius himself was silent and unmoving in the center, ears flat against his head, crouched to spring.

Beyond her terror, Eliana took enormous satisfaction in the fact that he was almost twice as big as the biggest of the rest. Who were *huge.*

"Love," said the Alpha, very neutral, from beside the Queen. "Have you something to say?"

The Queen took a step forward, another, and another. She moved down the steps of the dais slowly, her gaze on the group of snarling animals, her posture relaxed. She finally stopped just shy of the circle.

"Demetrius." Her voice was odd and flat. "I've been wanting to meet you."

Viscount Weymouth—voice throbbing with fury—said, "*Demetrius!* This is the one who defied orders, who took it upon himself to kidnap a prisoner who was rightfully ours, who *dares* to enter your home in such a hostile, threatening manner—" He pointed at Eliana. "He's just as dangerous as her brother!"

"Probably more dangerous," the Queen said, still with that flat tone. "But for very different reasons."

"Thank you!" the viscount crowed, vindicated, and then, to the circle of panthers, "*Attack!*"

"Stand down!" said the Queen forcefully, her hand held up. There was a moment of confusion, of hesitation, until she said, "He won't be harmed, at least not yet. Everyone, stand down."

"Majesty!"

"*Viscount.*" Jenna turned her head and gave Weymouth a look that snapped his jaw shut and sent him sinking back into his seat in lip-trembling, pale-knuckled fear.

Deadly soft, the Queen said, "Let me repeat myself *again* so there is no possibility of misunderstanding. I said, *stand down.*"

Leander sighed and crossed his arms over his chest.

There was disgruntled hissing, a slow slinking back on silent paws. D watched with wary eyes until they withdrew to a safer distance, but he still didn't Shift back to human form, and Eliana waited, feeling like her heart was choking her, to hear what would come next.

To D, the Queen said in a reasonable tone, "Please, Shift. We need to talk."

He looked from her to Leander to the viscount. Slowly, his muzzle curled back over his fangs.

"I understand," she said, sounding as if she actually did, "but we really need to talk."

He made a sound in his throat, a low, chuffing noise of discontent. The Queen waited patiently, unmoving, her expression revealing nothing. His flattened ears came forward, and he tested the air with his nose. Finally the enormous panther shimmered and dissolved to a floating cloud of Vapor, which then coalesced into the form of a man.

A tattooed, very, *very* naked man, muscular and tall and huge.

Everywhere.

The Queen spun around, turned her back on him. Her face turned red, and her eyes were enormous and round. Her hand flew to her mouth, and she coughed into it, ladylike. "Thank you. You'll be needing clothes. I, um, I don't know what we have that will"—she coughed again—"fit you, but I'm sure the viscount can arrange for something." She glanced up at him with a wicked glint in her eye. "Perhaps you could offer him your trousers, Viscount."

This wasn't a question.

Eliana didn't even have to look at him to feel his outrage. She probably couldn't have looked at him, anyway; all she could see was Demetrius. Beautiful, powerful Demetrius, staring past the Queen, at her, his eyes shining and ferocious and dark.

"*Majesty!*" The viscount was apoplectic.

"Your trousers," the Alpha repeated icily, staring in open disapproval at his red-faced wife. Clearly this was not how he envisioned this meeting going. "*Now.*"

Seething, the viscount unbuckled his expensive-looking black pants, slid them over his legs, and handed them over. Leander tossed them at D, who caught them and put them on.

They were inches too short, the thighs inches too tight, but he managed to stuff himself into them and zip them up. The waist was too large and sagged down around his hips. He crossed his arms over his chest and stared with hooded eyes at the back of the Queen's head.

He casually drawled, "All in, m'lady."

Eliana fought the sudden, insane urge to laugh. Leander, however, did not appear to find any of this in any way funny. He watched D with the laser-like intensity of a predator contemplating a meal.

The Queen turned to face him again, her composure regained. "As the viscount so helpfully pointed out, you've broken quite a few of our most sacred laws."

D said nothing.

"But Eliana has broken them all."

"Your laws aren't ours," D said, steel in his voice. "And she is guilty of nothing except putting her trust in the wrong place."

The Queen appeared unimpressed. "Even if what you say is true, that kind of misplaced trust has its price. Especially when it results in the death of innocent people." Her voice darkened. "Especially when it means we will be hunted even more fiercely than before. Everything will change now, for the worse. There must be proper punishment."

D stepped forward with a low snarl, and Leander did, too. The two of them squared off on either side of the Queen, who, judging by her expression, was more irritated than alarmed.

"By all means, Warrior, go ahead and try to intimidate me. But when I Shift into a dragon and eat you, it will be too late to regret your mistake."

D looked at her a moment. Then, very quietly he said, "Dragon?"

Leander snapped, "Big as this room, you bloody oaf. So choose your words carefully, and show some *respect*."

The Queen smiled sweetly. "Or maybe a Kodiak bear, so I don't damage the frescoes again." She glanced at the high, vaulted ceiling above, and D followed her gaze, as did Eliana.

There among the pastel clouds and feasting gods and dancing cherubs painted on the ceiling were long, deep gouges and cracks, and three craters where the plaster had been crushed and torn away as if something had smashed into it. Something big.

At D's look of incredulity, she shrugged. "Learning how to fly is a nightmare, let me tell you. I should never have attempted it indoors."

D said between gritted teeth, "Celian said you were reasonable, but now I can see he was wrong."

"Oh, on the contrary! In fact, I have a very reasonable proposition for you."

His jaw worked. With a livid, threatening glance at Leander, he said, "Which is?"

The Queen's sweet, sweet smile never wavered. "Give your life in her stead, and we will let her live."

This shocked the entire room, even Leander, whose head whipped around as he stared in confusion at his wife. But no one was more shocked than Eliana, who leapt to her feet.

"No!" she shouted. "He was only trying to protect me—"

"Well, *someone* has to pay," said the Queen, drolly. "I'm sorry, but it's one of our oldest laws. A traitor's life is forfeit. So either he dies for you, or—"

"Yes," said Eliana, instantly comprehending. "I will die for him."

The Queen gave her the oddest of smiles then. Feral and eerie and satisfied, as if she'd just won a bet with herself.

D shouted, "No!"

Leander moved in front of the Queen, and he and D snarled at each other, crouching, readying themselves to spring. She said to Eliana, fiercely, "You will take the punishment he has earned by his own acts of disobedience?"

"Yes."

"And you will not resist in any way? You will allow us to proceed as we wish?" She lifted a hand toward the draped machine in the corner.

Eliana nodded.

D snarled, "If any of you bastards lays so much as a finger on her, I'll kill you all!"

"Demetrius—"

"No, Ana, I'm not going to let you do this!"

"This isn't your decision!"

"You should know it will be much worse now that you're paying for him, too," interrupted the Queen, still smiling that strange smile, paired now with a withering stare. "It will take much *longer.*"

It was that smile that finally did it. It hardened something inside her.

In a voice that was cold and iron heavy, Eliana said, "Do. Your. *Worst.*"

It came from some place inside her that she didn't know existed, a place devoid of fear or doubt, and the Queen knew the truth of it, as did D, who let out an outraged, deafening roar.

The Queen's head snapped around. She said to him, "Just remember what she offered to do for you, Warrior. And remember it was *before* she knew."

The Queen reached out and seized his hand.

And Eliana watched in horror as the proud, fierce warrior was consumed.

His eyes popped wide, unseeing. His mouth fell open. His jaw went slack. A tremor passed through his chest. Then, with slow, supple grace, he sank to his knees on the floor in front of the Queen and bowed his head.

The Queen closed her eyes and made a low, humming sound low in her throat. She inhaled, long and deep, and when she exhaled it was as if a weight had been lifted from her.

"Winston Churchill once said, 'A lie gets halfway around the world before the truth gets a chance to get its pants on.' And you've proven him right, Warrior." She looked down on D at her feet, bare-chested, dressed in another man's pants, and laughed softly. "Literally."

"Jenna?" Leander stepped forward.

She turned, glanced briefly at her husband, then finally let her gaze rest on Eliana, and spoke directly to her. "You were right. Truth *is* an absolute. Even with a minority of one. Or, in this case, two."

So dry, her mouth, so loud, her heartbeat. And so, so wild, this thrum and chaos in her blood, like a windstorm descending. She tried to swallow and couldn't. She tried to move and couldn't. It was as if someone outside of her was controlling her entire body, some powerful force had ripped away her will and left her frozen. Breathless. Thunderstruck.

"Jenna." Leander's voice was firmer.

She looked back at Leander and smiled, a true smile, one that lit her whole face to radiance. "She's innocent. And so is he. Neither of them are a danger to us."

The tension in the room relaxed as if a held breath had been expelled. One by one, the panthers who'd retreated Shifted to Vapor and hung there in the silence of the great hall in small, glittering clouds.

"Eliana," the Queen said, still holding D's hand. "I apologize. That was a test, one I hope you can forgive me for. I'm not going to harm him, or you. Come here."

Quaking, that wild hum still singing in her blood, Eliana found the will to move. She climbed slowly to her feet and crossed to the Queen, staring all the while at Demetrius, who was still on his knees, immobile, transfixed.

The Queen held out her other hand. Smiling, she murmured, "Are you ready for Truth with a capital T?"

Again, Eliana's mouth would not work. Her lips would not form words.

"Don't be afraid. There's just something you need to see, if you'll let me in." Her gentle smile grew blinding. "Butterfly."

And so Eliana took her outstretched hand and finally, *finally* understood.

FORTY-ONE

As Good As Dead

Truth, like honor and courage and love, does not come in shades of gray. You either have it or you don't—there is no in between.

Sometimes it takes a lifetime to uncover it, and sometimes it is clear and simple as a sunrise. Also like honor and courage and love, sometimes the truth can be lost, and you have to find your way back to it, crawling over fields of broken glass and dead bodies, your knees and hands bloody and raw, until you get to it and it's even sweeter than before because of what you suffered on the way.

Eliana was filled with that grateful sweetness now, filled so full her heart could burst. She had seen and felt everything D had seen and felt in the past three years—in *forever*—and now she understood. She understood everything.

And she loved him all the more for it.

"You couldn't tell me—you couldn't tell me it was Constantine," she whispered, voice breaking over every other word. The Queen still held both their hands, providing a connection that allowed her to see inside D's mind, and him to see inside hers. "He was protecting you from my father…and you were protecting me from him, too. All those years, you watched over me, making sure nothing happened to me. Making sure I was always all right. And then, at the end…"

A scene like a painted picture in her mind: a circular, stone room, two men fighting, a naked woman chained to the wall. Her father plunging a knife into the other man's back, the man falling to his knees, the woman screaming. D in one doorway and Lix and Constantine in another, watching in horror. Her father throwing another knife at D; its blade sunk deep into his chest.

Constantine, loyal and protective of his brother, broken down from years of abuse from her father, pointing a gun at him and pulling the trigger.

Her father falling slowly to the ground.

Then the *Bellatorum* helping a wounded D to his feet, Constantine handing him the gun so he could carry him, Eliana skidding to a stop just outside the door.

"He found out—about us—about you and I," D said hoarsely, trembling as badly as she was, his face fraught with the weight of so many memories, so much pain and loss. "He would have killed me, he would have killed us all if Constantine—"

"I know," she sobbed, on her knees beside him. "*I know.*"

She tore her hand from Jenna's and threw her arms around D's neck.

"But you didn't when you said you'd die for me," he whispered, his voice harsh. "You didn't know and still you… you…"

"Because I love you, idiot." She choked it out. Tears ran down her face and dripped off her chin, her entire body shaking. "It took thinking I'd lose you all over again to realize you're all the best parts of me. I'm never as good as when I'm with you, and if I can't be with you then I'm as good as dead anyway."

Then his arms came around her, and they knelt there like that together in silence, rocking gently, until his lips found hers and he kissed her with all the hunger and possession and tenderness and love he'd always felt for her, all of it between them, bright and burning and so sweet it hurt.

I love you, God how I love you, how I'll always love you, until the day I die.

Someone cleared his throat.

"Pardon me," Leander said, freezingly polite, "but perhaps you'd like to…ahem…freshen up after your long journey. And then we can all talk more later."

D broke away, breathing hard, and nodded. But Eliana could only stare back at her beloved warrior, unwilling to let her eyes stray from his face, even for a second. He rose to his feet and gently pulled her along with him, wrapped his arm tight around her shoulders and tucked her under his arm, and still she stared up at him, rapt.

"My colony," D began, but the Queen interrupted him.

"They're safe from us, Demetrius. But unfortunately, I can't guarantee they'll stay that way. The Expurgari know about the existence of all the confederate colonies except the one in Brazil. Which is why most of Sommerley has been moved there. They haven't made a move against us yet, but after today and what happened at St. Peter's…"

Her voice trailed off.

"Rome will be the first place they'll look," D said, his voice dark.

The Queen nodded. "And they'll want vengeance for having been deceived for so long. You're welcome to go to Brazil—it's large and well hidden, and better fortified than we are here. Otherwise, I'd recommend establishing a new colony quickly, somewhere secure. And as I told Celian, you're welcome to join the Council and the confederacy, on your own terms. The choice is yours. Either way"—she held a hand out to Leander, who grasped it, pulling her against him with a hard look to D that indicated he wasn't fully on board with this plan—"we consider you family now. We'll do everything in our power to help you, whatever you decide."

Something in D's face softened. He looked from her to the Alpha, who was protecting Jenna with his body in exactly the same way D was protecting Eliana with his. He inclined his head—a move that was both thanks and grudging admiration—and then looked down at Eliana, at her bare legs and the coat she wore over absolutely nothing.

"Nice jacket," he murmured.

"Nice pants," she murmured back.

He smiled. "Between the two of us we make a suit."

She laughed weakly and hid her face in his chest.

"There's a suite of rooms in the north wing you're welcome to use, as long as you like," said Leander, his voice a little less tense than before. "The viscount can show you the way."

There was a squeak of indignation from the viscount, which she might have imagined because of the roaring in her ears, but then he had moved to the door, shirttails dangling against his bare thighs, which, as he stiffly moved, parted to reveal a pair of baby blue silk boxers. His face was livid, and Eliana knew by the look in his eyes they'd made an enemy.

And so, perhaps, had the Queen.

But D moved to follow, and she let herself be led away, wrapped in the circle of his arms.

FORTY-TWO
The Color of Happiness

The wedding was a simple and solemn affair, vows and rings exchanged under a canopy of pine boughs and wildflowers deep in the ancient, wild woods at Sommerley.

Eliana had insisted it be outdoors, and at night. Number two and three of her top three favorite things, she said, and D knew without asking what number one was, because she showed him every day in a million different ways.

Lix and Constantine were there, of course, along with Celian, who officiated. Jenna and Leander were the witnesses, as were a host of tiny, unseen woodland creatures, drawn in curiosity to the small clearing ringed in candles, the play of light through the trees and the sound of voices, hushed and reverent.

D repeated the words he'd said to his love before, and now she said them back, the vows of honor and loyalty, the ritual words that would bind them for life.

In truth, they were already bound beyond what any words could prove. They were bound by chains that could never be broken, the chains of love that bind stronger than the most flame-tempered steel. And as he looked into his beloved's tear-filled eyes as she solemnly swore her oaths to him in a soft, shaking voice, D couldn't help but feel something he'd never felt before in his life.

Blessed.

The past few months had been an extraordinary blend of happiness and hope, chaos and confusion, and life-altering changes for them all. After an initial meeting between the *Bellatorum* and the Council of Alphas, the Roman colony had joined the confederacy and accepted Jenna as their Queen. And what a meeting it had been! Expecting to find D and Eliana jailed or tortured—or worse—the three other members of the *Bellatorum* had arrived at Sommerley mere hours after D. They'd burst into the manor in much the same way he had, and they'd been brought to their knees as he had, but for a far different reason.

A beautiful, pure white peregrine falcon had flown into the high-ceilinged throne room through an open window. It made three lazy turns above the warriors' heads, soaring with silent grace as they stared up with craned necks and open mouths, then sailed down and perched atop the carved wooden back of one of the thrones, shook out its tail feathers, and waited with unmoving patience while Leander approached, holding out a robe of heavy, embroidered ivory silk. The white falcon turned into a shimmering cloud of mist and funneled inside the robe, slowly ruffling and filling the fabric, until the shape of a woman emerged. The woman tied the sash around her waist and turned to face the warriors with a warm smile of welcome.

One by one, silently, they had taken a knee and bowed their heads in respect.

And when the Queen of the *Ikati* inquired as to why, it was Celian who answered her, by shrugging off his coat and lifting the sleeve of his shirt, displaying the tattoo of the Eye of Horus on his muscular left shoulder, the tattoo all the *Bellatorum* shared.

An ancient symbol of protection and royal power, the Eye of Horus was the crest of the Egyptians' patron god, one of the oldest and most significant gods of Egypt, the city from which the *Ikati* of the Roman catacombs traced their lineage.

God of vengeance, god of war, Horus was always depicted in the ancient texts and hieroglyphs as a peregrine falcon.

It was taken as a sign. And when the *Bellatorum* found out that he and Eliana were well, had been declared friends and family, and furthermore that no harm would come to any of them or their colony by the Queen's decree, it was taken as another sign.

The choice to join the confederacy had been easy after that.

What hadn't been easy, for D at least: accepting Alexi.

He begrudgingly admitted that the man had stayed true to his word. He'd helped all the remaining members of Eliana's small colony in Paris reunite with their old colony in Rome, and he'd made sure no trace of them could be found for any of their enemies who might be looking. But that didn't make D like him any more.

It made the Queen like Eliana more, however. As it turned out, the two of them were of one mind when it came to seeing humans and *Ikati* live together peacefully. The Queen herself was half human, after all. It was a goal that looked highly unlikely in light of what Caesar had done, but a goal the two of them had decided to work toward nonetheless. Their existence was no longer a secret, and the threats to them had multiplied a thousandfold, but the Queen had refused to leave Sommerley, and Eliana had refused to leave the Queen.

"She knows what it's like to be a woman in a man's world, Demetrius," his love had said. "Besides, I've always wanted a sister." Then she'd given him a toe-curling kiss that made him forget what they'd been talking about in the first place.

So they'd stayed the last few months at Sommerley, planning for the future. Planning for this beautiful wedding, which was now coming to a close.

"You may kiss your bride," Celian murmured with a glance at D and a slow, lazy grin spreading across his face. Celian unwound the silk cord that bound D's wrists to Eliana's and stepped back, his hands clasped behind his back.

And when Eliana blinked up at him, her cheeks flushed, her eyes shining, her pulse fluttering wildly in the base of her throat, D cupped her face in his hands and lowered his forehead to hers.

"To forever," he murmured.

"Forever," she murmured back, a tear slipping down her cheek.

Then, with his heart like a hammer in his chest, D pressed his lips to hers.

Light through lashes.

Fingertips brushed lightly across his lips.

D opened his eyes and looked into Eliana's. It was morning, and they'd only been at Sommerley for two days. Realizing what had just happened, he began to chuckle. He wrapped his arms around her and drew her to his chest, laughing into her hair.

"What's so funny?" she murmured.

"Just had a dream."

She went still. "A dream-dream, or a Dream, capital D?"

He pressed his lips to her hair. "Both."

She lifted her head and looked at him, a quizzical furrow between her brows.

They were naked in a very large bed, pillowed with very fine sheets, in a very fine room that was far too fussy and finicky for his taste. The Queen and her Alpha had put them up for the last several days, which they'd spent mostly in this bed, talking a lot, making love even more.

They had to make up for three years' worth of lost time, after all.

"Well, are you going to tell me about it?" Eliana insisted, poking him in the chest with the tip of a finger. "Was it good? Was it bad? Was it—"

"It was perfect. It's all going to be perfect," he whispered, then leaned in to give her a kiss, soft and warm. His hand slid up her arm to cup her face.

When they broke apart, they were both breathing faster. "You're not always going to be able to distract me like that, you know," she complained, not really meaning it.

"Oh yes, I am." Just to prove it, he kissed her again.

When he pulled away this time, it took her a moment to open her eyes. When she did, they were heavy-lidded and full of heat.

"Damn." She sighed. "I hate it when you're right."

His brows lifted. "Thought you'd be used to that by now."

This earned him a glare. "Don't push your luck."

"Hmmm." He trailed his fingertips slowly down the length of her spine, enjoying her little shiver, the satiny softness of her skin. "You're sure you don't want to grovel a bit more?" he murmured, teasing. "I was getting to really like your groveling."

And she had been. Ever since the Queen had shown her the Truth with a capital T as she liked to call it, he'd had apology after apology, all heartfelt and sincere, every one of them stopped with a kiss from him. They weren't going to look back anymore. They were going to look forward.

Because now he knew exactly what they had to look forward to.

But she took him at his word. Her glare faded, replaced by instant, lip-biting chagrin. She stammered, "I—I should have trusted you from the beginning. I should have let—I should have let you explain before I left. I'm so—I'm so—"

That's as far as he let her get. His lips were on hers before she could say it again.

"I'm starting to think this is all excuses for kisses," she murmured against his mouth when he drew back. Her lashes lifted and she gazed at him, her eyes soft.

His brows rose. "Are you complaining?"

"No. I love your kisses." She snuggled closer to him, pressing her pelvis to his. "Almost as much as I love some of your other things." Then she giggled.

His hand trailed lower, past the curve of her hip, to her bottom, so perfectly round and soft he couldn't help but give it a pinch. She yelped, complaining.

"You're lucky all I'm doing is pinching, baby girl. I think you deserve something a little more *stringent* for running off without my permission to see your gangster friend Gregor."

She'd told him all about Gregor, about how he'd helped her and been a friend—purely platonic—and he was going to make sure the man stayed safe, because she was worried about him. And what she worried about, well, that became a priority for him.

"Your permission?" She repeated it in an innocent voice, playfully batting her lashes. "Right. I'll be sure to remember that next time." She gave him a grin that said she would absolutely *not* be remembering that next time.

"Just going to have to spank you, baby girl," he warned, spreading his big hand over her behind and glowering down at her.

"Ugh. You're obsessed with spanking!" She pushed against his chest, but he had her in a tight grip and didn't budge.

"Please," he scoffed. "Don't act like you don't like it."

She looked mortified. "Of course I don't *like* it—"

He cut her off again with a kiss, this one harder and more demanding. He pressed his body against hers, rolled half on top of her, and when she wrapped her arms around his neck he took both her wrists in his hands and pressed them down to the pillow above her head and held them there, captive.

"Truth with a capital T, remember?" he said, his voice husky, eyes burning into hers.

She managed to look outraged, for about two seconds. Then she dissolved into laughter. "Okay. Maybe I like it *a little* bit."

"Better," he said, smiling now. He released her wrists and brushed a lock of blue hair from her cheek. He tugged at the strand. "I've been meaning to ask you about this."

Her hand flew to her head. "What? You don't like it?"

"Actually…I do. But you told me before you changed it to blue with black to match your mood. Your usual mood."

"And?"

"Well"—he brushed his lips across her forehead—"what if that's not going to be your usual mood anymore? Would you change the color?"

She blinked up at him, suddenly coy. "How do you know it's not going to be my usual mood anymore?"

"Because I plan to ensure it, that's why."

A smile spread over her face. "Well, in that case—yes, I'd change the color."

"To what?"

The smile grew dazzling. When she really smiled, she smiled with everything she had. D's heart soared.

"I don't know," his beloved said. "What's the color of happiness?"

They stared at each other in silence, the future unfurling between them like the loosed strings of a kite.

"You know things are about to get worse," he whispered. "Things are about to get very bad for us all."

She nodded, her smile fading. "I know. First the Expurgari, now that group, Section Thirty…"

D stiffened in anger, remembering what the Queen had shown him, Eliana's memories like a sped-up movie inside his own mind. He'd already taken his revenge on that bastard Keshav for putting his hands on her—he didn't think he'd be walking anytime soon—but the images of the cold-eyed German doctor were what really stuck with him. Looking into those eyes was like looking into an abyss. His dream had revealed nothing of the German.

"You think they're another religious outfit?"

Eliana exhaled and shook her head. "Worse—corporate."

"How is that worse?"

"Religious fanatics, I can almost understand. They're following a belief, and however warped that belief might be, it's still based on something they think of as sacred. It makes them more predictable, their goals more clear. They want us dead because they think we're evil; it's cut-and-dry, simple. We know what to expect. But with a corporation, only one thing matters…"

"Profit," he realized, with a slow, sinking feeling in his gut.

Her eyes, gazing up at him, grew troubled. "If they're after us because of money, because they think somehow they can profit from us…" She swallowed. "The Expurgari just want us to die. But there are far, far worse things than death, Demetrius."

He didn't reply, only gazed back at her, knowing without doubt she was right. Worse than death was life in chains. Worse than death was bondage. Slavery. Being captive guinea pigs.

Greed was one of the seven deadly sins for a very good reason.

"I know." His voice grew soft. "Like being apart from you, for instance."

She started. "Something you'd like to tell me? Is that what your dream was about?"

He drew her even nearer, cupped her face in his hand, and looked into her eyes. "Baby girl, you're just going to have to trust me about the dream. Can you do that?"

"Oh," she breathed, her eyes locked on his, "I think I need more practice with the trust thing…maybe we need to be in a shower for that. It worked pretty well at Alexi's." Her lips curved into a slow, mischievous smile.

He smiled back. Then in one lightning-fast move, he tore the covers off both of them and threw Eliana over his shoulder.

There was little time to prepare for what lay ahead. With the death of the pope and the slaughter at the Vatican, the entire world now knew of their existence, and the entire world was in an uproar because of it.

The future, dark and uncertain, loomed large. But right now, here in this little oasis in the middle of an ocean of insanity, D and Eliana had each other, and they needed more practice at a little thing called trust. So with a sharp smack on her behind that had her cursing in outrage, D set off for the bathroom with his woman over his shoulder, kicking and squealing, pummeling his back with her fists.

"Resistance is futile, *principessa.*" He gave her another smack, a broad smile on his face. "How many times do I have to tell you that? Resistance is futile."

Damn, but he loved his Gift. And her, the spitfire on his shoulder. His future bride.

He loved her most of all.

EPILOGUE

The serum had been removed, the lab that produced it totally destroyed, along with all their records. It had been shipped ahead in the large freight containers with the cache of weapons. The cases of money he wasn't taking any chances with and had them loaded onto the yacht he'd rented that was currently en route to their final destination.

Zion, land of gods, hidden deep, deep within the African rainforest, would have to wait. Eliana knew he planned the stronghold to be built along the banks of the Congo, so he'd changed his mind and was headed to Spain.

He'd always wanted to see those Gothic cathedrals and Gaudi's fabulist sculptures, watch the bullfights and drink sangria on a sun-drenched beach.

Meet a few sloe-eyed flamenco dancers and see if their screams outdid those of the cancan girls in Paris.

It was only him and the five others who'd helped him on Christmas Day now; naturally, Silas couldn't be trusted. There in the pope's private chambers, after the Swiss Guard lost their nerve en masse and fled from the sight of his bullet-riddled body regenerating itself, Caesar had ensured Silas met with the same end he'd so spectacularly failed to execute on him.

Caesar had slit his throat from ear to ear, and then he'd driven the blade of Silas's own dagger straight through the back of his neck.

He died facedown, twitching and wheezing into a growing pool of his own blood.

Too bad, so sad, and good goddamn riddance.

The irony wasn't lost on Caesar that his entire past had been defined by what he couldn't do, and now his entire future would be defined by what *only* he couldn't do, but everyone else on Earth could: die.

His body rejected death the way a vending machine rejects a torn bill. It took it in, assessed it for a moment, and then spat it unceremoniously back out.

No, we're not having any of that nonsense, thank you. Try again.

In the last week, he'd tested it himself. Drowning, electrocution, a high fall, an even higher dose of prescription medication, hanging, a straight shot to the brain with a gun—just in case the first shooting was a fluke—seppuku, and the ever-popular self-immolation. Nothing worked. He would actually die, quite painfully, too, but in moments his body would simply regenerate, and that, as they say, was that.

Really, could anything be better?

He'd believed himself unblessed. UnGifted. Everyone had. But now Caesar understood he'd been given the greatest Gift of them all.

Immortality.

He couldn't Shift to Vapor, he couldn't Shift to panther, but so what? He also couldn't cease to *be.*

Oh, happy, happy day.

Oh, beautiful day!

As Caesar stood at the helm of the yacht next to the swarthy hired captain—who of course would also have to die at the end of this trip—feeling the salt wind sting his face, the wind whip his hair into his eyes, he knew that all his tomorrows would be even better.

ACKNOWLEDGMENTS

As always, I must first thank my wonderful editor at Montlake Romance, Eleni Caminis, whose name and feisty spirit were the inspiration for Eliana. You're a joy to work with. To the rest of my friends and family at Montlake, you are an amazing team, and I'm grateful to have found a home there with you. I also owe thanks to my agent, Marlene Stringer, who gives the best advice. Here's to future adventures! To Melody Guy, thank you for all your wonderful ideas and feedback, and to Jessica Fogelman, thanks for your incredible eye for detail.

Without my readers, of course, the stories of the *Ikati* would be gathering dust on a shelf. I am profoundly grateful that you have taken the time to buy this book and continue to support the Night Prowler novels with so much enthusiasm and generosity. And to the fantastic book bloggers who have introduced my books to their communities, I'd like to give a special thank-you. Your dedication to reading and reviewing books is such a crucial service to readers. I'm humbled and thankful so many of you have taken the time to recommend my books.

Writing a novel is a long, lonely process, and without the support of my family I wouldn't be able to do it. Or much of anything else, for that matter. Mom and Dad, thanks for being cheerleaders and for instilling in me a lifelong love of reading.

And to Jay, my amazing, charming, brilliant, funny, capable, courageous, cheerfully combative, and most excellent husband…I've said it before, but it's true—I'd be lost without you. You are the kind of person I've always wanted to be.

ABOUT THE AUTHOR

Photo by Jay Geissenger, 2011

J. T. Geissinger's debut novel, *Shadow's Edge,* was published in 2012 and was a #1 Amazon US and UK bestseller in fantasy romance and romance series. She is a 2013 finalist for the prestigious RITA® award from the Romance Writers of America for best paranormal romance for her second book in the Night Prowler series, *Edge of Oblivion.* A native of Los Angeles, she currently lives there with her husband and is at work on her next novel.